...n Jess-Cooke is the author of *The Guardian Angel's Journal*, which was an international bestseller. Also the author of the award-winning poetry collection *Inroads* (Seren, 2010) and four academic titles, Carolyn is published in over twenty languages. She was born in Belfast, Northern Ireland in 1978 and now lives in Gateshead with her husband and three children.

Carolyn's website is www.carolynjesscooke.com.

the Boy Who Could See Demons

CAROLYN JESS-COOKE

piatkus

PIATKUS

First published in Great Britain as a paperback original in 2012 by Piatkus

Copyright © 2012 Carolyn Jess-Cooke

The moral right of the author has been asserted.

*All characters and events in this publication, other than those
clearly in the public domain, are fictitious and any resemblance
to real persons, living or dead, is purely coincidental.*

A CIP catalogue record for this book
is available from the British Library.

ISBN 978-0-7499-5313-3

Typeset in Bembo by M Rules
Printed and bound in Great Britain by
Clays Ltd, St Ives plc

Papers used by Piatkus are from well-managed forests
and other responsible sources.

MIX
Paper from
responsible sources
FSC
www.fsc.org   FSC® C104740

For Phoenix
my precious son

Demons do not exist any more than gods do, being only the products of the psychic activity of man.

— Sigmund Freud

The greatest trick the Devil ever pulled was to convince us all that he does not exist.

— Charles Baudelaire

A LOVE SONG FOR ANYA

1

RUEN

Alex

People look at me funny when I tell them I have a demon.

'Don't you mean, you have *demons*?' they ask. 'Like a drug problem or an urge to stab your dad?' I tell them no. My demon is called Ruen, he's about five foot three, and his favourite things are Mozart, table tennis, and bread and butter pudding.

I met Ruen and his friends five years, five months and six days ago. It was the morning that Mum said Dad had gone, and I was at school. A bunch of very strange creatures appeared in the corner of the room beside the canvas we'd made of the Titanic. Some of them looked like people, though I knew they weren't teachers or anyone's parents because some of them looked like wolves, but with human arms and legs. One of the females had arms, legs and ears that were all different, as if they had belonged to different people and were pieced together like Frankenstein's monster. One of her arms was hairy and muscly, the other was thin like a girl's. They frightened me, and I started to cry because I was only five.

Miss Holland came over to my desk and asked what was wrong. I told her about the monsters in the corner. She took off her glasses very slowly and pushed them into her hair, then asked if I was feeling all right.

I looked back at the monsters. I couldn't stop looking at the one who had no face but just a huge red horn, like a rhino's horn, only red, in his forehead. He had a man's body but it was covered in fur and his black trousers were held up with braces that were made out of barbed wire and dripping with blood. He was holding a long pole with a round metal ball on top with spikes sticking out of it like a hedgehog. He drew a finger to where his lips would be, if he had any, and then a voice appeared in my head. It sounded very soft and yet gruff, just like my dad's:

'*I'm your friend, Alex.*'

And then all the fear left me because what I wanted more than anything in the whole world was a friend.

I found out later that Ruen has different ways of appearing and this was the one I call the Horn Head, which is very scary, especially when you see it for the first time. Luckily he doesn't appear like that very often.

Miss Holland asked what I was staring at, because I was still looking at the monsters and wondering if they were ghosts, because some of them were like shadows. The thought of it made me start to open my mouth and I felt a noise start to come out, but before it grew too big I heard my dad's voice, again, in my head:

'Be calm, Alex. We're not monsters. We're your friends. Don't you want us to be your friends?'

I looked at Miss Holland and said I was fine, and she smiled and said OK and walked back to her desk, but she kept glancing back at me with her face all worried.

A second later, without crossing the room, the monster who had spoken to me appeared beside me and told me his name was Ruen. He said I'd better sit down otherwise Miss Holland would send me to talk to someone called A Psychiatrist. And that, Ruen told me, would not involve anything fun, like acting or telling jokes or drawing pictures of skeletons.

Ruen knew my favourite hobbies so I knew there was something strange going on here. Miss Holland kept looking at me like she was very worried as she continued her lesson on how to stick a needle through a frozen balloon and why this was an important scientific experiment. I sat down and said nothing about the monsters.

Ruen has explained many things to me about who he is and what he does, but never about why I can see him when no one else can. I think we're friends. Only, what Ruen has asked me to do makes me think he's not my friend at all. He wants me to do something very bad.

He wants me to kill someone.

2

WAKEFUL DREAM

Alex

Dear Diary,

A ten-year-old boy walks into a fishmonger's and asks for a leg of salmon. The wise fishmonger raises his eyebrows and says, 'Salmon don't have any legs!' The boy goes home and tells his dad what the fishmonger said, and his dad starts to laugh.

'OK,' the boy's dad says. 'Away off to the DIY store, pick me up some tartan paint.'

So the boy goes off to the DIY store. When he returns, he is feeling very humiliated.

'OK, OK, I'm sorry,' the dad says, though he's laughing so hard he almost pees himself. 'Here's a fiver. Go get us all fish fingers and use the change for some chips for you.'

The boy threw the fiver back in his dad's face.

'Here, what's all that about?' the dad yelled.

'You can't fool me,' the boy shouted back. 'Fish don't have any fingers!'

This is a new diary that Mum bought me for my last birthday when I was ten. I want to start every entry with a new joke so I can keep in character. That means I can remember what it feels like to be the person I'm playing, which is a boy called Horatio. My acting teacher Jojo said she's rewritten a famous play called *Hamlet* as a 'contemporary retelling of twenty-first century Belfast, with rap, street gangs, and kamikaze nuns', and apparently William Shakespeare is OK with that. Mum says my getting into the theatre company is a really big deal but not to tell anyone in our street as I might get beaten up.

We're performing the play at the Grand Opera House in Belfast City which is cool cos it's like a ten-minute walk from my house so I can make rehearsals every Thursday and Friday after school. Jojo said I can even make up my own jokes. I think this joke is funnier than my last one about the old woman and the orangutan. I told it to Mum but she didn't laugh. She is sad again. I have started to ask her why she gets sad, and each time the reason is different. Yesterday it was because the postman was late, and she was waiting for a Really Important Letter from social services. Today, it's because we've run out of eggs.

I can't think of a more stupid reason to be sad. I wonder

whether she's lying to me, or if she actually thinks that it's fine to burst into tears every five seconds. I think I'll ask her more questions about what the sadness is like. *Is it because of my dad?* I wanted to ask this morning, but then I had what the bald counsellor called a Wakeful Dream and remembered my dad the time he made Mum cry. Usually she was really really happy when he came to visit, which wasn't very often, and she'd make her lips red and her hair would look like ice cream piled up on her head and she'd sometimes wear her dark green dress. But there was this time that he came and all she did was cry. I remember I was sitting so close to him that I could see the tattoo on his left forearm of a man who Dad said starved himself to death on purpose. He was saying to Mum, *Don't give me the guilt trip*, leaning across the kitchen sink to tap his cigarette into the sink. Always three taps. *Tap tap tap.*

Aren't you always going on about how you want a better house than this? This is your chance, love.

And just as I reached out to touch his jeans, the left knee almost worn through from where he'd always bend down to tie my shoelaces, the Wakeful Dream faded and it was just me, Mum, and the sound of her crying.

Mum hasn't talked about Dad in about a million years, so I think she might be sad because of Granny, because Granny always looked after us and was tough with nosy social workers and when Mum got sad Granny would slam her hand on the kitchen bench and say things like, 'If you don't stand up to life it'll knock you down,' and then Mum seemed to snap out of it. But Granny doesn't say that any more, and Mum just gets worse all the time.

So, I do what I always do, which is ignore Mum as she walks around our house with her face all dripping wet, and I hunt through the fridge and kitchen cupboards and under the stairs for something to eat, until finally I find what I'm looking for: an onion and some frozen bread. Unfortunately I don't find any eggs, which is a pity because it may have made Mum stop crying.

I stand on a stool and chop up the onion underwater in the sink – like Granny taught me, so the juices don't make my eyes flood – and then fry it up with some oil. Then I put it all between two slices of toasted bread. Trust me, it is the best thing in the world.

The second best thing in the world is my bedroom. I was going to say drawing skeletons, or balancing on the back legs of my chair, but I think they're third best, because my bedroom is so high at the top of our house that I don't hear Mum crying when I come up here, and because it's where I go to think and to draw, and also to write jokes for my part as Horatio. It's freezing up here. You could probably store dead bodies. The windowpane is cracked and there's no carpet and all the radiator does is make a big yellow puddle on the bare floor. Most of the time I put on an extra jumper and sometimes a coat, a hat, woolly socks and gloves when I get up there, though I've cut the fingertips off my gloves so I can hold my pencils. It's so cold that Dad never even bothered to rip all the old wallpaper off the walls, which he said has been up since St Patrick kicked all the snakes out of Ireland. It's silver with lots of white leaves all over it, though I think they look like an angel's feathers. The last person who lived here left all their stuff, like a bed with only three legs, a wardrobe, and a tall white chest of drawers which was filled with lots of clothes. The person who left them was probably just lazy but it's worked out OK as Mum never has any money to get me any new clothes.

But that's just the best thing about my room. You know what the best *best* thing about my room is?

When Ruen comes, I can blether on at him for ages. And no one else can hear.

So when I found out that Ruen is a *demon* I wasn't scared because I didn't know a demon was a *thing*. I thought it was just the name of the shop near my school that sold motor-bikes.

'What's a demon, then?' I asked Ruen.

He was Ghost Boy then. Ruen has four appearances: Horn Head, Monster, Ghost Boy and Old Man. Ghost Boy is when he looks like me, only in a funny kind of way: he has my exact same brown hair and is as tall as me and even has the same knobbly fingers and fat nose and sticky-out ears, but he has eyes that are completely black and sometimes his whole body is see-through like a balloon. His clothes are different than mine, too. He wears trousers that are puffy and gather in at the knees and a white shirt with no collar, and his feet are bare and dirty.

8

When I asked what a demon was, Ruen jumped up and started shadow boxing in front of the mirror on the back of my bedroom door.

'Demons are like superheroes,' he said between jabs. 'Humans are like maggots.'

I was still sitting on the floor. I'd lost our game of chess. Ruen had let me take all his pawns and bishops and then checkmated me with just his king and queen.

'Why are humans like maggots?' I asked.

He stopped boxing and turned to me. I could see the mirror through him so I kept my gaze on that rather than look him in the face, because his black eyes made my stomach feel funny.

'It's not your fault your mum gave birth to you,' he said, and started doing star jumps. Because he's like a ghost his jumps looked like scribbles in the air.

'But why are humans like maggots?' I asked. Unlike humans, maggots look like crawling fingernails and they live at the bottom of our wheelie bin.

'Because they're stupid,' he said, still jumping.

'*How* are humans stupid, then?' I said, standing up.

He stopped jumping and looked at me. His face was angry.

'Look,' he said, and held out his hand towards me. 'Now put yours on top of mine.'

I did. You couldn't see the floor through mine.

'You have a body,' he said. 'But you'll probably waste it, everything you can do with it. Just like free will. It's like giving a Lamborghini to an infant.'

'So you're jealous, then?' I asked, because a Lamborghini is a really cool car that everyone wants.

'A baby driving a sportscar would be a bad idea, wouldn't it? Somebody needs to step in, stop the kid from doing more damage than it needs to.'

'So demons look after babies, then?' I said.

He looked disgusted. 'Don't be ridiculous.'

'What *do* they do, then?'

And then he gave me his Alex Is Stupid look. It's when he smiles with only half his mouth and his eyes are small and hard and he shakes his head as if I'm a disappointment. It's the look that makes my stomach knot and my heart beat faster because deep down I know I *am* stupid.

'We try and help you see past the lie.'

I blinked. 'What lie?'

'You all think you're so important, so special. It's a fallacy, Alex. You're nothing.'

Now I'm ten I'm much older so I kind of know more about demons and Ruen's not like that. I think everyone's got it wrong about demons, just like they did about Rottweilers. Everyone says Rottweilers eat children but Granny had one called Milo and he always just licked my face and let me ride him like a pony.

Mum never sees Ruen, and I haven't told her about him or about any of the demons who come into our house. Some of them are a bit strange, but I just ignore them. It's like having loads of grumpy relatives tramping through the place, thinking they can order me about. Ruen's OK, though. He ignores Mum and likes poking around our house. He loves Granddad's old piano that sits in the hallway. He'll stand beside it for ages, leaning down to have a closer look at the wood as if there's a miniature village living in the grain. Then he lowers down to press his ear against the bottom half, as if there's someone inside trying to talk to him. He tells me this was a *stupendous make of piano*, once upon a time, but he's very irritated by the way Mum keeps it pressed up against a radiator and doesn't get it tuned. *Sounds like an old dog*, he says, rapping it with his knuckles like a door. I just shrug and say, *Big deal*. Then he gets so cross that he vanishes.

Ruen sometimes turns into the Old Man when he gets cross. If I look like him when I get older, I'll honestly kill myself. When he's the Old Man he's so skinny and withered he looks like a cactus with eyes and ears. His face is long as a spade with lots of wrinkles grooved so deep he looks sort of scrunched up, like tin foil that's been reused. He's got a long hooked nose and his mouth reminds me of a piranha's. His head is shiny as a silver doorknob and is covered in wispy tufts of fine white hair. His face is grey like a pencil but the bags under his eyes are bright pink, as if someone's ripped the skin off. He's really ugly.

But this isn't as bad as what he looks like when he's Monster. Monster is like a dead body that's been underwater for weeks and is dragged up by the police on to a small boat and everyone pukes because the skin is the colour of an aubergine and the head is three times' the size of a normal person's head. And that's not all: when he's Monster, Ruen's face isn't a face. His mouth looks like someone blew a hole there with a shotgun and his eyes are tiny like a lizard's.

Here's another thing: he says he's nine thousand human years old. *Yeah, right*, I said when he first told me, but he just tilted his chin and spent the next hour telling me how he could speak more than six thousand languages, even the ones that no one spoke any more. He went on and on about how humans don't even know their own language, not really, and don't even have proper words for big things like *guilt* and *evil*, that it was *idiotic* that a country with so many different kinds of rain should only have one word for it, blah blah blah, until I yawned for about five minutes solid and he took the hint and left. But the next day, it rained, and I thought, *Maybe Ruen isn't such an eejit after all. Maybe he actually has a point.* Some rain is like little fish, some is like big globby chunks of spit, and some is like ball bearings. So I started to borrow books from the library to learn some words in lots of cool languages, like Turkish and Icelandic and Maori.

'*Merhaba*, Ruen,' I said to him one day, and he just sighed and said, 'It's a silent "h", you imbecile.' So I said, '*Góða kvöldið*' and he snapped, 'It's still only mid-morning,' and when I said, '*He roa te wā kua kitea*,' he said I was as obtuse as a gnu.

'What language is that?' I asked.

'English,' he sighed, and disappeared.

So I started reading the dictionary to understand the weird words he uses all the time, like *brouhaha*. I tried using that word with Mum about the riots last July. She thought I was laughing at her.

Ruen also told me all this stuff about people I had never heard of. He said one of his best mates for ages was called Nero, but that Nero preferred to be called Seezer by everyone and still peed the bed when he was like twenty years old.

Then Ruen told me he'd stayed in a prison cell with a guy called Sock-rat-ease when Sock-rat-ease was on a death sentence. Ruen told Sock-rat-ease that he should escape. Ruen said that he even had some of Sock-rat-ease's friends offer to help him escape, but Sock-rat-ease wouldn't, so he just died.

'That's mental,' I said.

'Indeed,' said Ruen.

It sounded like Ruen had loads of friends, which made me sad because I didn't have any except him.

'Who was your *best* friend?' I asked him, hoping he'd say me.

He said Wolfgang.

I asked, *Why Wolfgang?* and what I meant was why was Wolfgang his best friend and not me, but all Ruen said was he liked Wolfgang's music and then he went quiet.

I know what you're thinking: I'm crazy and Ruen is all in my head, not just his voice. That I watch too many horror movies. That Ruen's an imaginary friend I've dreamed up because I'm lonely. Well, you'd be incredibly wrong if you thought any of that. Though sometimes I am lonely.

Mum bought me a dog for my eighth birthday that I

named Woof. Woof reminds me of a grumpy old man cos he's always barking and baring his teeth and his fur is white and tough like an old man's hair. Mum calls him the barking footstool. Woof used to sleep beside my bed and run down the stairs to bark at people when they came into the house in case they were going to kill me, but when Ruen started appearing more often Woof got scared. He just growls at thin air now, even when Ruen isn't there.

Which reminds me. Ruen told me something today that I thought was interesting enough to bother writing down. He said he's not just a demon. His real title is a *Harrower*.

When he said it he was the Old Man. He smiled like a cat and all his wrinkles stretched. He said it the way Auntie Bev tells people that she's a doctor. I think it means a lot to Auntie Bev that she's a doctor, because nobody in our family ever went to university before, or drove a Mercedes and bought their own house like Auntie Bev.

I reckon Ruen is proud of being a Harrower because it means he is someone very important in Hell. When I asked Ruen what a Harrower was, he told me to think of what the word meant. I tried to look it up in my dictionary but it described a gardening tool, which makes no sense. When I asked again, Ruen said did I know what a soldier was. I said, *Duh, of course I do*, and he said, *Well, if a regular demon's a soldier, I would be comparable to a Commander General or Field Marshal*. So I said, *Do demons fight in wars, then?* And he said *No, though they are always fighting against the Enemy*. And I said that sounded paranoid, and he scowled and said, *Demons are perpetually vigilant, not paranoid*. He *still* won't tell me exactly what a Harrower is, so I've decided to make up my own definition: a Harrower is a manky old sod who wants to show off his war medals and hates that only I can see him.

Wait. I think I can hear Mum downstairs. Yep, she's crying again. Maybe I should pretend that I don't notice. I've got rehearsals for *Hamlet* in seventy-two and a half minutes. Maybe she's just doing it for attention. But my room has started filling with demons, about twenty of them sitting on my bed and huddled in corners, whispering and giggling. They're all talking excitedly like it's Christmas or something, and one of them just said my mum's name. I have a funny feeling in my tummy.

Something is happening downstairs.

'What's going on?' I just asked Ruen. 'Why are they talking about my mum?'

He looked at me and raised one of his caterpillar eyebrows. 'My dear boy, Death has arrived at your front door.'

3

THE FEELING

Anya

The call came this morning at seven-thirty.

Ursula Hepworth, the senior consultant at MacNeice House Child and Adolescent Mental Health Inpatient Unit in Belfast, rang me on my mobile and mentioned a ten-year-old boy at risk of possibly harming himself and others. Name of Alex Broccoli, she said. Alex's mother attempted suicide yesterday and has since been sectioned, while the boy has been taken to the paediatric unit at the City Hospital. Alex was at his home in west Belfast and had spent an hour alone with her, trying to call for help. Eventually a lady coming to collect Alex for a drama group intervened and took the pair to hospital. Quite understandably, the boy was in quite a state. Ursula informed me that a social worker named Michael

Jones had already had contact with the boy and that he was concerned about his mental health. Alex's mother has attempted suicide at least four times in the last five years. Eight out of ten children who witness a parent self-harm will go on to repeat the action on themselves.

'Typically, *I* would be the lead clinician on this boy's case,' Ursula explained, her Greek accent sliced up by Northern Irish tones. 'But as our new child and adolescent psychiatry consultant I thought I'd pass the baton over to you. What do you say?'

I sat up in bed, greeted by a swathe of boxes all over the floor of my new flat. It's a four-room place on the outskirts of the city, so close to the ocean that I wake to the sound of seagulls and the faint smell of salt. It is tiled floor to ceiling in a tomato-red tile that burns like the inside of a furnace every sunrise, on account of the fact that the flat faces east and I haven't had the chance to buy curtains. I haven't had time to furnish it either, such have been the demands of this new job since moving back from Edinburgh two weeks ago.

I glanced at my watch. 'When would you need me to come in?'

'In an hour?'

The sixth of May has been circled in my work schedule as a day off for the past three years, and was agreed at the point I signed my employment contract. It always will be for the rest of my working life. On this day, those who I count as my closest friends will arrive bearing consolation offerings of cheesecake, tender embraces, photo albums of me and my daughter in happier times, when she was alive and relatively well. Some of these friends will not have seen me for months, but even when their hair colour has changed and other relationships have ended, these friends will show up on my doorstep to help me purge this day out of my calendar for another year. And it will always be so.

'I'm sorry,' I said, and I began to explain about my contract, about the fact that I've booked this day off and perhaps she could interview the boy for today and I could catch up on his notes tomorrow?

There was a long pause.

'This is really quite important,' she said sternly.

There are many who feel intimidated by Ursula. At forty-three, I like to think I am past such things as an inferiority complex, and in any case the staggering reality of Poppy's fourth anniversary already had me on the verge of tears. I took a deep breath and informed Ursula in my most professional voice that I would gladly meet with the rest of the Child and Mental Health Services team first thing tomorrow morning.

And then something happened that I still can't explain, something that has happened only a few times before and which is so unlike any other feeling that I've named it, quite simply, The Feeling. It defies words, but if I'm to attempt to verbalise it, it goes like this: deep in my solar plexus, there's at first a warmth, and then a fire, though not a sensation of heat or pain, that creeps up my neck and jaw, right into my scalp until my hair stands on end, and at the same time I feel it in my knees, my ankles, even my sacrum, until I am so conscious of every part of my body that I feel like I'm about to lift off. It's like my soul is trying to tell me something, an urgent, tingling message that so fills my capillaries and cells that it threatens to burst if I don't listen.

'Are you all right?' Ursula asked, and I told her to give me a moment. I set the receiver on my dresser and wiped my face. In ten years of training I have never come across a single piece of literature to inform me why this thing happens to me sometimes, nor why it tends to happen on the most significant of occasions. I only know that I have to listen. Last time I didn't, my daughter decided to end her life and I was not able to stop her.

'OK,' I told her. 'I'll be there this morning.'

'Appreciate it, Anya. I know you'll be wonderful on this case.'

She told me she would contact the boy's social worker, Michael Jones, and have him meet me at the reception of MacNeice House in two hours. I ended the call and glanced in the mirror. One of the effects of Poppy's death is that I now wake frequently during the night, resulting in sallow patches beneath my eyes for which no make-up seems to compensate. I looked over the jagged white scar on my face, the flat of my cheek there sucked inward by the ribbed pattern of dead tissue. Usually I spend a considerable amount of time each morning arranging my long black hair in a way that shields this ugliness. I made do with sweeping my hair into a chignon spiked by a biro and threw on the only item of clothing that I'd unpacked – a black trouser suit with a crumpled white shirt. Finally, of course, I draped my silver talisman around my neck. Then I left a note for the friends who would come and find, to their astonishment and fear, that I had actually crossed the threshold of my home on the anniversary of Poppy's death.

I took the coastal road instead of the motorway in a bid to distract myself from thoughts of Poppy. Maybe it's a consequence of approaching middle age, but my memories of her these days are not visual, rendered instead by sounds. Her laughter, light and infectious. The melodies she used to make up on my old Steinway in our Morningside flat in Edinburgh, using one finger. The phrases she'd use to describe her condition. *It's like . . . it's like a hole, Mum. No, like I am one. A hole. Like I'm swallowing darkness.*

MacNeice House is an old Victorian mansion located in an acre of wilderness, high in the hills that look down on Belfast's bridges named after British monarchs. Recently refurbished, the unit offers inpatient and day-patient treatment for children and young people between the ages of four and fifteen suffering from any mental illness noted in textbooks – anxiety disorders, autism spectrum disorders, behavioural disorders, depressive disorders, obsessive compulsive disorder, psychotic disorders, and then some. There are ten bedrooms, a common room with computers, an art room, an interview or therapy room, a toy room, a dining room, a swimming pool, a small apartment for parents who need to stay over occasionally, and a restraining room – strictly referred to in-house as 'the quiet room'. Inpatients require education, and so an onsite school is available and provided by specialist teaching staff. After completing my training at Edinburgh University I worked at a similar unit there for two years, but the reputation of MacNeice House attracted me back home to Northern Ireland – a move I am still tentative about.

I spotted a new vehicle parked beside Ursula's gleaming black Lexus in the car park – a battered bottle-green Volvo with a 1990 registration plate – and I wondered if Alex's social worker, Michael Jones, had already arrived. I raced across the gravel car park using my briefcase as protection against the pouring rain, when a tall man in a navy suit stepped out from behind the stone pillars, opening a golf umbrella in my direction.

'Welcome,' he called. I stepped underneath the umbrella and he shielded me until we were well inside, where Ursula was waiting at reception. She is tall with an imperial air, her red suit, thick black Diana-Ross mane streaked with grey and handsome Greek bone structure more suggestive of a high-profile businesswoman than a clinical psychologist. She was also one of the panel members at my interview for this post, and it was because of her that I was sure I hadn't got the job.

You originally trained to become a GP. Why the shift into child psychiatry?

At the interview I had slipped my right hand beneath my thigh, looking over the faces of the panel – three male psychiatrists and Ursula, internationally renowned as much for her developments in child psychology as for her boorishness.

My original interest lay in psychiatry, I had replied. *My mother had a long battle with mental illness, and I had a desire to find answers to the riddles posed by such illnesses.* If anyone knew the devastation caused by mental illness – its social taboos, disgraces; its ancient, fearful association with shame at just how far the human mind can plummet into itself – it was me.

Ursula had watched me carefully from behind the panel desk. *I thought the cardinal sin of any psychiatrist was to suppose that all the answers can be found,* she had offered lightly – a joke with a jag. The panel Chair – John Kind, Head of the Psychiatry Department at Queen's University – had glanced uncomfortably from Ursula to me and attempted to forge a question out of Ursula's thinly veiled joke.

Do you believe you've found all the answers, Anya? Or is that your intent by taking up this post?

My heart said *yes*. But, at the time, I smiled and gave the answer they were looking for.

My intent is to make a difference.

At reception, Ursula gave me an overly wide smile, then extended a hand and shook mine firmly for the first time since my interview. It is not entirely uncommon for psychiatrists to clash with psychologists, given the disparity in our approaches, though I assumed from her phonecall that whatever issue she had with me at the interview had been resolved.

She turned from me to Michael, who was shaking out the umbrella and slotting it into the coatstand.

'Anya, this is Michael, Alex's social worker. He works for the local authority.'

Michael turned and flashed a crooked smile. 'Yes,' he said. 'Someone has to.'

Ursula regarded him through heavy eyelids before facing me. 'Michael will talk you through the details. I'll meet with you later to discuss management of the case.' She nodded curtly at Michael before walking back down the corridor.

Michael held his hand out for a shake. 'Thanks for coming in on your day off,' he said. I wanted to tell him it was more than a day off – it was the anniversary of my daughter's death – but found a lump forming of its own accord in my throat. I busied myself with signing my name into the register.

'You know, we've already met,' he told me as he took the pen from my hand.

'We have?'

He signed his name with an illegible flourish. 'At the Child Psychiatry conference in Dublin in 2001.'

The conference was six years ago. I had no memory of him at all. I saw he was rangy and wide-shouldered, with steely green eyes that held a stare several seconds longer than was comfortable. I guessed him to be in his late thirties, and there was a weariness about him that I'd encountered many times with social workers, a cynicism detectable in his body language, the slightness of his smile. His voice bore the rough edge of too many cigarettes and from the cut of his suit and the shine of his shoes I suspected that he had no children. His blond hair was worn messy and long over his collar, but a scent of hair gel told me this was deliberate.

'What was a social worker doing at a child psychiatry conference?' I turned towards the corridor behind us that led to my office.

'Psychiatry was my original discipline, after a spell studying for the priesthood.'

'The priesthood?'

'Family tradition. I liked your paper, by the way. "Addressing the need for psychosis intervention in Northern Ireland," wasn't that it? It struck me that you're passionate about changing things around here.'

'Change is probably a bit ambitious,' I said. 'But I'd like to look at the way we handle younger cases of psychosis.'

'How so?'

I cleared my throat, feeling an old defensiveness rise up. 'I think we're missing too many signs of psychosis and even early onset schizophrenia, allowing these kids to flail and even harm themselves when treatment could very easily help them live normal lives.' My voice had started to wobble. I heard Poppy's efforts on our piano in my head, her voice softly humming the melody she was trying to match on the keys. When I looked back at him I noticed he was staring at the scar on my face. *I should have worn my hair long*, I thought.

We reached the door to my office. I tried to remember my entry code, given to me the week before by Ursula's secretary,

Josh. After a few seconds I punched the gold number on the lock. I turned to see Michael looking up and down the corridor, his expression wary.

'You never been to MacNeice House before?' I asked lightly.

'Yes. Too many times, I'm afraid.'

'You don't like it?'

'I don't agree with psychiatric institutions. Not for kids.'

I opened the door. 'This isn't a psychiatric institution, it's an inpatient unit . . . '

He grinned. 'Tomayto, tomato, eh?'

Inside, Michael remained standing until I pointed out two softbacked armchairs at a white coffee table and offered him a drink, which he declined. I poured myself a herbal tea and sat down in the smaller armchair. Michael leaned back in his chair, his gaze turned to a poster on the wall by my bookcase.

'*Suspicion often creates what it suspects,*' he said, reading the poster. There was a question in his tone.

'C S Lewis,' I said. 'From *The Screwtape Letters*. Have you read . . . ?'

'Yes, I know,' he said, his face twisting at the sight of my herbal tea. 'I'm wondering why you framed a quote like that?'

'I guess it was one of those things that made sense at the time.'

'I have the T-shirt for that one.'

There was a pause as he pulled out a file from his briefcase. The name at the top read ALEX BROCCOLI.

'Alex is ten years old,' Michael told me, his voice softening.

'He lives in one of the poorest parts of Belfast with his mother Cindy, who is a single parent in her mid-twenties. Cindy has had a hard life herself, though that's probably a conversation for another time. You'll know she recently attempted suicide.'

I nodded. 'Where's Alex's father?'

'We don't know. There's no name on Alex's birth certificate. Cindy's never been married and refuses to talk about him. He didn't seem to play much of a role in Alex's life. What we do know is that Alex is deeply worried about his mother's health. He acts fatherly towards her, exhibiting all the hallmarks of a child deep in the clutch of the trauma of parental suicide attempt.'

He spun a document around on the table to face me – a compilation of notes from Alex's consultations with several different paediatric psychiatrists.

'Interviews with his mother and schoolteachers have flagged multiple psychotic episodes, including violence towards a schoolteacher.'

I looked up. 'Violence?'

Michael sighed, reluctant to divulge. 'He lashed out during an outburst in the classroom. He claimed he was provoked by another child and the teacher didn't wish to make a big deal out of it, but we still record these events.'

A quick scan across the notes told me that Alex had all the classic first-rank symptoms of mild high-functioning ASD – Autism Spectrum Disorder – such as being quite concrete in his thinking, prone to misunderstandings, violent outbursts, language that is slightly more sophisticated for his age, no friends, and eccentricity. I noticed a detail about his claiming to see demons. Then I saw that no medication or treatment had ever been prescribed, and for a moment I was lost for words. I had been warned repeatedly by colleagues in Scotland that *things are different in Northern Ireland*, 'things' being the practice of psychiatric intervention. Those words rang in my ears as I scanned the file.

After a few moments I became aware that Michael was watching me. 'So what brought you back to Northern Ireland?' he asked when I caught his gaze.

I sat back in my seat and clasped my hands. 'Short answer, the job.'

'And the long answer?'

I hesitated. 'An off-hand remark from a PhD candidate doing a placement at the unit I worked at in Edinburgh. She mentioned that even those kids in Northern Ireland who have never experienced the Troubles, who have never been fished from a swimming pool and wrapped in tin foil during a terrorist threat, who have never measured distance by the sound of a bomb and who have never even seen a gun are experiencing psychological effects because of what the older generation has suffered.'

He cocked his head. '"Secondary impact", isn't that what it's called?'

I nodded. For a moment my memory heaved up the muffled thud of a bomb. From my bedroom window in Bangor – a coastal suburb on the fringe of Belfast – I could hear the explosions; sickening, hollow. A memory I have never shaken.

'There's a higher prevalence of psychological morbidity in the adult population here than anywhere else in the UK.'

'Well, that explains a lot about my job, then.' He rubbed his eyes, suddenly deep in thought. 'Did *you* ever get fished out of a swimming pool during a bomb hoax?'

'Twice.'

'So you reckon every poor sod who's been involved in the Troubles has a higher chance of a mental breakdown?'

I shook my head. 'No one has any ability to estimate the impact of an experience on a person's mental health. There's too many other factors . . . '

He frowned. 'Alex has never been involved in the Troubles.'

'No?'

'We've interviewed him and Cindy about things like that. I mean, yes, they live in a rough neighbourhood, but Cindy has made it clear that it was the abuse she suffered at home as a child that impacted on her so greatly.'

Another form of secondary impact, I thought. 'How long have you been involved with Alex's case?'

'I've had intermittent contact with him since he was seven. His family situation is very vulnerable, and his living conditions aren't exactly ideal, either. The powers that be threatened to place him in foster care last time Cindy attempted suicide.'

It struck me that this might not have been as bad an idea as Michael clearly believed, though I figured I would give him the benefit of the doubt for the time being.

I tapped the thick wad of notes on the table in front of me, thinking.

'What's needed?' I asked quietly, noticing Michael's voice grow louder at the mention of foster care, his pale face beginning to flush red around his jaw.

'A Statement of Special Needs, for a start.' He paused. 'When I heard we had a new child psychiatrist in town . . . well, you can only imagine my relief.' He smiled, and suddenly I felt afraid of letting him down.

'Be specific, Michael. Please.'

He leaned forward, elbows dug into his knees, his eyes falling on my legs. With a cough he brought his gaze up to meet mine.

'The thing is, Dr Molokova, I'm an advocate of Signs of Safety.'

I stared at him.

'You know, the Australian model for child protection . . . ?'

'I know what Signs of Safety is,' I said flatly. It was in my interests to. Signs of Safety is a type of child protection plan based on working closely with families to build a system of safety and, ultimately, family-centred treatment. Most of its advocates staunchly reject the types of intervention that form the basis of my job.

Michael seemed agitated. 'Look, I need you to promise me you won't separate this family. Trust me, they need each other, not some bureaucratic, by-the-book, form-ticking procedure that lands this boy in care . . . '

'My only agenda is to find out what treatment the boy

needs.' I said it clear and slow, hoping it would reassure him. If we were to work together on this case, we needed to sing from the same hymn sheet.

He eyed me with a degree of nervousness, a hint of pleading. This boy meant a lot to him. Not just professionally, either – I saw that Michael had become personally involved in this case. I perceived he had a touch of the hero complex about him – the weathered, tired air was a result of his frustrations. After a long pause he broke into a smile, before pouring himself a mugful of my nettle tea and necking it with a prolonged shudder of disgust.

I stood up to leave, noting our appointment with Alex was in twenty minutes' time. Michael shuffled his notes and slid them neatly into his briefcase.

'You look exhausted,' he said, smiling to show the comment was born out of empathy, not criticism. 'Shall I drive?'

4

'WHO GAVE YOU THAT SCAR?'

Anya

And so we headed off in Michael's Volvo – which, oddly, bore a strong smell of fertiliser inside – to the paediatric unit of the Belfast City Hospital.

It was important that my approach was gentle and provided Alex with a high degree of space and assurance. Before leaving MacNeice House I had instructed Michael to contact Alex about where he would like to meet with me, and to confirm that the time was suitable, so that my arrival did not cause anxiety. Alex had not been concerned about either; he simply wanted to know how his mother was doing and when he could see her at the hospital. He had subsequently been promised a visit with her once she had been treated medically.

Michael entered the room first, after a knuckled *rat-a-tat-tat* on the door. Children's interview rooms in psychiatric units are always the same: a corner full of sensory toys and, invariably, a doll's house. In this case the room had just a doll's house, a child's whiteboard on a stand, a tatty blue sofa and a table with two chairs. Over Michael's shoulder I spotted Alex on a chair behind the table, balancing on its hind legs.

'Hello, Alex,' Michael said lightly. At the sight of Michael the boy slammed the chair back down on all four legs and shouted, 'Sorry!' Michael waved his hand in the air to indicate no harm done. Then he held both hands towards me as if presenting the prize on a quiz show.

'I'd like to introduce you to Dr Molokova,' he told Alex, who gave a polite smile and a nod in my direction.

'Call me Anya,' I told Alex, smiling back. 'It's nice to meet you.'

'An-ya,' he repeated. I looked him over briefly. I noticed he had a touch of the street urchin about him: chocolate-brown hair in need of a cut and a good wash; pale, Northern Irish skin; wide denim-blue eyes; a cheeky mushroom nose splattered with fat freckles. More striking was his dress sense: an man's oversized shirt with brown stripes, buttoned-up wrong; brown tweed trousers with thick turn-ups at the hems, a man's tartan tie, and black school shoes that had been carefully polished. Slung over the sofa I spotted a waistcoat and blazer. I wouldn't have been surprised if I'd spotted a cane and pipe. Alex had clearly been independent for a long time, and was trying to be much older than his years. To support his mother,

I guessed. I was anxious to work out whether this was a manifestation of another personality, or if he was just plain eccentric. The room was filled with the smell of onions.

Michael pulled a chair close to the door and sat down, careful not to intrude on my meeting with Alex. I walked towards the table.

'Very cosy in here, isn't it?'

Alex watched me, nervously. 'Is my mum OK?' he asked. I glanced back at Michael, who nodded.

'I believe she's safe and sound, Alex,' I said, choosing my words carefully: it is always my utmost resolve to be honest with my patients, but when it comes to young children, tact is highly important. Though Alex had seen me hesitate and glance at Michael, and the smile he offered back was fractured with worry. This was not surprising, given what he had been through. It is rare for me to work with children who have had pleasant childhoods, yet despite the catalogue of traumatic life stories I've racked up so far I still find it upsetting to become part of yet another narrative that is marred by so much harm at such a young age. Too many times I know the ending out-right, and I can never erase the faces of those children from my memory. I find myself mulling over their life experiences in my sleep.

But Alex did not appear what we in the psychiatry field call 'flat'. His eyes were lively, questioning, and haunted.

A psychiatry consultation is a little like an interview with a celebrity: it moves in inward-bound spirals, circling the crucial issue through a series of related topics. Only, a psychiatry consultation needs to achieve that by allowing the interviewee to steer the conversation. I looked for cues. On the whiteboard beside the doll's house, a fresh picture of a house had been sketched in blue marker with noticeable care. I pointed at it.

'What a beautiful drawing. Is this your house?'

Alex shook his head adamantly.

'Is it a house you've seen before?'

He got up from his seat and walked carefully towards the whiteboard.

'It's the house I'd buy my mum if I had enough money,' he explained, rubbing a stray line around the carefully arched front door. 'It's got a yellow roof, and there's flowers in the front garden and lots of bedrooms.'

I was keen to pursue this topic, seeing his shoulders begin to lower. 'How many bedrooms?' I asked.

'I'm not sure.' He picked up his blue marker and continued adding to the house with surprising artistic skill – a cockerel-shaped weather vane on the roof, two small bay trees beside the front door, a dog running up the garden path. I watched on, saying nothing, mentally taking notes.

He drew a small circle in the front garden of the house and filled it with dots – a strawberry patch, he said, because his granny used to grow strawberries to make jam. His final addition to the drawing was a huge set of wings at the top of the picture, in the sky.

'What's that?' I asked.

'An angel,' he said. 'To protect us from bad things. Though

I've never seen an angel.' As soon as he said it he appeared to shut off, withdrawing eye contact and raising a hand to his mouth, as if he was afraid he'd given something away.

I asked Alex if it would be OK for me to open a window. I find an open window often acts as a reassurance to patients that they are not trapped, that there's a physical exit, should they require it, even though it would take a set of ladders and a Spider-Man dexterity to climb out these windows. He nodded and took a deep breath. Already, he was relaxing. Step one.

I sat cross-legged on the multi-coloured foam floor tiles and pulled out a notebook and pen from my satchel. Alex fidgeted a bit, glancing at Michael, who was sitting on the sofa at the other side of the room. Eventually, Alex sat down opposite me.

'Do you mind if I take notes during our conversation, Alex?'

He made himself comfortable, crossing his legs and holding on to his ankles. He nodded. 'I write stuff down, too.'

'You write?' I asked. 'Stories? Poems? A diary?'

At the third attempt, his eyes lit up.

'Me too. I find writing things down helps me clarify them,' I said, holding up my notebook, but he was still staring at the corner, deep in thought.

'How did you get that?' he said when he spotted my facial scar.

'It's nothing,' I said, fingering the jagged groove on my cheek, reminding myself to keep my emotions in check. 'Have you ever fallen off your bike?'

'I cut my knee once.' A long pause while he reflected on this. Then: 'Why are you wearing a bottle top for a necklace?'

He was looking at the silver talisman around my neck. I showed him. 'It's not a bottle top. It's called an SOS talisman. It's to tell people what treatment I need in case I experience something called an anaphylactic shock.'

He repeated the words *anaphylactic shock*. 'What is that?'

'I'm allergic to nuts.'

His blue eyes widened. 'Even peanuts?'

'Yep.'

He considered this. 'And peanut butter?'

'That too.'

He cocked his head. 'Why?'

'My body doesn't like them.'

He held me more firmly in his gaze now, inspecting me like I might explode at any moment or grow a second head.

'So what would happen if you ate, like, a Snickers or something?'

I would probably stop breathing, I thought, but instead I said: 'I would fall straight to sleep.'

His eyes widened. 'Do you snore?'

I laughed out loud. 'Michael tells me you've got some great jokes. I *love* jokes. Can you tell me your favourite?'

He looked back at me and, after a moment of contemplation, slowly shook his head. 'I can't,' he said, very seriously. 'I've too many favourites.'

I gave him a minute to think, then: 'Shall I tell you one of my favourites?'

'No, I've got one,' he said, and cleared his throat. 'Statistically, six out of seven dwarves aren't Happy.'

It took me a second or two to get it, but when I did, I laughed so hard that Alex's face lit up like a Chinese lantern.

'I didn't write that one,' he said quickly.

'You write your own jokes as well?'

'It's for a play I'm in. I'm playing someone called Horatio.'

'You're in *Hamlet*?'

He informed me that the play was a modern version of Shakespeare's original, that he would be performing it at the Grand Opera House in a few weeks and would I like to come along?

'I'd *love* to,' I said, and I meant it. 'I bet your mum is really proud. Have you shared any of your jokes with her?'

He nodded and looked immensely sad. 'She hasn't laughed in a long, long time.'

'Sometimes people don't laugh on the outside,' I offered, 'but they still laugh on the inside.'

He contemplated this, but I noticed his right hand had crept up to his shirt collar and was tugging at it as if it had suddenly become too tight. I allowed the silence to move past the point of discomfort.

'You mean, people laugh *internally*?' Alex said at last. 'Like, internal laughing instead of internal bleeding?'

The association took me aback, a little. I let him continue.

'I think I know what you mean,' he said slowly. 'I used to laugh internally when my dad was still alive.'

I tread lightly on this topic. 'Can you tell me what you mean?'

Alex glanced at me warily. His hand had not dropped from his collar.

'Sort of. Or more like, I'd do stuff that I liked to do but when he was around I'd do it quietly. Like writing and drawing. That made me happy in here,' he pressed a fist against his chest, 'even though my granny said my dad should go to Hell for what he did.'

He quickly drew a hand to his mouth as if he had revealed something of himself that he didn't wish to.

'It's OK,' I reassured him. 'You can say that, I'm not here to punish you.'

He nodded and fidgeted in his seat.

'I run,' I said, to break the tension. 'Running makes me happy.' I laughed, but Alex's face dropped.

'I don't want to,' he said tensely.

I cocked my head. 'What?'

He glanced at the corner, as if someone was there. Then he took a deep sigh. 'OK,' he said resolutely. I waited for him to continue. Finally, he broke into a wary smile and said: 'Ruen wants me to say hi.'

I stared at him. '*Ruin?*'

'Ruen's my friend,' Alex said, with a hint of confusion in his voice, as if he already expected me to know. 'My *best* friend.'

'*Ruin*,' I repeated. 'Well, thank you. Hello back to Ruin. Can you tell me who Ruin is, though?'

Alex chewed his lip, his eyes dropping to his feet.

'Ruin's an unusual name,' I said. Then, after a long pause: 'Is Ruin an animal?'

He shook his head, his eyes focused beyond me. 'Some of them are, but Ruen's not. He's . . . we're just friends.'

'*Some* of them?' I asked. He nodded but said no more. *Imaginary friends*, I thought.

'Can you tell me a little bit about him?'

Alex looked up, thinking. 'He likes my granddad's piano. And he *loves* Mozart.'

'Mozart?'

Alex nodded. 'But Ruen can't play the piano.' A pause. 'He says you do, though.'

'Yes,' I said, my smile withering. 'I've played the piano since I was a little girl. Mozart's not my favourite composer, though. My very favourite is Ra—'

'Ravel,' Alex said, matter-of-factly finishing my sentence. 'Ruen says Ravel was like a Swiss watchmaker.'

'A *Swiss watchmaker*?' His accuracy shocked me. Ravel had been my favourite composer for decades. I set down my pen and folded my arms. This kid was full of surprises.

Alex leaned sideways, as if he was listening to something. Then he straightened up and stared at me. 'He means Ravel wrote his music like he was making a really expensive watch.' He lifted his hands and twisted imaginary dials. 'Like all the cogs fitted.'

It wasn't out of the question that he might know about Ravel, though still fairly astonishing. I was intrigued. 'And how does Ruin know all this?'

Alex didn't blink. 'Ruen is over nine thousand years old. He knows lots of stuff, though most of it is really *boring*.'

'Does he tell jokes, too?'

Alex raised his eyebrows and started to laugh, his head arched right back. When he recovered himself he said, 'No way, Ruen thinks my jokes are *stupid*. He's more serious than the Terminator.'

I must have looked puzzled, because Alex read my face and told me, 'You know, the film? With Arnie?' He put on a surprisingly decent Arnold Schwarzenegger voice: '*It's in your nature to destroy yourselves.*'

I gave a sufficiently generous chuckle though I note his interest in films older than he is as unusual. 'Does Ruin look like Arnie, too?'

'No, he . . . ' His eyes searched the room. 'He says you are *delectable.*'

Alex's voice had a tone of surprise to it, and he pronounced 'delectable' in a lowered tone and slightly English accent.

'Do you know what that word means, Alex?'

He searched his mind. 'No,' he said. 'I skipped most of D.' He started to reach for his collar again. 'Can we talk about something else now, please?'

I nodded, but when I looked up I realised it wasn't me he was asking. He was still addressing the empty space in the corner.

'We can talk about anything you like,' I said, but he was starting to shake his head furiously. 'Stop it!' he shouted. I felt Michael rise to his feet behind me, and I raised my hand to prevent him from intervening.

'Take it easy, Alex,' I said calmly. His face was pale, his eyes wild. 'Is Ruin bothering you?'

He was rocking back and forth now, rubbing his hands together as if he was trying to start a fire from the friction. I set a hand lightly on his arm and he snapped out of it.

'Sometimes he does,' he said, when he had calmed. 'He says he's a superhero but really he's just a pain.'

'A superhero?'

Alex nodded. 'It's how he describes what he really is.'

'And what is that?'

Alex hesitated. 'A demon,' he said innocently. 'My demon.'

I thought back to the notes Michael had showed me in my office. A mention of demons, though I was certain the note was dated three years ago, when Alex was seven. I paused, noting the lack of fear in his tone. A mention of 'demons' is usually accompanied by aggressive or angry behaviour, but Alex said it calmly, as a matter of fact.

'Is Ruin a character, like the one you're playing in *Hamlet*?'

He shook his head, then paused. I allowed him time to consider, but he remained adamant. 'Ruen is real. He's a demon.'

'You're an excellent artist,' I said, nodding at the picture of the house on the whiteboard. 'Could you draw a picture of Ruin for me?'

'What, the way he looks right now?' Alex asked, and I nodded.

He took a few breaths, pondering. Then he stood up and reluctantly removed the picture of the house with the eraser.

When the whiteboard was clear, he began to draw a face. As he sketched, I made a few notes on the environment, my thoughts during the interview, and a memo to investigate superheroes named 'Ruin'.

'There,' he said, a few moments later.

I looked at the image on the sketchboard and frowned. It was a self-portrait of Alex, replete with sunglasses.

'That's Ruin?' I asked.

Alex nodded.

'But he's very like you,' I said.

'No, he's much different. He's the bad Alex, and I'm the good Alex.'

This gave me grave cause for concern. I opened my mouth to ask, *What makes the bad Alex bad?* but then I closed it, aware that I had reached the core of Alex's issues, the root of this 'Ruin'. I needed to tread carefully in understanding how Alex conceived of himself as 'good' and 'bad'.

'Has Ruin ever hurt you, Alex?'

He shook his head. 'Ruen is my friend.'

'Oh, I see,' I said. I struggled silently to come up with ways to find out why Alex had chosen a demon to project his emotions, whether Ruin was the imagined figure responsible for his mother's episodes of self-harm, and if Ruin had plans for Alex to harm himself. Alex's conceptualisation of 'bad' might well involve self-punishment.

Just then, Alex walked right up to me and pointed at the scar swirling over my cheek.

'Who gave you that scar?' he said.

I opened my mouth but no sound came out.

He blinked. 'Ruen said a little girl did that to you because she was angry.'

I glanced over at Michael, but he was looking out the glass door at a couple of doctors walking up the corridor, too distracted to notice what had just happened. I looked back at Alex, my heart racing.

How the hell does he know all this? I thought.

'Ruen said you hurt that girl,' he persisted, his tone questioning, puzzled.

I struggled to retain my focus. 'Does Ruin say how I hurt her?'

Alex glanced to his right. 'Ruen,' he snapped. 'That's not nice.' Then he turned back to me. 'Ignore him.

I swallowed. 'What did Ruin say?'

Alex sighed. 'Rubbish, really. He says she was trapped in a dark, dark hole, and there was a ladder there but you pulled it up so she got stuck.'

'Is that how you feel, Alex?' I asked, though my voice had shrunk to a distant whisper, as if there were two of me: one asking the questions I've been trained to ask, the other a grieving mother, my arms suddenly aching to hold my little girl again.

But, too late. Alex withdrew, closed for business. I watched him he walked over to the whiteboard, beginning to draw his dream house a second time.

'I'll come and see you again tomorrow,' I said, rising to my feet, my hands trembling.

But he was engrossed in his drawing, touching up the wings above the house.

'How did it go?' Michael asked as we headed down the corridor towards the front entrance.

I kept three paces ahead of him so he couldn't see the strain on my face. I could feel my phone buzzing in my bag with text messages from my friends who were all probably out of their minds with worry. I was training my thoughts on a series of numbers that scrolled in my mind backwards from ten, but I had already reached zero and still my heart was pounding in my chest, tears pricking the corners of my eyes. I felt the wounds of Poppy awaken in their deep places. I had only so long before I broke down.

'I'll compile my notes this afternoon and meet you and the others in the morning,' I told Michael quickly.

We had reached the hospital foyer. Michael stopped me as I approached the entrance.

'Dr Molokova,' he said, his voice terse. I looked up sharply, rattled by his tone. He combed a hand through his long blond hair, visibly perplexed.

'Look, please just tell me you're not going to split up that family. I have one of the best therapists in the country working with his mother . . . '

'That's good,' I said. 'But—'

'But what?'

'I think Alex may be a danger to himself. I'd like to book him into MacNeice House for sustained assessment.'

Michael's face fell. 'Alex's aunt Beverly is on her way up here from Cork as we speak, he can be assessed in his own house with his own flesh and blood . . . '

I felt suddenly exhausted, full of regret at breaking my resolve to stay indoors. 'In my opinion Alex could seriously harm himself if we don't keep an eye on him. Frankly I'm appalled he's not been given proper treatment until now.' A scene of Poppy flashed before my eyes. She was holding a knife at a table in a restaurant, the people around us beginning to turn and watch. The soft light from a chandelier danced on its blade.

I made to walk away but Michael grabbed my arm. 'I want what's best for this boy.'

I stared at his hand on my bicep, my blood boiling. Finally, I pulled my arm free. 'Then let me do my job,' I said quietly, walking past him to the exit and towards the taxi rank.

Many of the parents I encounter in the course of my job tearfully confide in me that they worry in case their child is possessed. It is a very real and terrifying possibility to confront: you may never have given the notion of God or Satan the time of day, but suddenly the bizarre, frightening and occasionally violent actions of your son or daughter force you to ask yourself questions you never dared believe would cross your mind. Such questions haunted me every day for most of Poppy's life – and, if I'm honest, I don't think I've ever found the real answers. After many years of watching her behaviour deteriorate, I had grown tired of specialists telling me that my beautiful, intelligent, and sensitive child was merely 'hyperimaginative', a label which progressed as she got older through the spectrum of apathetic and uninformed childhood mental health diagnoses: attention deficit disorder, disassociative identity disorder, bipolarity, Asperger's syndrome. All wrong, and with these wrong diagnoses, the wrong meds, the wrong kind of treatment. So after medical school I trained in child psychiatry, doubled up by a PhD based on a hunch about Poppy's condition: childhood schizophrenia.

Like Michael, I had wanted us to stay together as a family. But it had cost her her life.

As I pulled through the busy streets of Belfast in a taxi, I heard her voice. *I love you, Mummy. I love you.* And then I saw her, clear in my mind. Her coffee-brown eyes curved with laughter, her thick black hair swept across one shoulder. She was turning to me, the white sheen of a curtain brushing against her face. *The hole is gone*, she said, smiling.

She was only twelve years old.

5

'TELL HER WHO I AM'

Alex

Dear Diary,

Today I met a lady doctor at the hospital who asked a lot of questions about Ruen. I felt very confused when she asked about him. I've never told anyone much about him because that was our deal. But then he asked me to introduce him and it confused me because usually he hisses at me like a cat to keep quiet and pretend that he doesn't exist, at which I say something like, 'But, Ruen, you're such a charming fellow, surely you want me to tell the whole world about you?' and he narrows his horrible eyes at me and says, *Sarcasm only gestures at one's impotence*. Then I blow a raspberry and he disappears in a huff.

When Ruen first came to stay, he said he was simply here to be my friend because I looked lonely. Then one day we had an argument and I told him to go away, and he said he couldn't. He said he'd been sent to study me because he and all his friends had never come across a human being who could see demons like I did. He said I was very special. The most anyone had ever seen of demons was a glimpse, he said, and these people usually thought they were seeing things. I remember he was very, very excited that I could see him and said it was very important that he study me, like a lab rat or something. I said I didn't want to be studied, that sounded like there was something wrong with me, and all my life people have been saying that there is something wrong with me. I hate it, because I am totally fine and want to be left alone. But Ruen promised me something if I let him study me. I'm not going to say what. It's our secret.

The lady doctor had a big Harry-Potter kind of scar, but on her cheek, not her forehead. She was pretty and smiley and had small dark brown eyes and long black hair that looked like chocolate sauce being poured out of a bottle. One of her teeth had a chip in it and sometimes I could see her bra through her shirt. Dr Molokova, she said her name was, but to call her Anya. Peanuts make Anya fall asleep. I ate some when she left to see if they'd make me fall asleep but they didn't.

When Anya asked me about Ruen I think I must have blushed and got twitchy. Ruen told me to tell her who he was. I was very confused. The lady doctor asked me what was

48

wrong. Ruen said it again: *Tell her who I am.* So I did. She was very interested to hear about Ruen and Ruen must have met her before because he told me some things about her, like she played the piano quite well and that her daddy had been Chinese, though she never really knew him, and her mum had a lot of problems. Just like mine.

When she left Ruen had a funny look in his eyes, the kind of look Woof gets when he sees Ruen. Worried. Afraid, almost. I asked him what was wrong and he said nothing and then started asking lots of questions about Anya and about *love.* I was *so* sick of questions by this point, though I was a bit freaked out by the fact that I had to stay in hospital when it was Mum that had something wrong with her, not me, and that no one had come to collect me yet. So I answered his questions, even though they were very strange.

He said: 'What does love feel like?'

I said: 'You'd have to ask a girl.' And then I thought of Mum and how much I love her and so I said: 'Like you'd do anything for the person you love.' And then I stared at him for a long time and worked it out by myself.

'You love Anya,' I said.

'I most certainly *do not*,' he said.

'You do,' I said, laughing. 'You *fancy* her.'

I was having great fun getting my own back after he teased me mercilessly about fancying Katie McInerny just because I let her share my locker.

He got all angry, then disappeared so fast he made a slight pop, and I laughed myself to sleep.

When I woke up, it was really dark outside. All the rooftops of the houses across the street looked like a zigzaggedy dinosaur spine against the sky. I could tell Ruen was in the room because I was colder than frozen sausages even though it was May, and sometimes he does that. All the hairs on my arms were standing straight upright. I said, 'What is it now, you creep?'

He took a step out of the shadow beside the window and said, 'I want you to tell Anya all about me.'

I sat up in bed, trying to keep the blankets tight around me. 'I was right, wasn't I? You really *do* fancy that lady, Ruen.'

And for some reason I thought of my dad just then. I saw his face in my head, all blurry, his eyes blue just like mine, Mum said. Then I saw the policeman, his face turning towards me in slow motion, angry and scared at the same time.

Ruen scowled at me. I snapped out of my daydream and rolled my eyes at him.

'Fine, Ruen. I'll tell her about you, OK? Does that make you happy?'

He gave a tiny nod and then he vanished and I thought, *What a nut.*

I slept all night at the hospital and in the morning Anya came and said I could see Mum. She was more smiley today, though her eyes looked sad and she was wearing black square glasses. I didn't tell her what Ruen had said because I was so excited to see Mum.

'How are you today, Alex?' she said as we walked through the hospital.

'I thought of a new joke,' I said, and I told her it: 'How do you make a hot dog stand?'

She shrugged.

'You steal its chair.'

She laughed, though she sounded like she didn't find it funny.

'I bet you're excited to see your mum,' she said, and I nodded. 'She might not look like her usual self, though. Is that OK?'

This to me could only be a good thing, so I gave a big grin and Anya told me to follow her. We walked down loads of hospital corridors until I thought my legs would fall off, and then finally we came to a small room where Mum was in a white bed.

At first, when I went in, she didn't look up. She was just lying there with white bandages around her wrists and a tube in her arm. Her face looked like someone had taken a rubber to it and erased Mum out of it. Then she turned her head and smiled at me, and it was as if someone had put all the colour back into her face. Her hair turned yellow again with black roots and her eyes changed from grey to sky-blue and even the tattoos on her arms and neck seemed brighter. Someone had taken out the hoop in her nose but that was a good thing because I thought it made her look like a bull. I wanted to ask if they'd taken the one out of her tongue as well, but I didn't.

'Hello, love,' she said as I walked in. Her voice was hoarse. I felt nervous to go in, in case Ruen appeared.

'Come here, Alex,' she said. I stepped forward and she put her arms around me and squeezed me. Her arms felt cold and skinny.

'Are you feeling better yet?' I said.

'I've had better days,' she said after a long, long pause, and she smiled but her eyes were wet and small. 'How have you been?'

I shrugged. 'They don't have TVs here.'

'What a shame, eh? You can watch TV when you get home.'

'Yeah, but I've missed loads.' And I started naming all the programmes I'd missed and counting them off on my fingers.

Mum just stared at me. 'How's the barking footstool?'

'Woof's OK,' I said. 'Though who's feeding him, Mum? Won't he be hungry?'

Mum's face looked worried. Then Anya stepped forward and touched Mum's hand with her fingers.

'I'm Anya Molokova,' she said, and her voice was suddenly very soothing and kind. 'I'm a consultant at MacNeice House. I'm here to take care of Alex.'

I wanted to say this was a lie because Anya wasn't cooking me pizza or onions on toast or anything like that. Mum nodded. I pulled a chair close to her bed and she reached out and ruffled my hair.

'Cindy, I'm aware that you'll be kept in here for another few weeks?'

'Yeah?' Mum said, in a way that made me wonder if Anya was doing something wrong.

'I'd like Alex to stay at my unit for a little while. Just so I can assess him.'

Mum's face tightened. 'Assess him for what?'

Anya glanced at me. 'I wonder if we should discuss this in private ...'

'No,' Mum said loudly. 'It's about him, so he should be here.'

Anya sat down on the other side of the bed, then took off her black square glasses and used her shirt to clean them.

'In light of recent circumstances, I think Alex may have a kind of illness that requires ongoing assessment and monitoring. It might be in his interests to have a stay at MacNeice House.' I wondered what sort of illness she meant and if MacNiece House had TVs.

'Isn't that a place for nutjobs?' Mum said.

Anya's smile turned real. 'Not at all. It's where we do some of our most important work for families in the region.'

Mum scowled. 'Last time some woman in a suit tried to take Alex away from me.'

Mum and I stared at Anya. I noticed she was wearing a suit, too. She swallowed. 'If we were to do this, I'd need your permission—'

'Well, you don't have it,' Mum snapped, and her voice wobbled until I squeezed her hand and she looked at me and smiled. 'I'll get myself out of here soon, I promise,' she said.

'You sister Bev is here,' Anya said softly. 'She came up from Cork to take care of Alex. Part of the arrangement, if Alex was to stay at MacNeice House, was that Bev would look after him at weekends . . . '

Mum widened her eyes. 'Bev is here?'

Anya nodded.

Mum lifted a hand to her face and started to cry. 'I really don't want her seeing me like this,' she said, and she started pressing her hair down with her fingers because it was sticking out all over the place like she'd been electrocuted.

'She'll only visit when you're ready. Everyone's very aware that you need time. I'll drop Alex home this afternoon, but if you're not happy with him coming to MacNeice House I need to get permission to visit with him every day for the next week for us to have a chat.'

There was something about the way Anya said 'have a chat' that sounded like she meant something much more serious. Mum seemed to think so too. She stared at Anya very hard.

'You mean, about me?' Mum said.

Anya glanced at me. 'And other things, too.'

Then she stood up and said she'd see if she could get one of the nurses to let me watch TV. She went out of the room and I didn't look at Mum because just then Ruen appeared and I jumped about three feet in the air.

'What's wrong now, Alex?' Mum said.

But I ignored her. I was nervous, because I could see that Ruen was Monster. Only, he wasn't looking at me. He was looking at something in the doorway. I tried to see what he was looking at but there was no one there. Ruen was so angry that he was growling. Three seconds later he disappeared.

When Anya came back she told me they would let me watch TV, then she saw Mum was upset and I was curled up on the floor.

'What's happened?' she asked Mum, who just shook her head and whispered something.

'Is there TV now?' I said, and I saw that Ruen was gone so I stood up.

Anya smiled and went to say something, but then she just said, 'Follow me.' So I went out and sat in a smelly room with the tiniest TV I've ever seen that had yellow lines running through all the channels. About five minutes later Anya came in smiling and told me I could come and see Mum again, but only for a little while because Mum was very tired.

I sat beside Mum and a lady came with a tray of food that Mum didn't want.

'Do you want it, Alex?' Mum said, and I nodded and tucked into the beans and potatoes.

'Did you know Alex is in a play?' I heard Mum say to Anya.

'Yes. *Hamlet.* You must be very proud.'

I felt Mum stare at me. 'I could hardly read when I was his age. He's top of the class in English. He hasn't got any of that from me, I can tell you. He's so clever.' Then there was a long pause as I used the last piece of toast to mop up the juice from the beans.

'Sometimes I think I'm holding him back,' I heard Mum say, and her voice was very small.

'How do you think you're holding him back?' Anya said.

Mum's colour looked like it was fading again. 'Do you

think there's ever a chance for a kid that starts out in life like me and Alex did? Or do you think it would have been better if I'd just never been born?'

Anya looked from me to Mum. Then she leaned forward and took Mum's hand. 'I think some of us have really big challenges in life. But I think everything can be overcome.'

Mum leaned over and gave my cheek a gentle tap, and even though she smiled at me there was this look in her eyes that made a knot in my belly until I couldn't eat my toast. I saw Ruen in the doorway but didn't look up at him.

Auntie Bev is Mum's sister, though she looks nothing like Mum, not even slightly. In fact, you couldn't really tell they're sisters. She's older than Mum by eleven years and ten months and two days, but she looks actually younger and finds everything funny and she doesn't have any tattoos, except for a black squiggle on her left ankle which she says happened when she was *out of her tree in Corfu*. She says weird things like, 'I nearly took a buckle in my eye.' Her hair is short and white like Woof's fur and her job means she spends all day shining a torch down people's ears and mouths. She wears a small gold cross on a chain around her neck though she's not Catholic any more, and I'm never to say the name *Lawrence* in front of her because that's the name of the husband who took all her money. When she moved into my house the first thing she did was put a shower pole in the doorway of our living room. I stood for a few minutes, wondering if her brain had slipped out of her ears in the night.

'For this,' she said, when she worked out why I looked so puzzled. She held on to the pole and started pulling her head up over the bar with her arms. She did it three times before I noticed her feet weren't touching the ground.

'Oh,' I said, though I still had no idea why she'd done that. Then she laughed and jumped down and the next thing I knew she'd hooked both her feet over the bar and was hanging like a bat.

This morning she came up to my room and knocked on the door, and when I noticed she wasn't out of breath I said to her:

'Why don't you sound like an old dog?'

She looked at me funny and asked what I meant, and I told her Mum always made a noise like this (I went *hah-hah-hah* with my tongue hanging out) when she climbed all three floors of our house. The lines in Auntie Bev's forehead disappeared then and she giggled, then flexed her arm muscles, which I thought was a funny thing for a girl to do, though they were big and made me think of onions in a sock.

'That's what wall climbing three times a week will do for you,' she said, slapping her arm.

'Wall climbing?' I said. 'Can you take me wall climbing with you?'

'Of course,' she said, her face all shocked. 'We should find one close by. It's been that long since I lived here that I can't even remember where a wall would be.'

'There's a wall outside our front door,' I told her.

She rolled her eyes. 'That's not the kind of wall I meant,

Alex.' Then she looked me up and down for a long time, her eyes like gobstoppers. 'What in the name of Mary and Joseph are you *wearing*, Alex?'

I looked down at my clothes. I'd forgotten to roll up my trousers.

'A suit?'

Auntie Bev laughed really loudly and she sounded like an owl. 'Dearie me, we need to go shopping, don't we?'

Before I could answer she dragged me downstairs for some food, but she wouldn't let me chop the onions in case I cut myself.

'But Granny taught me how,' I told her, and suddenly her smile slipped off her face and she looked out the window. It was starting to rain.

'Was your mum happier when Granny was around?' she asked very quietly.

I shrugged. 'I think so. Though Granny didn't like my dad so that made Mum sad.' At the thought of Granny, I felt my whole body stiffen, though I wasn't sure if it was just the cold.

'I really miss Granny.'

Auntie Bev reached down and squeezed my hand. 'I miss her too, Alex.'

And when I looked back, Auntie Bev's face was all misty and our breaths hung in the cold air like smoke.

6

THE SILENT TOLL

Anya

I sleep late and avoid my morning run. My leg, back and neck muscles feel like I've been on a rack all night and when I look outside it's raining. I make a conscious effort to compile my notes from yesterday and catch up on emails instead. I don't return any of the phone calls from my worried friends, not even Fi, my best friend from primary school, who has called nineteen times since Poppy's anniversary and left four messages ordering me to ring her back. Instead, I hide behind the faceless deletability of email, cutting and pasting the same 'Hey, I'm fine, sorry I missed you' message to each of the friends who knew Poppy. I will apologise and explain later. First, there is the issue of Alex. I shower quickly, then head to my office. Unpacking will have to wait.

When I moved to Edinburgh to go to medical school, people always asked, *What was it like growing up in Northern Ireland?* with an occasional sense of awe, as if I was the first person to have done it. It was only when I'd left that it struck me how dangerous this mild but otherwise down-at-heel and volatile land of my birth appeared to others – like a treasured friend whose social graces often do them a disservice in the eyes of strangers.

From a professional viewpoint, Northern Ireland's social scars run deep, and not just through the psyches of those who experienced the violence first-hand. Although the politicians are celebrating what they call 'peace', those of us working behind the scenes are finding anything but. The history of violence here is usually measured in terms of its death count, but there is another silent, and more alarming, toll: one in five Northern Irish children will experience major mental health problems before their eighteenth birthday, with case studies flagging self-harm as a response to confrontation and shame for family involvement in violence. I empathise with Michael for wishing to keep Alex and Cindy as a family unit, but I have not returned to my homeland to perpetuate a failing system. I am here to begin rebuilding lives.

I pull up into the car park of MacNeice House at 8.59 a.m. For some reason I half expect to see Michael's battered Volvo parked in my space, his tense, brooding stare forcing me to sign off Alex's report as A-OK, as if he's passed an exam to qualify for a decent family life. If only it were that simple. I should have realised it sooner – Michael perceives me as the enemy. He wants me close so he can have a better chance at keeping Alex out of – Michael's terms – the 'nuthouse'. And I suppose it is in this respect that Michael and I share a common goal – despite myself I have bonded with this child, sensed something very familiar about his predicament, something that lies close to the bone. And I feel I can help him – though it may not be in the way that Michael desires.

Inside my office, I flick the switch on the kettle and browse the few shelves of books I've finally managed to stack in my bookcases. My collection comprises psychiatric journals and textbooks, naturally, but also literature, drama and religious texts – the truth about the human psyche doesn't always reside in the factual and academic tomes.

As I leaf through a handful of old, yellow-paged books by C S Lewis and John Milton, I reflect on Alex's claim that he can see demons. As far back as the first century, the symptoms of mania and schizophrenia have been linked closely to super-human manifestations and hallucinations. God, angels, superheroes, martyrs . . . they've all played across the stage of schizophrenia throughout the recorded delusions of the last two thousand years. Patients claiming to see demons are not entirely out of the ordinary, but Alex's case strikes me as unusual. He claimed that a demon was his best friend. And he seemed to know about Poppy. At the very least, a ten-year-old with such powers of perception is extremely rare.

The kettle trembles with heat. Poppy's voice rattles in my head. *It feels like a hole, Mum. A hole instead of a soul.*

The red switch clicks.

I think of Cindy at the hospital, her tired, thin face filled with the weariness of a woman maybe three times her age, how she had admitted that she did not feel good enough. I jot down some notes to the effect that Alex is struggling to understand his dark colours, and most likely those of his mother. I make another note to pursue aspects of shame and guilt in his character; why he feels both of these and how I might help him come to understand that they are natural elements of his being. How to deal with them when they cause him rage and potential self-harm, as well as the risk he may pose to others. Helping him understand why his mother turns to the pills and razor blades every time a black cloud passes will be much more difficult.

I stare at my page of scribbles. On the open textbook beside me I circle a passage from Milton's *Paradise Lost*, not because of any insight it offers me into Alex's situation, but because it clouds me in an overwhelming sense of déjà vu:

> *The mind is its own place, and in itself*
> *Can make a Heav'n of Hell, a Hell of Heav'n.*

I tap my pen on the desk for a few moments, trying to remember where I came across this quote before, and why it should feel so familiar, and then it all comes back. It was a gift from a fellow student during the first year of my psychiatric training, when the questions surrounding Poppy's behaviour were pounding my brain, when I felt launched beyond the natural maternal impetus to make everything all right into a quest worthy of Superwoman: to make Poppy's Hell a Heaven. It never happened.

That doesn't mean it *can't* happen, I remind myself. The Hell that psychotics live with can be relocated, if not redecorated, so to speak. 'Hell' is when no treatment is given – or the wrong sort – and when the mind is left to plummet into itself without proper intervention. My thoughts turn back to Alex. Michael wishes me to write a report that will enable him to give Cindy and her son the kind of family support they should have been receiving for years – counselling, better housing, care assistance. But something nags at me. Poppy's voice in my head morphs to Alex's when talking about Ruin: *He's the bad Alex.*

There has already been some speculation in Michael's notes that Alex is bipolar, but I am not convinced. With a deep breath I write 'Schizophrenia?' at the top of my notes as, in many cases, it has virtually been ruled out from the get-go on account of early onset schizophrenia affecting one in ten-hundred-thousand children under the age of twelve years old. Some psychotic disorders may be a result of physical and/or sexual abuse in childhood. I will ask after the boy's father and other relatives who have played a part in his life so far. Has the mother had lovers, and how much have they been around Alex? Very often, mothers in Cindy's position end up using their lovers as babysitters: has this been the case? Abuse will be my primary area of enquiry, although I need to explore the history of Cindy's depression and its impact on Alex: a much harder thing to investigate.

First, I contact Alex's school and leave a message with the secretary to speak with Alex's teacher, Karen Holland. Then I Google the name of the theatre company that Alex belongs to – Really Talented Kids Theatre Company NI – and discover a sophisticated website with a photograph of several dozen children grouped on a stage, Alex's smiling face among them. A cluster of logos for high-profile businesses in the region feature under the banner 'Our Sponsors', beside which is an attractive woman with sharp cheekbones, a melon-slice white smile and a wild nest of backcombed red hair. I recognise her as Jojo Kennings, an actress in a TV series I much admire. Like me, Jojo is originally from Belfast, and has returned after twenty years in London to boost regional participation in the arts, enlisting the help of her celebrity friends such as Kenneth Branagh to mentor the kids in the theatre company. I am impressed by her passion, and feel a sense of hope that Alex is involved in the project. I type a message into the 'contact' box on the website, delete it, and rewrite one that sounds less formal.

To: jakennings@rtktheatre.co.uk
From: A_molokova@macneicehouse.nhs.uk
Date: 08/5/07 09.21 a.m.
Dear Jojo (if I may),
I'm writing to ask if I might have a brief chat with you about one of the children involved in your production of *Hamlet* in Belfast next month, Alex Broccoli. I'm a consultant with the CAMHS team at MacNeice House

and am assessing Alex in the light of some recent
changes at home. I'd be keen to find out more about his
involvement in the play, and the performance in general.
Might there be a suitable time to meet?

Kind regards,
Dr Anya Molokova

I hit 'send' and return to my notes. I glance at the word
'schizophrenia' and sigh. I've made myself very unpopular in
some circles because of the number of children on whom I've
slapped the label of early onset schizophrenia, like a dentist's
smiley-face sticker. *How come all these kids are suddenly coming out
of the woodwork?* is the heckle I normally get at conferences, or,
in other words, why the sudden incline in cases? Is it because
kids as young as three really are exhibiting the hallmarks of
schizophrenia – severe confusion between fantasy and reality,
extreme moodiness, violence, mental disturbances, paranoia
and unusual perceptual experiences – or is it just that doctors
like me are keen to define a set of disorders that might just be,
say, characteristics of a dreamy kid or merely a childhood phase?

The thing is, when you spend eighteen years of your life
dealing with a schizophrenic mother and twelve years dealing
with a schizophrenic daughter, neither of which was ever
properly diagnosed or treated, you tend to have a particular
investment in the proper diagnosis of what is an absolutely
horrific, crippling and misunderstood mental illness that shat-
ters families with the force of a bomb.

My computer bleeps a tone – B natural – that indicates a new email has come through. The sender is Jojo Kennings.

To: A_molokova@macneicehouse.nhs.uk
From: jakennings@rtktheatre.co.uk
Date: 08/5/07 09.25 a.m.

Yeah no worries – having a rehearsal at GOH 2night 4–5 p.m. – could speak to you just before, that OK?

JOJO xoxox

I glance at my diary. I can make it. I send an email straight back confirming the meeting and asking if 'GOH' means 'Grand Opera House'. A reply zings back.

To: A_molokova@macneicehouse.nhs.uk
From: jakennings@rtktheatre.co.uk
Date: 08/5/07 09.27 a.m.

Yes, at the Opera House. See you then.

JOJO xoxox

I only half read her reply because the chime of the email hitting my inbox has chimed another tone, its echo threading back, back, into the past. The curse of perfect pitch. In a heartbeat my senses have returned to the moment a B natural key of the piano in my Morningside flat was struck by my daughter four years ago.

In my mind's eye I see Poppy's dark head behind the brown lid of the baby grand piano, singing out the melody in her head. I had taught her piano as, first and foremost, a family tradition. *You aren't a Molokova if you don't play*, my mother used to say. But Poppy's dabblings with music – and they were, sadly, no more than dabblings – achieved something more important. They worked wonders in calming her, in channelling energy that would otherwise spark into aggression, in keeping her focused for more than a handful of seconds. And she loved music.

'Try a note higher, baby,' I call to her, and she looks up at me.

'Thanks, Mum.'

I can see her face – heart-shaped like my mother's, small dark eyes from our Chinese ancestry on my father's side, and a high, intellectual forehead that she meticulously covers with a thick sharp fringe. Even at twelve years old she has the air of an older spirit about her; a soul burdened by its penetrative perceptions.

Several months previously, she began an intensive programme of treatment for EOS – early onset schizophrenia – including a stay at a residential psychiatric unit. She hated me for it. But, to my relief, she had started to show signs of improvement since she returned. For the first time in many years, I knew what it felt like to have a 'normal' child – a child who tells me she loves me.

Nonetheless, the drill still stands – I glance across the open space of the living room before I leave to run her bath, assessing the room carefully for any sharps, wires, breakables or flammables. Poppy pauses, then strikes the B above middle C once more to begin her new composition.

I can hear her singing now. Satisfied that she is calm and content, I head through the kitchen to the bathroom, shutting the door tightly behind me as I turn on the taps.

The rushing bathwater drowns out the chime of the piano and for a moment I wonder if I should go back and check she's all right. *She is fine*, I think. *Let her play*. I remember the holiday we had booked that summer to Paris, of the possibility of picking up her piano tuition again with another teacher. I tried teaching her myself, but we had always ended up laughing.

As I rummage through the bathroom cupboard for bubble bath I feel a sensation of warmth flood across my skin, seeping into my heart, my lungs, telling me that something is wrong. *Something is wrong*. I scan the contents of the wall cabinet – no pills or sharps. *Nothing is wrong*, I think, and immediately I chide myself for letting my emotions dictate to my logic. It was a core part of my training – and essential to the success of Poppy's treatment – that I heed science and not my feelings.

But the sensation grows stronger, an instinct shouting at me that I need to go back into the living room and check on Poppy. I wrench at the tap, shutting off the water. I look at myself in the mirror of the bathroom cabinet, frowning at the scar on my face that is still an ugly raw pink, not quite old enough to hide. A breeze from outside brushes my hair across my face, trapping itself in my lips. I lean over and shut the window.

The window.

Earlier that day the sun had made a rare visit to Edinburgh in all its glory, filling Princes Street Gardens with shirtless workers and sunglassed women, forcing me to open our living room window for a gust of cool air. Of course, the window has a safety catch. And Poppy has turned a corner, her consultant has assured me. Her treatment is working.

The window.

I glance out the door. 'Poppy?'

There is no sound of her music. I see the wing of the piano, shining with the pink and blue lights from the city. In the distance, Edinburgh Castle sits at the top of black volcanic rock, as if it has evolved from tectonic clashes as a status of Scottish victory. When Poppy's medication made her too weak to walk up the steep hill there, I would point at the castle from our living room. To her, it was more than beautiful. It was a symbol of hope.

I step out of the bathroom into the narrow hallway that leads to the open plan living room. Our long L-shaped sofa is empty, the corner lamp beaming in the corner. I see movement at the window, a flash of white curtain.

'Poppy?'

She is on the windowsill, a silhouette obscured by the night sky, her bare legs curled up to her chest. I feel a sense of alarm.

'Poppy, there's no need to sit so close,' I say quickly. 'Come on, move back. You could fall off.' My heart stops. 'And why is the safety catch off?'

I move forward, but as I do so she swings both legs over the ledge and looks at me, her face a blank.

My heart clangs in my chest. I hold up both hands in a calming gesture. I am no longer talking to a twelve-year-old girl. I am talking to a child who suffers from schizophrenia. Her age and our relationship shift into a different kind of focus in the light of her illness: what matters now is keeping her calm.

'Poppy,' I say, 'can you play your music again for me?'

'Someone built a bridge last night,' she says, smiling. 'From our window to Edinburgh Castle. It's cool.'

I reach out my hands to her.

'It's bed time,' I hear myself say, though my voice sounds far, far away from the panic in my head. 'Poppy, love, come away from the window.'

She leans forward, brushing her leg against the cool air, and I cry out.

'Mum, it's fine,' she says. 'There's a bridge. It's made of solid iron. I won't fall.'

'Poppy, there is no bridge,' I say firmly. 'Come back inside.'

But her face has changed. 'You don't believe me.'

My mind is racing with ways to distract her. 'Come inside and I'll make you supper. What would you like? Pizza?'

I am walking slowly towards her, careful not to charge in case she tips herself right over that ledge. There is no balcony, no fire escape – nothing to break her fall on to the pavement ten storeys below.

'Pizza, yes,' she says, and I feel gripped by relief.

'Tell you what,' I say tentatively, inching past the piano, 'I'll make you a cheese-crust pepperoni with olives if you come inside right now.'

I am close enough to feel the cool night air rushing in. If I charge there's a chance I could grab her.

'I love you, Mummy,' she says, smiling.

And then I lunge at her. She leans forward and drops, she drops into the black depths, and I am scrambling halfway out of the window, yelling as I reach hopelessly after her. For a split second she is almost close enough to my fingertips for me to grab her hand. But despite my efforts she is beyond me, and by some deep instinct of survival I remain half inside, half outside the window, crying and reaching as my daughter shrinks into the distance.

7

THE GHOST

Alex

Dear Diary,

OK, so I have a new joke that I tried out tonight and every-one laughed, though according to Jojo it's incorrect politically. There's an Irishman, an Englishman and a Scottish bloke washing the side of a skyscraper. Every day at lunchtime they sit on their balcony overlooking the city and eat their sand-wiches. One day, the Englishman opens his lunchbox and gets really angry. 'Ham *again!*' he says. 'If my wife packs me one more ham sandwich I'm going to throw myself off this bal-cony.' The Scottish bloke opens his lunchbox and finds a cheese sandwich. 'Cheese sarnies *again!*' he says. 'If my wife packs me one more cheese sarnie *I'm* going to throw myself off this balcony.' The Irishman opens his box and finds a tuna sandwich, and *he* threatens to throw himself off, too.

The next day, the Englishman opens his lunchbox and finds a ham sandwich. 'Right, that's it,' he says, and he throws himself off the balcony.

The Scottish bloke opens his lunchbox and finds a cheese sandwich, and he throws himself off the balcony. The Irishman finds a tuna sandwich and shouts, 'You stupid woman!' before throwing himself off, too.

At the funeral, the English, Scottish and Irish wives are consoling each other. 'I thought he *loved* ham,' said the English wife. 'And I thought my husband loved cheese,' said the Scottish wife. 'I don't understand it,' sobbed the Irish wife. 'He always packed his own lunch.'

Jojo said she didn't like the joke but then she said actually the sinister undertones probably matched similar ones in *Hamlet*. She said it's important for us to tell our own jokes because comedy is actually a way of working out stuff that bothers us. I told her I didn't like ham, cheese or even tuna, so I don't think I'm really working through anything.

Though tonight something weird happened and it wasn't just because Anya was there or because Katie McInerny kissed me.

Tonight was a full run-through of *Hamlet* and I was very surprised and pleased but also nervous, because when I arrived I saw Jojo talking to Anya. Anya looked very happy when she saw me walk in and her eyes went big and her smile was huge and red because she was wearing lipstick. She looked pretty. I could see her silver necklace – the one that tells people she'll fall asleep if she eats peanuts – flashing in the spotlight as the technician Terry is rubbish and is always pointing the lights the wrong way.

'Hello, Alex,' Anya said to me, and Jojo said, 'Aren't you lucky to have a groupie, Alex? A sign of things to come.'

'Anya is a psychiatrist, not a groupie,' I said, and Jojo didn't seem to know what to say, which I thought was interesting because Jojo *always* knows what to say. Jojo is tall and thin and she always wears a bright pink leotard and leggings with black legwarmers and an army jacket big enough for three people to fit inside. She sounds like she's reading the ten o'clock news on television even though she's from north Belfast and is really superstitious about things like saying the word 'Macbeth' on stage and putting our shoes on the dressing room table and forgetting lines during rehearsals. If any of us forget our lines we are to *improvise*, she says, not just stand there in the spotlight with our mouths open like dumb twits. I gave a thumbs-up to Jojo and Anya and they smiled back.

I dumped my rucksack in the cloakroom and saw that Katie McInerny was in the male dressing room again, which she says is important because she is playing a boy, which is weird. Katie is two years and one month older than me but about seven and a half inches taller. A little bit taller would be OK but seven and a half inches is like she's half giant or something. What's really wick is that she never brings her script and always asks to share mine, and I can't even open a can of Coke without her wanting some, and I bet you like a million quid she's forgotten her locker key tonight and wants to share mine.

'Hiya, Horatio,' she said as I walked into the dressing room.

'Hiya, Hamlet,' I said, and I noticed she was wearing a white bandage around her right wrist. 'Did you get that from fencing?' I asked.

She looked down at it as if she had forgotten she was wearing it. How stupid.

'No,' she said. 'I didn't get it from fencing.' Her eyes were sad and had that look in them that I used to see Mum give my dad, as if there was something she wanted to say but wanted me to guess it instead of just coming out with it. I hate games like that.

Just then, Ruen appeared. He was his Old Man self, short and baldy and his face all twisty and scrunched up like scrunched-up paper. I could even smell his disgusting tweed jacket. It smells like a wet dog that's been dead for about ten years.

'Are you OK?' Katie said.

'Do you want to share my locker?' I said. I needed to get rid of her and find out why Ruen was here. Her face glowed like a Christmas tree.

'Yes, that would be lovely ... ' And she leaned over and made to kiss me but I moved my face so instead of hitting my cheek she kissed my ear. No one's ever kissed my ear.

I took the key out of my pocket and pressed it into her sore hand and she yelped but I didn't say sorry because Ruen was walking away. I ran after him. He walked on to the stage and looked up.

'What is it?' I asked.

'Look, you silly boy. Use your God-given eyes,' he sneered. And so I looked up and I saw Terry the technician unscrewing the old loose screws from the big brass spotlight and holding the new screws in his mouth.

'Bad idea for a boy with an attention deficit disorder to be fiddling with the set, don't you think?' Ruen said, clasping his hands behind his back.

'So?' I whispered, careful not to let anyone see my mouth moving. I saw Anya down below but I didn't say anything, though I noticed Ruen staring at her. 'So what?' I asked him again.

Ruen looked like he was making a plan. 'So. He would be easily distracted. Doesn't Katie's mother always make a big fuss at the end, coming on stage and hugging her in front of everyone?'

I thought about it. There's something about Katie's mum that I don't like. She always claps the loudest when she comes to see Katie, but her smile is false and sometimes she smells of alcohol. And even though she's small and works as a school patrol lady, Katie looks scared of her.

'I'm not doing it,' I told Ruen.

'Please yourself,' he said, walking away. 'Only I daresay Katie'll miss out on her big night.'

My legs thought they were jelly for a total of nine seconds.

I watched after Ruen and opened my mouth to shout because suddenly what he meant dawned on me like someone just poured a bucket of ice down the back of my collar. He meant that if I didn't do something to Katie's mum, Katie's mum would hurt Katie on purpose so she couldn't perform.

Just then I saw Jojo waving at me with her arm, as if she was cleaning windows too high to reach. I blinked.

'Oh, you're back with us, are you?' she said, though I hadn't been anywhere.

I nodded my head.

She grinned. 'Got a new joke for the rap scene, Alex?'

I said *Uh-huh* and tried to remember it. I told the joke, though suddenly I felt that the word 'Irishman' sounded weird inside this place and Jojo wasn't laughing like she normally did. I remembered the time last week when she came by my house to pick me up for rehearsals and instead she had to phone an ambulance for Mum. I thought of the way her hands shook when she tried to find Mum's pulse.

Jojo shouted at us all to regroup and run through Act Three. I ran after Ruen.

He was in the wings now, his face in the shadows.

'You could always help Katie out, couldn't you?' he said calmly. 'All it would take is for you to shout up at Terry at just the right moment.'

I could feel my heart beating really quickly. *Ba-dum, ba-dum, ba-dum.*

'Alex?' I heard Jojo call.

I stepped closer to Ruen. 'But wouldn't that hurt Katie's mum?'

Ruen's eyes were like tiny little knives in his horrible face. He smiled. 'But doesn't *she* hurt Katie?'

'Alex!'

I spun round and ran back across the stage to take my position. Jojo walked towards me, her eyes watching me strangely, and I started to panic in case she'd spotted Ruen. She bent down in front of me. 'Are you OK, Alex?'

I nodded like I was definitely OK.

'You sure?'

My nod said I was *absolutely* OK. Jojo jumped up, clapping her hands above her head.

'OK! New plan, everyone. The Opera House manager has told me we've a little more time tonight, so we're going to take it from the top *again* and smooth out the creases.'

Some people groaned and some shouted, 'Hooray!' If we were starting from the beginning then I was on first. I tried to remember the new joke I wanted to tell but it wouldn't come to my mind. It felt as though my brain had turned into the stuff I sometimes pull out of the pipe of the vacuum cleaner.

And then Ruen came back, but he was no longer the Old Man. He was Ghost Boy, and as he crossed the stage he turned around to me and gave me a smile and his eyes were black. The lights went down and everything went dark until my eyes adjusted. Gareth and Liam stumbled across the stage, with guns, towards Ruen and I almost cried out, thinking they were going to run into him.

'Who's there?' Liam shouted. The smoke machine started dribbling out a blanket of silvery fog. A projector above me started to whir, but a second later James turned on some music to cover the noise. The projector threw a movie of a man – who's one of Jojo's famous friends – on the wall just behind Liam. The projection was shadowy and the man's face was hard to see and he really did look like a ghost. He was walking though he never got any closer. Liam didn't see him.

It was my turn to go on. I stepped forward through the black curtains of the wings. 'What's all this talk of ghosts, then?' I said in a big voice, and Gareth and Liam almost jumped out of their skins.

'We thought you were it,' Liam said. He spun round, pointing his gun at blank space. 'Two nights in a row now we've seen this . . . *thing.*'

'Thing?' I said, and as Liam told me about the ghost the fog grew thicker. Ruen was on the other side of the stage, right beside the projection of the ghost. He was just standing there, smirking. And then his voice appeared in my head.

Alex, he said.

I blinked, trying to ignore him. The ghost turned and started to walk again, but it looked like he really was coming towards us.

'Aye, this ghost, demon, whatever you call it,' Liam said fearfully, fluffing his lines a bit. 'You'll think I'm crazy, but I think it looks like the dead king.'

I took a step beside Liam, remembering what Jojo said about keeping my shoulders turned to the audience at all times. I knew my line, as it's important because it's straight from Shakespeare's play and Jojo said it was *vital to the men with money that we keep some of Shakespeare in the play* and so I made sure I learned those bits really carefully.

'It harrows me with fear,' I said, but my voice sounded really far away.

Liam looked at the projection of the man walking towards us, and as he walked, Ruen marched beside him too and I felt dizzy at seeing double. Liam started to yell and the music got louder and sounded like a heartbeat – *ba-dum, bad-dum, ba-dum* – and I was supposed to lift up my fake gun and point it. But instead I looked down at it in my hand, and when I looked up at Ruen standing about ten feet away I saw he had one, too.

'Don't,' I said as he lifted his gun, but he just grinned. The gun shone in the spotlight. The music got louder. Someone shouted.

Ruen lifted his gun higher and aimed it at Liam, and I felt the crack of the gun deep in my gut. Liam's head snapped back. Blood shot out of his forehead. He dropped to the ground.

'Liam!' I yelled, and I ran to him and fell to my knees beside his body. The blood was coming out and making a shiny puddle around his arms but it wasn't really red like in films. It was black.

Then the music stopped and the lights went up.

I looked around. Ruen wasn't there, and the projection was less ghostly and more like a home video against the wall on the stage. Liam leaned forward and I saw there was no blood on his body. He looked at me funny.

'You're shaking,' he said as he sat up, and I went to answer but I was panting so heavily that I couldn't form any words.

Jojo ran on stage and she looked really shocked. 'Alex!' she shouted. 'That was *brilliant*! So real, so convincing! Did you just make that up on the spot?'

'I ... I ...' was all I could say, and then I saw the gun in my hand and I dropped it. Jojo was using her hand to talk to the lights team. 'Let's go again. Same, please, Alex,' she said, but I shook my head.

'I don't want to.' I felt dirty and horrible and like I wanted to take a really hot bath.

Jojo looked up. 'Are you OK?'

I shook my head. 'I need to go,' I told her, and she nodded like she understood.

'OK, everyone, back to Plan A. Act Three. Assemble!'

I whispered, 'Thanks' to Jojo and then, 'Sorry' and she told me, 'It's all right, Alex, just take it easy,' but already I was running off stage and pulling open my locker and when I got home I sat in a hot bath until my fingers turned pink and squidgy.

8

DEMON HUNTING

Anya

Yesterday I had the opportunity of meeting Jojo Kennings and seeing a run-through of the adaptation of *Hamlet* she is putting on at the Grand Opera House in a couple weeks' time. Alex seemed comfortable, if not a little shy, though I saw him beaming over at me once or twice when Jojo applauded his efforts. Admittedly I hadn't been inside the Grand Opera House for many, many years – my memories were still fresh of when they pulled the shutters down and scheduled the beautiful building for demolition at the height of the Troubles. Jojo remembered this, too. 'It's one of the reasons I pushed so hard for this project,' she explained, during a brief tour of the auditorium and the stage. A teenage kid was attempting to reposition a light overhead, and although Jojo assured me that he was trained and equipped to be hanging precariously from a height of some thirty feet above, the clanks and creaks made me look up frequently.

I followed Jojo down the small narrow steps from the Grand Circle to the front of the stage. A young girl with a long pink wig and a shell suit – Bonnie, Jojo told me, who was cast as Ophelia – ran up to Jojo and asked her for change for the vending machine. Jojo sighed and dug her hand deep into her enormous jacket.

'There you go,' she told Bonnie, who wrinkled her nose as she smiled. 'Don't tell the others, mind.'

'You give the kids money?' I said, once Bonnie had gone out of earshot.

Jojo gave a dramatic sigh. 'I can't help it, they've started to feel more like family than my cast.' She stopped and looked up at the ornate ceiling above us. 'None of these kids recall anything beyond the Stormont Agreement, and most of their home lives are so colourful that the outside world is alien and insignificant. They aren't in touch with their heritage.'

I felt there was a little more to her drive for the project than heritage – the power that lies in handing people their dreams, for example. 'What about Alex?' I asked. 'Why did you pick him for this project?'

'Talent is a difficult thing to put into words,' she said, bending down to pick up an abandoned microphone. 'But Alex is gifted. He has a way of seeing right into the human soul, though I don't even think he knows he's doing it.'

'How so?'

She dusted down the mic. 'Despite his young age, Alex has the ability to perceive the angelic and the demonic in a human being. He sees the good and the bad and he understands a lot more than your average ten-year-old.' She paused. 'Though now I think I know a little more about why that might be.'

'How has he taken to working as part of a group of children? Have there been any fights? Outbursts?'

She looked at me knowingly. 'We had a team of social workers here for the first few weeks. You've met Michael, I presume?'

'Of course.'

'He usually comes to check up on Alex, make sure he's hunky-dory. And the parents are always welcome.' She glanced at a handful of men and women seated at the top of the auditorium. 'Alex's mother has never been. And to answer your question, Alex has been the most affable and easy-going of the bunch. I was very concerned when I found his mother in that state, of course. I didn't even realise he had a problem until . . . ' She looked down. 'Until your email.'

I could see my email had unsettled her. Suddenly her plan to pluck Belfast's diamonds from the rough and put them into the spotlight had revealed a flaw – what if one of them cracked on opening night?

At that, Alex made an appearance on stage, directly under the spotlight, which was starting to sound as if it was going to fall off any minute. Jojo shielded her eyes and looked up at the boy amongst the rafters.

'Everything OK up there?'

A voice shouted down. 'Fixed it.'

'One more thing,' I said quickly. She fixed a pair of silver eyes on me. 'Could I get a copy of the script?'

'Absolutely.' She jogged backstage and returned a couple of minutes later with a scrolled-up bundle of white paper. 'Here you go.' She paused, nervous for the first time during our meeting. 'You think you can fix it?'

'Fix what?'

She fluttered her fingers as if 'it' was an ethereal concept. 'Whatever it is . . . that's bothering Alex?'

I nodded and held up the script she'd given me. 'This is wonderful, thank you very much.'

Alex looked down at Jojo intently. 'Are we ready to start again?'

She threw me a smile. 'See? He was *born* for the stage.' Then she clapped her hands together and shouted: 'Everyone back for the third act!'

I thanked her for her time and waved up at Alex. He stood stock-still in the centre of the stage, lit up by the spotlight, his eyes fixed ahead.

I spent the rest of the evening reading Jojo's script. From my limited memory of the original play – about a young prince who's devastated by his father's death and his mother's hasty remarriage – I was able to pick out those parts of the play that Jojo had retained intact and those she had tweaked to comment on contemporary Belfast. Some of the more heavy-handed alterations – 'To riot, or not to riot,' Hamlet says at one point – made me wince, though parts of the retained original made me wonder whether Alex's participation in the play was doing him as much harm as it was good. He was confident and believable on stage, no doubt about that.

But there was a scene in there that made me wonder, a scene that could easily provoke a young boy's sense of reality and fantasy: when Hamlet and Horatio see the looming ghost of the dead king, Horatio cries out, 'It harrows me with fear and wonder,' comparing it to a demon. 'I swear,' Horatio adds in Jojo's version, 'I wouldn't believe that I could see this demon without the sensible and true guarantee of my own eyes.'

The reasons for Ruin's presence in Alex's life are becoming clearer. But the answers for his eradication are not yet in focus.

So today's task is to venture to Alex's home and meet his aunt Beverly, and also to scope out Alex's immediate surroundings. I am never satisfied with the picture of a patient that a general assessment affords me: Poppy was so much more than the individual she portrayed in psychiatric interviews. Alive in the Scottish Highlands, confident and thoughtful at Arthur's Seat, she was a product of her environment. In a way, I find myself considering Michael's push for Alex to stay at home, in a place where he obviously feels safe and more at ease. But I have learned there are ways to make the transition from home to residential unit much smoother, if one takes the time to understand exactly where a person has come from.

I put on my talisman and head towards the city on foot. I make it as far as St George's Market close to the Belfast Waterfront before my phone rings. It is Michael. I consider ignoring him. I feel awkward about meeting him again, given our conflict over Alex. I stare at my phone for a moment, then press 'Answer' on the screen.

'Man, you walk fast,' Michael says on the other end. He's panting and I can hear the drone of traffic in the background.

'Where are you?'

'Can you wait where you are for a sec? Am almost there.'

I look around me. A tall, blond-haired figure in a billowing black raincoat waves at the other side of the road. It's Michael. I frown and wave back. When the traffic lights turn he jogs across the road, his face beaming. A far cry from our encounter at the hospital. Though, as he draws closer, his smile fades into concern, then into a look of apology. He sticks out his hand, and when I shake it he pulls me gently towards him, pecking my cheek.

'How are you? Better than last time I saw you?'

I nod. 'Much.'

His eyes are searching. 'Look, I'm sorry about ... well, getting so worked up the other day.'

I felt myself soften. 'I know this case is important to you. And I should probably reassure you that I have only Alex's interests at heart.'

He nods. 'I know things probably seemed a lot simpler in Edinburgh. But it's different here. None of the kids I've witnessed being separated from their families have fared particularly well . . .'

We start walking, his voice drowned out by the hustle and bustle inside the market. We take a side street towards the City Hall where a man is busking. Michael stops to throw some change into the small red cap on the ground. As a result, he rises two notches in my estimation.

'Maybe you didn't hear me when I said I had no interest in separating Alex and Cindy,' I say lightly. 'And I actually meant it. But a spell at MacNeice House would ensure that Alex receives the correct treatment . . .'

Michael looks ahead, his hands deep in his pockets. 'Once bitten, twice shy, I guess,' he says.

'What do you mean?'

He hesitates, thumbing the corner of his mouth in thought. 'There was a guy who worked there a few years ago, same role as you. Manson. One of my cases was a twelve-year-old girl. Nina. Cute little blonde thing. Suffered from Asperger's, and also this rare disease called Cigarette Burns. Her dad even owned up to it. Mother kicked him out, pleaded with us to let Nina stay with her. But as soon as Manson finished Nina's treatment he sent her off to a foster family.'

We reach the end of the side street, the blare of the city traffic inching closer. I stop to let him finish.

'Was she reunited with her mother?'

'Yes, but there was a lot of unnecessary heartache caused. And I guess I'm just a sceptic anyhow. I think a lot of these kids make things up to get attention.'

It's at this point that my heart sinks. The team involved in assessing Alex's needs consists of a jocular, doughnut-obsessed occupational therapist, Howard Dungar, who remains mostly in the sidelines as a signature on the report; Ursula, whose presence in the case is surprisingly in the form of a stony silence of disapproval at meetings, her head firmly turned towards the event of her retirement; and Michael the skeptic, who doesn't believe in what I do.

'So what are you out here for, anyway?' he says, visibly forcing a smile on to his face.

I step out towards the road, waiting for a break in oncoming traffic.

'Sightseeing.'

'Sightseeing? I thought you grew up in Belfast?'

'Demon hunting, then,' I say with a smile. 'I'm investigating Alex's environment.'

Just then, he steps towards the road, sticks an arm out, and a few seconds later we're both bundling into a taxi.

'Just up the road, please,' he tells the driver.

'Where're we going?' I ask Michael.

His green eyes are serious, unsmiling. 'You said you wanted to hunt demons. We're hunting demons.'

The taxi pulls around the front of the City Hall and leads us out of town, taking us along a sprawling, congested street that has large murals on either side, some of them spreading across three or four walls. Michael leans across me, eyeing the rows of shops and houses.

'Alex's old school is around here,' he says.

'We're going to Alex's old school?'

He shakes his head. I catch a whiff of aftershave as he leans close. There's tobacco, too, lingering in his clothes. It is oddly reassuring. 'This is the route he used to take to walk there. Look.'

He taps the taxi driver on the shoulder and asks him to pull over. Outside, he jogs across the road towards one of the biggest murals. This one has an enormous oval in the middle in which are painted the words UVF FOR GOD AND ULSTER. There are five named faces above and four gun-wielding figures at the bottom, all featureless, all dressed completely in black. But one mural makes me double-take. It is a demon holding a gun, snarling at the viewer and stalking across the graves of dead Republicans.

'You never seen this before?'

'There are murals all over the city. I've seen dozens like this.'

'But not with demons in them?'

I look up at the portrayal above me. There is no denying that such a striking image witnessed daily by an impressionable boy could have an impact.

'There's more,' Michael says, tapping my arm and heading back to the taxi. Inside the cab he leans forward to the driver and gives directions. The driver does a sharp U-turn and pulls us through streets that show Belfast is in the process of being rebuilt: old, graffitied buildings en route to demolition, spewing the contents of interior rooms as if a giant axe has chopped them in half; smaller, newer buildings with silver cladding and artwork on the exterior. I am still undecided as to whether this is a good thing or not.

Finally, we pull up alongside a pub on a busy road, prompting some angry car horns behind us.

'Come with me,' Michael says, jumping out of the car and racing round to the other side to help me out. Despite myself, I'm warmed by his chivalry.

'What do you think?' he says, nodding at the wall in front of me.

Another mural. This time, it's a wall-sized portrait of Margaret Thatcher. Only, she has red eyes and blood trickling from the corners of her mouth. Another demon.

'So, can I ask a personal question?' Michael says, reaching for the sugar pourer. We are at a café on the Waterfront overlooking the River Lagan and the usual clouds of starlings looping around the Albert Bridge. An early evening coffee is the furthest distance I will travel in a professional relationship.

I stir my coffee and watch, amazed, as Michael dumps sugar into his with abandon. 'Go on, then.'

'What made you want to become a child psychiatrist?'

I take a gulp. The coffee is much too hot and I struggle not to splutter.

'You say it like I'm a lion tamer.'

'Not far off, though,' he says, grinning. He sets down the sugar pourer.

'That's the common assumption, isn't it? That us psychiatrists are all trying to tame the wild imaginings of damaged kids ...'

'No, it's just I ...' He loosens his tie with a flick of his thumb under the green knot at his throat. 'My parents sent me to a shrink when I was wee. Made me apprehensive about the profession ever since.' The admission makes him clear his throat and cross his legs.

'Apprehensive in the sense that you don't believe I can help Alex?'

He throws me a look. 'No, I do. It's just ... well, my stance on treatment is a little more grounded in the theory that medication only works on a short-term basis. In the long run, if we're to ensure Alex has a future in society, I believe we need to work with him *and* Cindy. And his Auntie Bev. I believe Bev is going to play an important role in his life now.'

'Doesn't she have to return to Cork?'

He shifts in his seat. 'You didn't answer my question.'

I retrace my train of thought. 'Oh. Long story. The short version is that I got a scholarship to medical school, then further funding to pursue child psychiatry.'

'Two scholarships?'

'Three, actually.' Usually I am self-deprecating, but not about my scholarships.

'Three?'

'I grew up in Tiger's Bay.'

Michael gives a whistle of surprise and raises his eyebrows, and I find myself heartened by the response. Tiger's Bay meant nothing to anyone in Edinburgh. To a Belfast boy, it means something akin to the Bronx in New York City, or South Central in Los Angeles. It means that, in all likelihood, I should have ended up at the other end of the social scale. The truth is, my childhood has earned me an invaluable amount of self-respect. Or, rather, what it took to climb out of there.

'How on earth does a girl from Tiger's Bay end up a child psychiatrist?' Michael presses his fingers against his head as if he's trying to stop it from exploding.

'The government was keen to give kids from single-parent families in the north Belfast area a head start to grammar school. Scholarship number one. Then a medical degree at Edinburgh University, scholarship number two. Followed by a scholarship to train as a child psychiatrist.'

He shakes his head in disbelief. 'If that's the short version, I can't wait to hear the long one.'

I rub my scar without realising. He notices. 'Has the long version anything to do with that scar?' he asks, half-jokingly. When I hesitate his smile fades.

'Sorry, that was rude of me.'

Before I can reply, a waitress approaches, asking if we want anything else to eat or drink. The café is starting to fill with couples on dates, friends meeting up for after-work drinks. Michael holds up a hand to indicate we're fine with coffee. He looks appalled at himself for the reference to my scar, a look of self-mortification so intense at his rudeness that I immediately let the comment go with a sense of relief.

I have a very convincing, very rehearsed story for this scar.

It is so deep and oddly situated, running from my cheek to my neck, that make-up doesn't cover it fully. It is the reason I grew my hair so long, though since turning forty it has started to thin at the ends. More and more I use this lie when my hair fails to conceal it. The lie I concocted – which revolves around an unfortunate coral encounter whilst snorkelling in Fiji – was to engineer ensuing questions (*Is Fiji beautiful? So you snorkel? What kind of coral?*, etc.) that deflected entirely from the truth and towards a much more pleasant direction of conversation.

Only, right now, I'm not in a lying mood.

'Actually, you're right on the money, Michael,' I say breezily. 'My daughter has ... *had* ... early onset schizophrenia.' I tap my scar. 'This was a result of my agreement to put her in an inpatient unit.'

Michael nods and clasps his hands, his face soft. 'I'm sorry.' There is a pause as he holds my gaze, fitting the scar to its imagined origin. 'It's one thing to treat other people's children. But to see your own child suffering, especially when you understood so intimately ... ' He shakes his head. 'I can't imagine how that must have felt.'

I open my mouth to explain how it felt, then find I am lost for words. The fact is, schizophrenia doesn't affect every sufferer the same way. Hallucinations, unshakable delusions and muddled thoughts are the most striking symptoms. In Poppy's case, her delusions were of a frightening physical nature. She'd see walls right in front of her that stretched up to the moon. She'd see bridges; vast, swelling rivers and oceans channelling down Princes Street. This was the cause of her outbursts. And she became increasingly convinced that she was stuck in a hole or being buried alive. She might have been sitting on the sofa watching television when suddenly she'd begin to scream for dear life, convinced that she was falling into a bottomless pit. '*Help me, Mum!*' she'd yell, her nails dug deep into the arms of her seat, as if they were the sides of the hole she was sinking into.

It took me a long time to understand what was happening when she did this. And when I wouldn't believe her, her reality would shift again: I was trying to kill her. She would become violent.

Michael's stare brings me back into the present. I clear my throat and remember where I'd got up to. 'She was the reason I trained in child psychiatry. My mother had suffered with what I now believe was schizophrenia. It was never diagnosed, of course. The GPs gave my mother all sorts of prescriptions for depression, told her to chew Valerian Root . . . '

Michael snorts. 'Fobbed her off, you mean.'

I nod. 'I heard there was a genetic link to schizophrenia. By the time Poppy was three, I had seen things in her behaviour that none of the paediatricians could explain. So I retrained. Three years basic psychiatry, then six months in child psychiatry.'

'As a single mother?'

I smile. 'Yes. I had a kindly neighbour who helped out with childcare. And I can live on four hours' sleep.'

'You must have seen an improvement in her after the treatment,' he says. 'If you still advocate inpatient units.'

'She *did* improve. Before that, she had no life. No friends, no ability to make friends, no hobbies ... but the problem with schizophrenia is it's unpredictable. Too many riddles for one person to solve.'

He lifts his head and looks at me, searching my expression. 'Riddles frustrate you. Don't they?'

I blink. 'Don't they frustrate *you*?'

He leans back in his chair, crossing an ankle over one knee. 'Riddles I can live with. Battered kids, I can't. Man, the stuff I've seen ... I mean, I know you probably deal with the most terrifying psychological nightmares ever ... but social work,' he grins, though his gaze stretches far into the distance, 'someone shoulda warned me. Someone shoulda warned me.' He uncrosses his legs. 'I bought an allotment for that reason.'

'You bought an allotment for *what* reason?'

'To detox,' he says, using his hands for emphasis, as if he's brushing an invisible cloud of smoke off his chest. 'To free myself from the tangle of all those messed-up families. Nothing like a turf fire and slug repellent to take your mind off a teenager who starved her baby to death because she was out dealing crack.'

The image makes me shudder and he sees it. The shadow of a smile returns to his face. 'So what do *you* do, then? Swim? Jog?'

I nod. 'Both. And I play.' I run my fingers up and down the table as if it's a piano.

He raises his eyebrows. 'Ah, the merry Joanna? Jazz?'

'Classical. Or post-impressionist, if you want specifics.'

'Always.'

I feel the conversation slide in a direction that makes me nervous. I change the subject. 'I read the notes from the primary consultations with Alex, but I doubt very much that he has attachment disorder,' I tell him.

'No?'

I shake my head. 'He's not bipolar either. I won't rule it out, of course, but it's my feeling, and I haven't been wrong in quite some time.'

He taps a spoon against his cup. 'What about childhood schizophrenia?' I sigh, and he looks up. 'What, that's a possibility?'

I am tentative. 'From what I've seen, yes. But a proper diagnosis requires admission and observation.'

His face looks heavier all of a sudden, his shoulders slumping. 'If Cindy gets home and finds Alex has been shipped off to some ... and forgive me, but *nuthouse* ... I don't think she'll be able to deal with it. I think it might be the final straw.'

The child's interests must come first, I think. But, clearly, much is at stake, and I am willing to give Michael's approach a little longer.

I look out over the darkening skyline, rush hour traffic forming a necklace of red brake lights across the bridge. The birds swarm and swoop as they settle in for the night. I meet Michael's gaze across the table, wincing at the concern in his eyes.

'For now, I'll assess Alex at home.'

9

INVISIBILITY

Alex

Dear Diary,

A convict escapes from prison by digging a tunnel which comes up outside the prison in a school playground. The convict is so happy when he crawls out of the mucky tunnel that he starts shouting, 'I'm free, I'm free!'

A little girl walks up to him in the playground.

'So what?' she says. 'I'm four.'

I've been sent back to school, which hasn't been good because all the other kids seem to have heard about Mum and they're starting to make up stories, like she's loony and I tried to kill her, or she tried to kill me and then herself. When

Auntie Bev picks me up at the front gates all the other parents look at me and smile but really they are talking and saying horrible things about Mum.

Also I'm not speaking to Ruen. When he promised me the special thing for letting him study me I was happy with it, but the other day I asked him why he still hadn't given me what he promised and he looked like he had forgotten all about it.

OK, so I know I said it was a secret but the special thing was a new house for me and Mum. When we first became friends and he told me I could have anything I wanted, I thought of asking for a new bike. I remember Mum was in my bedroom which was unusual and Ruen was the Old Man and he was standing over me with his arms behind his back as usual and his face in that tight fishy frown. I could see the bike I wanted in my head – it would be black and say 'Killer' on the side and the tyres would be thick and the seat would be a silver skull. Mum was scrubbing the windowsills with a liquid that smelled just like Ruen.

'You could grow mushrooms on these sills,' she said, and even though she was scrubbing hard enough to make her T-shirt all wet the black stuff wasn't coming off. The windows always looked like liquid, even when it wasn't raining.

'The council sticks people like us in places like this and for-gets about them,' Mum said, and her voice rattled because she was now on her knees rubbing the metal brush up and down and I hated the sound. I drew a picture with my fingertip in the wet glass of the window. Mum stopped to press the towel closer to the bottom of the wall to catch the drips. 'I mean, it's not like I want Buckingham Palace. A place that's not likely to kill us both from live wires might be nice.' She wiped her forehead with the back of her hand. 'Punishment, that's what it is.'

'Punishment for what?'

She tucked one of the long pink threads in her hair behind her ear. Some of the foam sat on the top of her ear like a cloud.

'For not being a perfect citizen. For living off benefits. For reminding the establishment of how it failed.'

'Who's the establishment, Mum?'

She nodded at me. 'Exactly.' She bent down to drip the metal brush in the bucket, then wiped the other side of her face and another little cloud of foam sat on her other ear. I tried not to laugh.

'That reminds me,' she said. 'I saw Fatty Matthews talking to you at the corner shop last night.'

I thought back to it. I didn't even know who Fatty Matthews was. I'd been buying milk and some big bald fat bloke came up to me and starting asking about school.

'. . . you tell me, OK?' she was saying. 'Because that powdery stuff isn't talc. Not even if he offers you lots of money.'

I nodded and finished my drawing on the window. After a few minutes Mum leaned back and stared at it and her face looked confused.

'What's that, Alex?'

'What's what?'

She stood up and the metal brush splatted foam on the floor. 'Your picture. What is it?'

I looked at it and thought, *Crap, Mum doesn't know who Ruen is*, and then I tried to think of a lie but Mum was staring at me.

'It's a man.'

'I can see that. Why did you draw it?'

I opened my mouth for a long time and said, 'Because I was bored,' but she was wiping her face now and knelt down in front of me.

'Alex, is there something you want to talk to me about?'

I shook my head, then thought better of it. 'I'm hungry.'

She tightened her hands on the tops of my arms. 'You know, what Dad did – it wasn't anything to do with you.'

I was thinking of asking Ruen for a burger now. Forget the bike. I'd seen someone eat a burger through the window of a shop in town: at first I thought it was like a totem pole or something, but no. It was a burger, with two fat round brown juicy slabs of burger meat and salad and a thick pink strip of bacon and cheese sliding on to the plate and it was so tall someone had stuck a flag in it like Mount Everest.

' . . . with chips, too,' I said, and Mum stopped whatever she was saying and looked at me with her eyes wide. She looked like me when she did that, because normally her eyes are small and puffy and sad.

'Alex, did you hear what I said?'

My arms were really hurting now. I nodded.

'Repeat it. Repeat what I said.'

I tried to think back, though my stomach was growling and I could actually *smell* it now, I could smell that burger.

She kept asking me to say what she'd said and so words came rising up in my mind like chips in a deep fat fryer, *police* and *Dad* and *blood* and *got what he deserved*.

'There are some things you're too young to understand,' she said, her voice growing softer, and I took a big breath because finally she'd let go of my arms. And then she raised a hand to her mouth and her eyes filled with tears.

'Oh, Alex,' she said. 'I'm so sorry.'

I looked down and where she'd held me on each arm was a big red mark in the shape of her hand. She tried to rub the mark with her palms but it didn't go away. So she pulled me close to her and my head was between her jaw and her shoulder and she was rubbing my back. I could smell cigarettes in her hair and also sweat and then Mum's smell which is quite nice. After a long time she leaned back and looked at me and there was a big smile on her face, which didn't happen very often.

'If you could have anything in the whole world, what would it be?'

'A burger with a slice of bacon and cheese.'

'No, really, Alex. What would it be?'

I looked at the picture I'd drawn in the window, which was starting to look like it was melting. *For Dad to come back*, I thought, but I didn't say that because I knew it would only upset her.

'What would *you* have?' I asked. She looked shocked and blinked three times.

'No one's ever asked me, I don't think,' she said. She stood up and stared at the windowsill.

'A new house,' she said then. 'Yeah. A brand new house. With a garden. And three ... no, *four* bedrooms, with a guest bedroom and everything. Maybe a gym.'

She started pacing up and down, describing every single room in microscopic detail, right down to the fact that we'd have no crappy attic with mould and no dead person's things all over the place and no mice and no drug-dealing neighbours either.

Later that day I told Ruen that the sort of house we'd like would have a garden at the back that gets some sun during the daytime, a kitchen big enough for two people to move in with an oven that works and hopefully a tap that doesn't drip, a toilet that flushes and walls that don't look like the last person living there took a pickaxe to them.

'Consider it arranged.'

'What?'

He narrowed his eyes at me in his Alex Is Stupid look. 'I'll sort it out, Alex.'

'How will you sort it out?' I asked. 'Do you have lots of money?'

He smiled and winked. 'I have powers of which you are unaware. A mere house is a trifle, my boy. If you'd asked me for a planet, it might have taken some time. But I could accommodate.'

I just laughed. *A planet*, I thought. What would I need a planet for? He's like that, Ruen. A bit of a snob, at least when he's the Old Man. He rolls his eyes when I play football and tells me my drawings of skeletons are *inept*, which means they're crap. According to Ruen, I should be reading something called *Chekhov* and am very *uncultured* for not learning the piano.

But then he tries to do what I see all the other demons doing: he suggests I do something mean, like drop the light in the Opera House on Katie's mum's head. I was too scared to do that. He told me later I was dumb for not doing it because really it would have been Terry dropping the thing and because Katie's mum hits her because she's a drunk and is jealous of Katie. *How can a mum be jealous of her own kid?* I asked him and he gave me The Look again, like I'm stupid.

And then last night Katie only came to rehearsals to tell Jojo she couldn't stay and when I saw her at the door she had a big black bruise on her cheek and her face was swollen and Jojo put her arms around her. She gave me a wave and ran off and I looked up at that light and thought, *Ruen was right*. Sometimes bad people need bad things to happen to them otherwise the bad things just go on and on and on.

I don't think I've ever done any of the things Ruen tells me to do, so I don't really know why I told Anya who he was when he asked me to. Sometimes his friends will come up to me and ask me to do things too, like steal from Mum's purse so I can buy her a Mother's Day card, or, once, one of them spent a long time plotting out how I can get back at our neighbours for breaking our window. I told them all to go away and leave me alone. I allowed Ruen to study me, but that doesn't mean I don't have a brain and will just follow what he says like I'm a stupid donkey or something.

Plus, I know what happened to Mum. I don't think Ruen realises this, and I don't tell him. But sometimes, when she gets sad, I see some demons surrounding her and talking to her, and the more they talk to her the sadder she gets. I tell them under my breath to get out. Usually, they just laugh at me.

I am very scared that they'll keep talking to Mum and she'll just keep taking tablets and never wake up. I want to tell this to Anya, but I'm not sure what she'll make of it.

Still, when Anya arrives at our front door, I am really pleased. I've made her onions on toast with a glass of milk and set it all on the table like she's a guest. Auntie Bev is really smiley. She wags her finger at me and says:

'He looks like a right wee Chaplin today, doesn't he?'

Anya looks at my clothes and says, 'What a lovely suit, Alex, and the bow tie's a nice touch, too.'

'Alex dresses himself,' I hear Bev whisper to Anya. 'I found a whole wardrobe of stuff left over from the old man who lived here before. I think he's supplementing his clothes with these old suits. I'm taking him to the shops tomorrow.'

Him, I think. It's rude for them to talk about me as if I'm not even here. I look at Auntie Bev's silver shower rail in the doorway and try to pull my head up, but I can hardly reach it. I climb up on the sofa then on to the lamp table beside it. I hold on to the door frame and lift my foot up over the bar to hang like a bat, the way Auntie Bev did.

'Alex?'

I can see Auntie Bev and Anya but they're upside down. Our dinner table looks like it's floating and the blue chair looks like it's stuck to the ceiling and everything looks so different I start to laugh.

Anya steps forward and holds my shoulders. 'Careful,' she says, slipping my feet off the bar and catching me as I drop slightly. Then she turns me the right way up and I feel dizzy.

'Well done!' she says. 'That's not easy to do, you know. Though maybe it's best if you warn me next time. Don't want you falling on your noggin.' She ruffles my hair and I feel surprised that no one's yelled at me. Anya sits down at the table, waiting for me.

'I'll just be in here while you have your chat, is that OK?' Auntie Bev tells Anya in a loud voice, pointing at the kitchen.

Anya nods. 'By all means. Are you making something nice?'

Auntie Bev ducks back out of the kitchen and wrinkles her nose. 'I'd love to, but all my sister has in the cupboards is ketchup and' – she glances at me – 'what the mice left behind.'

'You could make a nice risotto out of that, surely?' says Anya, though her face looks disgusted.

Auntie Bev presses her hand against her forehead and then crosses herself quickly. 'We'll go to M&S,' she tells me, then gives Anya the thumbs-up.

'What's risotto?' I ask Anya.

'Haven't you had risotto before?'

I sit down at the table and shake my head.

'It's like rice,' she says.

'Rice?'

She looks at me with her face all blank then says, 'You've not had rice either?'

I shake my head. Mum says she only has sixty quid a week for all the bills, and the way I go through sketchpads and cans of dog food for Woof we're lucky we don't have to live on air.

'Do you know you can buy enough onions for a whole week for less than a quid?' I tell Anya, and her face changes. She says, 'that makes sense.'

She leans forward and pulls a notepad from her bag, then a pen, then a fat pencil case and a big sketchpad. She hands the pencil case and sketchpad to me.

'What's this for?' I ask.

'I know you love drawing,' she says. 'I'd love it if you could draw some pictures for me.'

I unzip the pencil case and say, 'Cool!' because there's pastels in there as well as pencils, and I like the pastels because I can lick them and make the colours blurry which looks cool.

'What do you want a picture of?' I say, though I've already started licking the back of my hand and dabbing a yellow pastel in the spit. Anya doesn't say anything and just watches as I start drawing. I don't even know what I'm drawing but it makes sense to use yellow. I start off by drawing a sun with spirals instead of rays because the rays sometimes look like a spider and spiders are gross.

'Why don't you draw your mum for me?' Anya says.

I take out a peach colour and a brown and start to draw. I

begin with Mum's face which is an egg-shape with quite hollow cheeks, and then her legs which are like sticks. When I finish, Anya tilts her head and points at my drawing.

'Someone's carrying your mum. Who is it?'

I look at the picture and realise I haven't given myself a bow tie. I quickly find a red and draw it in. '*I'm* carrying Mum,' I tell Anya. Then I use a dark-blue for my eyes and find a light-blue for Mum's eyes.

'Why are you carrying your mum in this picture?'

I'm not sure. 'I think she might have a sore foot. Or maybe she's too tired to walk.'

Anya nods and frowns so I pick up a red pastel and dab some bits of blood from Mum's foot to show why I'm carrying her.

'What about Woof? Can you draw him?'

I find some white and black and draw Woof with his head under Mum's feet, because if I *was* carrying Mum like that he would definitely help me.

Anya takes a big breath. 'And what about your dad? Could you draw him?'

I look at my colours. I don't know what colour to use for Dad. I can't even remember what colour his eyes were and for a minute this scares me. Then Anya says: 'Even if you can't draw a picture of your dad, can you draw something that comes to mind when you think of him? Even if it's just a mark on the page?'

I blink my eyes four times. I pick up the blue pastel again and draw.

'Is that a car?' Anya asks. I nod.

'Did he drive a blue car?'

I shake my head, and she just nods and I stare at the picture. My hands feel tingly and my heart is pounding.

'I saw him in a blue car once,' I tell her.

Anya nods and smiles. 'What about Ruin? Or any of the people you see. Could you draw them?'

I had hoped she had forgotten all about Ruen. I wasn't happy when Ruen asked me to tell her about him but I felt I needed to be honest with her, and she seems like the sort of person I can be honest with. I look around me. There's a demon in the kitchen with Auntie Bev. You wouldn't think she was a demon as she is wearing a white dress tied at the waist and she's small with curly brown hair and looks like she eats a lot of cakes, but when she looks at me her eyes are black and I feel sick.

'Who's that?' Anya says, pointing at the picture.

'I don't know.'

'Is that Ruin?' she asks, tapping at the picture I've drawn of Horn Head, though I haven't drawn his red horn properly and it looks squiggly. I shake my head and rub it out with my thumb.

I fiddle with the scratchy corners of my bow tie and say:

'I *would* tell you more about Ruen, but I think you just think I'm crazy and that Ruen is someone in my head.'

She looks surprised. 'Does Ruin live in your head?'

I shake my head, very slowly. 'I'm not sure where he lives. Hell, probably. But for a long time he's lived mostly with me.'

'How long, would you say?'

I shrug. 'Since my dad died.'

She nods and writes something down in her notebook.

'Where does Ruin sleep?' she says, and she says it while she's writing.

'I don't think he sleeps. He comes and goes. Sometimes he disappears and I don't see him.'

'How long does he disappear for?'

I shrug. 'Sometimes a few hours. I usually see him every day, at least three times. Sometimes he just walks up and down our hall.'

'Why does he walk up and down the hall?'

'I think he gets bored.'

'What does he get bored of?'

Just as I'm getting sick of answering for Ruen he appears in the corner of the room. So I lean forward and look at him and ask, 'What do you get bored of?'

This shocks both Anya and Ruen, who is the Old Man just then. Auntie Bev is still in the kitchen, singing. Ruen looks very weird, like he's managed to crack his scowl into an open cave and his eyes are all droopy, like Woof's.

'Is he here now?' Anya says, her eyes all wide and round.

'He wouldn't dare miss a conversation about him, would you, Ruen?' I jeer at him and he scowls. 'What. Do. You. Get. Bored. Of?'

Eventually, he answers.

'Not being seen,' he says, and his voice is very hoarse like he's been smoking.

I thought as much. I tell this to Anya.

'Not being seen?' she says. 'You mean, because only you can see him?'

I say yes and then I remember something Ruen told me a while ago. 'He says that demons are old-school angels of Hell, which is a culture as old as the Earth. Demons have souls but they don't have human bodies. This is like a big deal to them so they get points for stuff they do.'

'What sort of things do they do?' she says, and she has to turn over her page because it's filled up with scribbles. I pause for half a minute because there's a demon right above Anya, and he's so fat his skin drips down around his body like a mountain of ice cream. It's like he's lying on her shoulders, trying to get comfortable. He yawns and then he disappears and I take a big breath of relief.

'I thought he was gonna squish you,' I say by accident.

'What?'

I shake my head and remember what she asked me. 'Ruen says he likes bringing a human to their lowest point. That's when demons get a prize called a human likeness.'

'They become human?'

I shake my head. 'No, they just *look* like a human. But even then they don't really get seen by anybody, not really. And I think invisibility's a very odd thing to be bored of,' I tell Anya. 'Being invisible would be so cool!'

I start to tell Anya all the cool stuff I'd do if I turned invisible, and she writes some of it down and then holds her hand up.

'Can I ask Ruin another question?'

I glance at him and feel a bit annoyed. I'm sick of talking about him now and wish I'd never bothered telling Anya about him in the first place because he's getting all the attention. He just stares. 'Yeah,' I tell Anya.

'Wait, where *is* Ruin?' she asks, looking around the room. I point at the spot he's standing in, which is right next to the window and beside the blue armchair.

'There,' I say.

Anya shuffles in her seat so she can make out the exact spot. She points. 'There?' Ruen looks taken aback by all this pointing and for a moment I think he's going to disappear.

'Yeah, there.' I get up and stand next to him. He looks down at me, frowning. He doesn't seem to be cross, just in a bit of a daze. I hold my hands out to my side. 'Right here.'

Anya nods. 'Can you hold your hand up, Alex, right so it touches Ruin's head? Just so I know how tall he is. Only you can see him, you see.'

I stretch up on my tiptoes to measure Ruen's height. My fingers brush the bald spot on top of his head and it feels cold and smooth.

Anya smiles and writes something down. 'Ruin seems tall for a boy,' she said. 'Didn't you say he was a boy?'

I shake my head. 'He's old.'

More scribbles in her notebook.

'Can you describe for me what Ruin's wearing?'

I tell her. I could tell her with my eyes shut: when he's the

Old Man he never wears anything else. Same dusty brown suit with the same smell of a dead dog. It makes me want to be sick. I don't mention that he's a monster sometimes, and I would never, ever tell her about Horn Head because when he's the Horn Head he just freaks me out.

'So you're both wearing suits?' She laughs. 'Is there some wardrobe copying going on here?'

I look from the straggling bits of black thread dangling from the hems of Ruen's suit to the shirt collar, so green and crusty it looks like someone gobbed on his neck, and I say: 'There's no *way* I dress like that.'

Then she asks something weird. 'Can you tell me what Ruin is *thinking*?'

I look at him. He looks at me and raises an eyebrow as if he's curious about that, too. I look back at Anya.

'Of course I can't tell you what he's thinking. That would make me a mind-reader, wouldn't it?'

She just smiles. Then it occurs to me: she thinks I'm lying. She really does think I'm making all of this up. I feel my cheeks get hot. I clench and unclench my fists. 'I don't want to do this any more,' I tell Anya. 'Can I see my mum now, please?'

'Hold on a minute, Alex,' she says quickly, setting her pen on her lap. 'I was enjoying learning all about Ruin. Maybe you can tell me what his hobbies are?'

And so I look at Ruen and he rolls his eyes. 'Tell her I quite enjoy genocide,' he says, and I go to say it but then remember what *genocide* means and think that she might look at me funny and so I stay quiet. When I don't say anything

Auntie Bev comes in from the kitchen with a big smile and bends down in front of me.

'If you tell the nice lady all about the things you can see, we can go visit your mum. OK, Alex?'

'Today?'

Bev looks at Anya and then nods. 'Yep. Today.'

And I feel really excited then and tell Anya that I can see all Ruen's friends, too, and that some of them are scary and look like dragons, and some of them look like human-looking robots with red eyes. 'Like the Terminator?' she says and I realise that yes, that's exactly how some of them look. And so I start wondering whether James Cameron who directed the film sees what I see too and maybe she could speak to him as well.

I hear Bev whispering something to Anya about 'masculinity issues' and Arnold Schwarzenegger and Anya nods and says, 'Potentially.'

'Let's talk more about Ruin,' Anya says, turning back to me. 'What does he like to eat?'

But I'm fed up now. I just want to see Mum. So I say: 'Why do you want to know so much about Ruen, huh? He's a miserable old fart who does nothing but make false promises and whinge about how crap our piano is.'

I glance over at Ruen, expecting him to be cross at me for saying this. And he does look very cross, just not at me. He is looking right past me at the doorway. I follow his gaze but I don't see anything.

'Alex?' I hear Anya ask.

'What's wrong?' I say to Ruen, but he doesn't reply. He is showing his teeth like Woof does when he's cross; his face is turning bright red. Then he changes into a monster right in front of me, his short skinny arms bursting out of his shirt and turning dark and shadowy and his eyes rolling back in his head. He grows so tall that his head bends against the ceiling and instead of his funny, purplish monster-skin he looks like thick black smoke with eyes and a hole like the middle of a tornado where his mouth should be. And in the middle of that hole are four long fangs. Then he turns and lunges towards me and I shout, 'Ruen!'

When I look up I see he's launched himself across the other side of the room in a kind of twist and crashes into the door-way of the living room, and I am screaming.

When he crashes, I feel very strange. There is such a sharp pain in my chest that I fall to the floor.

'Alex!' I hear Anya shout, then Auntie Bev runs towards me and Ruen lets out a huge, deep roar and then there is nothing.

10

THE THIN EDGE OF BELIEF

Anya

At my last session with Alex I met his temporary carer, his aunt Beverly, who drove up from Cork on the evening of Cindy's suicide attempt. I am relieved when I see her – she is lively, warm, and keen to put her all into helping Alex in whatever way she can. Beverly is Cindy's elder sister by eleven years and she works as an ear, nose and throat doctor. She has no children of her own and, having had a somewhat intermittent relationship with Alex over the years, is anxious to make up for lost time and be a support for her sister and nephew.

'I wish I'd come home sooner,' she tells me over and over at the back of the house, her face twisting as she looks over the smashed window in Cindy's kitchen, boarded up hapharzardly with cardboard and stickytape; the spots of mould above the sink. She pulls a cigarette from a fresh packet and asks if I mind. I shake my head and she opens the kitchen door, stepping out into the mossy yard.

'I knew Cindy was struggling. I should have come back for good, helped her out. I love Alex to bits. Cindy and I haven't always seen eye to eye but ... ' She trails off, taking a deep drag. 'We had such different childhoods. I've never under-stood Cindy. She's always kept things to herself. My mum did a good job of pulling information out of her, but she never opened up to me.'

I glance back at Alex, who is bringing his plate into the kitchen. He sets it on the bench and smiles at me. Bev waits until he is gone before she finishes.

'I only have so much time that I can take off work to care for Alex,' she says, giving up on her cigarette. 'But I'm all he's got until Cindy pulls herself round.'

'What about Alex's grandparents? Are they around?'

She stubs out her cigarette. 'Dad died when I was little,' she says quietly. 'Mum passed five years ago. She would be hor-rified by all this.'

'And Alex's father?' I ask. 'Does he have contact with him?'

She steps inside, shutting the door behind her. It won't close until she kicks it, making a dent in the base. She sighs. 'You'd need to talk to Cindy about that. The identity of Alex's father is something she chose to keep from all of us.'

I wonder why the decision has been made to hold it secret. I make a note to ask Cindy about it: even if Alex's father needs to remain unnamed, I still need more information about their relationship.

My session with Alex ends badly, though it reveals much about his relationship with his mother. When I ask him to draw a picture of her he sketches an image of himself carrying his mother, and I notice that his self-portrait is much larger than his sketch of Cindy. She looks baby-like, vulnerable in his arms, her own arms wrapped tightly around Alex's neck. From this I deduce that Alex has sensed her fragility and instability for a long time, which must have borne a huge impact on his sense of security and his role in the family as protector. His representation of his father is in the form of a blue car, which I believe is a memory from his childhood – most likely his father collected him in such a car during his visits.

He also tells me numerous things about the spiritual world, about what he can see and hear, and what he makes of it all. Most of it I can peg on the things I have witnessed in his surroundings, and there are connections to be made between his role in *Hamlet* and his interpretation of his home life. I notice his descriptions flit in and out of religious rhetoric – 'a dragon with seven horns', which I believe is in Revelations in the Bible – and the language he uses for such descriptions is far beyond his usual ten-year-old lingo.

'Ruen is not *bestial*, he says, he's a *committed intellectual*,' Alex informs me, when I query the portraits of some of the beings in the world he describes. His fondness for Ruin is palpable –

protective, even – and I believe there is something of Alex's feeling towards his mother projected on to his imaginary sketch of Ruin, and with good reason: whereas Alex cannot control his mother, he can control these other beings.

It is common for psychotics to construct a highly fantastical world with clearly defined boundaries and with a system of rules that derives from a system that exists in reality – in this case, the supernatural. Alex never mentions angels, which I find very interesting. No mention of God or any other deity either. However, he says there are demons everywhere, all the time, and that when he enters an empty room it is not empty, it is like a pub, with demons grouped in corners, plotting, huddled around any humans who happen to be about, tempting, cajoling, scheming.

When I press him to discuss Ruin in more detail, Alex erupts. His descriptions of Ruin ascend into a screaming fit, and to my horror he passes out in the chair opposite me.

Bev charges across the room and grabs him. He is limp and deathly pale, and for the first time during my assessment I feel afraid. I feel myself turn over the things he told me about demons, about spirits – immediately I dismiss the notion, but the fear lingers. On reflection, it astonishes me how frail a thing belief is.

After a few moments, Bev shouts, 'He's awake! He's awake!' I am in the kitchen getting Alex a glass of water. Then: 'He's going to be sick!' I grab the basin out of the sink and race into the living room, just in time to catch a spew of vomit from Alex's mouth.

'That's better, that's better,' Bev is saying, thumping him on the back and fumbling in her pocket for her mobile phone.

I kneel down in front of Alex and take his pulse. His heart rate seems fast, his pupils dilated. 'How do you feel, Alex?' I ask calmly. He blinks and tries to focus on me. Then he presses a hand against his chest.

'It hurts.'

'What hurts?'

'Here.'

Bev quickly unbuttons Alex's shirt. She gasps, and I look down to see three red stripes on his chest, as if something has just scorched his skin.

'Did someone at school do this to you?' Bev is shouting, and I try to tell her that these marks must have been made recently – as recent as my visit, in fact. My mind reels with questions, but just then Alex leans forward, his face pale and strained. I yank the bucket up, just in time to catch another fountain of puke. Bev dashes into the kitchen to find a cloth. When Alex collapses back in his chair he looks weak, but gives a little smile nonetheless.

'You feel better?' I say. He nods.

'Is Ruin still here?' I ask tentatively. He looks around, then shakes his head.

Bev returns, a tea towel in one hand, Alex's coat in the other. Alex is mumbling something about a diary.

'What should we do?' Bev splutters.

I look him over. 'We need to take him to hospital.'

*

We travel to the hospital in Bev's car, where an examination determines that he is absolutely fine. The doctor can't find any sign of the marks, despite Bev and I confirming that we saw them.

'Could have been from wrapping his own arms around himself too tightly,' the doctor offers. 'Maybe leaning against something. In any case, there's no bruising. In fact, no external marks at all.'

Bev turns and walks away in frustration. I thank the doctor for his time and jot down some notes while they're fresh in my mind. I note that Alex's separation from Cindy has intensified his anxiety, so I arrange for him to visit his mum as soon as possible. She is based in the psychiatric ward of this same hospital, and it strikes me as sad that both mother and son are hospitalised. Michael will be beside himself.

Once Alex is settled, I pull up a chair close to his bed and pull the curtains around us.

'Where's Bev?' he asks.

'She's getting some fresh air.' *She's outside, smoking.*

'Is she OK?'

'She's absolutely fine, Alex.' *No, she's hyperventilating.* 'How are you?'

'I'm OK. I really like Auntie Bev. I haven't seen much of her for a long time but she's really nice.' A pause. 'Did I scare her?'

'She just wants to know you're safe and well, that's all.'

He feels for his chest.

'Does it hurt?' I ask.

He shakes his head. 'Not any more. It was weird . . . '

'What did it feel like?'

He opens his mouth to describe it but can't seem to find the words. 'Like fear,' he says eventually.

'*Fear?*'

He gives a heavy sigh. 'Can I see Mum now?'

I pull my chair closer and look him over. He has a sweetness about him that makes me feel protective towards him. For a moment I hear a B natural note ring across the room from a dropped petri dish. Already my mind is turning to Poppy. Her dark head bending at the piano. *I love you, Mummy.*

I close my eyes and focus on what I want to ask next. It is important that I do not let Poppy enter this case. Alex is a patient, not a projection of my daughter. She is not an entity I can revive with another's breath.

'Alex, I wanted to ask you something.'

He stares at me. '*Please* not more stuff about Ruen . . . '

I shake my head. 'I'm going to take you to see your mum very soon. But do you mind if I stay, too?'

His face lights up. 'I'm going to see Mum?'

'Not this afternoon. But maybe tomorrow, when you're feeling better.' His eyes fill with tears. And, right then, he flings his arms around me and sobs into my neck. I feel tears rising in my own throat. His vulnerability is screaming at me, and, with only one exception, I have never felt as helpless in my whole life.

In the light of Alex's hospitalisation, it is crucial that we review the management of his case. I call a meeting at

MacNeice House tomorrow morning and arrange to meet with Michael later that day to prepare him about what I intend to put before the team: that I wish to move Alex into my inpatient unit.

I don't tell Michael why I want to meet, however, and he sounds flattered.

'OK,' he says on the other end of the line, after a long silence. 'I'm on my way back to the office from the Falls Road. What say we meet somewhere less formal than your office?'

'*Your* office, then?'

'How about the Crown Bar?'

'So be it.'

Michael arrives late. I see him bobbing through a heavy throng of punters in the same dark-green jumper, his head gleaming golden in the bright lights.

'Evening,' he says, reaching down and kissing me on the cheek. He takes off his jacket and folds it neatly before setting it down beside me.

'G&T?' he asks, still out of breath.

'Orange juice.'

He gives me a look. 'You driving?'

I shake my head. 'I don't drink alcohol.'

He cocks his head. 'A teetotal child psychiatrist from Tiger's Bay. That's a mixture.'

I shrug. 'I like to take care of myself.'

Michael blinks at me for a few moments. Then he straightens

up, heads to the bar, and returns with two glasses of fresh orange juice.

I feel very guilty and dull – the Crown Bar is a jewel in a country which has transformed the act of drinking alcohol into a cultural art. 'Just because I'm not doesn't mean you can't,' I say, then wonder what has caused me to reduce myself to state the perfectly obvious.

He slides up next to me. 'And how gentlemanly would that be of me?'

His crooked smile is wider tonight, accompanied by a gleam in his eye and a ripe colour to his cheeks. In this light it strikes me that, under different circumstances, I would enjoy his company. And I sense it then, that old buttery flutter in my belly. Flirtation. Which I am reciprocating beyond my better judgement. I really, really don't want this. I think of Fi, her round blue eyes heavy with sincerity and kindness. She would tell me this is a *sign*. Fi is all about signs.

'A sign of *what*?' I once asked her when a wasp stung me on my face, of all places.

'A sign that you don't believe you're beautiful,' she said. She'd had a point: a garish scar on one's face is a powerful antidote to vanity. And then I think of her sitting at my kitchen table and taking both my hands in hers, saying:

'Repeat after me: "Poppy's death does *not* mean that I have to abstain forevermore from life's pleasures."'

At the time I squeezed her hands and let go. 'I can't say it, Fi. I can't.'

She had reached out and stroked my face. My oldest friend,

younger than me. A divorced mother of four, maternal and homely; at ten years old she was kissing my knee scrapes better.

But even Fi didn't understand why I wanted to stay single. Something changes inside when you lose a child. No, *everything* changes. This kind of loss is far different – I won't say worse – than becoming bankrupt or losing your entire belongings in a house fire. Poppy's death was a different kind of agony, a different loss, even, than watching my mother sink beneath the yellow waters of cancer. Add together all the men I ever loved, then multiply that sum by how bad it felt when they all left, one by one ... you still don't come close to what Poppy's death was like. The only way I can describe it – and I rarely describe it, not even to Fi – is that in order to continue living and breathing in a world where my child is eternally robbed of her opportunities to grow up, fall in love, build a career and have babies means that I must remain my own personal fortress. I run, I don't drink, and I watch what I eat so that no one ever has to take care of me. I save sixty per cent of everything I earn in a high interest account so that I never have to depend on anyone. And I will not love again, because I can never, ever experience that degree of loss again.

There is a heavy pause as I realise Michael is staring at me. He has said something that I'm certain requires a response other than a blank stare.

'Sorry, could you repeat that?'

He half smiles and finishes his glass of orange juice.

'Actually, I was saying that I had Googled you. Quite an impressive list of awards, Dr Molokova. The Freud Medal for Excellence in Child Psychiatric Research, no less. And a Rising Star from the British Association of Child and Adolescent Psychiatry.' He gives me a small round of applause. 'I should get you to sign this beer mat.'

I grin, until he presents me with a pen and holds up the beer mat. I am laughing now, and the sound feels alien and delicious to me. Eventually, I sign it, and he tucks the mat into his jacket pocket.

'What else did Google tell you?'

He lowers his eyes, and I know he has read about Poppy. 'Only about your outrageous toothpick fetish, your blazing passion for bathmats . . . '

I take my chance. 'Can I ask *you* a personal question?'

'Yeah.'

'Why did your parents send you to a psychiatrist?'

He widens his eyes. 'Wow, that's a curve ball down memory lane. I had an imaginary friend. Why d'you ask?'

I make a mental note of the 'imaginary friend'. Seems he and Alex have a lot in common.

'It's just that you portray mental illness units as bad places, Michael. A lot of kids with even the most extreme psychosis can live a relatively normal life when they're properly treated. That's why I'm here.'

His smile is fading. He stares at a spot on the table for a long time. When he looks up, his eyes are hard. 'You want to move Alex. Don't you?'

I tell him what happened earlier that day, about the marks on Alex's skin. 'If he has psychosis, he will need treatment at the proper facility with the requisite medication and medical staff. Just as if he had to have surgery.'

'Surgery,' he repeats, unconvinced.

'The success rate of MacNeice House is impressive, Michael. Really.'

He shakes his head. 'To you, maybe. To those of us who've been in Belfast for the last seven years . . . not really.'

I try another tactic. 'I'm concerned about his long-term living arrangements, in any case. I mean, have you seen the state of his house? Do you know how many health and safety hazards I spotted?'

'How many?' he says, his voice hollow, far away.

'More than fifteen.'

I tell him energetically about the electrical socket I saw hanging off the wall and occasionally flicking blue sparks; the ancient, leaking radiators; the cracked ceiling; the smashed window at the back of the house covered up with tape and cardboard. Conditions that no human being should be forced to live in, and certainly not a mother and a child with mental health issues.

Michael mulls it over, drains his glass, then says, 'Excuse me,' before stalking towards the front door of the pub. For a moment I wonder whether he's clued in to what I'm *really* doing, and has responded by simply leaving me here, high and dry. I sip on my juice and check my phone for messages.

A few minutes later, I see him threading his way through punters towards me.

'Done,' he says with a wide smile, thumping down on the seat beside me. Though, I notice, not as close as before.

'*What's* done?'

He slaps his mobile phone on the table. 'I just phoned a friend of mine who works at the housing association, told him everything you told me. He says he'll have Alex and Cindy at the top of the re-housing list first thing tomorrow morning.' He raises his eyes to meet mine. 'It's your call if you want to put Alex in MacNeice House. I know what I know. That's all.'

Then he heads to the bar and brings back another OJ for me and a pint of Guinness for him.

11

STRAWBERRY PICKING

Alex

Dear Diary,

So there's this man who walks into a doctor's office with a carrot up his nose, a cucumber in one ear and a banana in the other. 'Help!' he says to the doctor. 'I don't know what's wrong with me!' The doctor looks at him and says: 'Clearly, you're not eating properly.'

Well, I'm in hospital now, not to see Mum though. I'm in hospital because Ruen went mental and turned into a monster and attacked something that he said was an angel, though I didn't see any angels. He came last night when everyone had gone home and I could hear the nurses' feet clapping up and down the corridor. I hope I don't have to miss rehearsals tomorrow. Everyone kept asking about the pain in my chest but it's gone now and so has Ruen.

He came just after Anya left. At first I was a bit nervous to see him because he really frightened me before. He was Ghost Boy then and he had a blue table tennis bat and a small white ball which he was trying to balance on the bat.

'Pity you're stuck in here,' he said. 'Otherwise you could come and play a game with me.'

He stood by the bed and started bouncing the ball up and down and counting.

'Stop that,' I said. 'Someone will hear you.'

He looked at me with his horrible black eyes. 'Are you soft in the head? No one ever hears me.'

'But they *feel* you, don't they?'

He stopped bouncing the ball. 'What you mean?'

'Don't be stupid, you know what I mean.'

He sat down on the bed next to me. I saw the blanket crease under his legs and I tugged it back because I was cold.

'Go on, then,' he said, smiling and folding his arms. 'Since you're the one who can see both worlds, why don't you fill me in? How do people *feel me*, Alex?'

'They just know, OK? They smell you, that's how.'

He pouted and I hope I don't look that girly when I pout. 'Why do you always have to be so mean? All I ever do is try and help you.'

I went to tell him he was a right whinger but then I wondered whether he really was trying to help me.

'That's what I was doing before, you know,' he said.

'What you mean?'

'Oh, so you actually want to hear, now?'

I sat up and looked around. The other people on the ward were asleep and the light above kept flickering and I could hear the nurses laughing in the tea room. One of them kept snorting and it sounded like a pig. Then another laughed and sounded just like a horse and I realised I'd never been to a farm.

Ruen picked up the ball and balanced it on his head.

'You can't see everything, you know,' he said. 'You never see angels. They're *so* annoying.'

I was thinking about what a farm might look like when it occurred to me he was right: I'd never seen angels. I'd never even thought about it until Anya mentioned it before. *How come you don't see angels?* she'd asked. *And what about God? And the Devil?* I said God was a man with a white beard and a red suit and a jolly face and the Devil was red too and he also smiled but was *inherently evil*.

'Is that what you think you are, Alex?' Anya had said, and I asked her what she meant and she said *never mind*. I told her angels had long golden hair and huge white feathery wings and usually lived on top of Christmas trees.

I told Ruen about this and he wrapped an arm round his waist and chuckled. 'Oh, you *are* thick, Alex,' he said. 'Angels don't look like that at all. In fact, angels keep trying to hurt you.'

This is the thing with Ruen when he's Ghost Boy. He's

constantly trying to prove he's smarter than me but sometimes he says stuff that makes me think and think.

'I thought angels were good and they protected people.'

Ruen keeled off the bed and staggered across the floor, dragging his feet and holding his stomach and making hacking noises as if my braindeadedness had stunned him to the point of death. Finally he slumped to the floor and gave a big sigh as if he'd actually died.

'Ruen?' I said, and I felt a sharp pain in my chest in case he'd actually died.

He jumped up to his feet and gave a big stupid grin. 'It's *me* that's been protecting you!' He walked up to me and leaned very close. 'They know you have a gift to see into our world. And they don't like it.'

'Why?'

Ruen looked around again in case someone saw us talking. The nurse that sounded like a pig was still snorting and I started wondering what it would be like if a cow wandered down the corridor. Ruen sat on the bed beside me.

'Because everyone thinks angels are beautiful when in fact they're hideous creatures. And they'd rather everyone believed the opposite.'

'So angels are trying to attack me?'

'Haven't you seen the white lights appear every now and then?'

I shrugged with one shoulder which means maybe I had but who cares? But really, I had seen white lights. They happened sometimes when I was getting scared or when Ruen was trying to make me do something and they looked like a bit of sunlight had drifted out of the sky and into the room. Ruen picked up his bat and ball and looked like he was going.

'You off, then?' I said, trying not to sound like I could give a rat's backside whether he was or not.

He turned and grinned. 'You want me to stay, don't you? You're *scared*.'

'Am not,' I said, but when he turned and sat back down and put his arm around me, I gave a big sigh of relief.

When I started to fall asleep Ruen said I was boring as a granny's picnic and left. Then I had a dream which was really lovely and really horrible at the same time. It was horrible mostly because I didn't want it to be a dream, and when I woke up I sat with the balls of my palms pressed against my eyes and sang the only song I knew over and over again which was 'Away in a Manger'.

My dream was about Granny. Granny reminded me of a Doberman, which sounds funny but I mean that she was really snarly and people were scared to say the wrong thing to her but when she liked you she'd protect you and scare bad people off. One time two men called bailiffs knocked on the door of her neighbour Doris because they wanted Doris's sofa. Granny ran out with a broom and whacked the men until they left because she said Doris hadn't done any harm to anybody, though I wonder why they wanted Doris's sofa cos it had cat hairs all over it. Granny lived a bus ride and four-and-three-quarter minutes of walking away from us and everyone called her 'Granny', like she'd been born with that name. She was short and the skin on her face shook when she laughed and most of her teeth were metal stubs screwed into her gums like a pirate and she smoked so many cigarettes that her voice was deep like a man's. Sometimes she lit another one while one was still making spirals of smoke in her ashtray. She was ill for years and years. I remember she said she'd *rather burn out than fade away* and at the time she was holding a cigarette in each hand.

Granny was very proud of her back garden because not many people we knew actually had back gardens and she'd always grown up with a yard made of concrete. So she decided to grow strawberries, which were red as postboxes and big as fat men's noses. The only time Granny ever told me off was when I ate them because she said she needed them to make jam.

'Jam keeps for ever,' she used to say, 'but strawberries only last a season – or a few minutes once *you* get your mucky paws on them.'

So in the dream I was in her kitchen and she told me to go outside to collect strawberries to make jam. Outside it was really sunny, and the clouds looked like balls of wool in the sky. I walked down into the grass which was really deep. There was a snake in the grass and at first I was really scared and backed away, but when I looked again I saw it wasn't a snake, it was a shadow. Then I noticed that the shadow was really long and I couldn't see what was making the shadow. I followed it all the way through the grass towards the end of the garden and when I looked up I saw Ruen standing in front of me. He was the Old Man. The shadow led right up to a thread hanging down from his suit which I thought was mental.

'What do you want?' I said. He looked down at the shadow. That's when I saw that it split in two, like a fork. One of the forks led to Ruen, and the other led to me and it was wrapped around my chest.

'What's this?' I asked him.

Ruen just did that thing when he flares his nostrils and tweaks his ears and I could see the tufts of white hair in them. It means he's annoyed, but I just stared at him. Then Granny called out the kitchen window.

'He wants to hurt you, Alex.'

This was weird to me because Granny had never seen Ruen and in the dream I wondered if maybe they'd met.

I turned around and shouted back to her. 'What you mean?'

She started waving. 'Come on inside, Alex. He's no good for you. Leave him well alone.'

I shook my head. 'No, he's OK, Granny. Ruen's my friend.'

She gripped the edge of the window ledge and looked very cross. 'No, he is *not*, Alex. He wants you to think you're nothing. He wants to hurt your soul.'

'My *soul*?'

When I turned around Ruen was gone, and then when I looked back at Granny the kitchen window was closed, though I could see Granny there doing the dishes at the sink, just as I remembered. I turned to the strawberry patch but beneath their green leaves they weren't red and juicy as usual. They were like big fat blobs of shadow and they smelled like poo.

I picked them anyway and brought them inside. I went to set the basket down on the table and tell Granny about the strawberries. I wanted to tell her it wasn't my fault they'd gone bad. But she picked them out of the basket and they were red and beautiful and I thought I'd gone daft, so I said nothing else. Granny was humming and happy and there wasn't even a cigarette in sight.

'Will you stir these, Alex?' she said, plopping the strawberries into a big boiling pan on the stove while she got some sugar from the cupboard. I took a ladle from the jar on the bench and started to stir, and the strawberries bubbled and smelled delicious.

Granny poured in the sugar and said, 'Memory's a funny thing, Alex. Sometimes it can hurt us without us realising.'

I nodded but had no clue what she meant. I figured this was what old people said when they were about to lose their marbles.

But then I looked inside the pot I was stirring. The jam had already gone from being a big boiling mass of lumpy goo like something Woof had barfed to a cold stew that Granny could pour into the jars that she'd lined up on the kitchen table.

'Now, Alex,' she said. 'You have to hold each jar in place so I don't knock it over as I pour.'

I stopped stirring the stuff in the pot and walked over to the table. Granny nodded at the six jars on the clean spotty tablecloth and I gripped one with both hands.

'Hold it tight,' she said, so I did. Granny went and got the pot and slowly tipped it over the jar I was holding. The jam plopped out into the jar.

Granny said: 'You can make jam out of strawberries, but you can't make strawberries out of jam.'

I looked at her. 'What do you mean?'

She set the pot down and stroked my face. 'Ruen wants to try to change you into someone you aren't. I want you to remember who you are, Alex. Do you know who you are?'

I nodded. 'How do you know Ruen?' I said. She smiled and the room started to fill with a bright light. The light grew and grew until it squeezed everything out of view.

And then everything changed. When I looked around I wasn't in Granny's kitchen any more. I was in a street with houses and lots of people. I recognised the street but didn't know how I did. The street was small with a black wet road in the middle with small stone shops at either side and there was a post office on the other side of the road. People were running on the pavement and I was outside a church. I think I might have been singing in a choir because I could hear singing and I knew the words.

In front of me I saw a man in a black mask and a black jacket and jeans. He raised his gun and pointed it right at me. And then it was like time went on hold. There were pigeons flapping in the air and they still had their wings outstretched so I could see the white feathers. Someone's Coke can was floating, liquid pouring out of it like a brown ribbon. A policeman next to me turned his face and his lip curled like he was afraid or angry. His face was blurry.

I turned back to the man in the black mask. I could see his blue eyes through the holes in the mask and they looked right at me. I could see his gun, black and shining and wet. He squeezed the trigger and I heard a deep crack. Beside me, the policeman's knees buckled and his arms flung up in the air like a puppet's. As he fell to the ground the man lowered his gun and started to take his mask off. I watched, and my heart was pounding and my mouth was open.

Just before I woke up, I saw his face.

It was me.

12

THE PAINTINGS

Anya

My mornings are filled with meetings with other inpatients at MacNeice House. Our youngest resident is a girl, Cara, aged eight years old. Autistic Spectrum Disorder. She is also a gifted artist, and our visiting art therapist, Iris, seems to have made a lot of headway in developing Cara's social skills and channelling a lot of her aggression through creative sessions. Cara brings one of her paintings to show me.

'Look,' she says, her hazel eyes wide as she points to a large painting on the wall of her room here at the unit. It is of four stick figures engaged in various activities of gardening, football and ballet. One of them seems to be fixing a car. 'There's me, there's my mum and dad and that's Callum.'

'It's beautiful, Cara,' I tell her, noticing the colours she's chosen. They are telling: instead of her usual preference for black, the painting features a mixture of sky-blues, pinks and yellows. Iris also highlights that Cara has started drawing circles as complete wholes instead of never-ending spirals – another sign of improvement.

Some of the other kids have more severe problems that remain to be as easily resolved – our fifteen-year-old inpatient, Damon, had been on a self-imposed hunger strike for four days before his parents brought him in. When I visit him in his room he refuses to make eye contact, let alone open his mouth to speak, and I am forced to have him restrained and put on a drip. Psychiatric assessments have indicated psychosis, and his medication seemed to be working: this sudden relapse is quite out of the blue. There are days when I feel the human mind is a jigsaw puzzle that I will never be able to solve.

The morning after Alex's transfer to hospital following his injuries at home, I call a review meeting of his case in the conference room, which involves Michael, Ursula, and Howard Dungar, an occupational therapist. Such meetings are necessary for me to present my findings and to get a variety of expert perspectives on the best programme of care for Alex.

Michael is already in the conference room when I arrive, warming his hands on an old radiator by the window.

'How's the allotment?' I ask, noticing his posture. He is stiff, frowning, ready for battle.

He turns and leans on the windowsill, digging his hands

deep into the pockets of his tweed trousers. The corners of his mouth twitch. 'My runner beans are four inches long,' he says blankly.

I shake my coat off and grin. 'I love it when a man says that to me.'

His mouth makes it all the way to a half-smile and I blush, wondering for a moment where my retort emerged from.

Ursula arrives, surrounded in her usual cloak of self-importance and wearing jeans for the second day in a row. The day before yesterday an advertisement went out for a replacement clinical psychologist, so her noticeable distancing from Alex's case is understandable. Howard shows up a minute after the hour, a white ring of sugar around his mouth and his fly undone.

When everyone has taken their seats, I begin the meeting with a brief commentary on my assessment of Alex to date.

'Alex Broccoli has witnessed his mother attempt suicide four times that we know of. He's also been privy to countless episodes of her self-harming. He has indicators of schizophrenia, including high vigilance, mild paranoia, bizarre behaviour and frequent and intense hallucinations. After an initial consultation at the hospital I arranged for him to undergo a series of physical tests to rule out any physical cause for his presentation. His brain MRI and EEG are normal and his blood tests proved fine.'

I look up from my notes to check everyone is still with me. Michael has his head raised slightly, his wide palms pressed into the wood of the table. Ursula is studying me through her small red reading glasses. Howard is picking at a shaving wound. I continue.

'As we'll all agree, there is a consensus that it is often better to keep the family together, but because of Alex's current state I feel it might be dangerous to keep him at home. It's my view that Alex needs constant assessment. Rest assured that I will do my best to maintain contact between Alex and his mother as regularly as possible.'

Howard looks up. 'Can you explain what you mean by "dangerous"?'

I nod. 'My interviews with him have revealed that he has frequent perceptual disturbances and delusions, including a strong attachment to an imaginary friend named Ruin. It's this character that I'm most interested in, because it tells me a lot about how Alex perceives himself.'

Ursula laces her fingers. 'How so?'

'He tells me Ruin is the "bad" version of Alex.'

She tilts her head. 'So Alex isn't saying *he* is bad?'

'No, but I believe Ruin is Alex's projection of himself. He also claims he can see demons, all the time, everywhere. I want to move him to MacNeice House for a period of at least one month for proper observation and assessment. Transferring Alex to MacNeice House requires his mother's consent. Cindy refuses to give it. She is currently being assessed to determine whether she is fit to make decisions for Alex as his mother, which makes me very sad. If she is found not to be, Alex will be moved to MacNeice House at the first opportunity.'

Michael leans forward. 'I think we ought to consider the

fact that Alex's mother is being treated at the adult psych unit. We're informed that she is currently there for another three weeks. Wouldn't it be a better idea to wait until she gets out?'

Ursula turns to him. 'Why's that?'

'As a matter of sensitivity to the situation,' Michael replies calmly. 'Alex and his mother are very close. If you wait until Cindy is released from hospital, she will be able to visit Alex at MacNeice House. This contact will provide security and reassurance for both mother and son, and will almost certainly make it easier for them to receive treatment.'

'What about the marks on Alex's body?' interjects Howard. 'Is the boy being abused?'

'Most likely self-harming,' Ursula offers loudly, folding her arms.

'If Alex *is* self-harming,' I say, 'we need to intervene as soon as possible.'

I look across at Michael, noticing his jawline beginning to grow red. I feel a sense of sadness that I have still failed to convince him that I am on his side.

'Both Alex and Cindy will be distressed about their separation,' he says quietly. Nobody mentions the irony that Cindy's suicide attempts have been efforts to separate the pair for good – Cindy's mental state doesn't perceive it that rationally.

'This is a medical problem,' I remind Michael gently. 'A medical problem requires medical intervention—'

'But you haven't given a diagnosis!' he shouts.

Ursula turns back to me. 'Didn't the notes mention Alex has ASD?'

I shake my head. 'Alex seems to have been passed around consultants like a guinea pig.' I can barely conceal the acid in my tone. 'One assessment pointed at Alex's enhanced vocabulary and his social difficulties as a possible indicator of ASD, but I'm keen to rule it out altogether. Which is precisely why I need him transferred to MacNeice House,' I say, but just then Howard and Ursula are consulting loudly and I feel my suggestion has gone unheard. For a moment, Michael and I stare at each other across the long table, two forces at opposing sides. I am the first to break off.

I clear my throat. Ursula looks up. 'Sorry,' she says, her tone brittle. 'Howard and I are of the opinion that a holistic approach to this case is the better option, an approach that takes in the whole picture. Frankly, Cindy is part of that picture.'

I see Michael nodding from the corner of my eye.

Ursula continues. 'For my part, I recommend a solution-focused approach to Alex's case. Michael, you've been working with this family for several years now, haven't you?'

He flicks his eyes at her and nods.

'Anya, perhaps it's best if you and Michael work closely from this point towards a programme that takes the individual contexts and requirements into consideration.' She glances at Howard. 'We can review again in a couple of weeks.'

I open my mouth to speak, but she is already standing up

to leave. Howard smiles awkwardly and follows suit, pausing to pour himself a cold cup of coffee from the stainless steel jug at the end of the room. Michael stays seated, his eyes lowered, and so do I.

He waits for Howard to slurp from his coffee cup and bustle noisily down the hall before raising his eyes.

'Anya,' he says quietly, 'look ... I just want to go easy on this family, OK? I appreciate that you're a mover and a shaker, and we're all just playing catch-up after years of too much shaking and not enough moving, you know?'

I feel my cheeks burn. I remind myself that Alex's case is not a battle of wills between me and my colleagues, and amidst the rush of blood in my ears I try and reason with myself that, maybe, waiting until Cindy is released is absolutely fine. But I am seized with an urgency to resolve this case and I hardly know why.

Michael stands up, walks around the table and sits down in the chair beside me.

'Are you OK?' he says then, and I see he looks worried. I raise a hand to my cheek and find, to my horror, I have started to cry.

I nod and laugh and try and rein in whatever emotions have slipped out of my grasp without my noticing.

'Yes,' I tell him, looking at my wet fingertips as if I expect them to announce the reason for their presence. 'I suppose I'm just trying to find my feet in this place. We just arm-wrestled each other in review meetings in Edinburgh, played some poker. None of this debate stuff.'

He smiles and I take the opportunity to run a finger under both eyes, mopping up the inevitable black smudge. Then I pull out the biro that's been holding my hair up. I want it long, covering up my scar. He stops smiling and reads my face, glancing at my new hairstyle. At my jawline.

'I don't mean to be a hypocrite,' he says carefully, 'but I think you should be careful not to become too involved in this case.'

'You think I've become involved?'

'I'm worried that the *real* riddle that bothers you is Poppy. And that you see much of Poppy in Alex's case.'

He adds the word 'case' hastily. I frown. 'I deal with dozens of kids with mental health issues all the time, what makes you think . . . ?'

He shakes his head firmly. 'Not with Poppy's illness, Anya. Not like this. You're afraid, aren't you? That he's going to hurt himself like your daughter did?'

I can feel the heat in my veins, and it is difficult to breathe, somehow. He is angered now, making claims out of agitation. I refuse to rise to it.

I stand and gather up my files. 'In the meantime,' I say, 'I intend on interviewing Alex's school teachers and his aunt Beverly. If I *do* find proof that he's self-harming or is a danger to others, I'm sure you'll agree that I have no option but to bring him in.'

To my surprise, Michael squeezes my hand and simply nods, before striding out of the room.

*

When I return to my office I find a new message in my inbox. I am relieved when I see it is from Alex's school-teacher, Karen Holland.

To: A_molokova@macneicehouse.nhs.uk
From: k.holland@stpaulsprimary.co.uk
Date: 12/5/07 13.44 p.m.

Dear Anya

I would be more than happy to speak to you – indeed I
recall Alex very clearly. I had concerns about him when I
taught him and am pleased he seems to be receiving
proper treatment at last. I have a couple of slots
available for a meeting here at the school – next
Thursday at 5 p.m., the following Tuesday at 4.30, or
perhaps today at 4 p.m.? Do you need directions?

Sincerely, KW.

I email her straight back to take her up on the offer of an appointment that afternoon. I change my heeled shoes for running shoes and transfer Alex's files from my briefcase to my backpack, then head off on foot, threading through the familiar streets around Queen's University. Amongst layers of students' advertisements pasted on lampposts and boarded-up buildings I spy a large, dazzling poster for Jojo's company 'Really Talented Kids'. HAMLET is spelled out in bullet-holes, and there are several pictures of nuns holding machine guns and kids doing gang signs with several movie-star endorsements beneath. I spy a small image of Alex during one of the rehearsals in his role as Horatio, and I smile at the thought of him attempting to concoct bad jokes for the part. Jojo had whispered to me that bad jokes were exactly was she was aiming for, though it was Alex's confidence that was the real reward – he had transformed from a stage-shy, nervous kid who was barely audible in the front row to a boy who was beginning to command his presence and find his feet on stage. I make a mental note to invite Jojo to MacNeice House.

I head on towards the school as the crow flies, cutting through the quad of Queen's University, its new buildings gleaming alongside the old red-brick ones I remember. I find myself thinking back to the days I spent as a teenager on a rug with a group of friends – it takes me a moment or two to remember their names – Blondie on the radio, a picnic of jam sandwiches and cold tea.

Was that really a quarter of a century ago?

I pass a gleaming new building bearing the sign 'The School of Music,' its clean, spacious rooms visible through large windows. A couple of students walk past, one of them on a mobile phone, another holding a Starbucks cup. I continue on towards the botanical gardens, then stop in front of the dome of the hothouse, where two patches of white tulips have been grown to form a pair of wings. They are so real, so richly bright, that they almost seem to move and the petals ruffle distinctly like feathers. I stop walking and spend a long time staring at them, feeling moved by the way they had appeared so differently from a distance – shaped in the form of a dove's wings, I realise, fanning outwards, the bird's head rendered by a smaller patch, its beak by primroses. The symbol of peace.

When Poppy was buried, I could not bear the thought of a tombstone. It seemed too final, too grim for my little girl. On her grave plot in Edinburgh, I had a craftsman cut a dove's wings from Portland stone – a kind of stone which whitens with time. The man took care to ensure he chipped each wing with precision, the feathers so lifelike that they appeared to move in the sunlight. I had hoped to bring her peace. It is my own peace that I have never found.

And I don't know how.

I arrived at St Paul's Primary School at 3.45 p.m., fifteen minutes early. Housed in a converted chapel, the school had a distinctly religious air about it that continued inside in the form of child-crafted murals on saints and religious festivals. I took note of the scenes of angels and Jesus in the stained glass windows, their colours and pathos ripe in late afternoon sun. A sign directed me to reception, where I found a young man typing at a computer.

'I'm here to see Karen Holland,' I told him. He nodded and asked me to sign a register before taking me to the staff room.

'Karen's in a meeting,' he said, nodding at the sink and

coffee maker opposite a square of sofas. 'Make yourself comfortable.'

In the corner of the room was an old black upright piano, candelabra curved like cactuses in its front panel, lid open. Its keys were yellow and chipped, like the teeth of an old man. I looked up at the doorway to check no one was coming, then slid my fingers over the notes that formed the opening chord of Beethoven's *Sonata Pathétique*. For a moment I was tempted to lean down, sound out the thick, hungry texture of that gorgeous chord, but I stopped short of pressing down on the keys. Slowly I lifted my hands and left the piano to its silence.

When Poppy died, I sold her beloved baby grand for a tenth of its value just to be rid of the sound of it. It seemed that even when the lid was closed the wind would find its way inside, brush across the strings, and Poppy's songs would rise up like ghosts. I had been playing since I was a child, tinkering on the old Yamaha at my school, then offered piano lessons by a teacher. It was important for me to teach her, to give her the same joy – but I had not anticipated how much the sound would dig deep into my veins after she'd gone. How much loneliness would suddenly infuse the music I had once loved.

'Dr Molokova?' a voice said. I turned around to see a short round woman in a rust-coloured wraparound dress standing in the doorway, her eyes hidden by tinted glasses. She had a helmet of thick amber-coloured hair, a ladder in her brown tights and hands that felt warm as toast when I returned her shake. She grinned broadly. 'I'm Karen Holland, how do you do? Would you like to come to my classroom?'

I nodded and followed her out of the room along a corridor lined with papier mâché mosaics of Africa and self-portraits sketched by thirty eight-year-olds. I searched for Alex's face but it wasn't there.

'I dug something out of my archives to show you,' Karen said when we were inside her classroom.

'Archives?'

I looked around. The walls of the classroom were covered in paintings, progress charts, rules, and a small film about elephants played silently on the whiteboard on the far wall. Karen walked past me to her desk where I could see a handful of large, childish paintings had been spread out for me to view.

'What are these?' I asked, unable to make sense of what seemed to be a series of large, misspelled phrases and small profile pictures in old, cracked black paint.

'I'm glad I kept these now,' Karen said, removing her dark glasses and rubbing her eyes. I could see her eyes were small and intensely blue, screwed up against the soft light from the window.

I turned my head to view the paintings from a different angle. 'Are these newspaper headlines?'

She put her glasses back on, sighing at the relief of dimming the light from her eyes. 'Alex did these when he was about six years old for a class project. We were imagining how the sinking of the Titanic might have been captured in headlines and how to use language concisely ... As you can see,

Alex deviated from the task in a way that always struck me as significant.'

I looked over the headlines. MONSTROUS CRIME, read one. Another bore a picture that looked like a swaddled baby Jesus and a title, ROT IN HELL. Then another: RUEND PEEPELS LIVES. I paused at the word 'ruend'.

'I've shown these to Alex's consultants in the past but they didn't see a link,' Karen said.

I glanced up at her. 'Did you ask Alex why he'd done these paintings?'

She nodded. 'He didn't seem to know why he'd done them.'

'But the task was about the tragedy of the Titanic ...'

I scanned the paintings again, tracing my conversations with Alex in my mind. He must have read the headlines on a newspaper.

'What was Alex like as a pupil?'

Karen raised a hand to pat her thick hair down. 'He was polite, quiet. An above average student. No friends, not really. I used to feel sad when he'd be the only boy in the class without an invite to so-and-so's birthday – but it happens, you know? I think it was this sense of exclusion that contributed to his anger.'

I stopped writing. 'Anger?'

She nodded, though I sensed some reluctance on her part to admit this. 'He had ... and they were occasional, mind you ... explosive rages that would end with him in floods of tears.'

I remembered what I'd read in the notes. 'Alex hit you, didn't he?'

She sighed. 'He lashed out, caught me full force in the chest with his fist. I think he was more shocked than I was. Still, I reported it to Alex's consultant at the time. He was growing more and more wound up by the day, I thought it was in his interests . . . '

'Did he ever hit another student?'

She shook her head. 'He never explained *why* he blew up, either. It was like a tantrum, but much worse. Cursing, shouting, threats.'

'Threats?'

'Yes. To me, to the other children. But they were . . . what I would call *blind* threats. As if he could hardly see who was there. As if he didn't recognise me or the people around him. As if he'd forgotten who we were.' She paused, upset by the memory of it. 'He would be completely devastated, an utterly different version of himself. When I spoke to his mother about it she seemed distressed, but refused to offer any suggestions.' She sighed. 'There's only so much we can do at school. The buck stops at home, which is unfortunate in some cases.'

When my page was filled with notes I thanked her for her time and began to close up my briefcase.

She took off her glasses again, her eyes immediately disturbed by the light. 'He isn't a bad kid,' she said. 'And something I never told the other consultant was that Alex wrote me a little note after he hit me that time.'

'Do you have it?'

She nodded. 'Of course I do. It's at home. I kept it, as I do all the gifts I get from my kids. He'd drawn a little picture of me with the word "SORRY" in capital letters, then signed it with kisses and hugs. Not every kid would do that, you know?'

I smiled at the thought of it, then wondered why no mention of that picture appeared in my notes about Alex.

'Karen, you taught Alex on and off for several years, didn't you? When would you say his behaviour changed?'

'December sixteenth, 2001,' she said briskly, and I looked up. She smiled sadly. 'The day Alex told me his father died.'

13

THE UNBESTED FRIEND

Alex

Dear Diary,

It's three sleeps 'til we perform *Hamlet* at the Grand Opera House. I like it loads in there. It's all red and I feel bigger when I'm on stage, like I'm a giant. I bet you could fit three of our house inside there. We had a rehearsal last night for *Hamlet* and for once everyone remembered their lines and Jojo's make-up ran and she hugged Cian, who she doesn't like normally, and then she made us all sit in a circle on the stage and talk about our Fears and Hopes for Opening Night.

Katie's hand went up first. 'I'm afraid my mum will go crazy,' she said, and her voice was flat. Jojo's smile came off her face and she asked Katie what she meant. Katie just shrugged and wouldn't say anything after that but kept snapping the elastic on her wristband until I told her to stop it.

I put my hand up. 'I hope the audience shouts, "Encore!",' I said, and Terry and Sean sniggered.

'I hope that, too,' Jojo said, giving me a wink. 'Though I think it's more likely that they'll applaud for a very long time if they like our performance.'

Then she held up her two index fingers which is a sign for everyone to be quiet. 'Now. Who thinks they understand why we're doing this play?'

We all looked at each other. Finally Bonnie Nicholls put her hand up. 'Because we're really talented kids?'

Jojo gave her a big smile. 'That's definitely one reason, thanks, Bonnie. Anyone else?'

'Because the play is famous?' Liam said. Jojo said yes but she said maybe we needed a hint. 'Where is this play set?'

'Belfast,' I said.

'Correctamundo!' Jojo said, and I felt proud. Then she looked serious and pressed a finger against her lips. 'But where did *Shakespeare* set his play?'

There was a lot of whispering. I saw Terry Google it on his mobile phone. 'Denmark,' he said.

'Yes!' shouted Jojo, pointing at Terry. 'And what does Shakespeare say about Denmark?'

'It's rotten,' I said quietly. And she opened her mouth to say *correctamundo* but I put my hand up again and she tilted her head.

'Are you saying that Belfast is rotten?' I asked.

'It *is* rotten,' said Terry, and everyone agreed.

'All of it?' Jojo said in a small voice. 'Or just some of it?'

Bonnie stretched her hand up high. 'I like Mauds ice cream.' You can't buy Mauds ice cream anywhere but in Northern Ireland which makes me feel sorry for anyone not living in Northern Ireland.

Queen Gertrude – actually her real name is Samantha but she makes us all call her Queen Gertrude – raised her hand. 'I like Helen's Bay.' Helen's Bay is a beach three miles from our house which I've never been to but Granny used to show me pictures and it looked nice.

'Good jogging,' said Jojo in agreement, pointing at Samantha. 'Anyone else?'

'I like it when nobody gets shot,' I said, and Jojo turned her head to look at me. For a moment everyone was silent.

'Hear hear!' said Liam. Then Bonnie said it, then Katie, then Samantha and Terry and everyone else. Even Jojo.

After a few minutes Jojo put her chin to her chest and folded her hands behind her back the way she does when she's thinking. We all knew to stop talking and the stage went very quiet.

'There's a line at the end of this play that gives a message. A message of hope. Who can tell me what it is?'

Hamlet wasn't really about hope as far as I was concerned. It was about a boy whose dad haunted him and made him kill someone to get back at him but it only made things worse.

'*We defy augury,*' I said quietly, because I wasn't sure exactly what it meant, but it was the final line of the play and Jojo had told us she chose that line for us all to end on because it meant that just because the future was predicted in one way didn't mean we couldn't choose a different path.

'What was that?' Jojo said, looking over us all.

'He said, "*We defy augury*",' Katie piped up. 'This play is about us saying that we don't care what's happened in the past cos we have a say in what happens to the future.'

Jojo's face lit up and she started to applaud and we all joined in, too. We clapped and cheered and then started chanting, '*Hamlet, Hamlet, Hamlet, Hamlet!*' which gradually turned into, '*Belfast, Belfast, Belfast, Belfast!*' Jojo waved her hand like she was conducting us and then, finally, when Liam and Gareth changed the chant to, '*Celtic, Celtic, Celtic!*' she held up her index fingers again. We all fell silent.

'Remember, folks. This is an important statement about who you are and where you want to be,' Jojo said.

'McDonald's,' Liam said under his breath. Some people giggled but Jojo just stared.

'This is more than Shakespeare's play. This is about what it means to rise up from the ashes of Belfast's past. Do yourselves proud.'

The other day after lunch I was thinking about the dream I had about Ruen and Granny and I remembered something: that when Ruen came to the hospital I saw he had a thread hanging down from his black jumper, just like in the dream. I have threads hanging down from my clothes all the time and in the hospital I had a gown on that had a long bit at the back, and I could have sworn there was a second when it looked like the thread from Ruen's jumper was linked to it. I don't know what this means but it makes me feel weird.

So I decided to tell him that I didn't want him to study me any more. I thought that it might make him cross. I didn't care about getting a new house. I thought that even though it would be nice and all, I just wanted Mum to get happy again and not cry any more. And I didn't know if being someone's friend means that you had to do stuff for each other either. Anya told me that she had arranged for me to go see Mum again very soon and I was so excited about this and also I was worried in case Mum died before I got to see her. Sometimes I think of the times she took all those pills and I think she actually knew that she would have died if the doctors didn't fix her. Why would she do that? Why would she *want* to die? And if she did, who would look after me then?

I hardly slept last night because I was scared that if I told Ruen that I didn't want him to study me any more, I wouldn't have a best friend. I still didn't know why he wants to study me. It's stupid actually because I'm just a ten-year-old boy from Belfast not a Prime Minister or a footballer or anything, and also he was starting to scare me. He used to be a right laugh and tell me comebacks. Like the time when Eoin Murphy got everyone at school to call me 'Azz' instead of 'Alex' and kept saying I was a *gay gypo psycho*. He had the whole class laughing at me and I felt so scundered that I couldn't think of anything to say back, not a single word. Then Ruen came up to me and whispered something in my ear. Right as Eoin was getting everyone to start chanting, 'Azz is a spaz,' I turned to him and repeated what Ruen had said.

I said: 'Eoin, the zoo just called. The baboons want their bums back, so you'll have to find a new face.'

Everyone stopped chanting and Jamie Belsey sniggered into his hand. Eoin's face went red. He looked at me and said, 'You think you're funny, psycho boy?'

Ruen whispered to me again and I repeated what he'd said:

'I heard your parents took you to a dog show and you won.' Then everyone laughed and Eoin got really angry.

'You wanna fight?' he said, shoving me backwards, but I stood straight and said what Ruen had told me to say:

'I would love to beat you up, but I don't like being cruel to dumb animals.'

Eoin punched me in the neck then which hurt but I still felt like I'd won somehow.

Ruen and me have had lots of fun and he's been a really good friend and we laughed about stuff like that for days. When he was the Old Man he was like a grumpy uncle who dared me to do naughty things, like jump off a bus while it was still moving or copy someone's homework or steal Miss Holland's cigarettes when she'd left her bag on the table. But he had gotten scary and angry and I felt weird when he was around. I reckoned he'd be cross at me but thought that maybe he could study someone else.

It made me so nervous to tell him this that I got up eleven times during the night to pee. My hands and feet were numb and when Woof refused to get into bed with me I got out from under the covers and curled myself around him on the floor.

When I woke up this morning Ruen was already downstairs. He was the Old Man and was sitting in Dad's old blue armchair with his feet up on Granny's old coffee table with his hands folded on his pot belly as if he was waiting for me. This surprised me. The second thing that surprised me was that he was very smiley. He looked like he'd just won a prize or something, twiddling with his bow tie and licking his palm to smooth down the strands of white hair that stuck up from his skull like dandelion clocks. When I came into the room he stood up with his hands behind his back and creaked his mouth into a smile that made him look constipated.

'Alex, my boy,' he said. 'I have some wonderful news.'

I didn't really want to hear his news. I was really tired and just wanted to spit out the speech I'd practised, which I'd cut short to just this: 'Ruen, I know we're friends and all but I don't want to be friends any more.'

I knew he wanted me to ask what the news was so I didn't. I stood there staring at him until Auntie Bev came out of the kitchen. She was wearing tight shiny shorts and a small shiny vest that showed the skin on her belly which meant she was going wall climbing. She put her hands on her hips and sighed at me.

'Do you *really* have to have onions on toast for the fifth morning in a row? That kitchen *stinks.*'

'Yes,' I said, and turned back to Ruen. Auntie Bev was

going on about *a nice Ulster Fry or even some porridge* but I ignored her and finally she went back into the kitchen.

Ruen headed for the hallway and waved his hand for me to follow. I yawned and trailed after him. I walked past the coats hanging on the coatstand – all of them Auntie Bev's, she's like a collector of coats – and kicked at the old red rug that's fraying on the floor. Ruen was standing beside Granny's old piano, both hands behind his back, a big stupid grin on his ugly face.

'Alex,' he said. 'I've found you a new home.'

At this my heart started to beat faster and I felt sorry for thinking how stupid he was. 'You have?'

Ruen took a deep breath and his smile grew wider. 'Later today Anya is going to tell you that you and your mother will be moving to a brand new house with a garden and all the things you requested of me.'

I just didn't know what to say. 'I don't know what to say,' I said.

'You can start by thanking me,' Ruen said, tilting his head to remind me.

I started to say it, because I was grateful, but I was still angry with him. He had scared me the other day and I was cross about it.

His smile turned back to his usual scowl. 'What is it, Alex?' he said. 'I thought you would be really pleased, now that I've given you the thing you wanted most. Don't you think that's a tad ungrateful?'

I looked at the red rug on the ground. It was so old it was

just a big bunch of threads clumped together, but I kept my eyes stuck to it so I wouldn't have to look up at Ruen. I felt scared in case we wouldn't really get the house but then I realised that this was Ruen and that he had helped me so much in the past and hadn't gone back on his word.

'And what is it your mother hates most?' he said, raising his eyes to the ceiling and clicking his tongue.

'People who don't say thank you,' I said.

'Exactly.'

Auntie Bev called my name from the living room. I looked through the doorway to see her set a plateful of onions and toast on the table.

'You should've been raised in France,' she said, before turning and walking back into the kitchen. I gave Ruen a look before going inside. I sat down at the table and looked at the onions. I didn't feel like eating them.

Ruen appeared in the seat opposite me. He looked very concerned.

'Alex,' he said, doing that thing with his hands where he makes a triangle with his fingers, only his fingernails are so long that his fingers don't touch. 'Is this because of the lady doctor, Alex? She *is* asking a lot of questions, isn't she?' His voice suddenly sounded like he was really concerned for me and I wondered if he really was. 'Is it starting to bother you?' he said. 'Maybe I can help with that.'

I knew Auntie Bev could hear what I said next but I didn't care. I looked at Ruen and said:

'Why are you studying me?'

'What, sweetheart?' Auntie Bev poked her head around the kitchen door. Ruen glanced from Auntie Bev to me. I felt a warmth around my heart and there was a big fat sob in my throat. I said it again.

'Why are you studying me? I'm not a footballer.'

Ruen laced his hands, making his triangle collapse, and his eyes grew small and angry.

'I don't like being studied,' I said. 'Not by you, and not by Anya. I just want my mum home, OK? And I don't care if she comes home to this house or a fancy house with a fancy garden. So you can *stuff* your house!'

Auntie Bev walked towards me and her face looked worried. She looked around at the window behind her, then at me.

'Are you all right?' she said.

I nodded and went to tell a fib about a bird landing on the windowsill and that's why I was shouting at it but then there was a big lump in my throat and I felt angry and sad all at once. Auntie Bev knelt down in front of me which made her smaller than me and I could see the freckles on her forehead.

'You're scared, aren't you?' she said, and I nodded but didn't say what I was scared of. She put her arms around me. She held me for a long long time and at first I wanted her to get off me but then I felt as if I could sleep right in her arms. After a few moments I got hot and needed to scratch so I pushed her away gently and she looked at me and smiled.

'I haven't held you like that since you were a baby,' she said, wiping my face, and I realised I had a tear on my cheek. 'You were born premature, did you know that?'

I had to think about what 'premature' meant.

'You were this big,' she said, holding her hands a very very small distance apart. She looked at the small space between her hands for so long that I expected a real baby to appear. Then she looked up at me and her eyes were shiny. 'You were like a little bird. All the doctors said it was amazing that you lived.' She lifted a hand to my face and tucked a piece of hair behind my ear. 'I had to go back to work the next day but Granny sent me photos, when she could get around to it. I promised I'd come and see you more often but . . . well, you'll know what it's like when you're older.' There was a long pause. I wondered if she'd finished but then she took my hands in hers and squeezed them tight. 'This I *can* promise, Alex. I'm here for you now.'

She was really close to my face and I felt the lump in my throat get bigger and I was afraid I was going to throw up so I pulled my hands free and ran up the stairs.

'Alex?' Auntie Bev was calling after me, but I ran all the way up to my bedroom and locked the door by pushing a chair against the handle.

A few seconds later Ruen appeared in the chair. I almost jumped out of my skin. He was Horn Head. I could see the blood all clotted on the barbed wire next to his furry chest and I felt trapped because there was no other way out. He had the metal mace in one hand and the light from the window made the spikes glint.

'Go and study bacteria,' I told him.

'You want to know why I study you?' Ruen's voice whispered in my head.

I wiped my eyes and folded my arms but said nothing. My chest felt like someone had scraped the insides out with a metal spoon and I felt angry with myself for pushing Auntie Bev away. Maybe she could get Ruen to leave. Even if I shouted I didn't think she would be able to hear. Mum never did.

'I would have thought you had already worked that one out, Alex,' Ruen hissed, and I closed my eyes. I hated that he had no face. Sometimes parts of his face appeared: a pair of blue eyes, a mouth like mine. But it was just so weird and horrible that I couldn't look at it.

'For whatever reason, we can't seem to tempt you. None of us seem to have much of an effect on you. And we need to know why that is.'

I went to ask why, but didn't. I kept my eyes shut.

'If you simply told me why this is the case, perhaps I might be able to stop studying you quite so intensively,' he continued.

I thought about it. After a while I forced myself to open my eyes and stare at him. I looked at the red horn coming out of his forehead. It looked like liquid floating upward.

'I guess I don't like people telling me what to do.'

'Admirable. Commendable,' whispered Ruen. Then he turned into the Old Man and I gave a big breath of relief. He stood up and walked to the window, his arms behind his back as usual. I glanced at the door and moved the chair away, but just then Ruen was back in front of me.

'I promise you, Alex, I won't tell you what to do. I already know you can't be tempted, so you have my word. I won't even try to tempt you. You're much too strong-willed, even for the likes of me.' He cackled and it turned into a cough. 'You will love this house, Alex. Are we still friends?'

I thought of the new house and felt happier. 'Yes, Ruen. We're still friends.'

14

MISTS OF THE MIND

Anya

I met with Cindy yesterday to ask her questions about Alex's home life and about his father. Usually, a parent is the first port of call when it comes to detecting any abnormalities – patterns of withdrawal, any indications of voices or hallucinations, a sudden slipping away from school and friends – but unfortunately Cindy's own depression has created a veil to anyone's issues but her own. A history of abuse, both as a child and as an adult, has been compounded by the breakdown of her relationship with Alex's father. Since then, repeated suicide attempts have been her method of dealing with it. Her 'bracelets', as she calls them, or the many white lines on her wrists from self-harming episodes, aren't easy to conceal. She thinks Alex is receiving counselling to deal with her suicide attempts, which is partly true.

For her own treatment, I am pleased to learn she's in the care of Dr Trudy Messenger, one of the most experienced and, dare I say it, warmest psychiatrists in the United Kingdom. She is renowned for making her patients feel like human beings after a single consultation. After years of feeling ousted, separate and vilified by the legions who don't understand mental illness, these patients experience a kind of homecoming in Trudy's office. Trudy has seen to it that Cindy is actively engaged in a variety of daily activities, mostly arts and crafts, and when I arrive she is completing a beautiful needlework of a small white dog.

'It's for Alex,' she tells me with a small smile. 'Woof. He loves that dog. Thick as thieves, those two. I know boys don't like crafty things but maybe he'll make an exception.'

I spend a few minutes talking about the facilities in the hospital before gently telling her that I have some concerns about Alex's mental health. She looks puzzled.

'Alex has seen a counsellor before,' she says. 'But they've never had any worries about him, not really. And he's spoken to Michael. You can hardly expect a kid from his side of town to be tap dancing with joy every day. That's my fault.'

'I don't think he's depressed,' I say.

'Then what do you mean?'

I tell her there are other possibilities that I'm investigating. I assure her I'm optimistic that he can be treated but that I'm keen to ensure he receives the correct attention.

'I'd like to know about Alex's father,' I ask softly, thinking quickly of my meeting with Karen Holland, Alex's paintings spread across her desk.

Her face darkens. 'Why do you want to know about Alex's father?'

My voice is gentle. 'A boy's relationship with his father is important in forming his identity and his place in the world.'

She sets down her needle and thread and folds her thin arms tightly. 'I haven't told anyone who Alex's real dad is. Well, except my mum.'

'I don't need names,' I say carefully. 'Would you say he was a good father?'

She looks out the window. A hand reaches for the other wrist, making a circle around it with her forefinger and thumb.

'He saw Alex every so often. Maybe a handful of days out of every month. Sometimes he'd stay with us for a week. Then we wouldn't see him for two months.' She raises her eyes. 'I named Alex after him.'

I nod. 'He was never abusive with Alex?'

She looks disgusted. 'No, never. He wasn't exactly over-joyed when I told him I was pregnant but he still provided for us. It was the reason he . . . ' She falls silent.

'It was the reason he what?' I ask.

She takes a breath. 'He'd take Alex to play table tennis sometimes, said it was good for his hand-eye coordination. He was thoughtful like that. He'd buy him toy cars. Alex hated cars.'

'When did Alex stop seeing him?'

She is lifting a hand to cover her eyes, lowering her head. I must watch my step.

'If it's OK for me to ask, what were the circumstances surrounding his departure from Alex's life?'

She shakes her head, her hand pressed to her forehead. I crouch down beside her.

'Cindy,' I say, lightly touching her hand. 'I promise you, I'm only asking these things so I can help Alex.'

She lowers her hand and fixes me with angry, burning eyes. 'You think he's crackers.'

'I don't,' I assure her. 'But he has mentioned some things that he can see which appear to be harming him.'

Her eyes widen. 'Someone's hurting him? Is it someone at that theatre company?'

I shake my head. 'Alex claims he has a best friend called Ruin. Several times now Alex has got quite aggressive during our sessions and claims that Ruin got angry. Have you ever come across any marks on his body, any unexplained injuries?'

She narrows her eyes. 'I'm not abusing him, if that's what you're getting at.'

'I think it's possible that *Alex* is hurting Alex,' I say softly.

She searches my face, her expression one of hurt and confusion. 'Why would you say that? Why would you say he's hurting *himself*?'

I hesitate, confounded by the fact that her own arms bear hundreds of scars from her own self-harm efforts and yet she cannot conceive of Alex doing the same. And, as if she knows what I'm thinking, she reaches one hand across her forearm, where sunlight is making silvery rivers of her scars.

'What if he's telling the truth?' she says, her lip trembling. 'I mean, Alex wouldn't do that. Would he? He's so talented and smart and braver than me.' She looks up at me. 'He wouldn't do that.'

'If Alex has seen you self-harm, chances are he'll do it too.'

My words smash around the room. Cindy's face crumples and she lets out a long, loose cry. It takes me a moment or two to realise why she is crying: she has never, ever considered the impact of her own issues on her child.

I walk across the room to retrieve a box of tissues. She plucks one out with a trembling hand and holds it to her eyes.

'Let me see him.'

Alex was brought to the hospital later that afternoon. I asked Cindy if it would be OK for me to stay around and observe their time together. I expected her to ask why, but it seemed my comment about Alex's potential self-harming had knocked the fight out of her. I wanted to ensure that I gathered the information I needed to answer these pressing questions: Is there a link between Ruin and Cindy? Or between Ruin and Alex's father? Is Alex's hallucination – and, indeed, his condition – linked to an incident in the past?

The adult psychiatric unit is on the same site as MacNeice House and is surrounded by a sprawling green lawn dotted with small patches of bright flowers, fenced off from the outside world by tall fir trees and an array of greenhouses which contain the potted plants and vegetables grown by inpatients. One of the nurses suggested Alex and Cindy take a walk outside – hinting at me to provide the necessary medical supervision – and so I carried three coats and an umbrella, in case the fat grey awnings of cloud toppled their load, and ushered us all outside. Cindy was keen to show Alex the result of her horticulture therapy workshop, and so we headed towards the greenhouses.

I let Alex and Cindy walk ahead of me, noticing the way Alex linked his arm with Cindy's. Many times he leaned his head on her shoulder. There was genuine affection between the two, and playfulness: on several occasions Alex made Cindy giggle, squeezing her waist to ensure the giggle became a substantial laugh, at which she clouted him across the head, visibly careful to ensure that the clout wasn't heavy-handed. They were almost the same height, though Cindy's frame was starkly birdlike beside his, the bones of her ankles and wrists jutting out like white buttons on the sides of her arms. I noticed that they had the same walk.

We reached one of the greenhouses, which was crammed with tomato plants and an array of hanging baskets exploding with lobelia. Alex and Cindy huddled around a toilet bowl outside that someone had filled with bright yellow daffodils. Cindy waved over to me and asked me to join them.

'I won a prize,' she told me, her face beaming. 'My first ever.'

'Where did you get the toilet, Mum?' Alex was asking,

inspecting the broken back of it and utterly perplexed by its incongruity beside the other plant pots.

'Never mind that, Alex,' Cindy said. She looked up at me again. I saw she was eager to share an achievement. '*You're* clever, aren't you?' she said to me. 'Can't you work out what I was doing?'

I looked over the arrangement, at the rather haphazard way the daffodils had been planted into the compost, though their fat trumpets indicated they were healthy and being taken care of. A good sign. I noticed she'd painted the word HOPE on the bulge of the toilet.

'Well, you're making a statement, aren't you?' I said, winking at Alex. 'Even when you're in the gutter you can become something beautiful.'

Cindy gave a big cheer. 'See, Alex? Told you she was clever. Daffodils mean hope. I thought that sticking them in a toilet bowl would be poetic, sort of. Plus they were throwing this out and I thought it would be a waste.'

Alex looked disgusted. 'But it's a *toilet*, Mum. That's *gross*.'

As we headed back to the ward, Cindy had her arm round Alex's shoulders and her chin leaning on his head, whilst Alex had his arms tightly around her waist. Both of them had slowed down their pace considerably, until I was forced to stop behind them and pretend to remove a stone from my shoe.

Just as the side entrance came into view, it felt like it was about to rain. The sky had turned from cloudy blue to wet slate in a matter of seconds, and the wind had started to move so fast that all the small white flowers I'd collected from the long grass flew out of my grasp as if someone had slapped my hands. I was about to shout to Cindy and Alex that it was time to go inside, when I noticed something very strange. Both of them were gone, and in fact the entrance to the adult psych unit was no longer in view, nor were the trees, the greenhouses, even the grass at my feet. I stood dumbly in a dark vacuum for a few seconds, rolling through a rapid list of possibilities. Fog? A blackout?

Right as I turned to find Alex and Cindy, a white light flashed in front of me, so bright that I staggered backwards, blinded for a few moments. When I recovered, the fog had disappeared. Alex and Cindy were ahead, still ambling towards the entrance. The sky was feathered with white clouds, and all around me was green lawn and bowing trees. Still, I felt shaken by the experience, unable to explain it. I asked Alex and Cindy if they had happened to have seen lightning, but they looked puzzled. All the way back to MacNeice House I felt on edge, raw with shock.

I cancelled a meeting with Howard, Ursula and Michael, went straight back to my flat and slept for nine hours straight. My head, I decided, had obviously been missing from my pillow much too often.

15

THE GREATEST DREAM
OF ALL TIME

Alex

Dear Diary,

A sandwich walks into a bar and says, 'A pint of Guinness, mate.' The barman replies, 'Sorry, we don't serve food here.'

I have to write really fast cos I have a dress rehearsal for *Hamlet* and Jojo is going mental with people who turn up late. Good stuff and bad stuff has happened lately. The good stuff is so good though that I'm not even sure I can call the bad stuff bad, it's just not even important any more. The first cool thing that happened was that Anya came and told me I could see Mum. I thought it would be a while before I could see her because she's chilling out and getting her strength back, according to Auntie Bev. But when I saw Mum I couldn't believe how much better she looked. Her hair had been washed and was shiny and soft and not like pasta that's been in the fridge for a week. Her cheeks were pink and her eyes didn't have dark bits under them and she was wearing a long white T-shirt which almost covered all the marks on her arms. It made me feel happy.

'Alex!' Mum said when I walked in, and her voice was normal and she hugged me so hard I coughed. 'How have you been?'

Then, before I could tell her about Auntie Bev throwing out all the onions and about the play and how I would love her to come, she said: 'You know what's weird? I had this dream about Granny last night and she told me I needed to give you a big hug.'

'Did she tell you to crack my ribs, too?' I said, rubbing my sides from her big bear hug and she laughed but I was serious.

Anya said she'd wait outside and Mum nodded and when Anya had gone she asked me if Anya was asking me anything that bothered me. I thought about Ruen but I didn't want to say anything to upset her.

'Has Anya asked *you* anything that bothered you?' I asked her.

'No,' she said. 'But my therapist keeps asking about my childhood. All she wants to know about is my favourite doll.' She made a clicking noise with her tongue then put on a voice, as if she was imitating someone. '"Why did you call her *Ugly*? Why did you dress her in black? Why did you put her facedown when your foster dad came in?"'

'Why *did* you put the doll facedown when your foster dad came in?'

She looked at me funny. 'Sorry, Alex,' she said, glancing down. 'I shouldn't have let my mouth go. Sometimes I forget you're not an old man, you know? How are *you*, anyway?'

I shrugged. 'When are you coming home?'

She bit her lip and ran her fingers through her hair. It was starting to go black again at the roots and I was about to tell her that if she came home I could help her put the sky-blue stuff in it to turn the roots yellow but she said:

'I just don't know.'

'Woof misses you.'

'*Woof* misses me?'

I nodded. She leaned forward and looked at me closely and I touched my face in case I had a black mark on it or something.

'You've never ... hurt yourself, have you, son?' Mum said.

I felt my cheeks turn hot. 'Why do you ask that?'

'I just wondered if what I'd ... I mean, you're different from me, aren't you? You're Alexander the Great, aren't you?'

Just then I had a flash in my head of someone else saying the words Alexander the Great, and I could see our living room but from a height. For a second I remembered my dad crying '*Alexander the Great!*' and I was on his shoulders and he was bouncing up and down, and then the memory was over.

Mum went to say something but then a nurse knocked loudly on the door and came into the room.

'Sorry for interrupting,' she said, though she didn't look sorry. 'Trudy thinks you should get out today, Cindy. Maybe take Alex to the greenhouse, show him what you did with the horticulturalist?'

Mum nodded. 'Okey-dokey. Come on, Alex, let me show you what you can do with a toilet.'

I didn't see Ruen all day after that. I remembered he said that Anya would tell me that we'd be moving house by the end of the day, but she didn't and I thought, *I'm definitely, definitely going to tell him I don't want to be friends next time I see him.* But he didn't turn up, which was nice because I got to go back home in the evening and Woof licked my face and whined as if he'd really missed me and slept on my bed all night.

And then Anya came to see me this morning instead of this afternoon because it's Saturday. She couldn't stop smiling. I asked her what was wrong and she told me to sit down, which I did, and she started taking lots of things out of her briefcase and spreading them across the table.

'This,' she said, 'is your new home.'

I could not believe it. I watched her arrange a set of photographs and drawings of our new house in front of me and Auntie Bev came in and asked all the questions I wanted to ask but couldn't, like, *Does Cindy know? How did this come about? Where is it? When can they move in? Is this for real?*

Anya kept wringing her hands and bouncing on the balls of her feet like she was moving, too. I think she was just really happy for this to happen even though she didn't even know that it was my Greatest Dream Of All Time. Auntie Bev said things like, 'Well, thank the elephant in the sky for that, then, this place is falling apart,' and, 'Is it seriously a council property? Looks stunning.'

'And there's more,' Anya said. 'The reason that some of the photographs look as though the rooms aren't finished is because this is a brand new property.'

'Brand new?' I said, and I tried to think of the last time I had something that was brand new.

'You can even choose your own wallpaper,' Anya said, her smile growing wider. 'Even your own kitchen units. The front door can be whatever colour you want it to be. The council are keen to ensure their residents have proprietorship over their accommodation.'

'What?' I said, because this made no sense.

Anya laughed. The sound was light and like bells and made me laugh even though nothing was funny. She turned to Auntie Bev, who was smiling and kept folding and unfolding her arms as if she didn't know what to do with them.

'They're calling the street "Peace Street",' Anya said to Auntie Bev, and they both found this really funny and laughed for about a decade. Apparently the politicians had knocked down one of the old streets where they used to barricade people in their houses and have riots, so they bulldozed the whole area and hired a poet to rename all the new streets and write a poem that would be carved on to a wall instead of a mural with gunmen.

'Which poem?' Auntie Bev asked.

'It's called "Belfast Confetti", by Ciaran Carson,' Anya said, and she pulled out a page and read it out loud.

'*Suddenly as the riot squad moved in, it was raining
  exclamation marks,*
*Nuts, bolts, nails, car keys. A fount of broken type. And the
  explosion.*
*Itself – an asterisk on the map. This hyphenated line, a
  burst of rapid fire . . .*
*I was trying to complete a sentence in my head but it kept
  stuttering,*
*All the alleyways and side streets blocked with stops and
  colons.*
*I know this labyrinth so well – Balaclava, Raglan,
  Inkerman, Odessa Street –*
*Why can't I escape? Every move is punctuated. Crimea
  Street. Dead end again.*
*A Saracen, Kremlin-2 mesh. Makrolon face-shields.
  Walkie-*
talkies. What is
*My name? Where am I coming from? Where am I going? A
  fusillade of question marks.*'

Anya put the page on the table. 'They're carving it in letters that will be three feet tall.'

I looked at the pictures for ages and ages as Auntie Bev and Anya chatted. The house was big at the front and didn't have other houses at either side and it had a garden. It had a big kitchen, which I knew would make Mum happy. There was a driveway at the front in case we ever got a car and didn't want to leave it on the street in case someone slashed the tyres. I thought of what it would be like if we got a car and all the places we could go to, like Helen's Bay and Portrush and the Giant's Causeway. My mind filled with so many thoughts and wishes that I got a headache.

'Well, Alex,' Anya said to me at last. 'What do you think?'

I didn't say anything, not because I wasn't thinking anything but because I was thinking too much, and I thought that if I opened my mouth all the words would just explode out like streamers from a party popper.

'You don't seem very excited, Alex,' said Auntie Bev, and I saw Anya reach out and touch her arm as though she shouldn't say that.

'Thank you,' I said to Anya.

After that she asked me loads more questions about Ruen and about demons and whether I could see angels.

'There are demons everywhere,' I said.

'Are there any here now?' she asked, and she seemed nervous. I looked at the fat man who'd appeared above her again. Sometimes I could only see a bit of him, like his toe or his belly with the bellybutton I could probably fit my head in. His eyes were black and when he grinned at me I saw his teeth were, too.

'Alex?'

I pointed up at him cos I could see all of him now. 'He's fat,' I said.

'Who is?'

'Your demon.'

She looked puzzled. 'I have a demon?'

He was stretching his arms out now like he'd had a really long nap, and the blanket that was covering up his willy almost slipped off. I looked away.

'Can you tell me what he's called?' Anya was saying. I looked back at him but he was disappearing.

I shrugged. So she asked me what demons looked like and why I thought I could see them and I was still so excited about the house that I can't even remember what I said. It was like there was a film of the house in my head and I could see every room really clearly and it was beautiful, just beautiful. Then she asked me something barmy which made the film stop suddenly and I was back in my own living room.

'Alex, have you ever been involved in a terrorist attack?'

I asked her what she meant.

'Like a bomb scare? Or a shooting? Did you ever get hurt in a riot, maybe?'

I thought about it. Granny's first husband died in a bomb and last year someone set a car on fire and rolled it down our street.

Anya nodded and wrote all this down. 'What about a policeman, Alex?' she said. 'Did you ever see a policeman get hurt?'

I felt sick and shook my head.

She looked at me very closely. 'Are you sure?'

I saw the policeman's face in my head, his mouth curling in a funny way as his head snapped towards me. I opened my mouth to say something but then I felt my hands make fists and I knew it was wrong to say anything, it was wrong, wrong, wrong.

'Deep breath,' Anya was saying, and when I opened my eyes I had both arms wrapped around me very tightly. When I felt normal again I said, 'I saw people on TV at a policeman's funeral. They were crying.'

She nodded. 'Did you feel bad for those people?'

I started to cry. Anya reached out and touched my arm. 'It's OK,' she said. 'Did you see what happened to the policeman? Did he get hurt?'

I nodded and wiped my eyes.

'Alex, was your daddy a policeman?'

'I want to go lie down now,' I said.

'Did you see something on TV, Alex? About a policeman?'

Her voice was starting to sound very far away. I stood up and my legs felt like they were made of melting ice cubes.

'We'll talk later,' Anya called after me, and I hoped she would just forget everything she had asked.

I said nothing and went upstairs to my bedroom. For some reason I knew Ruen would be there. As soon as I opened the door Woof ran out barking, then hid behind my legs and whimpered. I leaned down and stroked his head and I could feel he was trembling. I straightened and walked into my room.

'Hello, Ruen,' I said. He was Ghost Boy and was sitting in

the chair by the wardrobe as usual, his arms folded tightly like he was in a right huff. I smiled to myself.

I sat down on the bed and waved at Woof to come in, but he stood in the doorway looking at Ruen and growling. Eventually he whimpered and went downstairs. I thought of the photos Anya had showed me.

I glanced at Ruen. 'I want to tell you something.'

He looked up. He actually appeared a bit nervous, like I was going to tell him to go away. The knot that Anya had made in my stomach started to get smaller and I smiled at him.

'I want to say thank you,' I whispered.

'You want to thank me?'

'Yes,' I said. I stood up then, feeling better by the minute. After a few moments I was bouncing on the spot, thinking of our house. 'Thank you thank you thank you! Our house is fan-flipping-tastic! How did you do it? Where did you find it?'

His mouth hung open a bit but he didn't speak. I stopped jumping and started to cry again. He looked very confused. I sat down on the floor and held my face. My head felt like it was going to burst.

'I'm really, really sorry,' I said. 'I didn't mean to be ungrateful or horrible. I just . . . ' Really quickly my heart went from feeling ripped up like an old newspaper to feeling really warm, as if someone was hugging it. When I looked up, Ruen had vanished.

'Ruen?'

There was no one in the room but all of a sudden it seemed to fill with light, as if the sun had walked inside, and there was a smell of strawberries. I didn't know what was happening. I just felt happy. And for some reason I thought of Granny, which made me cry again because I hadn't thought about her for yonks. This would make Granny happy too, I thought, Mum and I moving into a new place. I was really, really young when she died but I remember her begging Mum to move into her house because she didn't like the thought of us being alone. She used to shout at our neighbours too and they wouldn't even shout back, they were so scared of her.

I must have fallen asleep because the next thing I knew I was in bed with all the covers over me and it was no longer sunny. I looked over at the chair and saw Ruen sitting there. 'Where did you go?' I said, but he didn't answer.

I rolled upright. All the pictures of the house came back into my mind and I started smiling again.

'Ruen, I don't even know enough words to say thank you for this.'

'You don't?'

I shook my head. 'There aren't even enough words in the whole of the dictionaries in the whole world to tell you how grateful I am. In fact, I'm more grateful than a whole field full of grated cheese!'

He looked at me as I started going on about grated carrots and great big sausages and Alexander the Grateful. He wasn't smiling his Alex Is Stupid smile but I didn't care.

'How about *showing* me how grateful you are?' he said.

I stopped laughing. 'OK. I'm grateful *this much*,' I said, stretching out my arms. 'No, *this* much,' and I ran to one side of the room and slapped the wall and then ran to the other side and slapped the other wall, 'times a billion.'

Ruen stood up. 'Can I make a suggestion?'

I nodded. He looked around. 'Find yourself a pen and paper.'

I searched my wardrobe for my sketchpads, then eventually found one under my pillow. The pen I picked up had been chewed up by Woof but after a few minutes I discovered a permanent marker in my sock drawer.

'OK.'

Ruen sat down again and made a triangle with his fingers, the way he always does when he's deep in thought.

'I'd like you to write down the following questions, and, when I tell you, I'd like you to ask them to Anya.'

'OK,' I said, and he started to talk.

16

THE BITTER SIDE OF FREEDOM

Anya

The weather has taken a turn for the better and I've started spending lunchtimes sitting on the grass in front of the City Hall, watching new blood circulating through Belfast's veins. It's still stunning to me to see my homeland so transformed, to see faces from all over the world walking through its streets. Even the hallmarks of globalisation make me feel relieved that the world has remembered Northern Ireland, and for the first time since I moved back I feel assured that my decision was the right one. I considered relocating back to Belfast when Poppy was about to enter primary school in Edinburgh. On the day that I had to decide, two car bombs exploded at an army barracks in Lisburn, about ten miles away from Belfast. The second bomb was deliberately targeted at medical staff treating those wounded from the first bomb. For me, the issue was no longer just about culture, about feeling a part of a nation, or whether my daughter could tick three nationalities or just one. The issue was about protecting her. Enough was enough.

Still, my return home has coincided with the beginnings of real peace in this land. Better yet, old friendships I thought I had for ever crippled with the move to Scotland have proved stronger than ever. My best friend, Fi, soldiers across the Albert Bridge every lunchtime to catch up with me, determined to make sure I stay put in Belfast this time round.

I arrive at the City Hall on the dot of noon after a morning spent consulting a new patient's parents about their son's dissociative identity disorder. A handsome, polite thirteen-year-old boy, Xavier is heir to his father's multi-million-pound fortune, excelling at private school, and is also a national chess champion. The problem is, Xavier has twenty-two different identities – a creation of personas usually developed in the wake of abuse or trauma, or chemical imbalance, and often a very disturbing illness for those who are close to the patient. The personalities can be of various ages, genders, temperaments, dialects and disposition. Coexistence is becoming increasingly difficult for Xavier's identities, and some of them are severely depressed. He has no history of suffering physical or sexual abuse, no drug problem. He has a loving, supportive family, who are heartbroken to learn that their beautiful boy is extremely ill. Cases such as his remind me that the biological factors of mental health are foremost, and that medical intervention is necessary. Michael, of course, would disagree.

I spread my coat on the grass, tuck my legs under me and make a start on my sushi. Ten minutes later my phone bleeps with a text message.

Meeting with the boss brought forward —
sorry honey! Meet up tomorrow? Will bring
CAKE! Fi xx

As I get up to leave, I spy Michael sitting cross-legged on the grass beside the Titanic Memorial. He is eating a packet of macadamia nuts, wearing a white polo shirt instead of his standard bottle-green jumper. He catches sight of me approaching and jumps to his feet.

'Dr Molokova,' he says, leaning in to kiss my cheek. 'Ursula's stretching the leash a bit far today, isn't she?'

'Can I join you?' I say.

He looks around him. 'I'm alone, aren't I? Have a seat.' He pats the space on the grass beside him. I hesitate, recalling the tension between us at the review meeting. Still, I am anxious to ask Michael about demons and all things pertaining to the supernatural dimensions that Alex continually invokes in constructing his fantasies. Michael has mentioned previously that he trained as a priest, before having a breakdown of conscience and switching to a career in social work. I think there's more to it than that, but I don't ask. I opt for a spot a little further away than indicated and sink down. The grass is warm and soft. For a moment the sensation of sitting is so intense that I want to fall asleep. Michael holds the bag of macadamia nuts in my direction.

'Would you like one?'

'Are you trying to kill me?' I hold out my talisman and give it a jiggle. He rolls his eyes.

'Oh yeah. *Allergies*. What, do you break out in a rash?'

'Something like that.'

He looks at me intently, carefully folding the plastic bag neatly into eight, before popping it into his shirt pocket. 'No, seriously. How bad is it?'

I take a breath, quickly recalling the last time I experienced anaphylactic shock. I was newly qualified as a child psychiatrist, chairing a symposium at Cambridge for the British Association of Child and Adolescent Psychiatrists. I hadn't had a reaction since I was in my teens, and so I'd been careless when it came to the catering. The chocolate cake had ground hazelnuts in the base, the chef admitted later. No more than a handful. Still, that delicious slice of chocolate cake was enough to start a reaction in just a couple of minutes. First, the familiar tingling sensation around my gums, then into my teeth. A feeling of dizziness. It was the metallic taste in my mouth that made me start to panic. But by the time I grabbed the person at the table next to me to tell them to phone a doctor, my airways had swollen so badly I could barely breathe, never mind talk.

I tell all this to Michael. When I'm finished, he unzips his briefcase, takes out a packet of antibacterial wipes and scrubs his hands. 'Just in case,' he says. I'm flattered by his attentiveness.

'I wanted to ask you about some of the religious undertones of Alex's descriptions,' I say carefully. 'Do you have a minute?'

He nods, his eyes lingering on my talisman. 'Shoot.'

'OK, so I've treated a handful of kids who've claimed to see demons, angels, what have you, but none of them have ever described the spiritual world with the depth that Alex has. There's a specificity to his descriptions that I need to explore. You're Catholic, aren't you?'

'Recovering,' says Michael with a wink. 'Doesn't make me an expert but I'll see what I can do. Define "specificity".'

'Alex told me that Ruin is a Harrower.'

'A *Harrower*?' Michael says, frowning.

I tell him about my meeting with Alex a few days previously.

'You say Ruin is a demon, Alex,' I had asked gently. 'What does that mean, exactly? Does that mean he's bad? Does he work for Satan?'

Alex had glanced to a spot next to the window, leaning towards it as if he was receiving instructions.

'Of course,' I tell Michael, 'I've seen a similar kind of attentiveness to imaginary friends before. But it was what he said next that astonished me. I mean, he's *ten*.'

'What did he say?'

I reach into my pocket and bring out my mobile phone. 'I

recorded it,' I tell Michael, hitting the tab on the screen. In a couple of seconds Alex's voice is audible over the blare of city traffic. He speaks slowly, with many breaks.

'A Harrower is a job title bestowed upon the kind of demon that's closest to the top of Hell's hierarchy,' he says, pausing to take another attempt at pronouncing 'hierarchy'. He continues. 'After which is Satan and his advisors. Whereas many demons are tempters, like worker bees, assigned the common task of fishing impromptu ideas and suggestions in the rivers of human weakness, hoping someone will take a bite, the more educated and experienced demons carry out the tasks of developing temptations into hobbies, habits, and into small axes that will eventually fell the whole tree.'

There is a break on the recording as I let Alex recover from such a wordy description.

'Why a tree?' I hear myself say.

Alex pauses, then attempts another metaphor.

'The ultimate goal of a demon is to take away choice. Choice makes for a very messy universe. Kind of like a garden that is left unattended for all the weeds to scatter wherever they want. Choice leads to all the bad stuff in our world. So we want to stop it.'

'We?' I ask.

I remember how Alex had glanced at the same spot. 'Sorry, I was just repeating what Ruen said. Shall I continue?'

I make a note of the 'we' and ask him to carry on. He coughs loudly.

'We see the removal of choice as a noble purpose. We have devised many methods to this end. Every demon's existence is dedicated to the fulfilment of his or her role, for which he or she trains for hundreds or even thousands of mortal years. Every demon who has any sort of role in the human realm, even a role as menial as tempting or discouraging, is a scientist, steeped in millennia of knowledge on human frailty. If a demon fails to achieve his or her purpose at any time, the punishment is severe.'

Alex stops. 'That's a bit harsh, isn't it?' he says to the spot by the window.

'What is?' I ask. He turns to me.

'If a demon fails, he's chained to the bottom of a pit a billion miles beneath the sun for a hundred years, and *then* he has to do his training all over again.'

I nod. 'I'd say that's harsh.' I refer to my notes. 'What is a Harrower?' This term clearly has great importance for Alex, and I want to know all the meanings he has attached to it.

Alex looks down, as if listening, then returns his gaze to me.

'What is it, Alex?'

'Ruen wants me to repeat his own words, as if he's talking now. Is that OK?'

I nod and watch him carefully. He blinks a couple of times, then opens his mouth to speak.

'I am a Harrower. My job is to go in after the barriers have been broken, after the action has been taken, even after regret has sunk its fangs deep into memory, and then I rake the soul until it is ripe for the seeds of doubt and hopelessness for which no human language has adequate lexicon. I could give you a thousand translations of "anguish" in the various tongues of the human realm, because all of them differ, and yet none of them come close to capturing its complexity. This is because there is no translation for the kind of work I perform. Nobody needs to be taken to Hell to experience it. We just grow despair inside the soul until it becomes a world in and around a human.'

Alex takes another breath, his shoulders relaxed, his eyes flitting across the room as if he is bored. Then he continues.

'Harrowing is an essential part of cultivating the soul to reject the idea of choice. Contrary to popular opinion, the soul is not like smoke on water; it is somewhere between liquid and metal, like the Earth's core. When one strokes it, grooves are made, impressions formed. The soul can only be removed by God, that is true; but, when the door is opened, when the path is made clear for my entrance, I can mould that slick substance into unlimited shapes and create hollows that channel through to eternity.

'There is much waiting around in this job. In order to do my work effectively, I must watch on as the other demons perform the complex tasks of analysing, tempting, suggesting, then deftly plucking away the scales of human realisation until remorse and horror pave the way for my entrance. It's no red carpet. By this stage, I am virtually alone, and there is no one to applaud the work I achieve. There is only the sight of a human falling deeper and deeper within themselves, toppling through the distances created by my grooves and hollows.'

When I'm sure that Alex has finished, I hit the 'pause' and 'save' buttons on my phone and scribble down a few notes. There is nothing I want to ask at this point. I need time to process the information that has been given. Just then, Alex says:

'Shall I ask her the questions now?'

He is speaking to the empty space by the window, not me. Still, I say:

'What questions?'

Alex nods. 'It's OK. He doesn't want to ask you just yet.'

I smile and thank Alex – and Ruin – for their time.

'Ruen says you are most welcome, my lady,' says Alex.

Michael sits in silence for a long time after I've played him the tape. Finally he says, 'Man, that's some serious stuff.'

'Is any of this regurgitated from a religious text?' I ask. 'Is the notion of a Harrower part of any faith that you're aware of?'

Michael scratches his head. 'In ten years of religious studies, I never came across the term *harrower*. I'll look into it and see if there're any passages in the Bible that refer to it. Though, to my knowledge, Alex's family isn't religious.'

'We don't know anything about his dad,' I say. 'Maybe he was. In which case, most of what he's saying could be working through a severely religious upbringing.' I pause to reflect on Alex's comments. 'What about that whole thing about choice?'

'*Butter and honey shall he eat, that he may know to refuse the evil, and choose the good.* Old Testament, Isaiah, chapter seven, verse sixteen. No, fifteen. Free will underscores most of Christian belief.'

'And you never found out about Alex's father?'

He leans forward, shaking his head. 'Cindy won't talk about him. The most Alex ever said was that his dad was dead and gone to Hell.'

'*Hell?*' I say quickly. 'Not Heaven?'

Michael shakes his head. 'He was, as you say, quite specific.'

I sigh. 'This kind of religious intellectual thinking is *not* that of a ten-year-old.' I pick up my phone and look down at it for a moment before putting it back in my pocket. 'What do you make of the questions Alex said Ruin wanted to ask me? Has he ever wanted to ask you questions?'

Michael considers it. 'No, I don't think so. Look,' he says, and there is something different about his tone, the look in his eyes. He strokes my arm. I pull it back, a sudden reflex, and he looks alarmed. 'What? I scrubbed my hands.'

'No, it's not that,' I say.

'What is it?'

You are forty-three years old, I tell myself. *You are quite capable of setting professional boundaries.* Still, I feel bashful when I tell him what *it* is.

'I'd rather us be colleagues. Full stop.'

He looks at me as if I've lost my mind, and I feel my cheeks burn. Still, in the past I've let men wander way beyond the iron gates of friendship, then watched their faces fall when I refuse to reciprocate a pass. I'd rather be upfront about it in case it gets in the way of Alex's treatment.

'Well, that's a pity,' he says lightly. 'I don't go to the Opera House with any of my colleagues, and here I was thinking we could share a taxi to Alex's performance of *Hamlet* tonight.'

I breathe a sigh of relief. 'I don't mind sharing a taxi.'

He looks visibly pleased. 'Good. I'll call past yours around seven. OK?'

I open my mouth to say, *Actually, I'll meet you there*, but he has moved on, telling me about his allotment, his Brussels sprouts. How we should share a bottle of his homemade orange juice sometime.

It is only when I attempt to find an outfit suitable for a trip to the Grand Opera House that I realise how much Alex's case has eaten into my personal time over the last few weeks – my flat is only partially furnished and filled with as yet unpacked boxes, meaning that I have no cutlery, plates, chairs, and only a small rack of clothes. So far, I hadn't noticed. I dig deep into a box marked CLOTHES and pull a dozen outfits on to the red Mexican tiles of my living room. Each outfit is black, and each is a variation of knee-length skirt or three-quarter-length shirt. Once I've assembled a row of possibilities, my mind turns of its own accord to Poppy. In my memories, she is standing beside me in our Morningside flat, shaking her head as I pull garments out of my wardrobe. Whereas I have absolutely no fashion sense, Poppy had an innate sense of style before she could form sentences, fumbling in the laundry basket, picking out the colours and textures she liked before draping them around her head and shoulders, then staggering around our little flat in a pair of my stilettos.

'What about this one?' I recall myself saying, holding another black dress against me. She rolled her eyes and shook her head.

'Everything you own is black,' she said, fishing through my wardrobe. 'Why not anything red? Or orange or even yellow?'

'Are those my colours?'

She flicked her eyes at me. 'Your skin tone is olive, your hair and eyes are dark brown.'

'I'll take that as a yes.'

She found a white dress lurking in my shoe rack. 'Aha! Here we go.'

I glanced it over, noticing the price tag still hanging from the label. A Stella McCartney, bought on a whim. Back then, my motto was, 'If you can live without it, live without it – unless it's Stella.' These days, I've trimmed the motto down a little. Poppy thrust the dress against me.

'*This* is it,' she said.

I shook my head. 'It's far too tight.'

More eye-rolling. 'Mother, you're skinny. Flaunt it, OK?'

And right as her precocious words chime in my ears, I spy something at the bottom of the box. Something I hadn't even remembered packing. A white puddle. I reach in and pull it out, noticing the label. It is the same dress. I didn't wear it the night that she insisted upon it. It wasn't *me*, I'd argued.

I strip down to my underwear and slip the dress over my head. Cut elegantly below the knee, one-sleeved, with a modestly straight neckline just under my collarbone and a discreet gold zip at the side, the dress still fits perfectly. And it still isn't me.

At seven o'clock a car horn sounds outside. I grab my briefcase and talisman and run outside to find Michael standing outside the taxi. He is wearing a navy suit and a clean white shirt without a tie, his hair combed back. He is holding the car door open.

'Evening,' he says.

I pause, certain that I've chosen the wrong outfit.

'You look lovely, Dr Molokova,' he said, giving me a small bow.

I smile back at him and jump into the back seat.

At the Grand Opera House I tell Michael to go ahead and find our seats while I search for a member of staff to take me backstage to ensure that Alex is all right. I spot Jojo's red head bobbing amongst the hordes in the foyer and shout her name. She turns at the sound, and I wave.

'Is everything OK?' I asked once we'd found a corner close to the stairwell. 'With Alex, I mean.'

Her face looks strained. 'Absolutely fine with *Alex*,' she says. 'Only we're a man down. Well, a girl, really. Katie, who plays Hamlet? I mean, thank the Lord we've an understudy to fill her shoes, but can you imagine? On opening night?'

'What happened?'

She presses a hand against her forehead. 'Had an accident, poor thing. Broke her leg in six places falling down a flight of steps. Anyway, we're sorted now. *And* there's a casting director from London here tonight. Roz Mardell, you heard of her?'

I shake my head. She tisks in disapproval.

'Roz is casting for the new Tarantino *Hamlet*, can you imagine?' She fans herself. 'I think Alex has an excellent chance.'

'You do?' I feel a sudden mixture of excitement and dread. Excitement at the opportunity this would afford him, but dread at what impact it might have on his emotions.

'You know his aunt Bev is here?' she tells me quickly. 'She's upstairs in a box if you want to say hello.'

A teenage boy in a black T-shirt bearing the REALLY TALENTED KIDS logo waves at Jojo from the other side of the foyer.

'I better go,' she says. 'You look beautiful in that dress, by the way.'

'Thanks,' I say, watching her squeeze her way to the other side of the foyer before I headed up the stairs to my seat in the Grand Circle.

Along the crescent of filled seats I spot Michael's blond head. I inch my way across handbags and legs and find my seat next to him just as the lights began to dim.

'Everything all right?' he whispers, leaning towards me. I catch his smell – the lime tang of aftershave, turf, and macadamia nuts – and forget why he should be asking me if everything is all right. I smile and nod, tugging the hem of my skirt self-consciously across my knees.

The curtain rises to the sound of a drumbeat from the orchestra pit. A soft mist brushes across the stage, where a figure holding a gun is wandering in a state of fear.

'Who's there?' a boy's voice calls. Another figure backs its way across the stage in the direction of the boy, a hand drawn to a holster at its waist. The figures collide.

'Bernardo?'

'Francisco?'

'What are you *doing* out here in the dead of night?'

'Taking over guard duty from you, you plonker. It's past midnight.'

'It is?'

Another figure crosses the stage, a boy I recognise instantly as Alex. Dressed in a camouflage suit, his brown hair slicked into an old-fashioned side parting and his feet in heavy black boots, he no longer resembles the nervous, timid boy with whom I have been consulting. Instead, he walks with an air of authority, and when he speaks, his voice is deeper, shot through with command. A wind whips up the mist around him, the sound of strings rising up from the orchestra pit.

'Francisco – where are you off to?'

A moment's banter. 'Bernardo's on guard duty. Good night.'

A second figure appears behind Alex, thumping his hand heavily on his shoulder to make him jump.

'Marcellus!' Alex shouts. 'Speak first, next time!'

Marcellus raises his gun to indicate he is armed, then nods

at Bernardo. 'You're more on edge than usual, Bernardo. Has the ghost been spotted?'

Bernardo shakes his head. 'Not tonight.'

Marcellus turns to Alex. 'Horatio says he won't believe what we've seen 'til he's seen it himself. Isn't that right, Horatio?'

Alex pulls the strap of a rifle over his head and sets the weapon in foliage by his feet. He settles down as if to sleep. 'No such thing as ghosts, you idiots.'

'There *is*,' Bernardo says, crouching to gather leaves and twigs together before creating a fire – or, in this case, a strip of red material blown upwards by a small wind machine, lit from behind. 'We saw it last night, just before one, looks just like the King.'

Marcellus crouched, too. 'It *is* the King.'

From the corner of my eye I see Michael turning to me, half his face in darkness, the other illuminated by the spotlight on stage. He throws me a smile in praise of Alex, which I return. The worry that had tugged at my heart on behalf of Alex – this being his first public performance, and at a time when his private life was anything but calm – is subsiding now, and at the sound of a slow piano melody rung out in the orchestra pit, a familiar song rose up in my head. Poppy's song, the one she was composing the night she died. My mouth turns dry. The events on the stage before me slide into the periphery of my thoughts, Poppy's face rising back into my mind.

But instead of recalling her by my side, instructing me on

the rudiments of fashion and laughing at my decision to wear *that* top with *those* shoes, I feel her absence keenly.

'*There it is!*' I hear Alex shout. '*A ghost! Oh, it harrows me with fear and wonder.*'

My thoughts enter a territory that is fenced off with rolling barbed wire, with armed guards at various posts keeping tres-passers at a considerable distance. I ignore them, crossing beyond the familiar planes of my memories with Poppy to the day I learned I was pregnant. Poppy's father was an acquain-tance from medical school: Daniel Shearsman, an American researcher spending a semester at University College London. We were never involved, at least not beyond a memorable weekend in Switzerland which started off in the lobby of a tatty convention centre for a postdoctoral conference and ended up in a minimalist hotel overlooking Lake Geneva. Daniel never knew about Poppy. I was eleven weeks pregnant before I found out, and, when I did, I kept her to myself like a guilty secret.

'*This ghost,*' Alex shouts on stage, his voice trembling. '*This ghost is an omen. A sign that something is not right in our nation. Something troubles it.*'

I walk on past the guards, recalling – with a mild aston-ishment – months of sleeping on friends' spare mattresses throughout my pregnancy, in case my mother – in the thick of her own psychosis – harmed the baby; then the birth; Poppy's small, creamy face presented to me in the nurse's arms, as if she was closing her eyes against bright sunlight; bringing her home to my new student flat, both of us curling up each night in a small bed against the window; Edith, the eccentric old spinster downstairs who swept the stone stairwell of our apartment block every single day, offering to look after Poppy while I finished my studies; the first day I noticed something was wrong with Poppy. Not wrong; *different*. It was the day Edith said she couldn't look after Poppy any more.

'Why?' I asked at the time.

Edith's brown eyes had always sparkled when I dropped Poppy off at her apartment, but lately her expression at the door had grown troubled, hesitant to receive my daughter. At my question, Edith's eyes lowered, her mouth searching for words.

'She killed one of my fish,' Edith stuttered, blinking back tears of disbelief. I thought of the large tropical fish tank Edith kept in her small sitting room, filled with small blue flecks and large purple swirls that looked like ribbons, but which Edith had told me proudly were Japanese fighting fish.

'Swiped him clean out of the tank, like a cat,' Edith continued, her lips trembling. 'Watched him gasp for air on the sideboard.'

'I am *so* sorry,' I said, horrified. I turned to Poppy, who was standing by my side, so easily bored that she was already doing a little dance and tugging my arm to leave. I bent down and cupped her small chin, turning her face to mine. I could see Daniel's face in hers, that high forehead, the dark curls bouncing off her shoulders.

'Poppy, tell Edith you are very sorry and we will buy her a new fish.'

Poppy rolled her eyes away from mine and continued to dance and bounce on the spot. Edith shook her head at me gravely, folding her arms. 'There've been other things,' she said. 'Small things, but strange . . . ' Her eyes darted down at Poppy as if she was something unclean.

'She's only three years old,' I reasoned, pulling Poppy away from Edith's legs. She was pretending to claw at her now, snarling and laughing.

'I'm sorry.' Edith had stepped backwards into the darkness of her hallway, closing her door for good.

I remember, now, that Poppy had never apologised.

'*That it should come to this . . .* '

I glance at Alex on stage, noticing that he has managed to keep his body facing the audience while addressing his fellow actors, his dialogue crisp and clear. I look down at the white hem of my dress bunched tightly in my fists, realising that now, in my forties, I am finally living a normal life. A life without excuses for Poppy's behaviour. A life without apologies to the parents of Poppy's classmates who sobbed after she lashed out, pleas to countless GPs to find the right treatment, rejection after rejection to potential lovers because my daughter needed a stability that a new relationship would rupture. A life without Poppy.

And, to my horror, a part of me is relieved.

When the first scene ends, a sudden burst of applause startles me out of the past and back into the room. I give a small jump, holding my hands up as if I've just landed in my seat. Michael turns to me.

'Are you all right?'

The stage clears, the orchestra picking up the theme tune as the wedding procession of Claudius and Gertrude begins to roll from the wings. I rose to my feet. 'I think I just need some fresh air.'

I make my way towards the exit, past the handbags and bent legs in the pew, through the doors to the stairwell, then taking the steps two at a time to the foyer downstairs. I ignore staff who ask if I want to buy snacks and souvenirs, pushing past a queue bristling at the ticket desk. Outside, I take off my shoes, relieved by the feel of the cold, wet pavement, the indifference of loud, busy traffic. I walk a little distance away from the front doors and lean my head against the cool wall.

'Anya?'

I turn to see Michael at the entrance, his navy suit jacket blowing open in the wind. He strides stealthily towards me.

'Are you sure you're all right?' His face is creased in concern. I turn away, anxious for him to leave. I don't want to have to explain myself and lying makes me fidgety. I fold my arms.

'I'm fine,' I say, turning back to him and forcing a smile. 'I just felt a bit hot, that's all.'

He nods, but the look of concern in his eyes doesn't fade. There is a moment where he should get the hint and go back inside. He decisively doesn't.

'Alex was great, wasn't he?' He grinned, plucking at the thin straws of conversation. I try to return his enthusiasm, but before I can speak I feel a sob form in my throat and my eyes well up. I raise a hand, embarrassed.

'It's OK,' I mutter. 'Really. Go on, you're missing the show.'

I glance out at the traffic, relieved by the sweep of cold air thrown up by the stream of cars, the lights of the Opera House dancing on each new shining vehicle. Michael is still standing there, both hands at his sides, watching me. I can make out the lines under his eyes, the slight fuzz of grey stubble around his jaw. I go to say *please*, but he steps forward. I look up, startled by the pain in his eyes. Without a word, he lifts a hand to my cheek. His thumb gently and deliberately rests across the scar inflicted by Poppy. I search his eyes, wondering what he is doing. It is as if he has ventured as close to the line I have drawn between our professional relationship and an intimate relationship as he possibly can. He doesn't move to kiss me, doesn't speak. He just holds his hand there, his eyes intense, burning into mine.

After a few moments he lowers his hand and walks back inside.

17

'Remember me'

Alex

Dear Diary,

I did NOT do this to myself, but everyone here thinks I did and I am really fed up. I don't know what happened. I feel so muddled and weird. Ruen wasn't around at the time and all Bonnie did was scream. An ambulance came and carried me out in a stretcher. There were lots of people in the street but also lots of demons.

All the doctors at the hospital kept asking me, 'Alex, did you do this to yourself? Did you throw yourself up against the wall? Did you punch yourself in the face?' and so on, and then when I wouldn't answer they asked me *why* I did it.

But something even weirder happened tonight, right when I was on stage.

I'll start at the beginning. It was like the craziest day all day in rehearsals, or I guess not all day but for about three hours before the curtain was going to come up and Jojo was getting sweaty and swearing a lot and everyone kept forgetting their lines. Katie didn't show up and everyone was worried and finally Jojo sat us down and told us Katie had had an accident and Aoife would be playing Hamlet. I thought about what Ruen had asked me to do to Katie's mum and felt bad for a moment. He was right. And if I had've done what he said, Katie would have been OK.

Then Jojo found out that a casting director was coming, which made her even more stressed out. 'Her name is Roz Mardell,' she kept saying, in case we met her and didn't call her by the right name which would be embarrassing, Jojo said. 'If she comes up to you, you shake her hand and compliment her on her outfit and mention that you would love to do a camera audition.' She fanned herself as if she might pass out. 'One of you could end up in a film!'

I looked in the mirror in front of me. *How amazingly cool would that be?* I thought, and I decided right then that I totally *would* act in films like all Jojo's famous friends and when I was really famous I would come back to Belfast and run a theatre company for kids, just like Jojo. But then I had a sinking feeling, as if a pit of quicksand had landed on my chest. There was no way I could ever end up in a film. I was just Alex from Belfast with a crazy mum.

Jojo made us all sit in a circle on the stage with our legs crossed and our hands on our knees and chant '*Um*', which made me forget the sinking feeling and I started to giggle. Then Liam changed the chant to '*Dumb*' and someone else said '*Rum*' and then it became '*Bum*', and everyone laughed.

Jojo said she'd hired professional make-up artists and technicians for the night, which really made it all feel real, and then when the orchestra turned up I felt sick with excitement. I know there was over twenty of us in the play but somehow I couldn't get it into my head that I was a part of something so cool. I had this feeling for a moment as if a warm wave of seawater had just passed over me, as if everything was going to be all right.

And then a second later it was as if another wave washed over me but it was icy cold and I had a thought in my head: *What if it all goes wrong?*

It was just after that thought that I saw Ruen. He was the Old Man then, strutting around the front of the auditorium looking over a big black piano that someone had just wheeled in. I could tell he really loved this one because he kept looking inside it at the strings and running his horrible hands up and down the keys.

When the curtain went up all the nervousness left me. I closed my eyes and told myself *I am Horatio*, and then I forgot about all the stuff that had happened before. I lowered my voice and thought of the way Jojo said Horatio would speak and how important he was at the end in continuing Hamlet's story.

The orchestra stopped tuning their instruments and all the people who were chatting in the audience went so quiet you would have thought they'd all gone home. But I knew they were there. The lights came on but just slightly. Everyone backstage went tense and nervous.

There were footsteps and shouts on stage. I heard Liam give his line.

Taking over guard duty from you, you plonker. It's past midnight.

It was my turn to go on. I looked down at my costume, which was a soldier's costume with shiny lace-up boots and a combat jumpsuit with labels from where I was meant to have done something brave. I had black marks smeared on my face and a big fake gun on my back. I took a deep breath. I stepped out into the spotlight.

'Francisco – where are you off to?' I said loudly. I turned my head to the audience but I could hardly see a single person, even though I knew they were all there. The spotlight was so bright that it seemed there was only me and Liam on stage. The projection of Jojo's friend appeared on the wall opposite. The projection always reminded me of Ruen because it looked like a real person but you could see the wall behind him. The orchestra started playing and it was loud, like scratchy, screaming violins. I gave my line: *Now I see it with my own eyes, I believe you. It is real.* But when I looked at the projection again it didn't look the same. The man was wearing a black balaclava now and a black jacket. I wondered if someone had changed the reel in the projector. He was just standing there, holding a gun.

Aoife came on stage then as Hamlet, and she looked at the ghost and reached to touch it. *He is my father*, she said. *He is my father! O Hamlet, progenitor, warmest father, namesake – tell me why you're here.*

The ghost turned and faced Aoife. The voice of Jojo's famous friend filled the auditorium.

I was murdered by that same traitor who has married your mother . . .

Aoife looked on as the ghost addressed her, telling her to take revenge for his death. She looked scared and clung on to me, and I felt numb.

Remember me, Hamlet.

I looked at the ghost and he held up his gun. And then it was like the stage and the smoke and the projection of Jojo's famous friend as the ghost and the audience all disappeared. And I wasn't even Horatio any more.

Remember me . . .

Aoife was no longer standing beside me. The stage had disappeared and instead of a black sea of faces, I was standing at the side of a road that looked like it was in Northern Ireland but I wasn't sure. There was a row of small stone shops behind me and a church and a post office. Some women were pushing prams along the narrow pavement and a little girl in a yellow dress was standing in a shop doorway eating a packet of crisps and throwing some for the pigeons. The road was black and shiny as if it had been raining. There were two policemen at either side of the road, one old, one young. A police car was parked just past me. *It's a police checkpoint*, I thought. I could see a camera in the back of it pointed at the patrol.

A blue car came up the road towards the checkpoint. *Enjoy them while they're young*, the policeman on the opposite side of the road said. *Not long before they start borrowing your car and bleeding you dry.* The young policeman spotted the car coming towards them and he walked into the centre of the road with his hand up.

The blue car came closer and I could see two men in the front. The man in the driver's seat was so small I could hardly see his face over the steering wheel, but as he got closer I saw he was old and bald with a white tuft of hair at the back. The other man's face was hidden behind a black balaclava. I could feel my breaths getting faster and my heart galloping because I knew who he was.

He was my Dad.

The policeman in the middle of the road shouted something to the older policeman who took out his radio and started talking into it. The policeman in the middle of the road reached for the gun in his holster at his waist and when the blue car stopped my dad jumped out of the car and pointed a gun at him.

It happened so fast I thought I must have missed something. There was a woman pushing a pram nearby and she screamed and ran into the post office and someone came out and grabbed the little girl who was feeding the pigeons and slammed the shop door. Another man just froze, as if he had turned to ice. The young policeman raised his hands.

'Don't shoot!' he said, and his voice was full of warning not fear but I was close enough to see his face, which was sweaty and strained. The older policeman had his gun pointed at my dad and I was very scared. I hid behind a pillar in front of the church.

But my dad wasn't. He kept his gaze on the policeman in the middle of the road.

'There's another patrol nearby,' the older policeman said, still pointing his gun at my dad. 'It's not worth it, pal. You won't get far.'

My dad turned his head back to the driver, as if he needed to ask him something, and in that split second the older policeman shot at him but the shot missed my dad and cracked the windscreen of the blue car. My dad spun round and aimed his gun and the younger policeman pulled out his gun but my dad shot him first.

I saw it like it happened slowly.

The man who had frozen like ice dropped his can of Coke.

The pigeons flapped up into the air.

The sky bounced off the wet road.

The policeman's head turned to me. His mouth was curled in a weird way and his face was a blur. Blood shot out of his forehead like a red horn.

My dad turned and I heard another shot. It was a crack, like a Christmas cracker only much louder, and with a kind of thud behind it that made me feel sick. The second policeman's arms flung forward and his knees crumpled and he fell. And when I looked back at my dad he was already in the blue car and the old man behind the wheel made the tyres spin and they drove away.

When I looked up again I wasn't at the police checkpoint or on stage. I was in my dressing room in front of a mirror and I wasn't wearing my combat suit any more, just my boxer shorts and my black boots. My face was wet and my mouth was red and I was shaking all over. I lifted my arm up to see the marks on it and it was shaking but I could see I was bleeding. Someone was behind me. It was Bonnie Nicholls.

'Alex,' she whispered. 'Alex, what happened?'

I glanced around the dressing room and for some reason it looked like it had been burgled. The dressing table was turned over with all four legs sticking up. One of the big photographs on the far wall was shattered and my locker was open with all the contents on the ground.

'What happened, Bonnie?' I said, but before she could answer my legs turned to jelly and I heard her scream and everything went black.

When I woke up I was in a hospital bed in different clothes and my body ached like I'd been trampled by dinosaurs. The nurses gave me some medicine which has pushed most of the pain into the distance. I had a huge black shiner and my nose was so swollen that every time I said, 'I didn't do it' it came out like 'I nin't noo it.' After the nurses a doctor came in and all he wanted to know is why I like drawing skeletons. I got so angry that I started to cry and I saw him write 'anger issues' on his notepad.

Anya and Michael and Auntie Bev came later on. I was so relieved to see them that I burst out laughing. This surprised

Auntie Bev but made her laugh, too, even though her eyes looked upset.

'You look like a queen,' I said to Anya, though I just meant to say she looked nice. She was wearing a clean white dress with no marks on it and her hair was up which made her neck look long and she had make-up on. She smiled though she looked like she wanted to cry.

'What happened, Alex?' she said. 'Did Ruin do this?'

Michael shut the door and Anya looked at some papers the doctors had written about me and then she started asking me more questions, but I felt sleepy and I just wanted some onions and toast with a cup of tea.

'Do *you* know what happened?' I asked Anya.

'We were hoping *you* would tell *us* what happened, Alex,' Anya said.

I pressed the balls of my palms into my eyes and took deep breaths. I felt so muddled. I thought, *Maybe I really am going crazy.*

When I moved my hands from my eyes I noticed that I'd said this out loud. Both Michael and Anya were looking at me really strangely. After a long time Anya said:

'Were you upset about your mum tonight, Alex? Did something happen earlier in rehearsals?'

I opened my mouth to tell her about the policeman and the shooting and that I had seen my dad, but when I went to speak no words came out, just long sobs and I started crying so badly that my whole body shook and my back started to ache.

Auntie Bev came and sat on the bed beside me and took my hand. Then she put her arms around me and held me for a long time.

'Was this an accident?' she said when she let go, and her voice was very small. 'Or did you do it to yourself? You can tell me, you know. I won't be upset. We all just want to help you.'

Just then, Ruen appeared as Ghost Boy. I must have jumped with fright because immediately Anya asked me what was wrong. Ruen stood at the end of the bed, staring at me. He was giving me the Alex Is Stupid look.

'I'm not stupid!' I yelled at him.

'It's OK, Alex,' Anya said, but I shook my head because I didn't mean her. I hated Ruen's eyes right then, it was like they were bigger than normal, like *bulging*, and even though they were black as two lumps of coal they could see right through me. I put my hands over my eyes.

'Tell them you did it,' he said, nodding his head and smiling.

The way he said it made it sound like he was offering more of a helpful suggestion than a command, like he knew something I didn't and that it would be a good idea to do as he said. He said it again. 'It's OK, Alex. Just tell them.'

I took a deep breath. 'I did it,' I said.

Auntie Bev let go of me slightly and Anya and Michael looked at each other and I regretted saying it. I wanted Auntie Bev to hold me again. I wanted to ask Ruen why he said I should say that so I just said, 'Can we talk about this more in the morning? I'm really tired now.'

Anya stepped forward and then crouched down so she could look me in the eye. 'You did this, Alex? Or Ruin did it?'

Ruen looked angry then. I thought back to the police checkpoint.

'My dad did something very, very wrong,' I said slowly, and Anya's face changed as if she'd seen something she hadn't seen before.

'Did your dad hurt you, Alex?' she said.

I shook my head.

'Did he hurt your mum?'

I shook my head.

'Can you tell me what he did?'

For a moment I was going to. But then I felt a new feeling. I felt really ashamed, which didn't make sense because it wasn't my fault. But I still felt like she would be disappointed in me.

'Maybe after a sleep you can tell me,' Anya said, and I felt so glad of that because I was so tired and sore and my brain felt like mud. I nodded and lay back and closed my eyes.

When I was sure they'd left, I said to Ruen, 'Why did you tell me to say that?'

He was just staring out the window as if he was looking for someone. He didn't answer so I asked him again. I was starting to get cross with him.

'Why would you tell me to lie?' I asked him.

He turned to me and pressed his face really close to mine. His breath smelled like a butcher's shop on a sunny day. I turned my face.

'But you *did* do this to yourself, Alex,' he whispered. And then he didn't look cross any more, but like he pitied me. 'Poor Alex,' he said, picking up the ball and batting it off the wall opposite. 'You don't realise, do you?'

'Realise what?'

'That you *did* do this.'

'And *how* did I do this?' I said loudly, though it hurt my chest. 'How would I lift myself up and fling myself into the chest of drawers?'

'Weren't you asleep at the time?'

'Hardly. I was getting ready for the third scene . . .'

He stopped batting and tilted his head as if he'd just thought of something that I hadn't. 'Or were you *dreaming* that you were getting ready for the third scene?'

My head felt like mincemeat now. I just wanted to sleep.

'I have to sleep now, Ruen,' I told him.

He nodded. 'I promise not to tell your mum about this.'

I thought to myself, *But Mum doesn't even know you exist*, but I said nothing because if I really did do this to myself I certainly didn't want Mum finding out. It would make her worse. And I felt glad then that Ruen was going to keep it a secret.

'Do you think Mum is OK?' I said.

'Oh, I'm sure she's fine. Would you like me to make sure she's OK, Alex?'

I nodded and felt so relieved. 'Yes, please. I would love that.'

Ruen smiled and leaned over me. 'Can I ask you to do something for me?'

I nodded.

'Tomorrow morning I'd like you to ask Anya the list of questions I gave you. Can you do that for me, Alex? I would be very grateful.'

'OK.'

And then I don't remember anything else because I fell asleep and dreamed of Granny all night.

18

RUEN'S QUESTIONS

Anya

Alex's latest predicament is a shock, to say the least.

I had returned to my seat in the Opera House auditorium just as Alex was on stage consoling Hamlet about the hasty marriage between his widowed mother and uncle. I looked over the other members of the audience – many were sat forward in their seats, eager to hear the counsel of this young man to Hamlet. I felt a swell of pride for him. And I wondered if he had crossed a bridge of sorts. I glanced at Michael and thought about Alex's treatment. *Should he receive treatment at home? Should I sidestep the furore that will be caused by having Cindy deemed unfit to act as Alex's mother and having him admitted to MacNeice House, a place she believes to be for lunatics? Is Alex demonstrating psychotic symptoms, or symptoms of post-traumatic stress?*

But something happened during the interval. When the curtain went down and the audience were rising in their seats, I spotted Jojo at the bottom of the auditorium, racing across to the other side. I saw her signal at a staff member, then turn to scan the pews as if she was looking for someone. I waved at her, but she didn't see me. I leaned forward to catch Michael's attention.

'Something's wrong,' I said to him.

'What do you mean?' He followed my gaze to the front of the auditorium, where two boys in REALLY TALENTED KIDS T-shirts were running to the door that Jojo had just exited. I started to make my way over. Michael followed.

When we arrived at the dressing room, Michael pushed past an obstructive crew member and saw the state of the place – it appeared to have been ransacked. Bonnie, the girl who played Ophelia, said she had heard a lot of noise coming from the dressing room. When she entered, she saw Alex crashing against the wall, then falling backwards on to the floor. He was unconscious for a few moments – Bonnie had thought he was dead.

I found Alex's aunt Beverly and told her that Alex had had an accident, though I still wasn't entirely sure what had happened. The Red Cross team had already taken Alex to A&E, a crew member told us, though he was more anxious about finding an understudy to carry on the performance than answering my questions. Beverly, Michael and I took a taxi and arrived at the A&E department of the City Hospital a short while later, where a nurse led us to a sideroom in the paediatric unit.

Alex looked terrible. Both eyes were bloodshot and his nose was bruised and swollen. A nurse informed me that he had bruising around his lower back that suggested he had deliberately thrown himself against the wall. The force by which the bruising had been caused was unusual in the case of self-harm: it looked like a much larger person would have had to have lifted Alex up and thrown him a distance of approximately ten feet.

I can only imagine that the strain of performing the play was too much for him. When I read through Shakespeare's original and Jojo's adaptation, I noticed that the relationship between Hamlet and his father was underlined by an eerie sense of debt, of carrying out revenge on his father's behalf. I have a suspicion that Alex's relationship with his father is something I need to investigate more, and I've made a note to push Alex a little to talk about it. But clearly I need to wait until he recovers physically.

I did not sleep when I returned home. Michael and I shared a taxi, making the journey together in silence. My mind was racing with hows and whys, circling the issue of the play's subject like a vulture. The truth was, I had already located my answer, but I wanted to pick the bones of it out of guilt. I should never have allowed Alex to perform in the play. I should have seen the kinds of pressures a major performance would have placed on him at such a vulnerable period in his life. And I should have insisted, *insisted*, that Alex be transferred to MacNeice House.

When the taxi pulled up outside my flat I turned to Michael.

'As soon as Alex leaves hospital, I am moving him to MacNeice House,' I said.

He chewed his cheek, keeping his eyes on the space between us. 'I know,' he said quietly. For a moment his eyes met mine – filled with a startling amount of want. Then he turned and looked out the window and the taxi pulled away.

When I went to see Alex the day after, he was already dressed. His aunt Beverly had been today, a nurse informed me. She had brought Alex's belongings. He was still wincing from pain as he sat upright, but had taken the time to get dressed, red bow tie furnishing his brown-and-white striped shirt. His hair had grown so long it was starting to cover his eyes. He had something in his shirt pocket which he revealed to be one of the photos of the new council house. He was keeping it close to his heart, he said. I was delighted that something I'd done had made him so happy.

'Where's Michael?' he said when I closed the door behind me.

'In his office, I expect,' I told him. 'Did you want to see him?'

Alex shook his head. I noticed his dressings had been changed but the silvery morning light revealed the bruising around his face to be travelling through the blue hues of deep impact. I recognised this was a very serious self-harm episode, completely undermining how happy he appeared on the surface.

'How are you feeling now?' I asked.

He seemed suddenly hesitant to meet my eye. He rubbed his bicep and said, 'Sore.'

'I bet.'

I pulled up a chair at the table, mulling over the best way to broach the subject of Alex's father. It was important that I eased him into the subject gently, establishing that whatever it was his father had done was not going to land Alex in trouble. On the table was a tray of food leftover from breakfast – a dilapidated fruit salad, a tub of warm Greek yoghurt and porridge sprinkled with pine nuts. I lifted it out the way and set it on the floor close to the door, handing Alex a cup of water.

'You can have some if you want,' he said, glancing at the tray of food. 'I'm not hungry.'

'Thank you, Alex,' I said with a smile. 'That's very kind. But I'm allergic to nuts, remember?'

'Nuts?'

I nodded. 'These are pine nuts,' I say, glancing at the porridge.

'Oh yeah,' he said. 'Nuts make you sleep, don't they?'

I remembered my lie. 'Yes,' I said.

'They don't even look like nuts. They look like tiny, little bullets.'

There was a depth to his tone that I recognised instantly. Some of the children I have treated recently have witnessed the violence in Northern Ireland first-hand. One girl, Shay, was blinded during a riot in Drumcree several years ago. She is being treated for clinical depression. Another fifteen-year-old boy from Carrickfergus was shot at point-blank range in the knee – 'knee-capped', they call it here – for his father's defection from a terrorist organisation. The trauma of that event has made him suicidal. Michael insists that Cindy and Alex have not suffered by the conflict in Northern Ireland, but I am uncertain. 'The Troubles' is a term most significant to those at a distance from the violence – to children who have grown up in the thick of it, The Troubles are simply a part of life.

'Have you ever seen a bullet, Alex? Or a gun?'

'You mean in real life?' he replied, keeping his eyes on the ground.

'Yes,' he nodded.

'Can you tell me where?'

He shook his head.

'Did a policeman come to arrest your dad?'

He stiffened at the mention of the word 'policeman', then shook his head briskly. Then he squeezed his eyes together tightly, his face scrunched up in concentration, both hands forming fists. I opened my mouth to speak, then waited for him to relax. A minute passed. I laid a hand on Alex's shoulder.

'I promise you won't get into trouble if you tell me what happened.'

He opened his eyes and looked past me. 'Ruen wants me to ask you some questions, is that OK?'

'Why does Ruin want to do that?' I asked gently.

Alex gave my question some serious pondering. 'I think he just wants to know more about you,' he said. 'Maybe because he and I are friends ... sort of ... and he wants to be your friend, too.'

'What sort of questions does Ruin want to ask me?'

'Um ... I'm not sure. Grown-up stuff, I think. Ruen's really weir—' He stopped short of saying 'weird', flicked his eyes to the right then laughed into his hand.

'If you answer my questions, I'll answer yours, is that OK?'

'About Ruen?'

'No, Alex. About your father.'

He blinked, then gave a small nod.

'All right – if I'm going to be interviewed, let's do it properly,' I said lightly, taking my mobile phone out of my pocket and finding the 'voice record' app. 'We'll record it, shall we? Like a proper interview.'

Alex shrugged. 'I don't care, they're not my questions.' He produced a piece of paper out of his trouser pocket. I leaned forward and looked down at what was a list of questions, scrawled in black marker.

He cleared his throat. 'Number one. Was your daughter called Poppy?'

I was unable to contain a gasp. This was more than a guess, and I am strict about not sharing personal details. I struggled to work out how he could possibly have known her name. Surely Michael would never have said? The sound of her name on his lips made beads of sweat form on my brow, between my shoulder blades.

Eventually, I said: 'Why do you ask, Alex?'

'Not me, *Ruen*.'

'Why does Ruin care about my daughter?' I said tensely.

He paused. 'I'm not sure.'

'OK,' I said, gathering my composure. 'Next question.'

'Did your daughter die four years ago?'

This time I felt my heart pound, and I wanted to leave. No, I wanted to run out of there. But I reminded myself that we had reached a critical point in Alex's treatment. He was at long last revealing clues to Ruin. So I counted to ten in my head and breathed slowly in an attempt to check my emotions. I needed to stay focused on the real reason why Alex might be asking such questions. When I opened my eyes I saw that he was visibly uncomfortable.

'I'm really sorry,' he said quietly. 'It's just ... I promised Ruen I would ask you these questions. I don't mean to upset you.'

I steadied my breath. 'Can you ask Ruin why he's so keen to know about Poppy?'

Alex turned and repeated my query to Ruin, who was purportedly standing behind him. After a few seconds' silence he turned back to me and said, 'Ruin says he really likes you and admires that you can play the piano.'

I remembered his comment about Ravel from our first meeting. 'I love the piano. But you already know that, don't you? Shall we move on to the next question?'

Alex shuffled in his seat and looked down at his list. 'Number three. Do you believe in God?'

'The jury's still out on that one, Alex,' I said, before correcting myself. 'Sorry, *Ruin*.' I decided to buy into the possibility of Ruin's presence in the room, noticing the way it instilled a confidence in Alex, his posture straighter, his eyes holding mine.

'That answers number four, then,' Alex told me.

'Which is?'

'Do you believe in Satan, the Prince of Hell?'

'What's the next question?'

'If you could have anything you wanted, what would it be?'

I felt my shoulders lighten at the breadth of the question. I exhaled, long and slow. *Poppy*, I thought, *alive and well*, and just then I caught sight of the NHS-standard canvas at the other end of the room. A field of poppies.

'It's OK,' Alex told me. 'Ruen says you've already given your answer.'

I blinked. 'Can you tell me why Ruin wants to know these things, Alex?'

He didn't answer for a long time. Finally, he nodded.

'I only have one more question,' he said quietly.

I felt disappointed that he was starting to evade direct questions. I took a deep breath and thought of ways to retrace our conversation about his father.

'Go on, then.'

He took a deep breath. 'Do you love Michael?'

I laughed, but instead of answering I watched Alex very carefully. He lowered his eyes to the table, as if he felt ashamed.

'Do I love Michael?' I repeated after a long pause. Alex nodded very slowly. Why did he want to know this?

'Next question,' I said.

'There isn't another . . .'

'*Next question*,' I said, with an insistence that surprised us both. Alex's lip began to tremble. He looked fearfully to his right, then turned to me again.

'It's OK,' he said, his shoulders lowering. 'Ruen says he already knows the answer.'

I watched him fold away the piece of paper before I discreetly held up my phone to record my own questions. 'Can we talk some more about your dad?' I asked him, changing position in my seat to appear more at ease. 'Can you tell me about him? What he looked like? What you remember about him?'

He nodded. A few seconds passed. I offered a prompt.

'Was he kind to you?'

He thought about it. 'Yes, I think so. He died when I was little, you see, so I only remember a few things about when he was alive.'

'What do you remember? Can you tell me?'

He took a deep breath. 'I remember he liked buying me toy cars. And we'd go swimming sometimes and he always brought bags full of food when he came to stay.'

'So he only came to stay with you and your mum? Did you ever stay at his house?'

He shook his head. 'Dad lived in lots of different places. I think he lived in America for a while and also in Dublin and Donegal. One time he said he was living in a barn.'

'A *barn*?'

He wrinkled his nose. 'He said it was very smelly and uncomfortable.'

'I bet it was. Do you know why he was staying in a barn?'

He seemed lost in the memory now, his legs – usually swinging from his chair – still, his gaze distant. 'He'd spend all day in the kitchen cooking weird food that Mum didn't really like but she ate it anyway cos she was hungry.'

'What sort of food?'

'I don't remember. It smelled weird and sometimes it made my eyes water.' A pause. 'He had tattoos on his arms.'

'Tattoos?'

'Yeah. There was an Irish flag here' – he clapped a hand around his left bicep – 'and words here.' He touched his right forearm.

'What were the words?'

'Actually I don't think they were words. They were letters. They stood for something. I don't know what.'

I held my breath, anxious not to push him too far. 'And when your dad died, Alex – how did that feel?'

He stared ahead. 'Lonely, I think. Until Mum bought me Woof and then it was OK. She cried and cried.'

'She cried when your dad died?'

'Yes, but she was angry, too. And scared. She tried to throw our piano out but Ruen said we mustn't.'

'Where is Ruin now, Alex?'

He looked around. 'He was here a minute ago. Don't know where he's gone.'

'Did Ruin hurt you? Or did he tell you to hurt yourself?'

A sudden fear passed across his eyes. 'The policeman . . . ' he said. And then he started to cry and I wrapped my arms around him, but he would say no more.

I left Alex at the hospital with instructions to contact me as soon as he was able to be discharged. In the meantime, I touched base with Cindy's therapist to find out whether she had given her permission for Alex to be treated as an inpatient.

'No, she hasn't.' Trudy sighed on the end of the line. 'But I've assessed her as unfit to act in the capacity of Alex's mother. His aunt has agreed to make this decision for him at present.'

There was a stretch of silence as both of us reflected on this sorry state of affairs. If Cindy had not given her permission, the news of her own sister going against her wishes would certainly be hard for her to take. And I felt extremely sorry that I had not managed to persuade her that treatment at MacNeice House would be in Alex's best interests – in fact, she was likely to perceive the move as a step towards the breaking-up of her family. I feel in a bind, and yet I am determined to treat Alex accordingly. It is, quite literally, his only hope.

The severity of Alex's hallucinations and the length of time they have been active indicate that his condition is deteriorating. Poppy was the same. In a short while, if left untreated, there is every chance that Alex will pose the same level of danger to himself or others as Poppy did. I can't let that happen to another child, another mother. In consultation with Ursula and Michael and with Cindy's permission, I resolved to prescribe a small dose of Risperidone. The effects will be monitored over several weeks, with regular consultations carried on throughout.

I returned to my office to write up my notes and compile a group email to Michael, Howard and Ursula.

To: U_hepworth@macneicehouse.nhs.uk;
H_dungar@macneicehouse.nhs.uk;
Michael_Jones@lea.gov.uk
cc: Trudy_Messenger@nicamhs.nhs.uk
From: A_molokova@macneicehouse.nhs.uk
Date: 16/06/07 17.03 p.m.

Dear all,

I am writing to inform you that I have arranged for Alex Broccoli to be transferred to MacNeice House where he will stay as an inpatient for approximately two months. I am treating him for early onset schizophrenia. I am happy to brief you further on my interviews with him and the programme of treatment, which I am currently compiling. Our next meeting is on 19/6 at 2.30 p.m. – I look forward to seeing you then.

Best,
Anya

I had barely hit the 'send' button when an email pinged back.

To: A_molokova@macneicehouse.nhs.uk
From: Michael_Jones@lea.gov.uk
Date: 16/06/07 17.03 p.m.

You do realise this will mean Alex is placed in foster care?

Sent from my BlackBerry

I stared at Michael's email, re-reading it, my mouth turning dry. I felt his hand on my face.

And suddenly I questioned everything.

The ghost I have seen
May be the devil: and the devil hath power
To assume a pleasing shape; yea, and perhaps
Out of my weakness and my melancholy,
As he is very potent with such spirits,
Abuses me to damn me.

William Shakespeare, *Hamlet*

19

ESCAPE

Alex

Dear Diary,

There's two fish in a tank. One turns to the other and says, 'Do you know how to drive this thing?'

I guess I don't need to write jokes any more as I won't be playing Horatio again because I'm in hospital and the doctors say there's *absolutely no way* I can get out to perform in the shows for the rest of the week. Though Auntie Bev told me something this morning that made me feel a wee bit better. She turned up wearing a blue headband and a thin blue vest with a Superman logo on the front which I thought was weird for a girl to wear. Her face was pink and sweaty and she was drinking from a lime-green water bottle.

'Have you been wall climbing?' I asked. She gave me a look that said she felt guilty.

'Sorry, Alex,' she said, and she sat so close to me I could smell sweat. 'I know you'd love to go. I'll take you once you get out.' She looked at the clock. 'Do you want to come and have lunch with me?'

'They're letting me go?' I said excitedly.

'I'm afraid not,' she said, lifting my shoes from under the bed. 'But we can go to the canteen just down the corridor. Would you like that?'

I said I would and stood up. I felt wobbly on my feet still but she held my elbow and helped me put my shoes on.

'I met the casting director before the show started,' Auntie Bev said as we walked slowly to the canteen. '*Roz*,' she said. 'That's her name. Turns out Roz has very bad sinusitis.' I looked up and saw Auntie Bev pull a face like she'd something really cool to tell me.

'What's sinusitis?'

'It's this horrible yucky illness that makes you feel like you've been punched in the face for about a week.'

I was horrified. 'You punched Roz in the face?'

Auntie Bev made that hooting sound that meant she was laughing.

'*No*,' she said, pushing a square silver button that made the doors open into the canteen. 'It means that she has an illness that falls into my area of expertise.'

We stood in the doorway, looking over the empty tables and chairs. I was glad it was really empty and the food on the shelves of the open fridge looked a lot nicer than the food they brought me on a tray. Auntie Bev took my arm and walked me to a table in a corner beneath a big clock with a picture of an ice cream on it.

'I told Roz all about you, you know,' Auntie Bev told me. 'I said you're a star in the making. That Quentin Tara-whatever-his-name-is would be glad to have you.' She sat down in the steel chair opposite me and clicked her tongue. 'And that I'd send her a top-of-the-range sinus irrigator free of charge.'

She winked. I didn't really get it but the way she was smiling made my heart beat really fast. I felt like I could breathe deeper than I ever had before. She flipped open the plastic menu and had a good long look.

'What do you fancy, Alex? A jacket potato with beans and cheese? Or what about a nice omelette? You can get it with bacon and peppers.'

I shook my head. 'Onions on toast, please.'

Auntie Bev lowered the menu and stared at me as if she felt sick. 'Really, Alex?'

I nodded and she looked sad.

'I know you and your mum don't have much money, but while I'm here let me spoil you. I love you. Honest, I'll get you anything you want on this menu.'

'Onions on toast,' I said, nodding. 'It's the best thing ever.' And just then my stomach gave a big growl.

Auntie Bev's smile came back and she set down the menu. 'Well, maybe I'm missing out, then,' she said. 'I'll have that too, shall I?'

She got up to tell the lady behind the counter what we wanted and I felt glad that Auntie Bev was going to eat the same as me. When she sat back down she smiled and said, 'Good thing I keep after dinner mints in my bag.'

When she left I felt good for a while but then I started to feel bad. I think I've upset Anya and I don't really know how or why. I tried to explain to her that the questions were Ruen's but I was stupid to expect that she would believe me when *no one* believes me at all. I don't even know why I ever told anyone about him in the first place. I don't know why Ruen told me that I hurt myself when I didn't. When all the doctors and nurses talk to me now they speak to me like I'm either really stupid or like I'm carrying a knife or something. When I ask about Mum they don't look at my eyes and they say things like, 'Oh, don't you be worrying about your mother,' and, 'Now, Alex, just you be patient while your mum pulls herself round. Why don't you get some sleep?' I just want to get out of here and check that she's OK.

I'm not going back to my old school for a while and when I leave hospital I am going to a new school at a place called MacNeice House. Just for a while and then Mum and I will move into our amazing new house. Anya showed me some pictures and kept saying I'd love it but I'm not so sure. It looks like a hospital on the inside but on the outside it looks like a posh house where you would expect servants and maids and things like that. I've been given homework until then but I feel like someone's attached a vacuum cleaner to my skin and sucked out all the energy. When I sit up it feels like the whole room wobbles and my head feels like an enormous cannon ball so that I have to keep putting my hands around my cheeks to hold it in place.

When the nurse brings me lunch she asks me what I'm doing.

I look up and say, 'My head is going to fall off.'

I think she might laugh but she actually runs out of the room, leaving my food tray too far away for me to reach, and I hear her shoes clacking all the way down the hall. When I look down, my bed is covered in vomit and my nails have blood in them from where I was scratching my neck. I don't remember being sick or scratching myself.

I'm starting to feel very strange, not like me at all.

When I wake up again my bed is clean and I am dressed differently. I can see my shirt and trousers hanging in the open locker in the corner. It's raining cats and dogs outside, Auntie Bev would say, and I imagine what it would be like if it really was chucking down kittens and Rottweilers.

I'm thinking of the RSPCA when someone comes into the room. I think it's a nurse and am afraid to say anything in case she gets scared again, but then I look up and see it's Ruen. He's Ghost Boy. He glances out of the door and holds a finger to his lips to tell me, 'Sshh.' I nod and about a second later a doctor comes in. He is holding a clipboard.

'How are you feeling, Alex?' he says.

'Fine,' I say. He puts two fingers against my wrist and looks at his watch and says nothing for a while. Then he puts a stethoscope under my robe. It makes me shiver.

'Any breathing problems?' he asks. I shake my head.

A nurse comes in and wraps a piece of material around my arm then squeezes a small black ball until the material gets really tight. 'One twenty over eighty,' she tells the doctor, and he writes it down. He nods and asks, 'Temperature?' The nurse says something I can't really hear but the doctor writes it down, too.

'OK,' the doctor says.

'Can I go now?' I ask.

This is apparently really funny.

'No,' the doctor says, handing me a cup with tablets in it. 'You have to take two of these twice a day for the next wee while. We need you to stay here to make sure they're doing their job.'

I frown at the round white tablets in the cup. 'What are they for?' I ask.

The doctor looks down at me through his glasses. The nurse says, 'To help you sleep better, Alex.'

'But I sleep fine,' I say.

The nurse smiles and hands me a cup with some water. I hold both cups in my hands and stare up at the nurse and doctor. Finally, the nurse says: 'Dr Molokova says you've to take them.'

She's says it like I should already know this. 'Who's Dr Molokova?'

'Anya?'

'Oh.'

I put the tablets in my mouth and they taste very bitter so I drink the whole cup of water in one go. She hands me a tray of food. It looks like Woof vomited on my plate.

'What is it?' I ask.

'Toad in the hole,' the nurse says. 'You want peanuts or chopped apple for your snack?'

'Peanuts,' Ruen says loudly, and I jump. I ask her for the peanuts and she looks at me funny, then she nods.

'Dessert is either meringue or bread and butter pudding.'

I glance at Ruen. 'Bread and butter pudding, please.'

The nurse slides the tray on to the table next to me and walks out, humming.

'I don't want to stay here,' I tell Ruen.

'I don't blame you,' he says, looking out the window.

I glare at him. 'I'm not your friend, by the way.'

He looks quite shocked. 'Whyever not?'

My face is very hot all of a sudden and my hands are shaking. When I blink everything looks blurred for a second. 'Because you made me ask Anya those questions and she got very upset. I didn't want to make her upset and it's your fault.'

He smiles. 'It is not my fault that she was emotional. I simply needed to discover a little more about her, that is all.'

Eventually my face goes cold again and my hands go still. It happened last time I took the tablets but then it went away after a few seconds. So I swing my legs round and put my feet on the floor.

'Then why didn't *you* ask her the questions, huh?'

'She's trying to get rid of me, Alex,' he says, turning his head to the doorway. 'She's trying to convince you I'm not real.'

But I've heard it before. And I decide he's got a big problem with being a demon and not being able to be seen. Which, I think, is *his* problem, because if I can see him surely other people can, too.

'Why do you keep hiding from everybody?' I say.

And then one second he is scowling at me at the other side of the room and the next he is crouching down beside me, his face close to mine, snarling with little bubbles in the corners of his mouth.

'I *don't* hide,' he says. 'Do you think I *want* to be invisible, you stupid boy? Do you think it's *fun* not being seen for what you are or what you can do? How do you think ... *Max Payne* would feel if all his heroic deeds went unnoticed, eh? Or Batman?'

He stands up and walks away. I frown at him.

'Batman wears a costume,' I say.

He turns. 'What?'

'Batman wears a costume. All the superheroes do, to hide their real identity. It's part of why they're superheroes. They don't want the glory for all the stuff they do. They just want to do good things for people.' *Unlike you*, I think.

Ruen stares at me so long and with such wide eyes that I wonder if he's actually died on the spot and is about to fall over.

'Ruen?' I say after a while.

He starts to grin. Then he starts to clap. And then – this is what really shocks me – he walks towards me, rubbing his hands, then he reaches out and ruffles my hair.

'What a clever boy,' he says, which is daft really because just then he's a boy, too. Then he points at me and starts to laugh.

'Why does everyone think I'm so funny today?' I say. But Ruen is laughing so much he can't speak. He walks up to the mirror above the sink and looks at himself. He straightens his back and looks dead chuffed with himself.

'A costume,' he says. 'Or a proxy.'

'What's a proxy?'

He turns to face me, still grinning like an eejit.

'You're no good to me in here, are you?'

'What?'

He shakes his head. 'Never mind. How badly do you want to see your mum?'

'*Very* badly,' I say.

'Right,' Ruen says, and clasps his hands together. 'Follow me.'

I get out of bed and immediately feel like I am on a ship. 'Steady now,' Ruen says, and I close my eyes and count the number of bones in an adult ribcage in my head and then I open my eyes and feel better.

'Grab your clothes,' Ruen tells me. I stagger to the open locker and pull on my shirt, trousers, shoes and blazer.

'Ready,' I say.

Ruen glances at my cap. 'You might be needing that. And your scarf,' he says. 'You'll catch your death outside. And then what would I do?' He starts to laugh.

Everybody else on the ward is asleep. At the end of the corridor Ruen holds a finger to his lips and I stop in my tracks, then hide behind a door as a nurse wheels a boy in a chair past me. Ruen gives a slight wave with his hand and I tiptoe after him. Ahead, I see the EXIT sign. I point at it. He shakes his head and tells me to follow him through a yellow door marked STAFF ONLY. When we get through that door there is a kitchen to my left and a fire exit to my right.

'Push,' Ruen says.

I lean against the bar across the door and push. And, easy-peasy, I am outside.

It is pitch-black and the rain is so thick I can hardly see through it. This kind of rain is like chain metal, I think. From here I can see the building that Mum is in, a tall white building with a thin bit at the top that occasionally flashes a blue light at night. It's about a ten-minute walk to Mum's building and already I am soaked right through my clothes. I decide to run. I run through the car park and then I see a lady in a long white coat walking towards me, so I duck behind a hedge and take a shortcut through a really muddy patch of grass. I keep the blue light in sight. Then, when the wind makes the rain come down sideways, I take off my coat and hold it around my head.

When I get to the front entrance I am panting like a dog. Ruen appears beside the door.

'You'll never get past the front desk looking like that,' he tells me. 'Besides, visiting hours are over.'

I frown. I am cold and tired and feel like if I fell over I'd probably stay there until someone stood on me.

'What should I do, then?'

Ruen shrugs and folds his arms like he couldn't care less. 'There is one thing,' he says finally, inspecting his fingernails like they're really interesting. 'But you have to promise to do something for me first.'

I am shivering now and my hair is dripping into my eyes and I can hardly speak. I am so cross with him for telling me to escape and then making me promise to do something else for him.

'Is it something to do with Anya?' I ask.

Ruen looks up from his fingernails and nods.

I feel a big wave of anger roll over me and I wrap my arms around my chest to keep warm. I'm shaking like I'm being electrocuted. 'Get stuffed, loser,' I say under my breath, because right now I hate his guts, and I turn around and start to walk through the curtains of rain towards my building.

Then Ruen appears right in front of me and I stop. My face is dripping wet and when I look up my eyes feel like someone's pouring a jug of water into them. He's Horn Head now, and I've never been this close to him when he's Horn Head. The red horn doesn't really look like a horn this close – it looks like it's liquid. I feel sick.

'It won't upset Anya,' he whispers in my head. 'It's a gift to her.'

'A *gift*?' I shout. 'Can't you see, you tosser – I haven't got any money! I'm only ten!' I keep my eyes on the ground and walk past him.

'Your mother needs you, Alex,' Ruen says in my head.

I feel a pain in my heart but I keep walking.

But just then, flashes of Mum rise up in my head: the last time I found her, curled up in her own sick on our bathroom floor, her head really limp and her tongue hanging out like a dog's. The time before that, when I walked into the kitchen and saw her at the sink, and I wondered why she was crying and chopping carrots, but she wasn't chopping carrots and the sink was full of blood. And the time before that, when I was gagging for the toilet and she wouldn't answer when I opened the door and she was in the bath, unconscious, her head about to go under the water.

And then I remember her watching me in the kitchen as I tried to make something called *gorgonzola and caramelised onion bruschetta* and then gave up and made onions on toast.

'You're so like him,' she said, leaning against the door frame.

'Like who?'

She looked at the food and smiled. 'Your dad.'

And then I think of coming out of the church that day when we were supposed to be practising for the school Christmas concert. We were singing 'Away in a Manger' and I remember I was fed up from standing so long and a teacher let me go to the toilet, but when I got there a big wind was coming through an open door and so I went outside.

On the street outside the church there were lots of shops

and people walking along the pavement. I saw a little girl eating crisps on the other side of the road and I thought maybe she'd give me some, but then I saw the policemen and I felt scared and then I saw the blue car. I had just wandered outside, right at the moment my dad arrived, like we were attached by an elastic band and turned up at the same time at the same place. I never told anyone I had seen him, not even Mum. I don't even think Dad knew I was there. I remember what people said at the policemen's funeral, that the man who killed them was evil and someone said he should burn and the policemen's wives were so sad and the little girl would grow up without a daddy.

And then something else rises up in my head, and when it does I know it's been buried in my brain for ages, like a needle that's been stuck in a chair and poking people in the bum all that time but they didn't know what was hurting them.

It's my dad, shaking something heavy out of a black shiny bag and putting it inside the piano where there should be strings. I remember he was wearing a blue T-shirt and I can see his tattoo on his arm, the one with just letters. I couldn't read then because I had just started school so I asked him what it said. He told me and I said, 'What?'

He smiled. 'It's a group, Alex. It's a group of men who believe in freedom.'

'And killing,' Mum said from the kitchen.

I was puzzled.

'Are you in that group?'

My dad put the last thing in the piano and shut the lid. 'Yep,' he said. 'And my dad was, and his dad, and his dad before that.'

In my head there was a big line forming of men I was linked to. Now that link reaches to me, only it's not something I'm sure I want any more, and it's like the link has split in two and it feels like I'm splitting down the middle.

I drop to my knees in the mud and start to cry. I cry so hard and the wind is so loud that I am able to scream out all the pain from way down in my belly and I know no one can hear me.

When I open my eyes, Ruen is still there, but he's back to being the Old Man. I sigh in relief.

'What sort of gift?' I ask, wiping my eyes.

'Follow me,' he says.

Ruen leads me to a side door at the back of the building where Mum is staying. Another fire exit. I try the door but it is locked.

'Be patient,' Ruen says, and steps back. I take a few steps back too and wait at the corner. A few moments later, two nurses come outside. Just as the door swings shut I run forward and catch it. Then I slip inside.

I spot a toilet to my left and go have a pee, then use lots of paper towels to dry out my hair and clothes. By the time I finish I see that Ruen isn't there. I open the door and look outside.

'Ruen?' I hiss.

There's no answer.

I step into the corridor. Still no sign of him. My fingers wriggle like worms at each other and I feel my neck and cheeks get hot. How am I supposed to find Mum now?

I walk down the corridor, digging my squirmy hands in my pockets and keeping my head down. Nobody seems to be about. My heart is racing and I feel sick.

At the end of the corridor is a list of signs. I scroll down the list and feel very confused. Where is Mum again? Then I see the word *Psychiatry* and it looks familiar so I follow the arrow.

The arrow takes me down another long corridor, at the end of which are women's voices. I stop at the corner and wait until I hear the voices stop, then walk very quickly round the corner.

'Can I help you?'

I freeze. There is a long reception desk right there with the sign PSYCHIATRY hanging above and a blonde fat woman in a nurse's uniform sitting behind it.

'Uh,' I say. I look around for Ruen.

'Are you lost?' the woman says. I nod. 'You shouldn't be here.' She tuts. She starts to get up from her seat to come around the desk to me.

I see my chance. I know Mum is just down the ward in a room to the right, four doors down, so I run past the woman and she yells 'Hey!' but I keep going until I reach the room. I push against the door but it is locked, so I stand on my tip-toes and look in through the small glass window.

I can see Mum inside. Her yellow hair is spread across the pillow and her face looks thin and she is fast asleep. I pound the door with my fists and yell, 'Mum!' but she doesn't wake up. 'Mum!' I yell again. *'Mum! Mum! Mum! Mum!'*

Then all of a sudden there are two men beside me grabbing me by the arms and I yell, 'Mum! I love you!' and I see her open her eyes and look around but she doesn't see me.

I don't remember much after that. I know I cried and I begged them to let me see Mum and I bit one of the men on the side of his hand and then I ran but they caught me and threatened to thump me if I did it again.

They took me to another reception area where a security guard was waiting and he asked for my address. I told him, but instead of taking me back home to Auntie Bev he took me all the way back to the building I'd come from.

This time, when they put me in my room, they locked the door.

I got into bed, pulled the sheets around me, and shivered and stared for ages.

A long time later, Ruen showed up. He was still the Old Man.

'Alex,' he said, smiling as if he'd really missed me or something. I ignored him. He sat down by my feet and looked at me.

'How was your mother?'

I said nothing.

'Alex, do you remember that I organised a beautiful home for you and your mother to move into once you both recuperate?'

I thought of the pictures of the house Anya had brought

me, the big back garden and kitchen. I felt excited at the thought of it but didn't want him to see, so I just nodded.

'And you said you would do something for me if I helped you find your mother this evening?'

I looked at him and glared. He could take a big hike off the tallest cliff.

'Well, I already told you that the something would be a gift to Anya. But there's something else now. For your mum.'

'Don't you *dare* talk about my mum,' I shouted. 'I didn't get to see her. The door was locked. Now they'll *never* let me see her!'

He swiped the air with his hand. 'Oh, they will. You'll see. Just wait until tomorrow morning, Anya will ensure that you get your visit. This is why we need to give her the gift.' He paused. 'And if you give her this gift from me, I'll do something else for you, too.'

'What *gift*?'

He stood up, glanced at the sketchpad in my locker and said, 'Have you got a ruler?'

I nodded.

'And a pencil?'

'Yeah?'

He turned to face me, all serious. 'I have composed for Anya a piece of music. She loves music so this will undoubtedly be a delight for her. It is composed in precisely the sort of style she prefers. When Beethoven and Mozart composed their opuses they always dedicated them to their friends, like Prince Karl von Lichnowsky and, on one occasion, Napoleon. I believe

Anya should be pleased to possess a piece of music that is not only dedicated to her, but written especially for her. What I require from you is to write it out for me exactly as I dictate.'

I stared at him. 'Whatever. What about the thing you'll do for my mum?'

He sat down, coughed and lowered his eyes.

'Has your mother ever mentioned your father, Alex? I mean, since he died?'

'No, but she was really upset about it, that's what landed her here in the first place. So if you think I'm going to bring that up—'

Ruen held up a hand. 'No, no. What I was going to suggest was . . . well, you may as well know.'

'Know what?'

He looked away and sighed very deeply. 'Your father is in Hell.'

I felt like I'd just walked into a wall.

'In *Hell*?'

'In the worst part of it, I'm afraid.'

My mouth opened and I went to speak but no sound came out.

'What's wrong, Alex?' Ruen asked, and I shook my head because I couldn't talk right then because my head was too full of memories about Dad. I remembered him coming to see us one day and he had a floppy black mask in one hand and a big heavy black bag in the other, and when Mum saw it she looked scared.

'You can't keep that stuff here,' she'd said.

Dad threw her a wink and headed towards the piano in our hall. He lifted the lid and set the bag inside and the piano made a sound even though no one touched the keys.

'What's in the bag?' I'd asked at the time.

'Nothing you need to worry about,' Dad said, and he ruffled my hair and lit a cigarette and told Mum she looked beautiful, and all the worry in her face went away.

And then I thought of the black mask and the blue car and the policemen. And I remembered what had happened after that. I remembered that Mum had cried and cried the day after and I knew that Dad had died. His face was in the newspapers and Mum warned me not to tell *a single soul* that he was my dad because then we'd be split up as a family and the headlines called him a *monster* and *evil* and said he should *rot in Hell.*

'Dad's really in Hell, isn't he?' I said to Ruen.

He gave me a long look that told me I was right.

I felt sick. Mum would be very, very upset if she knew this. I pulled the covers around my face.

'Oh, worry not.' Ruen groaned. 'You write this piece for me as a gift to Anya, and I'll release your father from Hell.'

I let go of the covers. 'You can do that?'

He looked very offended. 'Of course I can. Don't you think that would make your mother very happy, knowing he isn't in Hell? And I'm most certain your father would be grateful, too.'

'So he'll go to Heaven?'

Ruen grinned so wide I thought his face might crack.

Then I had a thought. 'Why did you write music for Anya?'

Ruen narrowed his eyes. 'The title is "A Love Song For Anya", my boy. Doesn't that give you a clue?'

'But you don't love Anya,' I said. 'You don't love anybody. You're a *demon*.'

Ruen sniffed. 'Penetrating as always, Alex. The simple truth is that reality lurks in the senses. If we are to prevent Anya from separating you and I then we must make her question what she believes to be real. Your questions have already begun that process, but what she *hears* when she plays this piece of music will surely finalise her self-questioning.'

'What the heck does *that* mean?' I said.

'Have we a deal?' Ruen said.

I chewed my nails. I thought of Mum lying in that room, all by herself. She looked very small in the bed. I wouldn't be able to tell her what Ruen had done for Dad, as she'd probably be very freaked out. But maybe, in a few years, I could. And she would be over the moon.

I nodded. 'Deal,' I said.

20

A Love Song For Anya

Anya

I grab a coffee on my way to the City Hospital. I go into the consultant office and look over Alex's recent notes. Observations during administration of Risperidone seemed fine, except for one, tiny, microscopic detail:

Last night, Alex ran away.

He made it all the way out of the building, across the court-yard and into the adult unit, where he subsequently pounded on his mother's door and sunk his teeth into a security guard.

I close my eyes and try to fill my head with the sights and sounds of the Caribbean. This is bad, bad news. It suggests problems with the security in this place, for certain, but it also indicates Alex's instability and a whole swathe of negative reactions to his treatment. It will also look very bad on my report.

I look up to find Dr Hargreaves, a cognitive behaviour therapy specialist who works at MacNeice House two days a week, standing in the doorway of the office.

'Alex is your patient, isn't he?' Dr Hargreaves says, glancing down his spectacles. We've spoken only a handful of times, and from the direction of previous chitchat I'm aware that he thinks I'm a psychotic disorder fascist.

'Yes, he is,' I say.

He nods. 'And you *do* know one of the side effects of Risperidone is akathisia?' Akathisia is extreme restlessness. I swallow, and he sees. It's entirely doubtful that akathisia would have made Alex go to such lengths, but the possibility makes me feel ill.

I head to the interview room. Alex is seated in a daffodil-yellow armchair beside the shatterproof coffee table, his ankles crossed and hands pressed inside his thighs. He looks very on edge.

'Hello, Alex,' I say cheerily. 'Sorry I'm a little late this morning. Did you sleep OK?'

He shakes his head, still looking down.

'No? Is that why you went for a walk?'

He shakes his head.

'Why *did* you go for a walk, then? And at three in the morning, I might add. Were you just sick of being in hospital?'

He looks up at me. His eyes are tired and hollow. 'I want to tell you something,' he says, ignoring my questions.

'OK,' I say, following his lead. I take out my notepad. He looks at it for a long time.

'Is this bothering you, Alex?'

He shakes his head. 'I don't care if you write it down or not. I just want you to listen.'

I set my pen down. He takes a deep breath.

'I know that you think I'm a danger to myself. But Ruen is real. And I have proof.'

He hands me a piece of paper. It is a piece of music with the title 'A Love Song For Anya' written at the top. The lines, notes and clefs are very awkwardly drawn, with evidence of much rubbing out and rewriting. But there is precision in its composition. There are accurate phrase marks, a time signature and octave sign, and at two points Italian terms are used: *andantino* and *appassionato*. A quick scan through the music indicates that it isn't a love song in the ballad sense.

But there is something else that causes my mouth to go dry, before I tell myself that it's nothing more than a coincidence: the opening melody is identical to the one Poppy composed on the night she died. A high B for three beats; a trilled A, G, A, each of them crotchets; another B for three beats; A, G, A; then a G for three beats; A for three; B again – a simple melody, and one that has passed through my head many times over the last four years, as if it held the secret to what happened the night she died.

'Where did you get this?' I ask him.

'Ruen told me that he composed it for you because you like music. He told me to write it down for you as a gift.'

'As a *gift*?'

He nods. 'He said it's only a short piece because I couldn't manage to score a whole symphony, not yet.'

Alex's voice is less animated than usual, and there is a firmness to his tone and manner that makes him seem to have aged several years since our last meeting. He seems reluctant, not excited, to show me what he's written. I stare at the piece of music. Alex leans forward and looks me straight in the eye.

'You ask my mum,' he whispers, his eyes darting around him. 'I don't know how to play music, never mind write it. I can't play any instrument at all. I can't even sing. So how would I be able to write that then, eh?'

I put our interview on hold until after his schooling session with a private tutor. I run outside, dial Michael's number, and leave a message on his phone to call me as soon as possible. He needs to know about Alex's escape attempt.

Just as I am redialling his number, my phone rings. It is Michael.

'Why is Alex on Risperidone?' are his first words. Aggressive and concerned at the same time.

'Did you know he attempted to run away last night?'

'Of course I do,' he snaps. 'The hospital told me to come in first thing. I'm worried that we're being over-zealous with the medication, Anya. The last kid I saw with a Risperidone prescription was eighteen and wiped off his face . . . '

'Alex's condition requires medical intervention,' I say levelly. 'Cindy shows no sign of getting out of the psych unit anytime soon. Would you wait a week before treating a broken leg?'

'Well, you should know that Cindy isn't doing so well,' he

replies stiffly. 'Not since she heard she'd been deemed incapable of acting as Alex's mother.'

That's not my fault, I think, then immediately feel guilty. I have had less than nine hours sleep over the last three nights – a combination of stress and playing catch-up with my other cases. I would do anything right now for a long, hot bath and a comfortable bed.

'I'm going to speak to Cindy later this afternoon.' I say. 'And there's something else.'

'What?'

'Has Alex ever had piano lessons?'

'Not that I'm aware of. Why?'

I mention Ruin's 'gift'. I tell him that, as a pianist, I am astonished by its complexity. Even if Alex *has* had some musical training, this is quite a coup. More importantly, the piece makes me wonder if Ruin is more than a projection – if he is a living person with whom Alex is having regular contact, and who is genuinely threatening his well-being.

'Where are you?' Michael says after a pause.

'Still at the adult unit.'

'Stay where you are.'

Ten minutes later, he's striding towards me across the car park. I expect him to follow me inside and grab a coffee while we kill time until I can speak to Cindy, but he tells me to get into his car.

'Where are we going?' I ask.

He keeps his eyes away from mine. 'I've arranged for us to

speak to someone at the School of Music over at Queen's University.'

'Why?'

'You said you wanted to prove whether Alex could have written it. Didn't you?'

'No, I . . . ' I tail off and glance at his car, parked badly on the kerb close by. 'What was all that about the other night, Michael?'

'You mean Alex?'

'*No*. You stroking my face.' I feel embarrassed questioning it, but I hate ignoring what must be confronted.

'Aye, there's the rub,' he says with a broken grin. 'Look, I was just worried about you, OK?'

'*Worried?* I said I was just getting some fresh air . . . '

I let him find the words he was searching for on the ground. When he looks up, his expression is sad. 'It won't happen again,' he says slowly. 'I promise.'

We head in Michael's car to the School of Music at the university, directly behind the botanical gardens.

'How's the running?' Michael asks.

I think of the fresh blisters on my soles from new track shoes, the suspicious bulge of fluid in my knee that suggests another steroid injection is due this year. 'Not nearly as exciting as keeping an allotment,' I tell him.

I notice a flash of colour in his cheeks at the mention of his allotment. He proceeds to tell me how his Green Windsor broad beans got blackfly and a rogue cockerel from a neighbouring patch took umbrage on his beetroot; how he's taken up horse riding just so he can collect manure and take it home afterwards ('Couldn't you just clean out the stables?' I ask, to which he responds, 'I'm too polite to take it without paying *something*'); how his new potatoes were in his belly an hour after being in soil.

I find my mind turning to my paternal grandmother, Mei, whose English was limited to the phrase she used often: *my yin and yang*, the balance of my life. She would say Michael is my yang, my opposite. The one who has been sent to teach me, and vice versa. Listening to him describe his rundown shed, Sundays spent up to his knees in compost, I feel the habits of my own life – a Waitrose basket filled with plastic-wrapped, pre-washed organic vegetables, a rented flat on a twenty-eight-day notice tiled from floor to ceiling, the ability to unclip myself from the artificial wall of twenty-first century life and drop into another at any moment – lose their appeal. The other night I dreamed I woke up in a solar-powered, wind-tur-bined house built entirely of wood, mud and straw on an island in the Hebrides, my plate filled with produce from my own garden. Five years ago this would have been a nightmare. Now, to my astonishment, it feels the kind of life I would embrace.

Michael's friend is a beautiful Californian blonde lecturer in musical composition with a PhD in Bach's fugues and per-formance diplomas in oboe, tuba, piano and kettle drums. She has so many letters after her name that it reads like a sentence. She tells me to call her Melinda, and we follow her into her office.

Michael hands her Alex's piece of music. She puts on her spectacles and glances at it.

'Gee, written by a ten-year-old, you say?'

I fumble for the right explanation. 'Well, sort of,' I tell her. 'He says he wrote it on behalf of . . . an imaginary friend.'

Melinda raises her eyebrows. 'Wowee, some imaginary friend, huh?' She glances at Michael. 'Well, it certainly ain't anything I've ever seen before. Some influences, here.'

She uses a short but immaculately manicured fingernail to point these out. 'A little Chopin here,' she says. 'Maybe some Mozart in the closing bars. Of course, influence is highly subjective.'

She stands up, music in hand, and walks from behind her desk to an upright Yamaha piano against the far wall.

'You play it,' Michael says, nudging me. 'It's *your* song, after all.'

Melinda turns. 'Oh, you play? Be my guest.' She pulls out the piano seat and gestures for me to sit down.

I wring my hands. 'I'm a bit rusty.'

'Come on,' Melinda says, smiling and patting the seat. 'Don't be shy. Let's hear this masterpiece!'

The truth is, I feel extremely nervous about playing the piece. I've already heard the melody in my head by cold-reading the notes, but I'm not sure how I will feel when I play those eight bars out loud. Poppy's song. It's a feeling far beyond my professional rationale and it makes me very uncomfortable. A coincidence, I tell myself, but the memories of my previous sessions with Alex are churning in my head, the unsolved riddles of the things he seems to know about her.

Nonetheless, I get up out of my chair, take a seat in front of the piano, slide my fingers up the smooth white keys, and begin to play. I hold my breath as I chime out the opening melody, gritting my teeth against thoughts of Poppy's dark head behind the piano in our Morningside flat. When I get to the second section, I allow myself to breathe out and focus on the technique of the piece. There is a simplicity, an impishness and a determination to it that grips me as I perform it. The melody of the second half is demanding, lyrical, passionate. I glance at the title 'A Love Song for Anya'. Then I note the smaller text beneath it: 'From Ruen.' *Ruen*. I had always thought the name of Alex's so-called demon was 'Ruin'.

When I finish, Melinda and Michael applaud me.

'I liked that!' Michael says.

Melinda nods. 'A very talented performer.' She winks, then walks over to the piano and bends down to have another look at it. 'Kid isn't very good with annotation, though. Needs a little practice with his treble clefs . . . ' She turns to Michael. 'You want me to run this through our software, check if it's plagiarised?'

Michael nods. 'Definitely.'

Outside the School of Music there is a moment when we are due to part ways.

'You want a lift back to see Cindy?' Michael asks.

'It's not far. I'll walk.' I start towards the botanical gardens and Michael follows.

'I'm parked this way anyway.'

'Thanks for contacting Melinda. She certainly was helpful.'

He searches my face. 'Something about that piece bothers you, doesn't it.'

It isn't a question. 'I don't think you know me well enough to—'

'Is it because you think Ruen actually wrote it?'

I glance at a car trying to reverse park close to us. It backs so close that its reflection pours across the other's bonnet. We walk on.

'I wonder if Ruen is Alex's father?' I muse.

'A *demon*?'

'No, I mean, if Alex is actually visiting with his dad. If the physical violence he experienced was at the hands of . . .' I stop. The thought that Alex's father is not dead at all but has been meeting with him on the sly is ludicrous. But I have run out of answers. The music, the attack, the way he asked about my scar the first time we met . . . And then I think of Ursula. Her urge for me to abandon labels.

We are at the foot of the botanical gardens now. A woman is jogging with two Dalmatians trotting alongside her. Michael sidesteps behind me so that he is between me and the dogs.

'OK,' he says, pushing his hands in his pockets and grinning. 'So let's consider the possibility. *Is* Alex seeing demons?'

I turn to read his face. He is serious. This is a side of Michael I haven't yet encountered. How could this intelligent, perceptive man even consider that there is such a thing as demons, that there is even the slightest possibility that someone could see them?

'You're kidding?'

We are close to the hothouses. Michael takes a step in front of me, tilting his head slightly to draw my attention away from the group of students.

'When I studied for the priesthood I did a lot of research into belief narratives. I read a lot of things by people who claimed they'd seen the unbelievable – angels, demons, God, what have you. People who said they thought they'd seen demons with forked tails, then realised that these tails were links that gradually grew fatter, binding them to the demon, destroying them.' He pauses. 'Crazy.'

'What made you so interested in that stuff?'

He takes his hands out of his pockets and gestures at a seat facing the green lawns of the university. We sit down. He takes a breath and combs his hand through his hair.

'I saw my sister when I was little. My parents have never spoken about her. I only found out she even existed last year. My nan let slip that there'd been complications during my birth because of the other dead baby inside my mother.' He leans close to me to avoid anyone else overhearing this sensitive conversation. I sense that he is offloading something that has made him feel lonely for a long time.

'I grew up knowing I had a sister named Lisa,' he continues, 'because *she* told me. I knew that she looked just like me, only she was a girl, and that only I could see her. My parents took me to psychologist after psychologist, changed my diet, and then when I was about eight and they were getting really sick of it, my dad threatened to put me through a glass window if I mentioned Lisa again. He said she wasn't real. One way or another, I stopped seeing her.' He chews his cheek. 'But I know she was real. She was.'

I nod, aware that I am probably the only person he has ever told about this, and I wonder why. I don't ask – instead, I choose a response that fits within the boundaries of our professional relationship.

'Is that why you studied psychiatry?'

'Sort of. Probably. I just . . .' He pauses, clarifying his thoughts. 'I suppose I needed to understand what the difference was between seeing things of a spiritual nature and having a mental health issue, you know?'

'You needed to explore whether you had a dissociative disorder as a child or were playing with the ghost of your twin.'

'Bingo. And here's the thing: I'm an atheist with agnostic tendencies.'

'Yet you were going to be a priest?'

'There's a whole difference between the religious and cultural motivations behind that career path. Few of the guys I met on that route were convinced of the great gig in the sky, ya know?'

'I guess both career paths are about believing in the unseen.'

'I know I saw my sister,' he says firmly. 'Mentally ill or not . . . you say "tomato", I say "tomayto".' He grins, his invisible guard of aloofness returning. 'I think there's just some things you can't explain away by science.'

'You think Alex is *really seeing something*?'

'Did *Hamlet* see the ghost of his father?'

'It's a *play*, Michael . . . '

He looks at me, reaching out to touch my arm. 'I'm not saying he's channelling the dead, Anya. There's got to be a reason why Alex has latched on to such a specific identity. What did Poppy claim to see?'

I think back to the moment that Poppy had tried to describe what it was like to be her. We were in a restaurant close to the Golden Mile in the centre of Edinburgh, her favourite place for steak. I wanted to break the news to her gently, in an environment where she felt comfortable and happy: she was going to spend two months at the Cherrytree Haven Child and Adolescent Inpatient Facility.

'The doctors say that you'll have your own room there, Poppy,' I told her. 'You'll be home at weekends. There's a swimming pool, a park outside, and lots of other kids.'

I swallowed. Despite training as a child psychiatrist, my professional expertise only got me so far when it was my *own* twelve-year-old daughter on the receiving end of treatment. The thought of leaving my little girl in a psychiatric unit for two months was heartbreaking, but I had absolutely no reservations that it was in her best interests.

But she had started to sob. I noticed her grip the sides of the chair, her face turning pale.

A waitress approached with two plates.

'Who's got the medium-rare?'

I looked from the waitress to Poppy. 'I'm *falling*, Mum,' she said, her voice rising to a shriek. 'Why aren't you helping me?'

I should have listened. I should have taken more time to understand . . .

People had started to stare. 'Is everything OK?' the waitress asked, and I nodded, bundling my wallet and phone into my handbag and searching for a quick way to drag Poppy out of there without too much ruckus.

'You don't understand what it's like,' she'd shouted. 'What this *feels* like, Mum! Have you ever even *asked* what this feels like?'

No, my love. Tell me now.

'Poppy, it's time to go home,' I whispered.

'*No.*' Her voice was firm, threatening.

The waitress stared, the plates in her hands like cymbals.

'Come on, Poppy,' I said, a little firmer this time.

And that was when she grabbed a steak knife from the table and plunged it into my face.

It could have been worse. She told me later she was aiming for my throat.

*

I step out of the memory. It takes a moment to untangle myself from its dark hooks. Her absence is a continual ringing in my ears of all the things I should have said to her, all the things I should have done.

Michael has said something to me. I raise my eyes to his, and he repeats it.

'I said I'm worried that you see Poppy in Alex,' he says. 'I know what it's like when a case hits close to the bone. At times like that you have to be sure you're keeping the right amount of distance. It's only human to get involved.'

Ironically, he says 'the right amount of distance' just as he takes a step closer to me, reaching out to touch my arm. I look down at his hand, and he draws it back as if his fingertips have brushed something hot.

'Sorry,' he mumbles, but for some reason my mind is turning to a moment of my past, a memory that strikes me as odd to rise up just then. I am in the kitchen of my Morningside flat, ironing Poppy's school shirt. *Keep your distance*, I tell her.

'What did you say before?' I ask Michael, my voice a whisper. He has stepped back now, unsure of what to do with his hands.

'When? About Alex?'

'When you asked about the reason he claims to see Ruen.'

He blinks. 'I said he was channelling the dead.'

'You said he *wasn't* channelling the dead.'

He looks on, his face full of confusion.

My darling, I'm sorry. I'm sorry ...

Words I can never tell her now. Unless ...

I smile at Michael and start to walk away. A thought has snagged itself on my heart. A thought that should not have arrived there in the first place.

What I wouldn't give to tell you I'm sorry.

Not a thought.

A temptation.

21

HELL

Alex

Dear Diary,

What do you call a boy with sticky-out ears, a wonky nose
and no chin?
  Names.

I started at my new school on Monday. It's a bit crap, just like
that joke. MacNeice House is like a boarding school in that
I have to sleep there and even though my new bedroom is
bigger than the one at Mum's house, I don't like it. It's all
white and the windows don't open and someone said the
doors are built so that if you try and hang yourself they'll fall
down. I run through all the doorways now just in case they
fall over, which makes the other kids laugh.

My bedroom in the new house will be cool though so I suppose it's OK in the meantime. Most of the teachers here aren't very friendly, though I like one of them. She's called Miss Kells, and she smells like a second-hand bookshop but she seems nice. She's my personal tutor and she meets with me after school every day in my bedroom for one hour. I get to go to her if I have any problems and we talk about stuff like maths and 2B pencils and *Hamlet*. Our classes only have ten other kids in them, which is cool because it's quiet and no one makes fun of me. But nobody talks to each other and some of the other kids are psycho. One of the girls is a year older than me and she says we're actually in a zoo and that there's a tiger on the desk and stuff like that. Yesterday she said I couldn't sit on the seat behind her cos there was a giraffe on it and I looked at Ruen to check there wasn't and he just rolled his eyes and yawned.

I'm really glad to have Ruen around because I miss so many things now, not just Mum. I miss waking up in the middle of the night and finding Woof asleep on my head. I miss onions on toast. I miss the way our tap drips all night and sounds like a heartbeat. I miss Auntie Bev and Jojo and the Opera House. I miss the way Mum wiggles her toenails on the footstool when she's drinking tea and watching *Coronation Street*. I miss Mum even when she's sad. I miss our house, even though there are no broken windows in this place and it's clean and warm.

I asked Ruen if Mum and I are going to lose the new house since Bev has gone home and there's no sign of Mum getting out soon, and he said that it was up to Anya now because she'd put me in here and even though Ruen could help me escape, I'd have nowhere else to go. For a moment, I thought, *Why don't I just go home and you can look after me?* But then I remembered that Ruen is a demon and he can't really do normal things, like cook and clean. Which is a pity.

Though I'm all excited and freaked out and curious about my dad. What was it like getting freed out of Hell? Is he really really happy? Is he grateful? Is he in Heaven or somewhere else? I really don't understand the afterlife, and when I ask Ruen about it he doesn't like to talk about it too much, particularly Heaven. He says it is *overly conceptualised and idealised* and that Hell is *pejoratively dismissed* and gets *bad press*.

Every time I ask about death he looks at me as if I'm stupid.

'It's the *end*, dear boy,' he says, tutting. 'No more body. No more chocolate cake. There are some advantages, but it depends where you end up.' And then I ask about where I might 'end up' and he starts going on about the *idealisation* of Heaven and the *denigration* of Hell.

Tonight, however, I want to ask him about my dad. I've never really found out much about how or why my dad died. I didn't go to his funeral and Mum has never taken me to his grave, and she has no pictures of him in the house. I'm not to tell anyone about him, she said. Only his name, because it's also my name. Alex. When I think of whether Dad is happy to be out of Hell I have a memory of me and Dad and Mum having dinner. We were sitting at our table in the living room and Mum brought in some bread rolls on a plate. Dad took two of them out and stuck his fork through one and his knife through the other and started bouncing them up and down the table as if they were feet doing a little dance. I remember the way the sunlight was strong and lit up the side of his face and the lines at the corners of his eyes when he laughed. I remember Mum flicking him with a tea towel, laughing and telling him to stop. She used to laugh loads back then.

When I think of this it makes me sad, but more confused than sad. I'm confused because when I think of him making the bread rolls dance and then I think of what I saw that day, of Dad shooting those policemen, it just doesn't make sense. Aren't evil people evil all the time? Aren't funny, kind people who bring toy cars for their son funny and kind all the time?

I was sad for a long time when I learned Dad had died. He just vanished one day, right after what happened at the checkpoint. I never asked Mum if he fell down a mineshaft or got run over or got the disease that Granny had because she was so upset all the time. She just cried and cried one morning and said, 'Your dad's gone,' and I said 'For how long?' and she said, 'For life.'

And then she went upstairs and didn't come down, which I thought was weird because I needed her to walk with me to school because I was only five. So I waited for about two hours, then went upstairs, checked the bathroom, then Mum and Dad's bedroom, and she was in bed. I gave her a push and shouted *Wake up!* but she didn't move. So I pulled all the covers off and stomped my feet and clapped my hands and tickled her feet. And then I noticed some boxes under the duvet covers. I knew what they were for because I was with Mum when she picked them up from the doctor's. All the pills were gone and I felt funny, like scared. Then Mum started coughing and I felt my heart pound because I was glad she made a noise. 'Have you woke up now?' I said, but she just leaned across and puked all over my feet.

I remember I ran downstairs and opened the front door by standing on the piano stool and ran all the way to Granny's. I told Granny that Mum was sick and there were white boxes in the bed sheets and that I was really hungry. Granny's face went shocked and her eyes were sad and wide and she told me to go make myself some toast and she made a phonecall, and then she walked quickly with me back to our house but instead of letting me go inside she said, *Go to school, go to school.* I went to school but I had a knot in my stomach the whole way which got tighter and tighter. And that was the day I first saw Ruen.

'Ruen,' I say now. I can only say his name when I'm sure that no one is around to hear me, which isn't very often. He is sitting on my bed and I am sitting on the floor of my room doing maths homework. When he's the Old Man he is starting to sit more and more, like he's tired. When he walks he sort of drags his feet and his scowl is becoming so pronounced that it's like his face is melting. After a few moments he looks up.

'What?'

'So did you get my dad out of Hell yet?'

He grunts.

'Is that a yes?'

He grunts again, and then starts to cough. He thumps his chest. 'Course I did.'

I sit upright. 'You did?' My heart is knocking in my chest and I feel like I need to pee. 'So what happened? Did you have to, like, break him out of there? Was there a big fight?'

He coughs once more. 'Yes, yes, all of that.'

My mind is racing now. I see Hell in my mind, a red, fiery place with loads of people. There is lots of screaming, and it's a city, only the city walls are pouring with orange lava and huge blasts of flame keep shooting out of windows, and there are creatures there like the demons I see all the time, only worse: these ones are like zombies with their flesh ripped off and blood pouring down their faces. Dragons are circling in the red sky and there's big black clouds of smoke there, too. I see Ruen striding towards a big black building with fire pits burning around the front door. There are big mean security guards outside holding long spears and wearing full body armour. Their helmets have horns sticking up out of the top like a rhino, and their armour is studded with spikes. When Ruen approaches they cross their spears to prevent him from entering. He stares at them, and his eyes are red. He tells them he's a Harrower. They fall to their knees and tremble before him. He lifts his leg and kicks open the door.

Inside the building it looks like the biggest cathedral you've ever seen, all naked stone and gargoyles and a ceiling so high you almost fall over when you look up at it. There are vile creatures with vampire fangs shrieking and hiding and swiping out at him with their claws, but Ruen calmly proceeds towards the place where he knows my dad is being kept: the room at the top of the tallest tower. He has to duck and dodge past loads of creatures but eventually he gets there, and my dad is so grateful, and when Ruen tells him, 'Your son sent me,' Dad cries. And then Ruen fights his way out of there with my dad close behind, only at this point Ruen is starting to sound German and is wearing a leather jacket. Outside is a Harley Davidson motorbike. He and Dad jump on the back and ride off to Heaven.

'Whoa!' I say to Ruen. 'That's just like *The Terminator!*'

He looks at me, very confused.

'Wait ... did you fight Satan as well?' I say, standing up. 'Was he riding a dragon and did giant hailstones of hot coal come falling out of the sky?'

'What are you talking about?'

'Saving my dad!' I shout.

I hear footsteps walking quickly down the hall so I lower my voice. 'Was he really grateful? Did you tell him about me?'

Ruen looks down as if he's thinking about it. Eventually he stands and smiles. 'Your father was released from Hell yesterday, on my command, of course. He was extremely grateful to me and told me he would remain indebted to me for the rest of eternity. In fact, he said he hoped his son – you, Alex – would attempt to pay some of that debt in his stead by remaining faithful to me and assisting in my research.'

I stare at him. I haven't a clue what he's just said. I'm still buzzed that he's done what he said he would do. And I think about Katie then, of what her mum did. That Ruen was right all along.

'Will you, Alex?'

'Hmm?'

'Will you remain faithful to me and assist in my research, just as your father requested?'

'Yes. Yes, of course. So did my dad seem happy, then? Did he like Heaven and did he ask about Mum and were there angels in Heaven?'

Ruen grunts.

Then something occurs to me. Something I should have told Ruen to tell my dad.

'Did you tell my dad that I love him?'

Ruen's face looks like a knot. 'Did you wish me to?'

I nod and suddenly my buzz wilts a little, like a goal I almost scored but didn't. 'Maybe he already knows. Do you think so?'

He shrugs. 'How would I know?'

'Did you . . . just get a sense that he knew that I loved him? You know, because I sent you to get him out of Hell? Did it show in his face?'

Ruen's expression tightens even more. You could probably hide stuff in between the folds of skin. When I think of this I remember the time I hid a fiver behind the radiator in my room and I wonder if it's still there.

Ruen snorts and flares his nostrils. 'My dear boy, love is a very *human* thing. I know nothing of love,' he says. 'And, if I did, I should be very, very angry.'

I sweep my hand over my head to show that everything he's just said is a bit psycho. He looks at the door. For a minute I think he's going to leave and I suddenly feel like pleading with him not to. But he just sniffs and sits back down.

'You know, Ruen,' I tell him. 'In a way, you're like my dad, too. I don't mean that I don't love my dad, it's just ...' Suddenly I don't even know what I mean. 'I'm just glad you're here.'

Ruen raises one of his fuzzy white eyebrows and snorts. I climb into my bed and pull the covers around me. Just as I do this all the lights shut off and it is pitch-black. They do this every night, even though I hate the dark.

It makes me even more glad that Ruen is here.

22

THE COMPOSER

Anya

Yesterday I went to the adult psych unit to talk to Cindy about Alex's piece of music. She was incredibly reluctant to see me. I had presented myself to the nurse doing the medicine rounds and overheard their conversation through Cindy's open bedroom door.

There's a lady here to see you, Cindy. Dr Anya ...

A sigh. *Tell her I'm not well.*

She says it's about your little boy, Alex?

Why does she keep coming here?

After a few moments the nurse emerged from Cindy's room and told me I could go in.

Cindy was seated beside the window, glancing out at the

rain, tapping both feet in a kind of sitting jump. Her hair was unwashed, her nails bitten to stumps. I hovered at the threshold, waiting for her permission to enter.

'Hello, Cindy,' I said warmly. 'May I come in?'

'Please yourself,' she mumbled.

I lifted a chair by the bed and set it down close to her, though not too close. 'I know you have an art session,' I said. I went to take off my jacket, then thought better of it. 'I won't keep you late.'

She flicked her eyes at me. 'I'm not going to no daft art session.'

I paused. 'No?'

She bit her nails in response and fixed her gaze out the window, drawing one bony knee up to her chest. 'What you here for, then?'

I kept my voice light. 'I wanted to ask if Alex ever had piano lessons?'

'*That's* why you're here?'

I nodded.

She sighed. 'Not to my knowledge. Couldn't afford stuff like that, ya know?'

'You have a piano at home, don't you? Did either of you play it?'

'No. It was a family heirloom. Hadn't rung a note in years.'

'What about at school? Does Alex take music classes?'

'He's much more into building models of castles, stuff like that. *Boy* stuff.'

'So he couldn't have written this, then?' Tentatively, I produced the piece of music. Cindy took it from me and glanced at it.

'No,' she said after a pause. 'He's never written music.' She tapped the writing at the top of the page with her finger. 'It does *look* like Alex's writing, though. Can I have a closer look?'

'Take your time,' I said. She pulled the page nearer to the light from the window and leaned in to the page.

'Actually I'd say this *is* Alex's writing.' She looked up at me, puzzled and happy at once. 'Fancy that, eh? My boy, a composer. Not that I'm surprised.'

'Why doesn't it surprise you?'

She shrugged and changed legs, drawing the left knee up to her chin, visibly excited by what she was seeing. 'Alex has always done things beyond his age. Stuff I never taught him, he just picked up somehow. You'd never think he was my son.'

I nodded. 'Alex says someone else wrote this.'

'No, it's definitely his writing . . . '

'I know. Alex said he wrote the music down, but someone else composed the music and told him to write it.'

She looked confused, then gave a shrug. 'Well, if that's what Alex says, I'd believe him.'

I bit my lip. 'Even if Alex says that person was a demon?'

She must have misheard me. 'What's wrong with him copying some music out? Just because he didn't actually compose it doesn't mean he isn't clever . . . '

'I didn't say that . . . '

She thrust the music back at me, her face angry and scared. 'Here,' she said. 'Stop asking about our piano, all right? It's none of your business.'

I took the music and put it back into my briefcase. She watched me intently, her hands still restless.

'They don't let you smoke in here, do they?' I said.

Her face softened. 'No, they don't,' she said, shaking her head. 'I'd give you a kidney for one right now.'

I smiled and pushed at the diversion of her frustration from me to 'they'. 'If I had one, you'd be glad to it.'

'Thanks,' she said, smiling weakly. She let both knees drop down on the chair. Whatever emotion had been wound tight by my questions was visibly lessening its grip. I leaned down to pick up my briefcase.

'Still, you'll be out of here soon enough.'

She glanced at me. Something in her gaze made me stop mid-rise.

'Won't you?' I pressed.

She was back to chewing her nails. I sat back down in my chair, sensing she had something left to say. After a few moments, she leaned forward, her eyes furtive.

'You have kids, don't you?' she said.

'What makes you ask?'

She scratched her head. 'Trudy doesn't have any kids, so I don't think she understands. But you know what I mean, don't you?'

'About what?'

She pulled her chair closer. 'That sometimes it feels like

they're the parent and *you're* the child. You know? Like they have more answers than we do.'

'You mean Alex seems older than his years?'

'He's always been so independent. Like he didn't even need me.' At last, her hands settled on her stomach, at rest. She turned her head towards the window, glancing up at the clouds that had begun to darken and gather. 'I never wanted to be a mother. Not a nice thing to say, is it? Then when Alex was born I fell totally in love with him. I was his number one fan. He's so amazing I can hardly believe he came out of *me*.'

I listened carefully as the weight of her words settled into the silence. It was beginning to rain when I spoke. 'Cindy, I think you and Alex should take a little holiday when you get out of here.'

She looked puzzled for a moment. 'When I get out of here?'

I nodded. 'It doesn't need to be anywhere expensive. But I think it would be a good idea for the two of you to have some fun together. Have you ever had a day at the beach?'

She shook her head, then laughed. 'How crazy is that? Three miles from the beach and we've never been. Then again, it's never sunny, is it?'

'Even if it's *snowing*,' I said lightly, returning her grin. 'When you get out of here I think you should make spending time together a priority.'

She lowered her gaze. 'Yeah. When I get out of here.'

*

This morning I woke, having finally fallen asleep at five a.m. on the floor of my bedroom, with the sound of Alex's piece of music in my head. I had to play it. I had to hear Poppy in the notes, to feel her close again. No, not just to feel close – to find answers. The echo of her composition in Alex's piece had rung out a series of echoes that filled my small flat. When she was born, she didn't breathe for two minutes. The doctors were frantic, flapping between my legs with a suction machine, counting – *one, two, three, come on, sweetheart* – until finally a midwife plucked her up by the ankles, held her upside down and gave her back a firm pat. She screamed, and I felt as if a flood of relief had poured across me.

Now, the trauma of that moment had a new echo – was that what caused it? Had the lack of oxygen caused something in her brain to go wrong? Did schizophrenia lurk in my gene pool, hitting my mother then skipping over me to reach Poppy? Was it something I had done?

And what else could I have done to save her?

I checked my phone. Missed calls from Fi and Michael, and a number I didn't recognise. I tried calling it back, but to no avail. Then, with a moment's hesitation, I called Melinda.

'Hey!' she said after I'd greeted her. 'The maestro! How you doing?'

I asked if it would be all right if I used one of the practice rooms for an hour or so.

'Yes, yes, of course,' she gushed. 'Absolutely. Come on over and I'll get you booked in. We've a Steinway in the main practice room, how'd that be?'

'That's perfect,' I said, and hung up. My fingers were already restless. I was aching to play that music. I was searching for an answer, a missing piece of the puzzle, and I didn't even know the question.

I arrived at Melinda's office clutching a Coke and a chocolate muffin that was the size of a ball of Aran wool. I had decided that my period was due, that my hormones were raging, hence the reason I was slightly off-kilter. That, and a temporary fling with insomnia. Melinda made drooling motions at the sight of the muffin in the clear plastic bag and took me to the practice room.

It was empty, except for a piano stool and a shiny black Steinway grand piano. At the sight of the 'no food or drink' sign, I shoved my Coke and muffin into a bin nearby.

Melinda frowned. 'I wouldn't have said anything,' she said, but I shook my head. I had no appetite, I told her. I just wanted to play.

When she shut the door behind me I began with a few arpeggios to warm up my fingers. In the last four years I had stroked the keys no more than a dozen times. What intrigued me was that despite such neglect my hands retained the ghostly fingerings of the pieces I used to play over and over again. I could no longer remember the key of Rachmaninov's second piano concerto, nor could I see in my mind's eye the notes for Ravel's '*Pavane Pour Une Infante*

Défunte', but my fingers found their way to the right chords without hesitation. I felt like a puppet in reverse, my whole body tugged and jerked by the strings of the piano.

Finally, I unfolded Alex's piece of music from my pocket. Though the melody was echoing in my head, my fingers were unfamiliar with it. I scanned the piece again, the image of Poppy's head bent over our piano rising up in my mind.

I love you, Mummy.

I creased back the page until it leaned against the music stand, and slid my fingers on top of the notes. I began to play, an emphasis on the B of the right hand, a waltz in the left. I hadn't made it past the first bar when I stopped, lifting my touch an inch off the keys, my heart clanging in my chest at the echo of the music in the cold empty room.

Whatever memory had been stirred by those opening notes had not simply flashed a picture in my mind. This time, memory filled my veins, my skin alive with the softness of her skin when I held her for the first time, cheek to chest, her whole head fitting neatly in my palm. The sensation of it was so real that it shocked me. But it was tantalising, too. I laid my hands back on the keys and continued. This time, I felt the L-shape of her shoulder blades pressed into my palms as I held her after a fall from her bike, as if the music was a conduit between me and that moment, no distance of time, no dulling of feeling.

I played on.

Rising up in my wrists, into my arms and through my

whole body now was the warmth of her, moulded against me in my bed after a nightmare, her feet clasping mine, her smooth hair against my chin.

By the time I had finished the first section of the piece, my heart was running and yelling through the streets of my body.

I was a few bars from the end when there was a loud knock on the door. I stopped. 'Come in?'

Very slowly, the door opened.

I expected it to be Melinda, or a music student who had overlooked my name written on the booking sheet stuck to the front of the door. Instead, it was a small and very old man, bald, hunched, dressed in a tatty tweed suit with a yellowing shirt and brown bow tie. I went to explain that I had permission to use this room until the hour was up, but I stopped short, realising that something about him was intensely familiar. I struggled to place him. A deeply creased, grey face, his mouth jutting forward, bald, save for a thick, snow-white bunch of hair at the base of his head. He inched over the threshold, dragging his feet.

'Can I help you?' I said politely.

He stopped, straightened up slightly, and smiled. I jerked back. Even for a man of his years, he was distinctly repugnant.

'Your right hand is a little too staccato,' he said, his accent difficult to place.

'Didn't you heed the phrase marks?'

I turned to the piece of music in front of me. 'Do you mean this?' I said.

'I am the composer of the music you are playing.' He bowed deeply. 'I wished to introduce myself.'

I watched him as he turned and slowly closed the door behind him.

'*You* wrote this?' I said.

'But of course I did,' he said, stepping forward. 'Do you like it?'

I stood, baffled, the hairs on my arms standing on end.

'Who are you?'

He was circling the piano now, arms folded behind his back, stopping occasionally to peer inside it. I bent down to pick up my briefcase. When I looked up he was right in my face, suddenly tall enough to meet my eyes. Only, his eyes had no irises. They were solid, cataractous, like grey marbles. I gasped and took a step backwards.

'Anya,' he said, watching me inch away. '*Anya.*'

I could feel my heart pounding, my hands trembling. I glanced at the door.

'Would you like this piano?' he said, grinning. 'Or one like it?'

He was pacing round the piano once more, tracing the black wing with his twisted fingers. I stood perfectly still, my body cold, my mind struggling to work out what was happening.

'You said you wrote this piece?' I said, curiosity rising up in me despite the feeling of threat he had brought into the room.

'Aren't you going to play some more?'

'Someone else I know said he wrote it,' I said. The man looked at the sheet of music and grinned.

'Do you know Alex?' I asked, watching him carefully as I edged towards the exit.

He glanced up at the door. I swear I heard it lock.

'Just give me a moment of your time,' he said, sitting down in front of the piano. 'I promise you won't regret it.'

I could feel sweat prickling my back and under my arms, and I was telling myself to stay calm, to stop freaking out as he was at least seventy-five years old and if I could not defend myself against a man his age then twenty years of circuit training had been a waste of time. But it wasn't about physical combat. I felt myself being stripped, seduced somehow, and the light seemed to have dimmed, with shadows closing in on the corners of the room, thickening.

I remembered my mobile phone. My hands shaking, I fetched it out of my pocket and began to dial. A second later, the screen went black. The battery had died.

I looked up at him. 'Alex says you're a *demon*,' I said, the words sounding ridiculous in the heavy air. 'Not a nice thing to call a family friend, now, is it? Any reason for that?'

He sat down in front of the piano and smiled.

'You go to university for that, then?' I said, inching for the door.

In a flash, he was behind me, against the door, his face menacing. I let out a sob. Something was very, very wrong here. For a moment I believed I was having a psychotic meltdown, my hands shaking quite violently now, the ground beneath my feet turning to water.

'Are you all right?' I heard him say.

I felt myself curl up into a ball on the floor, levelled by a dragging sensation in my heart that has only ever seemed as heavy once before. I felt the moment at which I saw Poppy at the window, and I lunged forward, but once again I am a half-second too late, my hands empty, the momentum of my reach continuing in everything I do now – her absence a space of reaching.

And then, it stopped.

My eyes still tightly shut, it was as though someone had filled my body with sunlight. The darkness retreated. Again and again there was the sensation of heat travelling through me and around me. I felt myself lift as if someone or something had scooped me up, then I felt weightless.

In my mind's eye, I no longer saw Poppy at the moment of her death. I saw her anxious, beautiful face right in front of me, her hands on my shoulders, shaking me. *It's OK, Mum. I'm here. I'm right here.* I wanted to open my eyes but didn't in case she faded. Instead, I saw my own arms reach in front of me, cupping her face.

She turned her head slightly to kiss my hand.

Mum, you haven't lost me. It's all really OK, you know?

I pulled her to me in a tight embrace, my chest heaving with both relief and disbelief. Eventually she leaned back and looked at me. She seemed older, teenage, her chestnut hair so long now, draped around her face in Botticelli curls, her brown eyes calm and without fear. Without darkness.

Go back, now, she said. *I love you.*

When I opened my eyes, Melinda was standing over me, slapping my face and shouting my name. I felt myself take an enormous breath as if I had just surfaced from the depths of the ocean. My legs and hands were numb and my head fizzed like a bad hangover. I caught a strong whiff of Melinda's heavy patchouli perfume and landed back on Earth with a sharp thud. The look on her face melted from horror to sheer relief when I sat upright.

'Oh, man – sweetie, I thought you were dead!' she cried.

I shook my head to confirm that, despite how I may have looked, I was pretty much alive. My body was tingling now, as if I'd just emerged from a warm bath or a day in the sun. 'I saw her,' I told Melinda. 'I saw Poppy.'

She threw me an odd look. I reached a trembling hand to my mouth.

Melinda took off her cashmere cardigan and wrapped it around my shoulders. 'It's *freezing* in here,' she exclaimed. 'Did you open a window or something?'

I shook my head, though the concern in her voice made me smile. It reassured me that I was safe. She laughed nervously.

'You'll never guess what,' she said as I rose to my feet, leaning on the edge of the piano for balance.

'What?'

She folded her arms and grinned widely. 'That piece you showed me. It's *one hundred per cent genuine.*'

I nodded in acknowledgement, glancing around the room.

'That kid is a genius,' she continued. 'A total child prodigy!'

I looked at the piano, then searched around the floor.

'What's wrong?' Melinda said, unfolding her arms.

'It's gone,' I told her. 'The music has gone.'

23

THE THINGS THAT ARE REAL

Alex

Dear Diary,

What did Pope Julius II say to Michelangelo?
'Sure, come on down, son, we'll paper it.'

I woke up really early today because today was a Saturday and I was going to see Mum at ten o'clock. It felt like Christmas morning. I set my alarm for seven so that I'd have time to get a shower before the others woke up and brush my teeth and clean out my ears and cut my nails. I was also afraid in case the laundry people forgot to wash my clothes so I made sure I'd have extra time to wash and dry them myself, but it was OK because when I checked my wardrobe my shirt and trousers and waistcoat were all there, really clean and nicely ironed.

I woke well before my alarm, so took a long, long time in the shower. I spent about an hour polishing my shoes and then I sat with a black marker colouring in all the scuff marks so they'd look extra clean. By this time it was only eight o'clock. So I rearranged all the photographs and drawings of our new house that I'd stuck to the walls and spent a while imagining Mum and me living there, cooking together in the kitchen, sitting in the garden when it got sunny, hanging up pictures of lilies and dolphins.

Then I drew Mum a picture and wrote a nice message inside. It said: 'Mum, I hope you feel better soon because I love you, and if you felt as good as much as I love you, you would feel really good.'

Mum was waiting for me in the living room that she shares with the other people in her ward. She was dressed in a pair of new jeans and a blue T-shirt. She had some make-up on, too, a pale pink on her eyelids and cheeks and her eyelashes were black. I was so glad to see her that I almost cried, and I felt she could see that I was upset and she almost cried, too.

When she let go of me I sat opposite her and smiled.

'How do you like this new school, then?' she said, though she said it like she wasn't glad I was going to a new school.

'It's OK,' I said. 'It's only temporary, isn't it?'

She nodded. 'What's this you've brought?'

I was holding my sketchpad. 'I've been doing lots of new drawings,' I told her. 'Anya said it's good for my recovery. Shall I show you?'

Mum gave a frozen kind of smile and nodded her head.

I'd deliberately avoided doing any more pictures of skeletons as they seemed to upset people, so I had drawn things like the flowers growing outside my bedroom window and a scene from my classroom and a portrait of Woof. When Mum saw the picture of Woof her smile dropped clean off her face. She touched the picture for a long time and held her hand up to her mouth.

'What's wrong?' I said.

She took a long deep breath and then held one of my hands in both of hers. 'Alex,' she said. 'I'm really sorry, but Woof has had to be moved to a new home, too.'

'What do you mean?' I said.

I didn't hear all the words she said because my heart was thumping so loudly, like it was in my ears, but basically it sounded something like Woof had been placed in a home for dogs when Auntie Bev had gone back to Cork for a week or so because there was no one at home to feed or walk him and Auntie Bev couldn't take him with her. When Mum said a home for dogs, I knew she meant the RSPCA. I thought of Woof being locked up there with all the other barking, miserable dogs, doing circles in a cage the size of our loo and wondering what he'd done wrong to end up in there.

I must have been panting because all of a sudden Mum put her arms around me and said, 'Oh, Alex. I'm so sorry, this is all my fault.'

'Can't we get him back?' I asked.

Mum hugged me tight and when she looked at me again her make-up was running down her face in wet black lines.

'Maybe,' she said. 'I won't make promises to you any more that I can't guarantee. So it's a maybe. If he's still there.'

I wanted to ask whether she thought the people at the RSPCA might put Woof down, because I overheard someone say that they had to do that all the time because they had too many dogs. But I was afraid of upsetting Mum even more.

'This is my fault,' Mum said again. 'If I hadn't got myself in here we'd probably all still be at home.'

At last I remembered my manners and pulled my handkerchief out of my pocket. I handed it to Mum and she smiled and dabbed her face.

'When *are* you coming home?' I asked.

Mum looked away. 'I don't know.'

I thought for a moment about what I could do or say to make Mum happy. Immediately I thought of Ruen saving my dad, but I didn't want to tell her the part about Hell because she'd definitely, definitely think I was loony.

So I said: 'I know you miss my dad, Mum, and I know you've been very sad since he died. But I think that maybe someday we'll be able to see him again. You know, in Heaven.'

Mum lowered my handkerchief from her face very slowly. She looked angry. *Oh no*, I thought. *I have made everything much, much worse.*

'Alex, what do you mean, *died*?' she said. Her face was very twisted now.

'I mean, when he died that morning that I found you in

bed with all the pills, and Granny phoned the ambulance and . . . '

I stopped talking cos she was looking at me as if I'd gone mad. Her mouth was opening and her forehead had a line into it that started to turn into a letter V.

'Mum,' I said after a few moments. 'I'm sorry, I suppose I shouldn't talk about it.'

Then she lowered her hands and gave a sigh that was so big her shoulders stooped.

'I'm so sorry,' she said, which was her twenty-ninth apology since I arrived. 'I thought you understood, Alex.' She looked out the window again and the sun lit up her face and for a moment she looked young again. 'Granny always said I treated you older than you were, that I expected too much of you. I suppose it was because you always *seemed* so much older. Did you know you were walking at ten months old?'

My stomach was starting to turn into a knot.

She was still talking as if someone else was in the room. 'The health visitor said it was remarkable, said she'd never heard of a nineteen-month-old talk like that. Like a three-or four-year-old, she said, especially since boys are so much behind girls, usually.' Her eyes smiled. 'You made me so proud, Alex. I felt so scared when you were born. Didn't know how I'd feed you, look after you. Didn't know how I'd manage. Didn't know how I'd give you what you needed. But you surprised us all.'

'Do you mean Dad *isn't* dead?' I demanded.

'You already know this, Alex. He's at Magilligan Prison,

remember? I tried to take you to visit him but you said you didn't want to . . . '

I fell back as if she had just punched me in the face.

'Alex?' she said, leaning forward with her arms held out. I felt my head turn from side to side on my shoulders, as if someone was turning it for me.

'It's OK,' she was saying, but then her mouth was opening and closing and I couldn't hear anything because my heart was beating so hard and it was as if I had forgotten how to speak because I couldn't get my feelings to come out as words. 'He . . . but . . . ' Then: 'Where's Magilligan?'

'It's about seventy miles from here. Just past the Giant's Causeway.' My mouth was full of spit. Mum sighed and rubbed her head.

'I want to tell you something, Alex.'

I got up and sat beside her but I felt like I was floating.

'You didn't deserve any of this,' she said. 'For a long, long time I've thought . . . well, that you didn't deserve me. That you deserve a much better mother than me. And I thought that it was because of me that my foster parents abused me. That I deserved it all.'

I nodded, even though I still wasn't really sure what she was talking about. Didn't 'foster parents' mean people who weren't your parents?

'But it takes time to feel good about yourself after feeling worthless your whole life.'

'What do you mean by foster parents?'

Mum frowned. 'See, that's the thing, Alex. I haven't been

truthful with either you or me. Granny wasn't my real mum, you see. She adopted me when I was about your age.'

I'm not sure what happened after Mum told me that. It was as if a huge glass tube suddenly came down from the ceiling and trapped me inside, the way people put upside-down jars over spiders and they can't get out, and all I could hear inside the tube was my own heart sprinting and my own thoughts. Which were:

Granny isn't my granny?
Auntie Bev isn't my real auntie?
Dad didn't die?
Who did Ruen get out of Hell, then?

But I must've been making all the right noises because Mum kept talking. I think she was discussing the new house with me and all her plans for decorating when she got out of the hospital, because she kept saying things like 'red paint, or maybe Tuscan orange' and 'lots of posh lamps'. And while she was saying all this, a thought clanked through my head like a midnight express train:

Ruen is lying.

Ruen is lying.

He didn't get my dad out of Hell.

There was no massive building or dragons in the sky.

And what was it he'd said? My dad wanted me to *pay the debt*?

In other words, Ruen felt he could spin me a big fib and get some payback while he was at it.

I stood up.

Mum was talking mostly to herself now, going on and on about how she always wanted carpet on the stairs. She was wiping tears from her eyes but smiling at the same time.

'Maybe we can make a fresh start,' she said.

I took her hand.

'Mum, I love you,' I said. 'But there's something I have to do.'

And I went, right when she was deciding between pink and peach tiles for the bathroom.

When I left Mum I got taken back to MacNeice House. As soon as we walked through the red front door there was a big smashing sound and a lady wearing a hairnet and an apron made me walk really slowly up the corridor in case I stood on any glass.

'Butterfingers today,' she said, holding up her fingers like she was surprised she had them on the ends of her hands. There were about eleven broken jugs all over the place and a big puddle of water. When I looked down in one of them I saw Ruen's face smiling back, but he was nowhere to be seen. He knew I was angry with him.

Miss Kells was waiting for me outside my bedroom. I walked up to her.

'I want to go swimming,' I told her.

She looked at me very seriously and I noticed her eyes and mouth were exactly like Michael's. I went to tell her this but then I thought she would only ask who Michael was so I shut up.

'Alex,' she said. 'I'd like to talk to you about something really important.'

'Right now?'

She nodded.

'I'm sorry, I can't,' I said, but I didn't say why.

I didn't say that I needed to have a chat with a nine-thousand-year-old demon who fibbed about busting his way into Hell and helping my father escape just so he could hold one over me. And that I needed somewhere quiet and private to do it, because if I started shouting in my bedroom they'd come in with restraints and more white pills.

'I need to work on my butterfly crawl,' I said, and I made a big show of looking at the sign for the swimming pool behind her.

Miss Kells crouched down next to me and I thought of second-hand books with their yellow pages.

'You know, Alex,' she said, 'you can tell me anything. That's the beauty about having a personal tutor. Nothing you tell me can ever get you into trouble, understand?'

I nodded. I didn't understand, but when she told me this I felt the knot in my stomach turn to butter and a feeling of warmth flood over me.

I opened my mouth. She nodded, encouraging me to speak. I wanted to tell her about Ruen. I wanted to ask her advice. So I said:

'Miss Kells, what would you do if someone you really, really trusted told you a really horrible lie?'

She smiled, and her eyes told me she knew why I was

asking what I was asking, and I wondered if someone had lied to her the way I'd been lied to. She came close to me and said:

'I would tell them I never wanted to see them again. Even if I loved them very much, I would never trust them again.'

I nodded and she took my hand, only her hand felt like warm air. 'Do you need my help, Alex?'

'Yes,' I said, but then I shook my head because I didn't know how she could possibly help me with this one.

'If you ever need my help in the future, all you have to do is ask,' she said.

'Thank you,' I said, and I went to ask her something else but when I looked again she was gone.

I did a lot of laps up and down the pool, thumping my body into the ripples with each stroke, imagining I was fighting with Ruen. Occasionally I'd take a rest at the end of a lap, clinging on to the side and muttering orders under my breath for Ruen to show his horrible stony face. But he didn't show.

Finally, I dragged myself out and went into the sauna. All the other boys were off playing football and the lifeguard was at the side of the pool, so I had the whole place to myself. I went in, lay down on a bench and imagined pure hatred oozing out of my pores.

A cough. I opened my eyes. On the other side of the room I could make out an old man through the steam. He was mean-looking and he had a piranha-fish smile and was wearing a suit that was threading at one side. And the thread snaked its way through the mist and ended at the hem of my towel.

'You called?' Ruen said.

'You're a liar,' I shouted.

'Oh?' He didn't seem bothered by the accusation, so I challenged him:

'You told me that you got my dad out of Hell, and you didn't.'

'And how did you come to that conclusion?'

I was standing now, pointing down at him as he sat on the bench opposite. 'Mum told me my dad is alive and well in Magilligan Prison. So I don't know who you dragged out of Hell, Ruen. In fact I don't think you dragged anyone out. I think you made the whole thing up. And I think I don't owe you anything.'

He stood up and looked at me very crossly. For a moment I thought he was going to change shape and become a monster just to make me feel scared. But he just glanced at a spot in the corner. When I looked, I saw another demon sitting there, unfolding behind the mist. He was dressed in a tweed suit like Ruen's but it looked new and he seemed younger and timid. He seemed to be writing stuff down in a leather notebook.

'Who's that?' I said.

The demon went to introduce himself but Ruen cut him off. 'That's Braze,' he said. 'He's an intern. Ignore him.'

I picked up my towel and made to leave. Just as I reached the door, Ruen said:

'Your mother lied, Alex.'

I clenched my fists, gritted my teeth and turned around slowly. '*What did you say?*'

'Your mother lied,' Ruen said calmly.

'Just *who* do you think you—'

He held up a hand. 'Please,' he said.

I was shaking with anger and my mouth felt tight as if I was really cold. He swept his hand from me to the bench, gesturing for me to sit down.

'You've got ten seconds to explain.' I didn't sit down.

Ruen sighed. 'The man I saved was your *real* father,' he said. 'The man in Magilligan Prison is not. Nobody knows your father isn't your real father. Not even your grandmother.'

All of a sudden I remembered what Mum had said about Granny: *She's not your real granny*. The memory and truth of it hit me so hard I had to blink back tears.

'Why would Mum lie about who my dad is, huh?' I yelled. 'How *dare* you call my Mum a liar—'

'I didn't,' Ruen said. 'I said she *lied*. There's a difference, dear boy. Your mother lied to protect you. Your mother lied because she loves you, and she knows all too well how much a revelation like this would hurt you. I only tell you now because you force me to.'

He glanced over at the other demon, who was still writing.

I couldn't stop the tears now, nor could I stop my heart from racing or my whole body pouring with sweat, dripping down my face and arms and fingertips. I took a deep breath. A sob wormed its way out of me, and then hot tears.

Eventually, Ruen approached me. I held my face in my hands. He patted my shoulder.

'It's OK,' he said. 'You weren't to know.' Then he turned and sniffed. 'You can make it up to me.'

24

THE NEWSPAPERS

Anya

I wake with a shout. A glance at the clock beside my bed causes momentary confusion as to the actual day. A quick calculation proves that I have been asleep for fifteen hours. Impossible.

I roll upright and look out the window. Bright sunshine lighting up the small park beneath my apartment block, cars threading along the motorway to Dublin, small and bright as boiled sweets. The River Lagan flicks to my right like a silver scarf, and the city sits in the distance, a cluster of bridges and boats, mint-green domes of old buildings and shining sky-scrapers.

On mornings like this, Belfast reminds me of an old fable I once heard of identical twin sisters, separated at birth.

After many years they were reunited, one haggard and hunched from years of service, her face dull and drawn, her eyes hollow and black. The other sister turned heads wherever she went, her eyes shining, her smile bright, her posture straight and upright. The beautiful sister made the haggard sister realise how she too could appear, and so she became beautiful for the first time in her life. There are many times when Belfast is that haggard, weathered sister, but there are days when you can catch a glimpse of the other sister's beauty.

The events of yesterday hit me like a cold shower. The sensation of passing out on the floor. Poppy. The man in the music room.

The missing piece of music.

I blitz slices of apple, kiwi and pineapple in my new blender and drink it while checking my phone for missed calls. The same unknown caller with the unfamiliar number is there. I dial it.

After five rings, someone answers.

'Anya, *hi*. It's Karen, Karen Holland.'

Karen, I think with a groan.

'Sorry, Karen,' I say, my voice still husky from too long in bed. 'I haven't found anything yet. Alex is at MacNeice House . . . '

'*I've* found something,' she said quickly. 'I think it's quite important. Do you have time for a chat?'

I glance at my watch. 'I've a meeting in twenty minutes. Can I see you later this afternoon?'

'Perfect.'

When I hang, up the events of the day before continue to rain down on me, stark and unnerving.

For even after a solid fifteen hours' sleep, I know I saw Poppy: I know I felt her hands on my face; I heard her voice; I smelled her hair, her breath. But I have no idea how to explain it. Nor do I understand the encounter with the old man. His face, rock-like, ancient, and those terrible empty eyes, all still throbbing in my head with a vibrancy I can't erase.

I had told Melinda about the old man's visit to the practice room shortly after I regained consciousness. She checked the visitor's register at reception, then CCTV footage, even contacted every security guard posted around the campus. When she couldn't find any trace of him, we reported it to the police.

'Ruen?' the police officer had asked as I sat in Melinda's office nursing another coffee. She was sceptical. 'As in *R-U-E-N*?'

'That's the only name he gave.'

'And about how old?'

'Somewhere between mid seventies and early eighties,' I said.

'Did he have a knife?'

I sighed. It sounded ridiculous just then. I didn't mention anything of our conversation, nor how I felt. I thought of kidnap victims who discovered they had been taken hostage not at gunpoint but by the barrel of a whiteboard marker pressed against their neck. Sometimes the imagination is the true predator.

Melinda asked to speak to me for a moment and the police officer stepped aside.

'This guy,' Melinda said. 'Did he *really* give his name?'

'Yes,' I said with conviction, then doubt crept in. Perhaps he hadn't said he was Ruen. Perhaps he hadn't said his name at all.

'Are you sure?' she said. 'It's just that from your descriptions it sounds like it could be one of the visiting professors.'

'He knew my name,' I interjected. 'He called me Anya.'

'Your name would have been on the booking sheet on the door, wouldn't it?' Melinda said quickly. 'The school's VPs don't come in that often and sometimes they just turn up. Some of them are very, very old. There's this one man who sounds very similar . . . He's a little, well, weird.'

'Have you got a picture of him?'

She nodded her head at the computer on her desk. I told the police officer to excuse us as we both walked around the other side to face the screen. Melinda gave the mouse a wave to shake the screensaver, then typed a name into the search bar. A few seconds later, the school's banner appeared in a web browser, followed by a list of staff and their photographs. Melinda scrolled down to a section marked 'Visiting Professors' and clicked on a small thumbnail.

'Here,' she said. The page reloaded. Staring back at me was a bald man, smiling, his grey eyes shielded by thick black glasses. A similar tombstone-shaped mouth, his top gum broader than his small yellow teeth. He was wearing a bow tie and tweed jacket. I leaned towards the screen, my heart racing.

'This is Professor Franz Amsel,' she said. 'He gave a paper at the music department a couple of nights ago. Do you think it might have been him?'

I looked over the wide smile and the glasses. The man I had seen looked older than this, I told Melinda. She scoffed.

'Most of these guys send us photos that are older than *me*,' she said ruefully. 'I know Professor Amsel is in his seventies, at least.'

'But he said *he* composed the music,' I spluttered, desperate to recall the event more accurately, devoid of emotion.

Melinda held up a hand. 'Let me contact him, find out if he was here yesterday.'

I swallowed and nodded in agreement. At the other end of the room, the police officer tapped her foot. Melinda lifted the phone and dialled a number, tucking a strand of hair behind her ear.

'Hi, Professor? This is Melinda Kyle here at the School of Music at Queen's University. Yeah, hi there. I was just wondering if you visited one of our practice rooms yesterday morning, we're just in a little pickle with security for not keeping our register of guests up to date. Uh-huh.' She nodded deeply. 'You *were* here.' I felt my heart sink. She looked relieved. 'Oh, thank heavens. No, nothing. That's OK Professor. I'll tell her. Thank *you*.' She set down the phone and rolled her eyes. 'He extends his *deepest* apologies and hopes he didn't upset you.'

Melinda threw me a smile while she approached the police officer, explaining in a smooth, affable voice that we'd had a little misunderstanding.

I sat numbly on the chair behind her desk, looking at the image of the professor on the screen. There was no denying the similarity.

I felt utterly, ridiculously *stupid*. How could I have let myself stray so far from reason? How could I have believed that the man was ... The thought of it was crazy now, and I felt angry at myself. Much later, I would leave my anger behind and feel harrowed with fear at the workings of my own brain. If I couldn't keep it together, what future had I as a child psychiatrist? How could I ever hope to rebuild the lives of others by helping them piece together their sense of what was real and what wasn't if I didn't know the difference myself?

My phone rings as I leave Karen Holland's classroom seven hours later, having chatted with her for almost an hour. What she has showed me there makes me want to run back to MacNeice House and speak to Alex immediately. I have already tried contacting Trudy Messenger, but to no avail, and so when the phone goes I assume it is her.

'Trudy, I need to tell you something about Alex Broccoli's father ...'

A cough on the other end of the line. 'It's Ursula.'

'Oh. Is something wrong?'

A pause. 'I need to speak to you immediately, if that's all right. Are you on your way back now?'

'Can I ask what this is about?' I say. 'Just I have some calls to make ...'

'I'll speak to you when you get here,' she replies stiffly, then hangs up. I make the journey back at a light trot, unable to merely walk.

At MacNeice House I meet Ursula in the foyer and sign into the register.

'You want to chat in your office?' I ask, taking off my jacket.

She smiles. 'Why don't we chat in yours?'

Inside my office I move the last of the boxes of books from the coffee table and invite her to sit down. I notice her surveying my posters and the dog-eared, incomprehensible paintings given to me by some patients as thank yous for their treatment – a gift much more meaningful than any other.

'How have you settled back into Northern Ireland?' Ursula asks, clasping her hands.

I pour us both a cup of water and sit down opposite her, catching my breath. I am still wearing my jogging shoes.

'I'm actually settling back home far easier than I would have imagined,' I tell her brightly. 'You never know, I might even stay.'

It is a light joke, offered to break the tension. She presses her lips together.

'I heard about what happened yesterday. At the university.'

I hold her gaze, feeling my heart sink. My excitement at the progress made in Alex's assessment withers. 'Yes,' I respond after a long, contemplative pause. 'I'm afraid I haven't felt myself lately.'

I explain to her about my unfurnished flat, how I still haven't properly unpacked. About my patients. About my progress with Xavier's case, the effectiveness of art therapy on our newest inpatient Ella. About Alex's situation.

'In fact,' I tell her, 'I've just had a meeting with one of Alex's old school teachers. I think I've made a huge breakthrough in his assessment.'

'I'm sure you have,' she says, reviewing her nails. 'But I'm afraid I have severe concerns about your ability to proceed with this case, Anya.' She lifts her eyes and I see nothing but disappointment. 'I'd like you to take a small period of sick leave.'

'*Sick leave?*'

'You must understand that your episode, or whatever it was, was ... well, it was worrying, frankly. Both in terms of the future of our practice and in terms of your own personal health. Any time police are involved it raises the level of seriousness a little, and with the kinds of funding bids MacNeice House is making, and with the recent interest from the Health Minister, we don't want it to look as if – and forgive me – the lunatics are running the asylum.'

I am stunned. I go to respond to her, but no words come. Instead, my mind turns of its own accord to what I have just seen in Karen Holland's classroom less than an hour ago – a photocopy of a newspaper from December 2001, bearing the headline RUINED PEOPLE'S LIVES. Beneath it was a large photograph of a shooting in action: a masked man by a car pointing a gun at a policeman. 'Read it,' Karen had said.

Yesterday afternoon two policemen lost their lives in what the Deputy First Minister described as a 'monstrous act of hate targeted at the newly-formed PSNI' at a checkpoint outside Armagh. Sergeant Martin Kerr, 29, the father of a two-week-old girl, was wounded by a single shot to the forehead at close range. Sergeant Eamonn Douglas, 47, died from his injuries last night at the Armagh County Hospital. Two men – Alex Murphy, 30, from North Belfast, and Michael Matthews, 69, from County Kerry – were charged this morning with first-degree murder.

I had lowered the newspaper and looked at Karen.

'It's the same headline as Alex's painting,' she said.

I frowned. 'But why would Alex be so disturbed by this?'

She opened a laptop on her desk and clicked on an internet icon. 'I found this online,' she said, opening a new page. I watched as the screen filled with rain–smeared footage of a calm street in Belfast, a church visible on the right side of the road, a post office on the other. The screen blurred as several women walked past pushing prams, their chatter audible but muffled through glass. Two policemen were on the road, stopping traffic and chatting to the drivers before letting them pass on. For a moment it seemed as if nothing was out of the ordinary – it was just another checkpoint, like so many I had witnessed in Belfast. A small figure in a red school jumper was visible outside the metal fencing of the church and a little girl in a white dress stood in the doorway of the post office.

Then, a blue car rolled up towards the checkpoint. Only one of the policemen stepped out. The other one remained at the side of the road and folded his arms. I watched, my throat growing dry, as a masked man jumped from the passenger side of the car. He pulled out a gun, pointing it at the policeman in front of him. For a moment he hesitated, and the screen blurred as people ran past the camera, positioned, I suspected, in the back of the police van. A gunshot resounded, cracking the windscreen of the blue car. The masked man hesitated, lifting his gun. A few seconds later, there was the low, sinister crack of a gunshot, and the first policeman on the road crumpled to the ground. A second crack. Someone pulled the young girl inside the post office. The policeman by the roadside flung his arms out and fell. The gunman paused and turned his head to the boy by the church, and I gasped, afraid that the boy would be next. The gunman lowered his weapon, taking a step backwards, perturbed by this young witness. The driver of the car signalled at him, and he promptly got into the car and sped off.

The footage had cut from there to a mugshot of the killer, a surly-looking man in his late twenties, strong lips, startling blue eyes and a feminine jaw, his shoulders well defined. His name flashed beneath the photograph in white letters: ALEX MURPHY. I leaned closer, noticing a familiarity about the eyes, the slightly turned-out ears.

The footage cut again to a journalist holding an umbrella

with one hand and a microphone with the other. '*It seems a dissident faction of the IRA was involved in what happened in this very spot just yesterday afternoon, when a masked terrorist opened fire on two policemen, supposedly in anticipation of their finding a heavy arsonal transported illegally from the southern border . . .*'

I tapped the spacebar on the keyboard, pausing the film. I had needed a moment to take in what I had seen. To understand its meaning. Karen walked across the room to close a window that was beginning to let in the din of the school run. I fumbled with the YouTube tabs, anxious to rewind the footage. There was something about the pixellated figure at the fence of the church, something familiar.

'Can we zoom in on this?' I asked Karen. She pressed something on the screen, enlarging the image. The picture was pixellated, but I was certain I knew that young, terrified face.

'You know, I recalled after our last meeting something Alex said more than once,' Karen offered. 'He said that his mother repeatedly told him that he was similar to his father. That he had his dad *in* him. What do you make of that?'

I hit the spacebar, starting the footage from the beginning again. Alex learning of his father's crime was one thing, but witnessing it . . . Even if he had somehow been present, there was every chance he would have blacked it out.

The footage refused to give up the boy's face. I turned to Karen.

'I think Alex knows his father was a murderer.'

*

' . . . just a couple of months,' Ursula is saying, and suddenly I am snapped back into my office at MacNeice House, listening to her make arrangements for my replacement while I 'recuperated'.

'Ursula,' I interrupted, keeping my voice and my gaze firm. 'I found out something this afternoon about Alex's childhood that affects *everything* about this case.'

She removes her glasses. 'Oh?'

'A new element of his past has arisen that puts everything about his condition in a completely new light. I need to speak to him and his mother as a matter of urgency.'

'You can write a report for Alex's new consultant,' she says with a heavy sigh. 'I'm sorry, Anya. But it's important that we remain vigilant as to the health of our staff as well as our patients. I'll email you the relevant forms for occupational health.' She rises to her feet. 'I'll initiate your period of sick leave with immediate effect.' Then, with a tilt of her head: 'Much better than an enforced absence. Or being fired.'

I close my mouth. She eyes me coolly before walking out.

25

SWAPPING CARDS

Alex

Dear Diary,

Our new house is gone. Gone gone gone gone gone gone gone gone.

Michael just came to MacNeice House to tell me. He said he was very sorry and swore a lot and said his so-called friend quit his job so the new person saw that we hadn't moved in yet and moved me and Mum down 'the list', as it wasn't really fair that some people were waiting for a house while we were in hospital. I just nodded as he walked up and down my room with his hands making fists, and then as soon as he'd finished I ran to the bathroom and threw up all my lunch.

Michael said he'd try really really hard to make sure we get a house just like it. 'But I loved *that* house,' I told him. He took a big breath and bent his knees so our faces were at the same level and his knees made a big crack.

'I *know* you loved that house, Alex,' he said. 'It's just the council decided ...' He made a fist and pressed it into his mouth and I wondered if he was actually going to bite himself. 'There are loads of new houses being built at the minute in Belfast. Lots of beautiful houses just like this one.' Then he leaned forward and I could see his green eyes and I felt a bit better because they told me I could trust him. 'I promise you, Alex,' he said. 'I will make sure you get moved to a better place.'

'But Mum liked that house, too,' I said, and I knew Michael already knew this but it was much more important than whether I liked it or not. I felt for a moment like I could hardly breathe and I was scared because I knew Mum would be upset. Michael stood up and said something else but I didn't hear because I was thinking of Mum sitting in the swing next to me at the park. It was a long time ago and both of us were swinging ourselves higher and higher. It didn't matter to me if I could swing higher, it just mattered that I could hear her laughing.

When Michael had gone I left my room and walked along the long white corridor. The other boys and girls staying here were all in the canteen as it was lunchtime. It was a Thursday which meant they were having a Sunday dinner with extra onions and toast. I didn't even care. My stomach was gurgly and I puked and then I ran into the communal loos, locked the toilet door and sat against it.

Before I even saw Ruen I saw the dark thread of shadow on the ground, which made me jump for a second because I thought it was a snake. I saw it slide across the white tiles of the floor and then it seemed to float up and snag on my jumper.

'Where are you?' I said, because even though I couldn't see him yet I knew he was somewhere.

Ruen appeared beside the bin as Ghost Boy. He was looking at me funny as if he wondered how I knew he was there. He had his table tennis bat and white ball in his hands, but instead of bouncing them he just folded his arms and scowled at me.

'Where's Braze?' I asked, because last time I'd seen him there was this other demon there too and Ruen said he was an intern.

'Shut up,' he said, and he lifted his leg and shoved me in the stomach with his foot and I fell back on to the ground.

'What are you doing?' I shouted, and quickly he pushed his face into mine and said: 'If you don't sit still I'll make your heart stop beating, and you'll die.'

I stopped moving and sat still as a stone on the floor.

'Good,' he said, smiling. I held my breath because I wanted to pant and my heart was pounding. I hated that Ruen looked so like me just then because he was so mean and I didn't even know why.

'I'm going to show you something,' he said, looking down at me. I felt scared but not of Ruen. I felt scared because the dark shadow that connected my jumper to Ruen was thicker than normal and moving the way a snake moves.

'OK,' I said to Ruen. 'Then can you go away, please.'

He bent down and his face looked like he was sorry for me.

'I want you to know that what I show you now is not a projection of your mind,' he said, and his voice was different, like a man's. 'You are not having a psychotic episode, Alex. All of this is very real, so pay attention.'

I nodded and looked away from the shadow beside me, then folded my arms across my body and pinched the undersides of my arms so I knew that I was still there and that everything was happening, because lately I haven't been so sure. I feel so dizzy when I take the tablets, especially on an empty stomach, that sometimes it feels like I'm on a ship and then sometimes I actually convince myself that I *am* on a ship and that we're floating out to sea, that my bedroom curtains are icebergs and the fields outside are the polar icecaps and the sky is really the Arctic ocean.

'Close your eyes, Alex,' Ruen whispered.

I shook my head. I was afraid of the shadow.

'Don't you trust me?' he said.

'Not any more,' I said without thinking, and our faces fell at exactly the same time because we both realised it was true. Ruen frowned at me.

'Do you want your mum to live?' he said in a cruel voice.

I gasped and shut my eyes tight.

'Look,' I heard Ruen say, and immediately there was this big cinema screen in my head filled with an image of Mum. It was clearer than a Wakeful Dream or a memory. It was even clearer than a film at the cinema because it was like I was right there in front of her. I could see her sitting in the communal room in a red chair at the adult unit and she was watching TV. She was wearing a long white T-shirt and her hair was tied back and her face looked blank. She kept changing position in her chair as if she couldn't get comfortable.

'Is this real?' I asked Ruen, opening my eyes.

'Of course it is,' he said, and I closed my eyes again and kept watching.

Mum turned to the lady in the chair next to her and said, *Do you have any smokes?* The lady looked at her as if she was stupid and shook her head. Mum said *thanks* in a voice that sounded annoyed and she left the room.

Then the image changed to Mum walking into her bedroom at the hospital. She looked upset and her hands were flapping and she walked up and down, talking to herself. She was saying things like, *Said I was no good; he was right*, and then she lay down on the bed. At first I thought she was going to sleep, and then I noticed she was reaching under her mattress for something.

I opened my eyes. 'What's she doing?' I asked Ruen.

'You'll see,' he said.

Part of me wanted to run out of here all the way to Mum and the other part needed to stay and see what happened.

But I already knew what was going to happen.

Mum reached her hand underneath the mattress and slowly pulled out a fat book. When she opened it I could see she had ripped out holes in the pages and hid round white pills inside, lots of them. She sat with the book on her lap for a moment and she looked at the door which was open and then back at the book, and I shouted, '*Mum, don't!*' because I knew what she was thinking. I opened my eyes but the image was gone and all I could see was the orange toilet door with black scribbles on it and a rusting handle. So I closed my eyes and immediately I saw Mum again, but this time there were no round white pills in the book and she was drinking a glass of water and crying. She rubbed her face and gave a big sigh.

I love you, Alex. You'll be so much happier without me.

I yelled and yelled and then I opened my eyes and scrambled to my feet and I felt my fingers fumble with the lock on the toilet door and then I raced out into the corridor, though I couldn't move fast enough. I needed to get to her, I needed to get to her. Every time I'd been able to stop her, but this time might be too late. I started to run but it felt like my legs wouldn't move fast enough, like they were made of Lego bricks and I had to drag them after me.

I was outside the toilets now and in the long white corridor with the long white lights in the ceiling like lightsabers. There was nobody around, not a single person.

'Help!' I shouted, but my voice sounded so small. I looked from one end of the corridor to the other.

Suddenly the lights flickered off and it became very dark. It was raining outside but the rain against the glass sounded like a hiss and I felt so, so scared. There was no one to help me.

I closed my eyes and I saw Mum asleep in her chair. I started to cry.

When I opened my eyes again I saw a dark shadow at the very end of the corridor. It started off like a big black balloon hanging in the air, and then it grew and grew until it sank and splatted like a puddle of black oil that spread across the floor. I felt like I couldn't move. I was just standing there frozen to the spot. Even if the building had exploded I probably would have just stood there. All I could think about was Mum. I watched the puddle as it spread to both sides of the wall and then it started to creep up the wall and I knew what it was.

The black liquid crept up both sides and then each floated into mid-air and joined and spread down to the floor to form a person. It was Ruen as Monster. He was almost as tall as the ceiling and as wide as the corridor and his eyes were tiny and yellow and his skin was a cross between black and purple. He had no ears or nose or hair and his mouth was big and full of sharp yellow teeth.

Then I heard his voice in my head, and it was soft and kind and gentle.

'Alex,' he said. 'Your mother is very, very ill. What will you do to help her?'

I turned and tried to run away towards the other end of the hall, but my legs still felt like they wouldn't work. I made it about four doors along, but Ruen was there again, right in front of me. This time he was the Old Man, and his arms were tucked behind his back and I could see the black thread hanging from his jacket and snaking up from the floor.

'Alex,' he said, 'your mother is going to die.' He said it like I was making it happen, like it was my fault.

I started to cry. 'Help me, someone!' I shouted.

Ruen reached out to me. '*I'm* here, *I'm* helping you,' he said, but I just wanted to run. I felt trapped. I turned to run again but this time I tripped and fell down with my hands outstretched and I hit my forehead on the floor. I wanted to get up but I didn't have the strength. I put my cheek on the ground and it was cold and I was numb.

Then I felt Ruen stand over me.

'There is still time, Alex, but you must act quickly. Get up, get up.'

I rolled over on to my back and looked up at him. I felt like it was all over, like I had nothing else in me, like I was empty. 'You're a demon,' I told him. 'Demons really do hurt people, not help people.'

Ruen grinned. 'It appears I'm the only one helping you right now, isn't that so?'

I looked at the ceiling. I could see the light flickering, trying to work. I wondered if there were angels out there. Or a God.

'Help me,' I whispered.

'I *am* helping you,' Ruen said, walking around me with his arms behind his back. 'Your mother will live. You just need to do one thing, Alex. Do you think you can do just one thing?'

I felt tears sliding down the sides of my face into my ears. I pressed both hands on my chest and felt myself taking breaths, in and out, and I wished I could give these breaths to my mum. There was nothing else, nothing nothing nothing that I wanted more than to stop her from dying.

Ruen bent down then, right beside me, so close I could smell him. It usually made me gag but it didn't then. He pressed something cold and sharp into my hand.

'Do you remember swapping cards with the other boys in the old school, Alex?'

I heard myself say yes.

'This is like swapping cards. For your mother to live, you need to send someone else in her place.'

I closed my eyes. I knew what he wanted. It was what Ruen had always wanted and even though he hadn't said so I knew it because I knew Ruen.

'You want me to kill someone.'

Ruen stopped walking. 'Don't you want your mother to live, Alex?'

I rolled up slowly to a sitting position and looked down at what he had put into my hand. At first it looked like a knife made out of glass. I brought it close to my face and saw that it was a broken handle of a glass water jug. The end of it was so sharp that when I tapped it lightly with my finger a small red line of blood appeared above my nail a few seconds later. Ruen looked at me as I held the weapon and gave a big smile.

'I can't do it,' I whispered, but then a new image of Mum flashed in my head, even though I had my eyes open. I saw her hand on the side of the chair, and even though she was asleep I saw her hand fall and I knew she was dying.

I looked up at Ruen. My mouth and eyes were sore and I felt like I was falling. I thought of my dad, my *real* dad, and what he said to Ruen: *My son will pay my debt.* And I thought of Mum, swinging beside me, going higher and higher and higher. She was laughing. When she laughed I felt like my heart would take off. I wanted to hear her laugh again.

Eventually I whispered:

'Who do you want me to kill?'

26

THE CALL

Anya

Trudy Messenger phones as I am at my flat, both arms filled with clothes and books that I didn't quite know whether to put back into their boxes or into the cupboards I have recently bought. I hear my mobile ring and expect it to be Michael.

She sounds both angry and relieved at the same time.

'Anya? I've been in touch with the secretaries at MacNeice House, they said you would be gone for some time ...'

I take a breath, my heart still heavy. 'What can I help you with, Trudy?'

Her voice softens. 'It's Alex Broccoli's mother, Cindy. She's in intensive care.'

'Intensive care?'

A pause. 'It's so rare when this happens, usually security is so tight ... Somehow she got hold of barbiturates and ...'

It is as if the ground around me has just plummeted ten feet. I can hear her rattle off the words *suicide attempt* and *coma* and *brain damage*, then times and procedures in a slightly shrill voice, but all at a great distance, as if a plane is taking off close by. Eventually, there is silence on the end of the line, and a terrible image unravels in my head: Ursula knocking on Alex's bedroom door with this news held in her mouth like a concealed weapon.

'Has anyone told Alex?'

'Not yet.'

I sink down on the bed, my mind racing with the necessary steps.

'I'm going over to see him now. When can I bring him to see Cindy?'

'That won't be possible,' Trudy says. 'Not at the minute. They're doing everything they can but I don't know … Cindy's sister's here. She's inconsolable. It would be really traumatic for Alex to be here right now. Let's wait until things calm down and we have a better idea of Cindy's condition.'

I nod at the phone, thinking hard about how I might get to see Alex without a confrontation with Ursula. Most likely, telling her about Cindy's suicide attempt would increase her efforts to block me from seeing him. Right at the moment he needs me most.

Michael's green Volvo pulls into the car park at MacNeice House a few seconds ahead of me. Ursula appears at the top of the steps, her arms folded. I get out of the car and walk quickly towards the entrance with Michael behind, feeling Ursula's stare and thinking quickly how to evade her.

It is Michael who speaks first. 'I think it's in the boy's interests that he speak to Anya, don't you?'

I am at the bottom of the steps, looking up at her.

'The boy is asking for you,' she says, pursing her lips. 'He's very upset about his mother.'

I feel a deep thud in the pit of my gut. 'You *told* him?'

She hesitates. 'Somehow he already knew. He even told us where she'd stashed the tablets.'

I ignore her, taking the steps two at a time. Just as I think she is going to tell me to leave or be forced to leave, she moves aside, letting us through.

'Don't sign the register,' she tells Michael and me as the three of us push through the front door. We follow quickly behind her as she sweeps up the corridor. Michael stops at the vending machine by the doors that lead to the staff offices, fills two plastic cups, one with water, another with espresso, and hands one to me.

'This is for Alex,' he says, nodding at the cup of water. 'You look tired.'

We catch up with Ursula at the therapy room. She turns as she reaches the door.

'I won't note that this interview took place,' she says candidly. 'Looks bad to the Trust if a member of staff on sick leave appears out of the blue.'

I glance past her and spy Alex through the glass panels. He is sat in the armchair facing us in a white T-shirt with a Bart

Simpson logo on the front and new denim jeans, and I notice he has had a haircut. He looks different in kids' clothes. Normal. Then he lowers his head in his hands, his fingers crawling through his long hair as if he wants to pull his head off. He begins to rock. I nod at Ursula, then watch as she turns the key in the door and pushes it open. I gesture for Michael to go inside first.

'No,' Alex says when he looks up. 'You.' He points at me.

Michael and I share looks. I turn back to Alex. 'You just want to speak to me, Alex?'

He nods. Michael shrugs and hands me the cup of water. 'I'll wait down the hall,' he tells me, lifting a hand to my shoulder, then dropping it. I wait until he has walked past and out of sight before I close the door behind me and sit in the chair opposite Alex. He watches me, his face pale and flat.

'What's that you're drinking?' are his first words.

I set my cup on the floor by my chair. 'Espresso.' I pass him the cup of water. He takes it but he doesn't drink it, nor does he say, 'Thank you,' which I note as unusual for Alex.

'How are you today?' I ask him gently.

'Scared,' he whispers.

Despite the relative stillness of his appearance, I know that his mind will be a tempest of questions and scenarios. I want to reach out to him, to wrap my arms around him.

'I don't think I want to do this,' he says suddenly, standing up.

I watch him pace for a few seconds.

'You don't want to speak to me?'

'No,' he says, shaking his head. He glances at my cup of espresso, then stops pacing. 'When can I see my mum?'

'As soon as the doctors say it's OK,' I say calmly. I remain seated, hopeful he'll sit back down. 'I promise, as soon as I hear . . .'

'But it will be too late!' he shouts.

Just then, a knock on the door. I jump up from my chair and find Michael, slightly breathless from a sprint. He lays a hand on my shoulder and leans close.

'Bev's on her way here now,' he whispers. 'She just left a voicemail on my phone.'

I feel my heart lighten. 'Any word on Cindy?' I say quietly. He shakes his head. Nonetheless, I feel slightly more at ease to hear that Bev is coming. Alex needs all the support he can get right now.

When I close the door again I hear Alex sit back in his seat. 'Are you OK, Alex?'

He flicks his eyes from the corner to me, then nods nervously.

Something is not right with him. To be expected, of course, but he is unusually jittery, on edge, and as he drains his cup of water I notice his hand is trembling. As I study him I recognise a familiar energy beneath his composure, the kind I have come to associate with Ruen's visitations. I think of my meeting with Karen Holland. The footage I saw. Alex watches me intently and I am careful not to let my smile slip. I want to ask him about his father and the shooting, but have already decided that today is not the day for such a discussion.

I pick up my cup and drain the espresso to show I'm at ease, relaxed. It tastes bizarre. I make a mental note never to get espresso from a vending machine.

Alex sits forward in his chair, wringing his hands. 'I remembered some things about my dad,' he says.

'You did?'

He looks uncertain now, and I notice he has yet to make full eye contact. Accordingly, I pull my chair adjacent to him instead of directly opposite to show I'm on his side, not confronting him.

'I mean, it's nothing important.'

'I think it *is* important. Can you tell me?'

His eyes drift back to the corner behind me. I resist from asking if he can see Ruen.

'It happened one Saturday morning,' he says slowly, his eyes gradually rising to my face. 'Maybe a Sunday morning. Dad didn't talk to any of our neighbours. In fact he'd usually come through the back door when he visited or he'd keep his baseball cap pulled down over his eyes. I was sitting on the sofa watching something on TV and I remember Dad was looking straight out the front window and then he stood up and walked to the front door. I didn't hear anyone knock. When I went after him I saw he was talking to Mrs Beaker from three doors up. She was on her way to the shops as usual. She was like a hundred years old and when she walked she was bent so far over she's staring at her feet. It was raining really heavy outside but she couldn't hold up an umbrella. So my dad said to her, "Where are you going?" And she said, "To do some shopping," and Dad shook his head and smiled and told her to give him her shopping list and *he'd* do her shopping. Mrs Beaker went back into her house and me and Dad went and bought all her groceries. Dad wouldn't even take the money off her. She was so happy she kissed him on both cheeks.'

His voice has raised several decibels and he is sitting upright. A few seconds pass. Suddenly his face crumples, his smile turning into a deep scowl. I notice he is holding something in his hand, hiding it between his legs. He must have picked up something when I opened the door to Michael.

'It's OK, Alex,' I say gently. 'It's good to remember nice things about your dad. It shows you are forgiving him.'

He struggles to speak, his lips trembling. 'But . . . but what would she have done . . . I mean, if she'd known . . . '

He doesn't finish. I glance out the glass panels of the door to watch for Michael, hopeful that we can see Cindy soon. When I turn back to Alex I see he has covered his face with his hands and I go to reach out to him.

'Alex,' I begin to say. But I stop short, overwhelmed by a sensation of nausea so strong that I cover my mouth in case I throw up. Alex looks at me.

'Are you all right?' he says, sniffling.

I nod. 'I think so. You were saying about your dad.'

'Are you feeling sleepy?' he whispers, and I shake my head. When I pull myself together he continues.

'My dad could be really kind,' he says, his teeth still chattering from the upset.

Just like you, I go to say, but then I feel a tingling in my mouth, a sensation of something creeping around my gums. I reach for my talisman on instinct, then realise with a stunned sense of horror that, for the first time ever, I've left it at home.

'But what about when someone is also a murderer?' Alex is saying. 'How can they really be kind if they're evil? How can anything that they did be true? It was all a lie, wasn't it?'

As I open my mouth to respond my throat tightens, and I feel like I'm choking. I lean forward to recover and take a breath, but before I know it I have fallen on to my hands and knees by the table, gasping for air.

Alex stands up, his face frozen as he watches me. Still, I see him reach behind his back, hiding whatever he's got in his hand from view. I know what is happening now, but I can't explain *why* it's happening. *Anaphylactic shock*, my mind screams, *anaphylactic shock. But how? How is this happening?* I keep my mind focused on taking short breaths, using what time I have left to think of a way to tell Alex what he needs to do.

'Are you sleepy?' I hear him say.

Why is he asking that?

Slowly I raise my head, watching him as he steps back against the doll's house. He is sobbing loudly now, his eyes streaming with tears.

'It's OK,' I whisper, and immediately it feels as if someone has put an invisible hand around my throat, squeezing tightly. I gag. 'Help me,' I tell him. 'Michael. Get Michael.'

But Alex turns away, facing the doll's house. It is then I see something that should not strike me as odd, but which makes me use the last of my strength to hold my head up and look closer. A plastic tub on the floor, tipped on its side, the kind you'd buy from a vending machine. A jelly bean tub, maybe. Or . . . There is trail of dust pouring out of it, like sand. And amongst the sand is a pebble. No, not a pebble.

A peanut.

Quickly I force my eyes to my left, spying my coffee cup which has rolled beside the table leg. I have to look twice, but it's there: on the rim of the cup is a small coating of the same beige dust.

My heart thuds in my chest, my mind racing in every direction.

Keep calm, breathe, breathe . . .

How did he do this? Just a minute ago, I wasn't looking . . .

Did he pour peanut dust in my coffee? He must have . . .

Why is he doing this? Does he realise what he is doing?

Does he realise he is killing me?

Alex is speaking fast and loud, pouring out apologies and explanations. My arms give way, dropping my face to the floor, cheek to carpet, my arms splayed awkwardly by my sides, my knees bent. It is vital to keep my breathing shallow, my heartbeat as slow as possible. I can feel saliva building up in my throat, and I start to panic. It feels like I am drowning.

I strain to open an eye. Eventually, it rolls back enough to show Alex standing above me. He is pacing, his face screwed up in a mixture of terror and grief. I hear him mutter 'Ruen,' and I understand. Ruen is making him do this, or rather the belief he has invested subconsciously in his self-image as the child of a killer – as an inevitable killer in the making. I think back to the footage, of a five-year-old Alex in the corner of the frame, watching on. Suddenly it makes sense to me. He was too young to process the meaning of what he had seen. The media coverage afterwards – newspapers, television reports – would have stirred up negative feelings towards a man he looked up to. A man he loved. His father.

I want to shout out to him the headline I saw amongst the paintings he did for Karen Holland's class. *Ruend Peepels Lives*. I want him to make the connection. *Ruen* is the embodiment of his conflict, a personification of his processing of what it means to be a murderer's son. I need him to understand his own feelings. Before it's too late.

My eyelid sags, plunging me into darkness. Nothing but the sound of my small little gasps. I hear Alex's feet edge closer, his whimpers of fear. A muffled scraping sound. He is pushing my chair against the door, the top of it wedged neatly beneath the handle.

'I'm sorry, I'm sorry,' I hear him say. He is pleading with someone or something, shuffling back and forth in front of me. 'I don't want to die. I don't want to die.'

I try to think of anything but the terrible alien feeling that has overwhelmed me, the thickness of my tongue in my mouth, the lulling urge to pass out. I mustn't. Using all my strength, I lift my head and open my eyes a fraction, enough to see Alex above me. At last, I see what he was hiding before: a thick shard of broken glass.

'Alex,' I whisper, though it's more of a gargle, phlegm and tears and saliva congregating in my throat. He bends down slightly, sobbing. The motion renews my strength, and the shivering that has overtaken me begins to calm. I feel my breaths get longer. I try. I try to tell him. It is all I can do to push back the blackness that laps at my consciousness. But I can't speak.

The last thing I see is Alex raising the glass shard high above him, the light from the corridor striplight glinting on the sharp edge.

27

THE PIT

Alex

Dear Diary,

I looked at Anya on the floor and I wanted to tell her I'm sorry. I wanted to tell her not to be afraid. I wanted to tell her more about Ruen, about what he had asked me to do and why I was doing it. In my mind I could see Mum in the hospital bed, her face the colour of vanilla ice cream. Ruen was beside me in the small room. I didn't expect Anya to get so sick. My hands were shaking and I thought, *She should just be falling asleep so why does she look like she's in pain?* I was so confused.

When Anya fell on the floor I felt really scared. I looked at Ruen, and he frowned at me and said, 'You know what you have to do, Alex.' I nodded and I felt sick.

I didn't understand. I had told him I would do it. I would kill myself.

I would do it to save Mum, that's what he said. He told me I had to do it in public, so everyone could see. In front of Anya. *Why?* I'd asked, but he wouldn't say. He told me to give her the peanuts if it made me feel better, so she would fall asleep straight away and not see it all.

I felt relieved then, but scared. I didn't want to die. At first I brought out the glass handle to show Anya, but then the black shadow trailed across the floor like a snake from Ruen and wrapped around me. He squeezed it and I knew what he was saying: if I didn't do it, he would.

I looked at Ruen in the corner of the room, standing close to where Anya lay on the floor, her body shivering like she was really cold. He was Horn Head again, a big red horn jutting out of his faceless forehead, his body covered in hair and barbed wire. I thought, *Maybe it would be better if I just went away*, because then Ruen would come with me and the only person he would hurt is me. Mum, Anya, Michael, even Woof – they'd all be much, much happier if I went away.

I wrote Anya and Michael a note in advance explaining all this. It's in my locker. I told them that Ruen showed me a film in my head of Mum hiding the tablets and then taking them out when she was sad and swallowing them. I told them that Ruen said the only way she would live was if I killed myself. And I told them why I thought he really wanted me to kill myself: he said I was nothing. He said I was like a maggot and I had nothing but a miserable life to look forward to and even if I did grow up to be big I would just end up hurting people like my dad.

I thought of Mum again, and the picture in my head was just like the first time I found her when she'd taken lots of pills. It was the morning Dad left, or the morning he got arrested for shooting those policemen. Mum knew he was going to be taken away for ever and she lost all hope. When I found her in her bed she was so limp and I thought she was already dead. It was what I feared more than anything, even her dying – seeing her again like that, *making* herself die. I couldn't understand that.

Do it, Ruen whispered, his voice in my head. But it wasn't his normal voice. It was a soft voice, not too deep and not too old and his accent wasn't English any more; it was Irish. It took me about three and a half seconds to work out why the voice sounded so familiar, and when I realised whose voice it was I got shivers right up my spine. It was my dad's voice. And when I looked at the red horn I thought of the policeman my dad shot in the head, the blood spurting out of it, and I felt sick.

'Alex!'

I turned around to see Michael pounding on the door with his fists, his eyes all wide and scared. He pushed his hands against the glass and looked down at Anya, then looked up at me. He looked really cross.

'Alex, open this door!'

I didn't move or speak. I could see the chair that I had pressed against the door handle budge forward each time

Michael slammed against it and I thought he'd kill me when he got in.

And maybe that would be OK.

My dad's voice whispered in my head again. *She's dying, Alex. Your mother is dying.*

'Please let my mum be OK,' I whispered to Ruen, because I knew he was angry that Michael was getting through the door and I was doing nothing to stop him. He had changed his appearance and was Ghost Boy now, standing opposite me with his hands by his sides and his eyes all black and angry, and his clothes were exactly like mine, as if I was looking into a mirror.

Michael was still banging on the glass, shouting, and there were lots of people behind him now. Then someone hit the glass with a hammer and started trying to break it. A big crack formed across the glass in the shape of a W.

I looked down at Anya, and for a moment it wasn't Anya lying there – it was the policeman lying on the ground, his right arm bent and covering his face, his left arm turned in a way that didn't look right. I wanted to reach down and fix Anya's arm to make sure she was comfortable. But before I could do anything there was a gigantic crash and I screamed. The glass in the door smashed and scattered to the floor.

'Alex! What's wrong with Anya?'

Michael reached through the broken glass and swept away all the shards with his hand before pushing the chair away from the door. I saw there was blood on his hand but he didn't notice. Then Ruen tightened his grip around me and I started to yell because it hurt a lot.

The only way to save her is to kill yourself, he said. *You're nothing. You don't deserve this life. You are unlovable.*

I bent down and lifted the glass handle from the floor. My mind was playing the image of Mum over and over, her hand on the bed opening loosely like a petal.

You're so like your dad, Alex. You're so like your dad.

I knew what Ruen was telling me.

I was going to grow up to be just like my dad. And that was a bad thing, because my dad was a murderer. I didn't want to hurt anybody. But I was already doing it. I was hurting me. I was hurting Anya. And I was never going to be free of him.

But Ruen had lied. He said I was unlovable. But the other day, Auntie Bev said she loved me. And Anya liked me, too.

And then I remembered something else. Ruen had told me that if a demon failed in his task he got chained in a deep pit a million miles under the sun for a hundred years. Ruen would be so bored, I had thought. Now I reckoned it would serve him right.

'I'm not nothing,' I told Ruen. 'I'm Alex. Alexander the Great. And I can be anything I want to be.'

I lifted the glass jug handle higher, but instead of hurting myself I brought it down over the thick black link between me and Ruen, and Ruen roared as the shadow shattered and every vein in my body felt like it was going to explode.

Someone grabbed my arms and Michael shouted, 'He's going!' and then there was nothing but blackness.

No one who, like me, conjures up the most evil of those half-tamed demons that inhabit the human breast, and seeks to wrestle with them, can expect to come through the struggle unscathed.

Sigmund Freud

28

THE ANSWERS

Anya

I woke up two days later in the intensive care unit at Belfast City Hospital, a venue in which I had never spent any time during the thirty years I lived here but which was now startlingly familiar. I was in a ward with two other women, my arm hooked up to a drip. A heart monitor bleeped steadily beside me. A bunch of red roses sat in a vase close to the bed. I sat for a few minutes in a blank daze as the wheels of thought warmed up again, wondering how long I'd been out for and – deep in the roots of my suspicions – if I really was alive. Gradually a series of aches and throbs announced themselves all over my body – my throat, my neck and shoulders, my stomach – and I realised with relief that I *was* alive.

A young black-haired nurse walked past and threw me a

smile, then doubled-back as it occurred to her that I had surfaced. She checked my vitals, read my chart.

'Well, well,' she said brightly. 'Back in the land of the living. How are you feeling?'

I tried to sit upright but the sudden exertion made my heart monitor bleep warningly. The nurse rushed over and pushed a cushion behind my back, supporting me.

'Where's Alex?' I asked.

'Who?'

'Michael,' I corrected myself, figuring she would probably be a stranger to the situation. Michael would know about Alex. 'Michael Jones, he must have brought me in. Is he around?'

She considered this while strapping a blood pressure gauge around my right bicep.

'I think he's just popped out, actually. Is that his coat?'

I followed her gaze to the chair by my bed, where a brown wool jacket was slung neatly over the back.

'I think so.'

The nurse flipped open my notes and scribbled a figure in a column. 'I'll arrange for you to get some soup.'

Just then, a set of footsteps made their way towards my bed. I looked up and saw Michael standing there, his face a mixture of astonishment and relief as he saw me sitting upright. The nurse glanced at me.

'This is who you meant?'

I gave her a nod. Michael had fresh silver stubble on his jaw, his eyes puffy with sleeplessness.

'How are you?' he said.

I hesitated, my mind a fog. Slowly the memory of what happened came creeping back like a slow tide: Alex's face, raw with tears and grief. The upended plastic tub. The trickle of beige dust on my espresso cup. The sensation of drowning.

'Where's Alex?' I whispered.

Michael's smile fell. He ran his fingers through his long hair, visibly reluctant to tell me. I felt my heart race.

'He's dead, isn't he?'

He swallowed and looked away. Then he pulled up a chair close to me and took my hand. 'You don't mind, do you?' he said. I shook my head.

And he told me.

When Michael had shattered the glass in the door and managed to open it, Alex collapsed to the ground. I was already unconscious, lying facedown by my chair with no immediate signs of what had happened. Ursula and Howard attended to Alex, who was also unconscious, while Michael tried to give me mouth-to-mouth resuscitation. He had noticed swelling around my throat, a small red rash gathering below my collarbone. Then he had remembered what I'd said about having a talisman. He rolled me on to my side and called an ambulance from his mobile phone.

'I thought you were dead,' he said, his voice breaking. The paramedics gave me an epinephrine injection in my thigh, which, he told me, made me open my eyes and stare right at him for a few moments, before sinking back into deep unconsciousness. Ursula shouted something about Alex's torso. She was leaning over him on the floor, raising his white shirt. There, garish on his pale skin, were several large burn marks on his chest.

'He had a medical examination just this morning,' Ursula had said. 'These marks weren't there.' With Howard's help, she tried to revive Alex, but to no avail.

'Is his heart beating?' Michael had asked.

Ursula nodded. 'Very faint.'

The ambulance arrived a minute later. With an oxygen mask attached to my face, the paramedics carried both Alex and me on stretchers and loaded us into the ambulance as Michael and Ursula watched on behind. Ursula's secretary Joshua came racing outside. He glanced at Michael before leaning close to Ursula to tell her about a phonecall, and despite Josh's best efforts at being discreet, Michael heard him clearly: Cindy was dead.

I sat in silence as Michael broke the news of her passing to me. I watched the thin floral curtains shuffle gently against the windowsill on the far side of the room. I thought of Cindy, a moment from the time I had observed her meeting with Alex. It was when she had showed him her creation in the greenhouse, when she felt proud. Alex had made her laugh and she'd turned to me, her blonde hair flung up and lit golden by the sunlight, her smile wide and easy, her blue eyes young and bright.

I thought of something she'd asked me when we first met. *Do you think there's ever a chance for a kid that starts out in life like me and Alex did?* Cindy's life had been one long tumble from one foster home to another. Rape, neglect, violence – until she was adopted by Beverly's mother at the age of fifteen. By then she was already pregnant with Alex, and her chances at a better life had been all but crushed.

But with Alex, I wasn't so certain that his chances were up. If anything, I felt assured that, despite everything, Alex had every chance in the world.

No, not despite. *Because of* Cindy. Because she loved him, and he knew it.

Michael began to speak again, telling me the pieces of the puzzle he had been able to put together – a necessary act, I understood, for him to feel resourceful in a challenging situation.

'The peanuts were from *this* hospital,' he said angrily, pointing at the floor, as if somehow the City Hospital catering staff should have had some ability to detect the potential of peanuts to be used as deadly weapons. 'Alex had stored them in his locker, then crushed them up,' he said. He shrugged and shook his head in bewilderment. 'I mean, how? *Why* would he do this?'

I knew Michael felt to blame for this. He believed he should have seen it coming, that he should have insisted on coming into the therapy room with me.

'How would he have known you would go into shock?' he said, shifting in his seat, restless with unresolved riddles. I spied traces of soil under his fingernails. His hands looked like he'd spent the last forty-eight hours sowing rhubarb.

'I don't think Alex intended to kill me,' I said, my voice no more than a hoarse whisper. Michael looked up sharply.

'It certainly looked like it to me.'

I shook my head, reaching for my throat. 'It's more complicated than that. He remembered what he had repressed so violently, the things he couldn't understand about his father.'

I remembered that Michael had not seen the footage of the shooting – that, in fact, he had no idea who Alex's father was. I would explain it to him, in time. But now, we needed to focus on the facts. Alex had lost his mother. His home. He had witnessed his father's killing of two men. His psychosis had no doubt been triggered by this event, compounded by his mother's suicide attempts. It was difficult for me to feel angry with Alex for what he had done. Instead, I needed to build a clear picture of *why* he had done it. Alex's future depended on that picture.

'Take me to him,' I told Michael after several minutes had passed.

He glanced at a wheelchair on the other side of my bed. Without a word, he stepped forward and helped me settle into it, with the IV at my side, and pushed me to the paediatric unit.

Alex had been moved earlier that morning from intensive care into a sideroom in the paediatric unit. Another social worker I'd met briefly – Joanna Close, an English woman in her sixties; short, feathery black hair and a grey trouser suit – was sitting outside. She rose to her feet when she saw Michael and me approaching.

'No lasting damage,' I heard her tell Michael. 'X-rays of his chest are clear. The doctor wants Alex kept in at least one more night for observation.'

I asked Michael to wait outside while I spoke with Alex alone. He made to grab my arm as I went inside, then stopped.

'It's OK,' I told him.

'Sorry,' he said, glancing past me and into the room. 'Just, after last time . . . '

'He's just been moved from intensive care. I don't think he poses a risk, do you?'

He sighed and glanced inside the room. Finally, he relented. 'I'll be right here.'

Alex was sitting upright in bed attached to a drip, his torso covered in bandages. As soon as he saw me he melted into deep, shuddering tears. I wheeled myself close, noticing at once the photograph beside his bed of him and his mother some years before: a tight embrace, their arms wrapped right around each other, both of them pulling a face. He saw me glance at it and wiped his eyes with his palms.

'Auntie Bev brought it,' he said when he'd recovered.

I hesitated. 'I'm so sorry about your mum, Alex.'

He nodded and struggled not to break down again. When he turned back to me, he seemed older, somehow. No longer the nervous, troubled boy I met in the psychiatric unit only two months ago.

'The funeral is on Thursday,' he said, wiping tears from his cheeks. 'Will you come?'

'Of course I will.'

He seemed relieved at this, enlivened by my support. He

took a few deep breaths, wincing with each breath. I glanced at the bandages across his chest and stomach.

'What happened there, Alex?'

He looked down. 'Ruen did it.'

'Ruen?'

He raised his head slowly and nodded.

'Can you tell me *how* he did it?'

'No,' he said firmly. 'Not really. I think it was because he had such a hold on me. He didn't want you to make him disappear.'

'Is that what he told you?'

He looked down again, wrapping an arm around his chest. 'It's just something I knew about him. When you're friends with someone you know things about them without them having to tell you, you know?'

I nodded. After a moment he looked at me and said, 'I never meant to hurt you. I'm so sorry.'

I thought quickly of the moment when I realised what was happening. The twist in my gut. The tightness of my throat. I closed my eyes, thinking how close I came to dying.

Would I have seen Poppy on the other side?

'Did you understand what you were doing when you put the nuts in my coffee?' I said carefully.

He looked deeply ashamed. 'Ruen said to ... ' He began to tell me about Ruen's revelation that Cindy was dying and his promise to save her if Alex took his own life. The images of Cindy in his mind. I waited until his wounds forced him to stop and take a long, slow breath. 'I just thought you'd go to sleep,' he said quietly. 'I didn't mean to hurt you.'

'Why did you want to make me go to sleep?' I asked firmly, my voice suddenly loud and clear. 'What did Ruen want you to do, Alex?'

He looked up. 'He wanted me to kill myself. He said I was nothing. He said I didn't deserve to live.'

I watched him, realising how lonely he must have felt all this time. How that loneliness must have imploded the moment he learned about Cindy.

'I just couldn't,' he whispered. 'Ruen wanted me to, but I couldn't, I just couldn't.'

I let him cry, listening as he broke into revelations here and there – about Ruen's different appearances, which I saw instantly were projections of how he had learned about his father's crime. About Ruen's offer to get his father out of Hell, which I suspected was linked to his self-blame, his willingness to make everything in his family better.

'I know about your dad,' I told him softly. 'I know what he did, Alex. Your father's acts, Alex – *not* your father – were evil. You are not your father.'

He was silent for a long time, contemplating my words. Finally he looked up, giving me a tilt of his head to indicate he understood.

There was much that remained to be properly explained. One of the doctors had suggested that Alex's burn marks might have been caused by a reaction to chemicals in the swimming pool at MacNeice House, though tests were still to be carried out and, I felt, the suggestion was far-fetched. Still, how else did he acquire three thick stripes across his chest? Were they self-inflicted? If so, how? The 'film' he claimed Ruen had put in his head of Cindy's suicide attempt echoed one of her earlier efforts, but its timing was an undeniably remarkable coincidence. And then there were my own experiences: Alex's piece of music, for instance. The man in the music room. Alex's perception of things far beyond his understanding, such as the scar on my face. Poppy.

When Alex had finished speaking, I identified the final thing I needed to know.

'Can you see Ruen now?'

He stared at me. Very slowly, he shook his head. 'Ruen has gone.'

'Gone?' I said. 'Gone where?'

'At the bottom of a pit a million miles beneath the sun,' he said with a smile.

'You said you could see other demons, too,' I asked tentatively. 'Can you see any now?'

He stared at me, looking over my head. 'No,' he said finally. 'I don't see any. Not any more.' He gave me a small smile – for the first time since we met – his eyes those of a ten-year-old boy. Untroubled.

That night I sat on a towel spread across the cold tiled floor of my flat. I was still without a sofa. But I had priorities. Alex's new programme of treatment involved paperwork. And it involved a new approach. I would have to lead him back, back to the moment he learned his father had murdered two men. I would have to guide him through that trauma, helping him understand the emotions he was feeling, the conflict that had split his psyche into the monstrous, the ghostly, the horrific and the evil forms that now comprised his vision of the father he had loved and idolised. And in order to prevent him self-harming or hurting others ever again, I would have to teach him how to overcome the biggest hurdle of all: his fear of becoming like his father.

I opened my laptop to compose a note to Trudy Messenger about Alex. In my inbox I found an email from Ursula, short and to the point:

To: A_molokova@macneicehouse.nhs.uk
From: U_hepworth@macneicehouse.nhs.uk
Date: 21/6/07 13.34 p.m.

Dear Anya

I hope you are feeling better. Please accept my apologies for what happened with Alex Broccoli; it has made me aware that our security needs to be drastically improved and measures are now in place to that effect. I can only hope that you can take my word for that without pursuing legal action.

I laughed to myself. She felt threatened now, afraid – even in the moment of her retirement – that I'd undo everything she had worked so hard to achieve. It was possible, and she was right – Alex's attack had underlined security issues that were part of a wider problem across the system. I was certain, though, that she meant what she said: the problem *would* be rectified. I read on.

> You'll remember I told you about the role I'm taking up as Chief Advisor to the government. The priority of this role is to address the damage the Troubles have caused to our youth. I recognise now that you have a similar passion for improving our provision of mental health services for children and young people. Should you wish to assist on the board at MacNeice House, please do let me know.

I read this passage twice. She was offering no small position – a role on the board would influence policy-making. It would give me a very large microphone in a noisy arena. It would enable me to do what I had returned to Northern Ireland to do: to make a difference.

I scanned the rest of the email, frowning as I reached her 'PS'.

> I hope you have found all the answers now?

I thought back to our first meeting at my interview for this post. She had asked it then, and I had trusted in my heart that it was possible to solve every mystery posed by the human mind with medicine and science. And when I had seen the similarities between Alex and Poppy, a deep part of me believed that, by solving his riddle, I could also solve Poppy's.

But Poppy wasn't a riddle. What had happened *happened*, just as surgeries go wrong, just as a driver looks down from the road for a moment too long. I had nothing left to solve. I just had to accept what I couldn't change.

And I knew now what questions I needed to be asking.

The doorbell chimed, sending a B note around the hard surfaces of the flat. For a moment I thought of Poppy again, her face when I had broken down in the music room. Her voice telling me that she loved me. I pushed it away, then immediately felt guilty. I rose to my feet and padded across the room. Laid my hand on the cold door handle. I had felt that, by refusing to let go of anything that reminded me of her, by holding on so tightly to her memory, I could somehow stop her from falling. I could somehow reach back into the past and make that extra stretch out the window after her. I could somehow save her.

I opened the door. Michael was standing there, his blond hair illuminated like a halo by the garish hall light. He held up his hand: bunched in his fist, the purple bulbs of beetroots at the end of their long red stalks, freshly ripped from the ground.

'And this, of course,' he said, raising a bottle of fresh orange juice in the other.

I hesitated. By letting him cross the threshold of my door, I was effectively breaking my own rules. I was crossing another threshold, too, one that left my old life far behind.

'Come in,' I said after a few moments' hesitation. 'If you don't mind sitting on the floor.'

He grinned, a flicker of nervousness passing across his face. 'I don't mind.'

29

A Friend

Alex

Dear Diary,

I'm in Auntie Bev's car right now and it's difficult to write because the car is so small and she drives like the roads are made of ice. We are on our way to Magilligan Prison to see my dad. She's been telling me jokes all morning and trying to make me laugh and she even bought me onions on toast at the fancy restaurant but I know why. She's trying to keep my mind off Mum and the funeral and she's worried how I'll feel when I meet my dad. I'm trying not to think of Mum's coffin and the way they lowered it into the ground. I didn't like that part, it made my insides twist and my heart feels broken. So I'm remembering the daffodils we made them plant all around the headstone, which makes me think of the day Mum was so proud of herself. I wanted to put Mum's toilet bowl on the grave but Auntie Bev said no.

'Have you heard from Roz?' I asked her as we were driving away from my old house. Jojo had let me keep my Horatio costume as a souvenir.

'Who's Roz?' she said, but then she took her eyes off the road and looked at me as if she really did know who Roz was and then the car swerved and we both almost died.

'Roz is that casting director who came to see me in *Hamlet*,' I said. 'You said you spoke to her.'

She smiled. 'Oh yeah, *that* Roz. I'm sure we'll hear from her soon enough.'

The last time I saw Anya she sat me down and told me some things about my dad that she said I needed to know. She said Dad's name is Alex Murphy. He was born in 1971, which makes him thirty-five, which is three-point-five times my age, though next month I'll be eleven which means he'll only be three-point-one-eight times older. Anya said he is staying at Magilligan Prison, just like Mum told me, so I know Ruen was lying. She said she had been in touch with him and he was really happy that I wanted to see him.

'Happy?' I asked.

She smiled. 'He was over the moon, Alex. I'll show you his letter, if you like.'

I nodded and said OK. 'Why do you think he killed those policemen?' I asked.

Anya's eyes looked sad. 'He was in an organisation that believes in killing people, Alex.'

That didn't make me feel any better. 'But did he *have* to kill them, or couldn't he have said he didn't want to?'

'I suppose the only way you're ever going to know is to ask your father. But . . . ' And she paused for a long time.

'What?' I said.

She looked like she was thinking carefully about what she wanted to say. 'I think you may only get the real answers after a long, long time. Sometimes an answer doesn't come in one go. Sometimes it has so many layers to it that it takes time for the person to tell you what they really mean.' Then she thought for a long time.

Anya looked at Auntie Bev then, who was sitting next to me, holding my hand.

'I think it's important not to openly condemn Alex's father, despite what you think of him,' I heard her tell Auntie Bev, and Auntie Bev took a deep breath and seemed upset. Anya reached forward and held Auntie Bev's hand.

'I know what he did was . . . well, it was what it was,' she said, which didn't make any sense but Auntie Bev nodded. 'A huge part of Alex's recovery will be to visit with his father when he can, maybe even write to him.'

Auntie Bev wiped her eyes and thought about it. After a while she looked at me and gave me a small smile. Then she said: 'Would your mum have wanted me to have taken you to see your dad, Alex?'

I nodded. 'Definitely. Mum loved Dad. He made bread

rolls dance.' And I told her all about him cooking bruschetta and the guns in the piano, and then about the blue car. And the policemen.

'OK,' she said after a long time. 'But first there's somewhere else we have to go.'

'Where?' I said, and just then Anya got up and went into the kitchen to make a pot of tea, but I think she was just being polite so Auntie Bev and I could chat in private.

Auntie Bev turned to me and for a moment it seemed that she didn't know what to say, or how she was going to say what she wanted to say. She pulled at her short white hair and smiled. 'I bought a house, Alex. You're coming to live with me.'

I blinked at her. 'A house? Not this one?'

'Is that OK? Would you mind?'

I think my eyes turned into saucers. 'No, I would *love* that!' And I started asking about the house – did it have a garden and a big kitchen and a driveway for her small fast car? And Auntie Bev said it had all of those. I was ready to burst. Then I thought about something.

'You mean, I'm moving to Cork?'

She shook her head. 'No, *I'm* moving up north,' she said. 'I want you to be close to Anya, so she can make sure you get better. And it'll be close for you to do more acting if you want, and you might not even have to change schools.'

She pulled out a map of Northern Ireland which looks like a witch's head, and Auntie Bev's new house is on the witch's nose. I pointed this out and she laughed. 'It's called the Ards Peninsula,' she said. 'Haven't you been there?'

I shook my head. 'Can we go?'

Auntie Bev put the map away and said we could, though we'd have to come back to my and Mum's old house a few more times to make sure we got all my stuff.

Anya came back in and shook Auntie Bev's hand and kissed her cheek. Then she bent down and took my hands.

'Remember what I said, Alex,' she whispered. 'You are *Alex*. Nobody is like you, and you are like nobody else.' She paused. 'In fact, you can be anyone you want to be.'

I nodded and felt my face go hot when she kissed my cheek, and then we waved her goodbye. Though not really goodbye, she said, because she would be seeing me again in a few weeks' time.

Auntie Bev flung her car around lots of sharp bends until we came to an industrial estate not far from the city centre. When she stopped I felt sick.

'Is *this* where we're living?'

She looked puzzled. 'No, Alex. Look.' She pointed at a big blue sign on a wire fence straight ahead of me. RSPCA. I stared at it. Why were we here?

'To pick someone up,' Auntie Bev said, smiling. And then my brain clicked.

'No way,' I said, because I didn't dare believe it.

She grinned. 'I bet he's missed you.'

I jumped out of the car and ran through the gate. All the kennels were quiet and Auntie Bev told me she would go and ask the lady at reception because she was certain he should still be here. For a minute I panicked. What if someone had taken him?

And then I heard it. Woof's bark, loud and frantic on his leash, walking in front of a lady who was wearing a big fishing jacket and black wellies and a hoop through her nose. As soon as he saw me he started pulling her behind him, his front paws paddling at the air to get him closer. I ran to him and he jumped up on me, licking my face and making lots of high-pitched barks.

The lady looked annoyed. 'He's missed me,' I explained to her, and I let him lick my face until he started to bite my nose and then I just wrapped my arms around him and held him. 'Hello, boy,' I said, and he whined and did a little spin and then climbed up on my knee and tucked his head under my arm. His fur was less white than usual and I could feel his ribs a little more than before but he was still the same Woof.

Auntie Bev came and signed some forms, and soon Woof was sitting on my lap in Auntie Bev's car and we were driving to our new home.

It took us a while to get there, and by the time we arrived Woof was snoring on my lap with his head between my knees and the sun was turning the sky gold. The city was replaced with lots of green fields and the blue ocean, and when the car started to get slower I knew we were almost there, but I couldn't believe it. We were driving up a long driveway with crunchy white stones towards the house I had pictured in my mind long, long ago. It was the exact same house, literally as if whoever built it had read my mind: it was a huge white house with a big red front door with two little trees in blue pots at either side of it. There were eight windows with curtains inside and a fake chicken beside the chimney pot. Even from the outside I could tell the kitchen would be massive. The only difference between the house in my head and the one we were in front of was that there was a huge willow tree right beside this house, and its branches looked like silver rivers.

'How many bedrooms does it have?' I whispered to Auntie Bev.

'Four,' she said, and I started to cry. I cried so hard that Auntie Bev looked very alarmed and asked if I'd hurt myself, and so I rubbed my nose on my sleeve and told her no: I was just really happy. Auntie Bev stopped the car on the white gravel path and as soon as I opened the door Woof jumped out and splashed in the puddles that were left by the rain, then raced up to the front door.

Auntie Bev got out of the car and gave a big stretch. 'What do you think, Alex?'

I got out and looked at the house. There were window-boxes hanging from the downstairs windowsills with flowers that looked like colourful hankies. 'Are all the gardens ours?' I said, because there was one at the front and it continued round both sides, and when I stepped to my right I could see a long one at the back, too. Auntie Bev said we had a quarter acre of gardens, which apparently is big enough for a set of swings and a strawberry patch.

'Hello,' a voice said as I was staring at the gardens. I spun round to see a boy standing on the white gravel path. He had bright orange hair that stuck up and was a little bit taller than me and his teeth were covered in metal braces and he was holding a green model airplane that made me think *wow*.

'Are you living here now?' the boy said.

I nodded. 'Do you live near here?'

He turned his head and pointed at the house on the hill nearby. 'I live there with my mum.'

'That's a cool airplane,' I said.

He looked at his feet for a moment. 'I'm Patrick.'

'Alex.'

He held up the model airplane. 'It's a jetfighter. My dad built it. He takes me fishing sometimes. It's boring.'

I shrugged. 'Do you think I could dress up as you and go in your place?'

His eyes went wide. 'We should give it a go.'

There was a moment when I was thinking of fishes and then sharks and I wondered if I could fit whole inside one. Then I realised Patrick was staring at me.

'Do you want to see my other airplanes?' he said. 'I've got tons more at home.'

I said yes and he said, 'Yes!' but much more excited and he ran off. About a minute later he turned and waved his hand for me to follow. I hesitated because I suddenly felt sad. I missed Ruen's jokes, especially the ones about the sandwiches. I missed him telling me what to say to people when they were being sarcastic. I missed him strutting around our house with his arms behind his back, lecturing me about the insights of Lucretius and dead languages and someone called Nero.

But I didn't miss him telling me I was nothing. And I didn't miss him telling me lies.

'Who're you talking to, Alex?' Auntie Bev said, slamming the boot shut.

'A friend,' I said. I saw Patrick waving from his house in the distance. 'I have a new friend now.'

Auntie Bev looked up and her face was worried. 'A *friend*? Where?'

'There.' I pointed at Patrick on the hill, running up to his house. He turned and shouted.

'Are you coming?'

Auntie Bev gave a long sigh as if she was really relieved.

'Do you want me to help you with the bags?' I said. She grinned and shook her head. 'Go on and play with your new friend.'

'OK.'

So I turned and ran up the hill towards Patrick where some fat grey clouds were hanging over his house. One of them looked just like Woof and another looked like a cheeseburger. One of them looked just like Ruen as the Old Man.

I stopped halfway up the hill.

'Come on,' Patrick shouted from his doorway. I looked up at the cloud, nervous because I could have sworn I saw Ruen's horrible eyes up there too.

But then a wind swept up and brushed the cloud on, and there was nothing in the sky but the first wink of stars.

ACKNOWLEDGEMENTS

First and foremost, I wish to thank my husband, Jared Jess-Cooke. Partners suffer so much during the writing of a book, not least in terms of having to watch their beloved become more and more zombified. Thank you, my love, for your patience, for Alex's jokes, for generally putting up with me while I wrote this, and for your endless encouragement.

I consider myself extremely fortunate to have *both* an amazing agent and editor. To my fabulous agent, Madeleine Buston, a kung-fu bow of respect, love and thanks for reminding me to follow my instinct, and for seeing the good when I could only see the bad – I am eternally grateful to have you in my corner. Thanks also to the team at Darley Anderson for all that you do. To my editor, the marvellous Emma Beswetherick, thank you for your infectious passion, careful eye for detail, for your utter brilliance – and for tons of fun. You are both just wonderful. Warmest gratitude to Lucy Icke for sterling suggestions. Thanks to all at Piatkus and Little, Brown for cheering me on.

The research I carried out for this book gave me a lot of

respect for the people involved in children's mental health in the UK, particularly in Northern Ireland. In this regard, I am indebted to Dr Marinos Kyriakopoulos, who helped enormously with my enquiries into early onset schizophrenia, and who was generous enough to do not one but two very thorough fact-checking reads of drafts of this book. Thanks also to Dr Stephen Westgarth for his help and advice on childhood psychotic disorders, to Dr Aditya Sharma for his generosity and insights, and to Helen Stew for information on social services. All errors – including my deliberate sidesteps from fact in the pursuit of good fiction – are mine. Thanks to the gifted Peter Tickell for assisting with the transcription of my composition 'A Love Song for Anya'. Thanks also to Sae Sae Norris for being a true friend.

Love and thanks to family who championed me throughout, especially my mother-in-law, Evita Cooke, who as always was there to help out with childcare at a moment's notice. Having someone who was willing to feed, bathe and put the children to bed while I was nine months pregnant and struggling to finish the first draft of this book was a true (and characteristic) act of generosity and kindness.

A warm thank you to those readers whose kind emails – often with the line 'Don't stop writing!' – serendipitously reached my inbox on those days when I most needed encouragement.

Finally, I want to thank my little ones – Melody, Phoenix and Summer. There is no greater inspiration in my life than the three of you.

LETTER FROM THE AUTHOR

Dear Reader,

I feel I should explain the origins of the piece of music at the beginning of this book.

Around the beginning of 2002 I had toyed with an idea I had for a screenplay about two guardian angels. Ultimately I never finished the story (though one day, I might) but a friend had recommended I read *The Screwtape Letters* by C S Lewis – which is about an older demon writing to a novice, giving him advice on how to tempt – for its take on angels and demons.

I read it – and fell in love. I hatched a plan for a film version that I would write and direct, one that would build a story around the idea behind *The Screwtape Letters* and began sending tentative emails to the companies and individuals who held the rights to Lewis's book.

Back then, I did a lot of composing, too, and one night I woke up thinking the radio had been left on. It wasn't – I just had a new melody in my head, blaring loudly. I fumbled around for a sheet of paper and a pencil and scribbled it down. By the time I worked out which note was which the music faded, but what I managed to jot down is now on the pages of this book. I didn't exactly know where the music would fit in the film I was writing, but I knew it had something to do with a demon character.

Eventually the response about the rights to *The Screwtape Letters* book hit my inbox – I would never get the rights. Not for love nor money. Still, the ideas and characters I had developed never left me.

When I started writing *The Boy Who Could See Demons* in May 2010, the demon character from the project I had had to abandon years earlier rose up again in the form of Ruen. I let the characters guide the story, careful not to plan too much in advance. So it shocked and intrigued me when Ruen asked Alex to give Anya a piece of music he had written. In the chapter where Alex is transcribing the music according to Ruen's instruction, the long-silent piece of music I had written during the night many years before came flooding back – as if a radio had been left on.

I knew it was Ruen's music.

THE BOY
WHO COULD
SEE DEMONS

Reading Guide

READING GROUP DISCUSSION POINTS

* How successfully does the author balance the Anya and Alex chapters?

* Which is your favourite character and why?

* How important is the setting of Northern Ireland in the story?

* Can you discuss the presentation of the demonic elements – whether Ruen is real or a product of Alex's mental illness?

* How sensitively does this story deal with the subjects of suicide and schizophrenia?

* Can you comment on the author's weaving of *Hamlet* into the story?

* Did Alex's ten-year-old voice feel authentic?

* How emotional did you find Anya and Poppy's story and how successfully did it complement Alex's own journey?

* Can you discuss the role of mothers in the story? You may like to talk about the part that Bev plays as well.

* How satisfying did you find the ending?

AUTHOR Q&A

Following the success of *The Guardian Angel's Journal*, how difficult was it to sit down and write your second novel?

I found it difficult to untangle myself from *The Guardian Angel's Journal*, but that had more to do with how involved I was with the story than its success. So pre-occupied was I with the 'world' I created in *The Guardian Angel's Journal* that I felt I had more exploring to do, particularly when it came to demons. I had become fascinated by Grogor (the key demon in that novel) and by the impetus and rationale for the evil he propagated. At one point in *The Guardian Angel's Journal* I wrote that demons were 'pack hunters' and that they were 'scientists of human nature' – this seemed to come out of nowhere, and I wanted to pursue it.

This book follows a few of the same themes as *The Guardian Angel's Journal*. Do you have an interest in the real world's blurring with the supernatural?

I am primarily interested in investigating the human

condition and confronting those universal questions of life and death. I don't believe either book to be fantasy or science fiction; rather, each uses the supernatural as a fascinating 'lens' through which to consider fundamental questions about humanity. I am curious about things we can't see and can never define or pin down: intuition, for instance, as well as inspiration and belief. It might originate from my Irish heritage but the immaterial has always been of a massive interest to me.

What made you decide to write part of this story from the perspective of a little boy and was it a challenge?

Alex's voice and character followed closely on the heels of the development of the idea for the book. I was interested in visiting some of the things I'd written about in *The Guardian Angel's Journal* and wanted to re-capture the idea of overcoming tough obstacles. Alex is beset by huge challenges and was a wonderfully charismatic character to write, but ultimately I had to sit back and let him tell the story. I was never quite sure if he would make it. . .

Why did you choose to set it in Northern Ireland?

In many ways Northern Ireland is a central character to the book, but I didn't plan it that way. Having been born and raised there my initial impulse is usually to opt for more exotic settings, but somehow I found myself returning again and again to Belfast and essentially exploring my own complicated relationship with that place. I wanted to write about Northern Ireland's shift from a long period of political unrest and violence to relative peace and prosperity, about the healing process. Alex is of a generation that is supposed to be enjoying the new face of Belfast, but as he told his story I discovered that ghosts arising from its past had affected him, too.

What prompted you to choose schizophrenia as your central theme?

It became an almost natural curve of the story once Alex comes clean about his ability to see demons. Instinctively I felt that this was the conclusion Anya might draw about his condition – when I researched the (vast) areas of mental health issues I found that the highly delusional aspect of Alex's claims (amongst other issues, portrayed in the book) made him a likely candidate for early onset schizophrenia.

This is a dark story, but Alex's voice is full of fun and life. Is this juxtaposition deliberate?

Alex's character was vibrant and buoyant from the outset, and this counterpointed the darker layers of his situation. Also, I wanted to be careful not to let the story sag into bleakness. It would have been too easy to let the subject matter darken the tone – I thought it would be clichéd and dull to write about demons in a typically gloomy way. Much more interesting when they're keen on bread and butter pudding.

Did anything in particular inspire you to write this story?

As my 'Letter from the Author' details, this story is grounded in a fascination I had with C S Lewis's *The Screwtape Letters*. In 2002 I wanted to make a film based on the book and started getting ideas for the music and plot, but ultimately I couldn't obtain the rights. I was pretty devastated as I loved the story and characters I had devised, but the idea lingered and ultimately inspired the creation of Ruen.

You're a mother of three young children. How do you find time to write and what advice would you give to aspiring authors in the same position as you?

The saying 'cut your cloth accordingly' rings true – you have to do what suits you and your circumstances. I fit my writing around my children and try to ensure nobody feels neglected, and luckily I've been writing for so long that I can write anywhere, anytime. I still don't even own a desk. The most important thing is not actually time to write – it's confidence to write. It's astonishing how much writing time can be gobbled up by doubt. Don't worry whether you're writing on a napkin or a Mac, whether you're writing poetry or prose, whether it's any good – just write. And remember that a vast majority of 'writing' happens in the head – don't be fooled if you ever catch me ironing. I'm actually plotting.

You're a celebrated poet and novelist; two very different disciplines. Which do you prefer?

I love both equally – honest! I think form is hugely important and worth taking time to explore; even if you are a committed short story writer you should dabble with poetry or novels or screenplays or radio dramas. Exploring the different genres of writing challenges you as an artist and profits your understanding of how a form can be used effectively. There are things a poem can do that a novel cannot – but it works the other way round. I find it very difficult to write both simultaneously; they seem to require different parts of my brain, which is a challenge that I enjoy.

What are you working on now?

Aside from my poetry, I am working on my third novel.

Read on for the opening of Carolyn Jess-Cooke's
internationally bestselling novel

THE GUARDIAN
ANGEL'S JOURNAL

A CELESTIAL PEN

When I died I became a guardian angel.

Nandita broke the news to me in the afterlife without any ice-breaking small talk or comfort-inducing chit-chat. You know the way dentists ask what your Christmas plans are right before they yank out a tooth? Well, I can tell you there was none of that. There was simply this:

Margot is dead, child. Margot is dead.

No way, I said. *I'm not dead.*

She said it again. *Margot is dead.* She kept saying it. She took both my hands in hers and said: *I know how hard this is. I left five kids behind in Pakistan with no papa. Everything will be all right.*

I had to get out of there. I looked around and saw that we were in a valley surrounded by cypress trees with a small lake a couple of metres away from where we stood. Bulrushes fenced the edge of the water, their velvet heads like micro-phones waiting to broadcast my reply. Well, there wouldn't be one. I spotted a scribble of grey road in the distance amongst the fields. I started walking.

Wait, Nandita said. *There's someone I want you to meet.*

Who? I said. *God?* This is the summit of Absurdity and we're hammering in the flag.

I'd like you to meet Ruth, Nandita said, taking my hand and leading me towards the lake.

Where? I leaned forward, looking amongst the trees in the distance.

There, she said, pointing at my reflection.

And then she pushed me in.

Some guardian angels are sent back to watch over siblings, children, people they cared about. I returned to Margot. I returned to *myself*. I am my own guardian angel, a monastic scribe of the biography of regret, stumbling over my memories, carried away in the tornado of a history that I cannot change.

I shouldn't say 'cannot change'. Guardian angels, as we all know, prevent our deaths a thousand times over. It is the duty of every guardian angel to protect against every word, deed and consequence that does not correspond to free will. We're the ones who make sure no accidents happen. But change — that's our business. We change things every second of every minute of every day.

Every day I see behind the scenes, the experiences I was meant to have, the people I was meant to have loved, and I want to take some celestial pen and change the whole thing. I want to write a script for myself. I want to write to this woman, the woman I was, and tell her everything I know. And I want to say to her:

Margot.

Tell me how you died.